P9-CCO-252

DATE DUE			
OC 12 '77	NO 05 '78	9-16-21	
OC 26 '77	JA 10 '79	9/24/21	
NO 09 '77		MAY 03 2022	
NO 15 '77	FE 07 '79	MAY 11 2022	
JA 03 '78	MR 04 '79	SEP 23 2022	
JA 17 '78		JAN 15 2023	
	MR 21 '79	MAY 04 2023	
AP 12 '78	MY 24 '79		
SE 13 '78			
OC 04 '78	OC 19 '79		
OC 05 '78	JA 16 '20		
OC 23 '78	11/19/21		

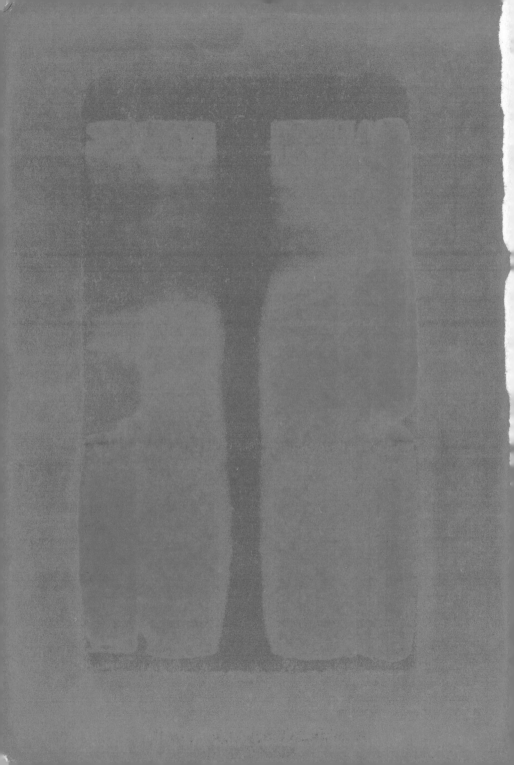

SWING IT, SUNNY

JENNIFER L. HOLM & MATTHEW HOLM
WITH COLOR BY LARK PIEN

graphix
AN IMPRINT OF
■SCHOLASTIC

Library of Congress data available

ISBN 978-0-545-74170-5 (hardcover)
ISBN 978-0-545-74172-9 (paperback)

10 9 8 7 6 5 4 3 2 1   17 18 19 20 21

Printed in Malaysia 108
First edition, September 2017
Edited by David Levithan
Lettering by Fawn Lau
Color by Lark Pien
Book design by Phil Falco
Creative Director: David Saylor

For Neelam and Neeta

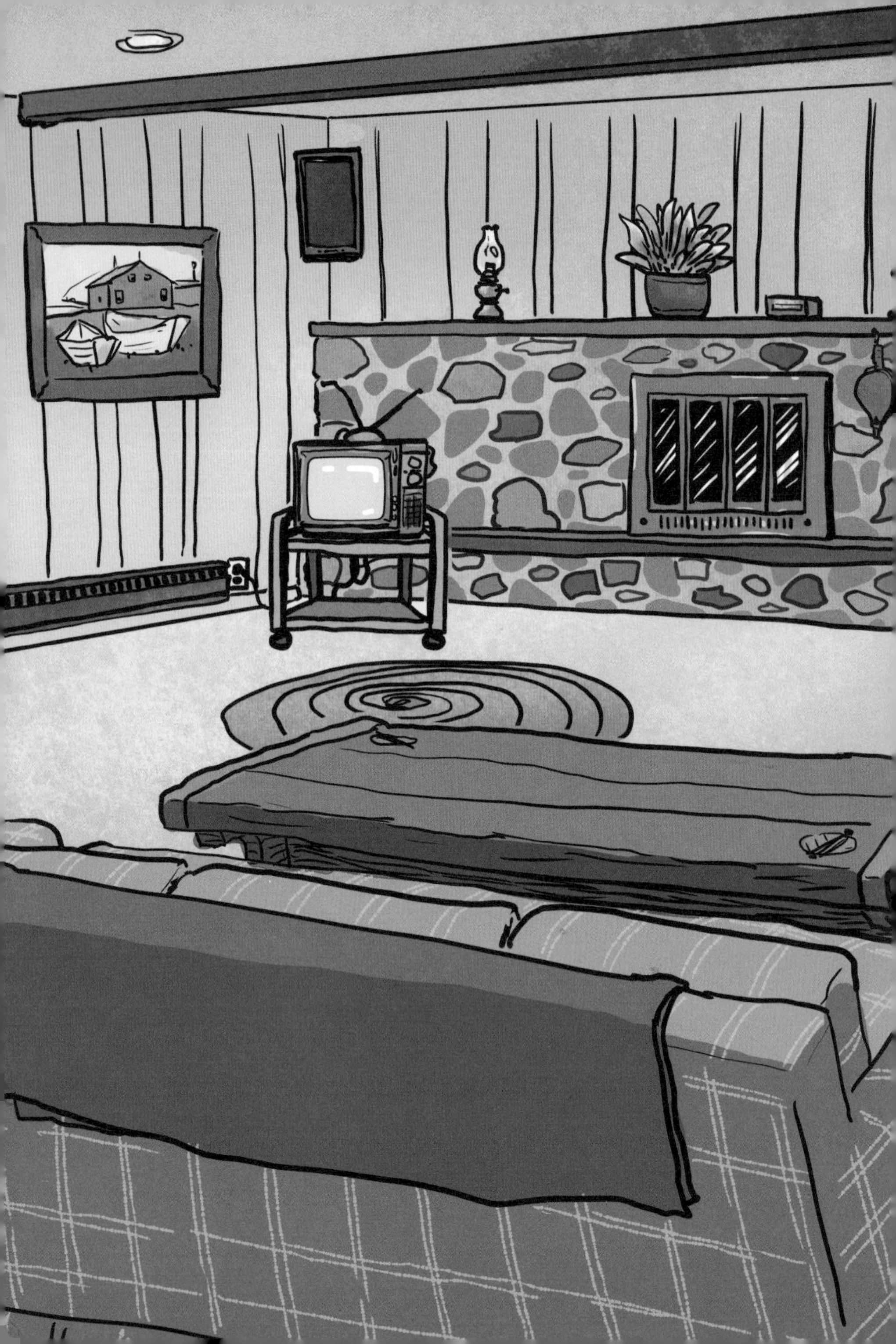

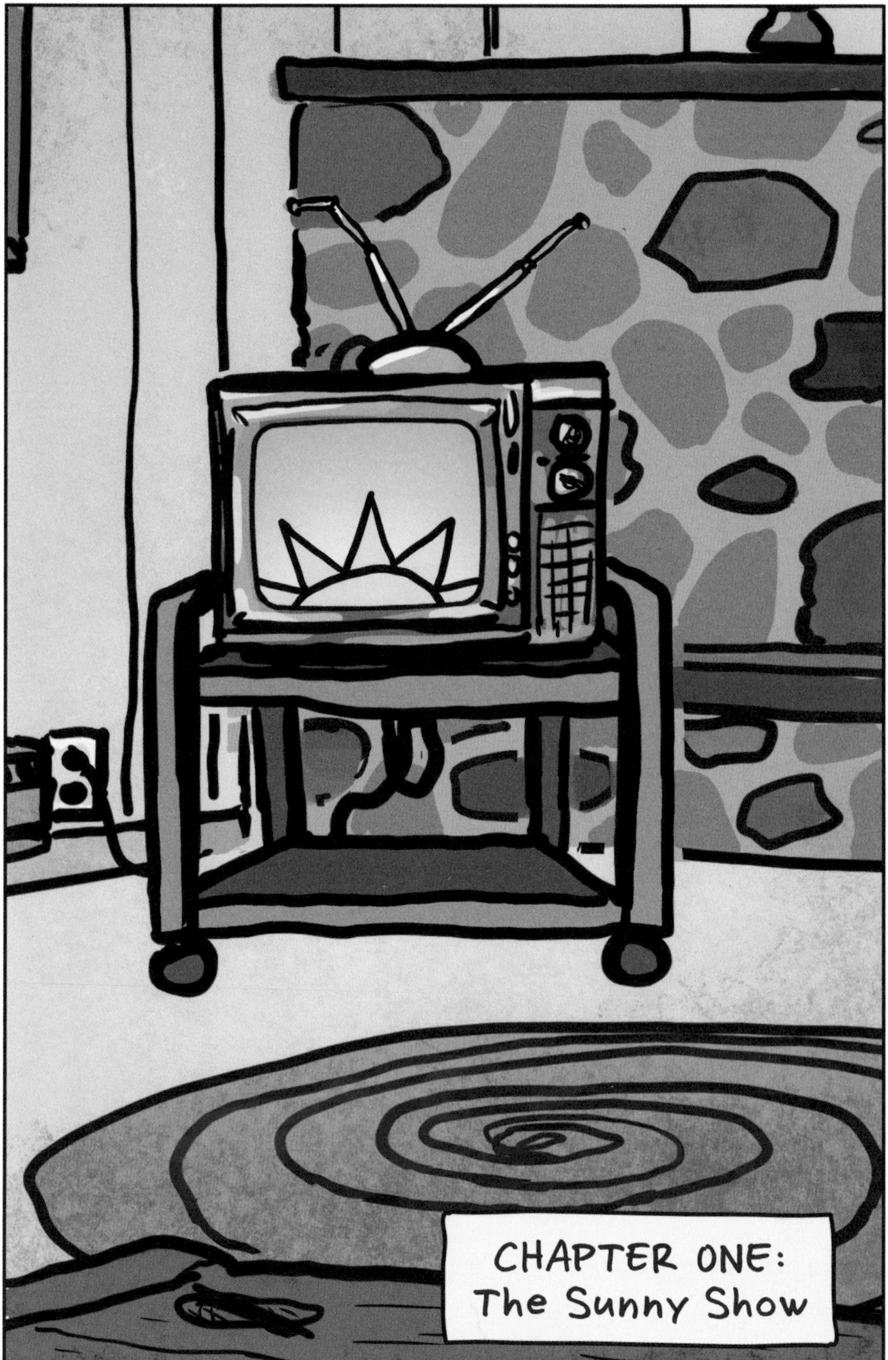
CHAPTER ONE:
The Sunny Show

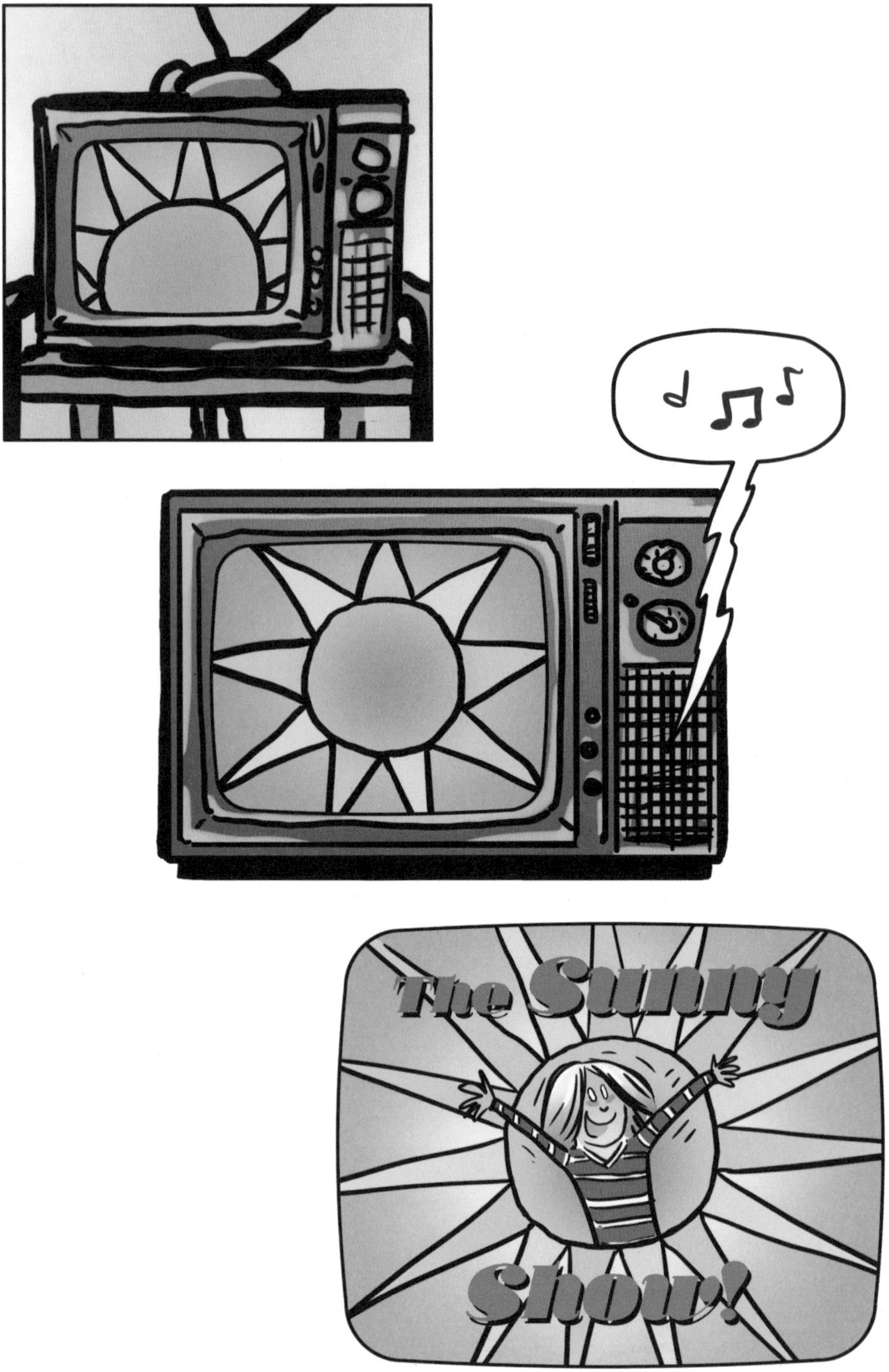
The Sunny
Show!

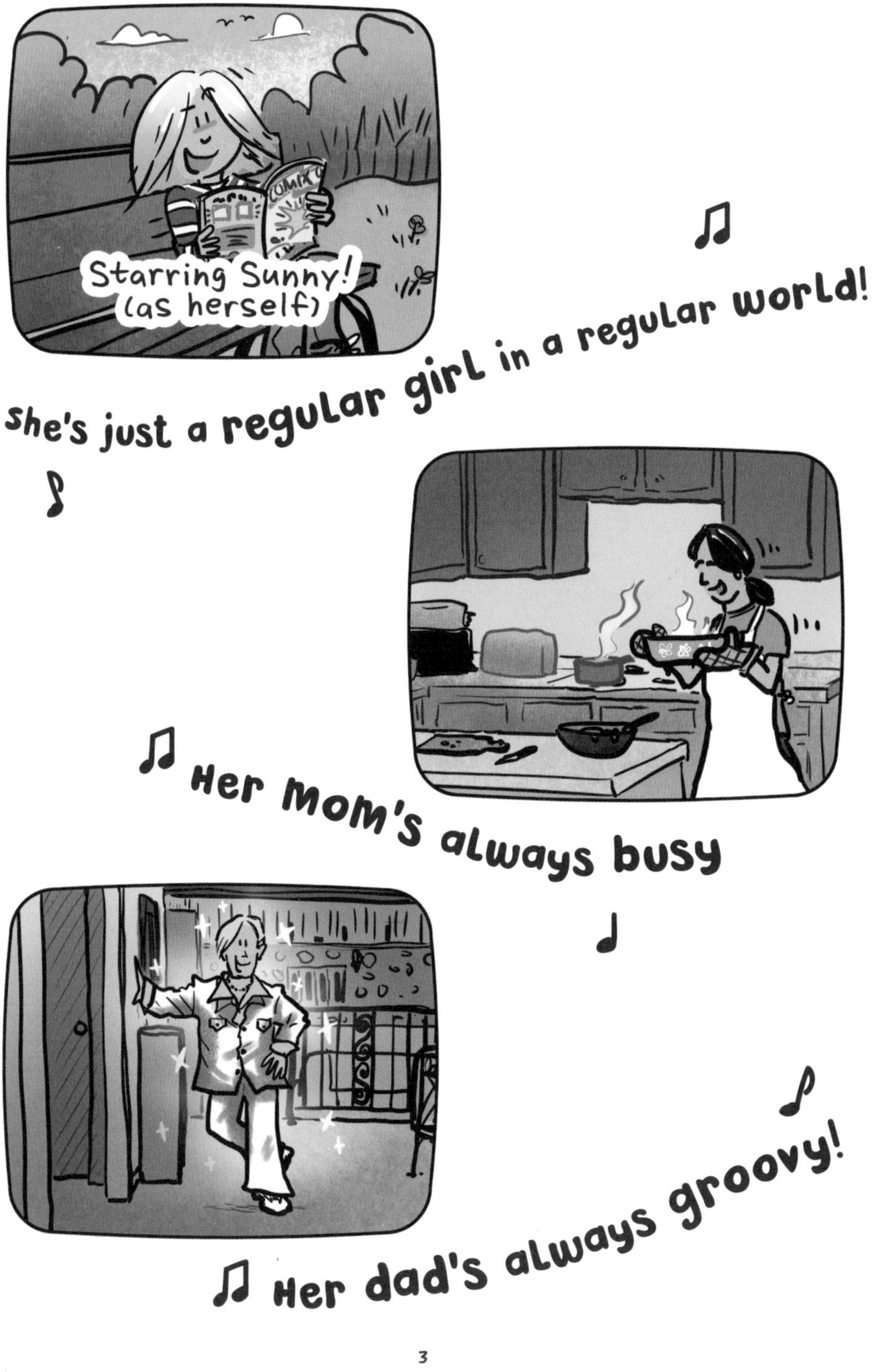
Starring Sunny!
(as herself)
She's just a regular girl in a regular world!
Her mom's always busy
Her dad's always groovy!

♪ ♫

Her little brother's always silly!

♩

There's her best friend, Deb! ♫

♩

And don't forget Gramps! ♫

♪

4

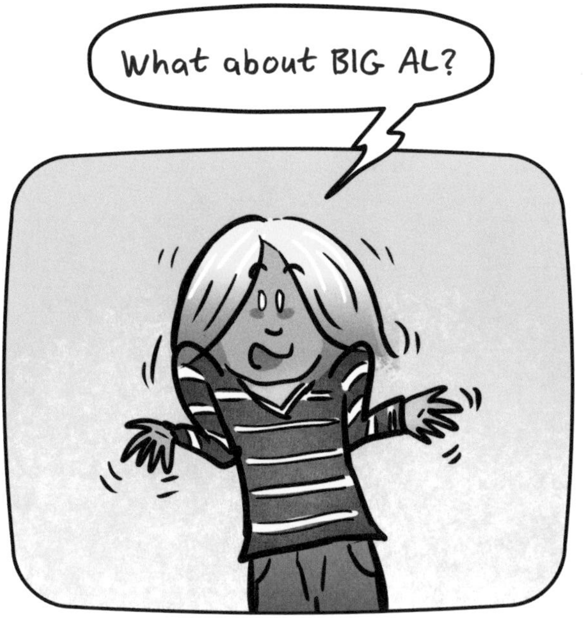
What about BIG AL?

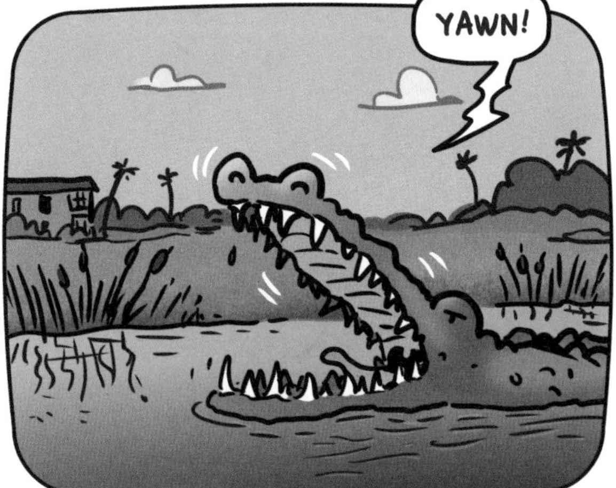
YAWN!

♫ And her favorite alligator! ♪

It's The Sunny Show!

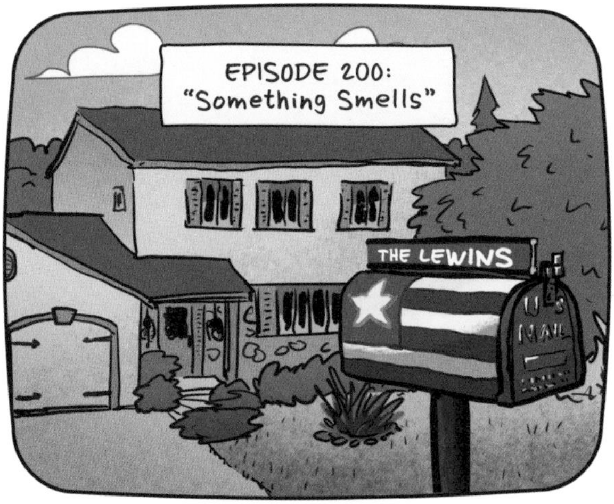
EPISODE 200:
"Something Smells"
THE LEWINS
U.S. MAIL

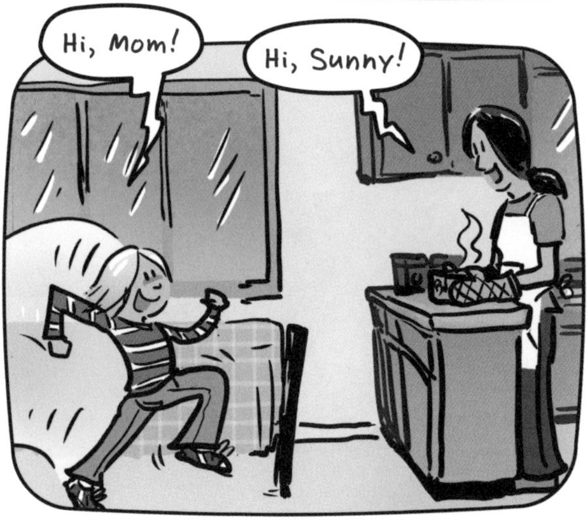
Hi, Mom!
Hi, Sunny!

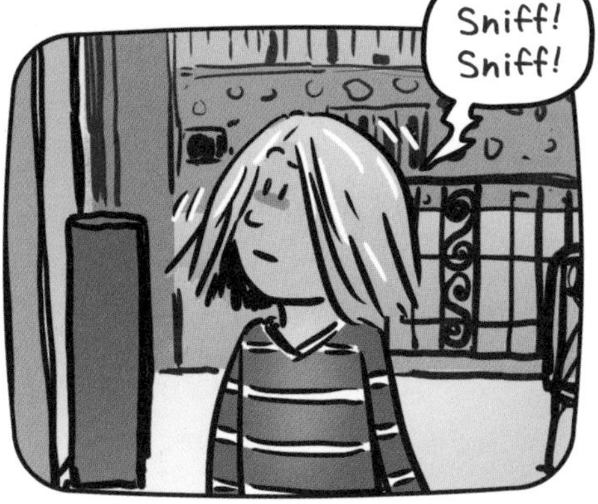
Sniff!
Sniff!

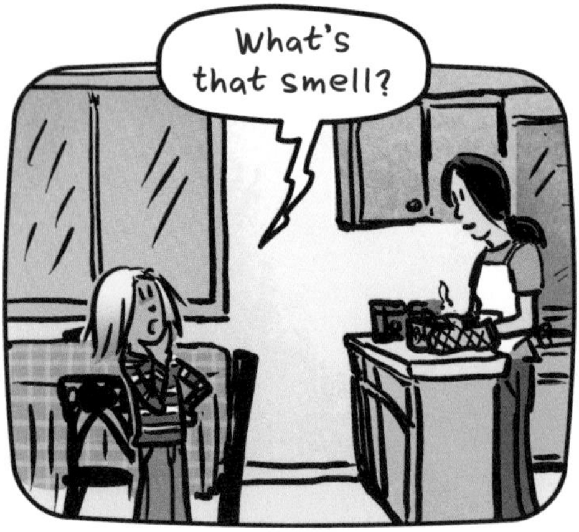
What's that smell?

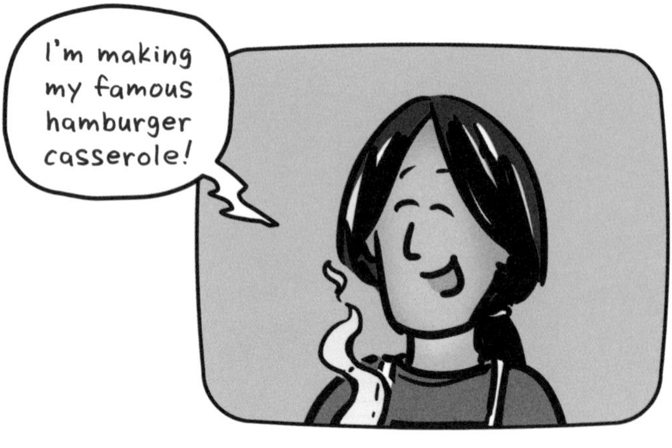
I'm making my famous hamburger casserole!

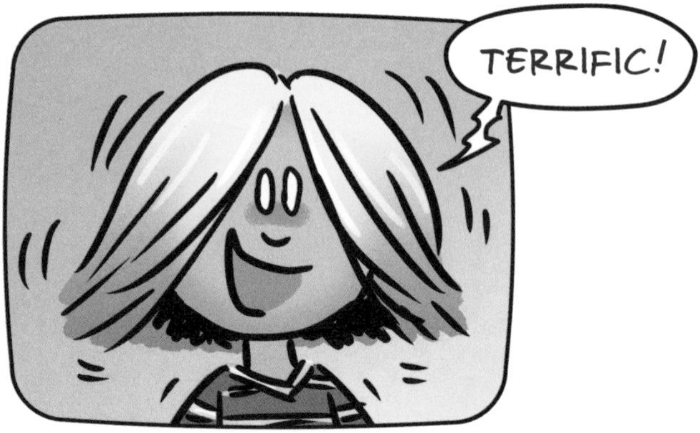
TERRIFIC!

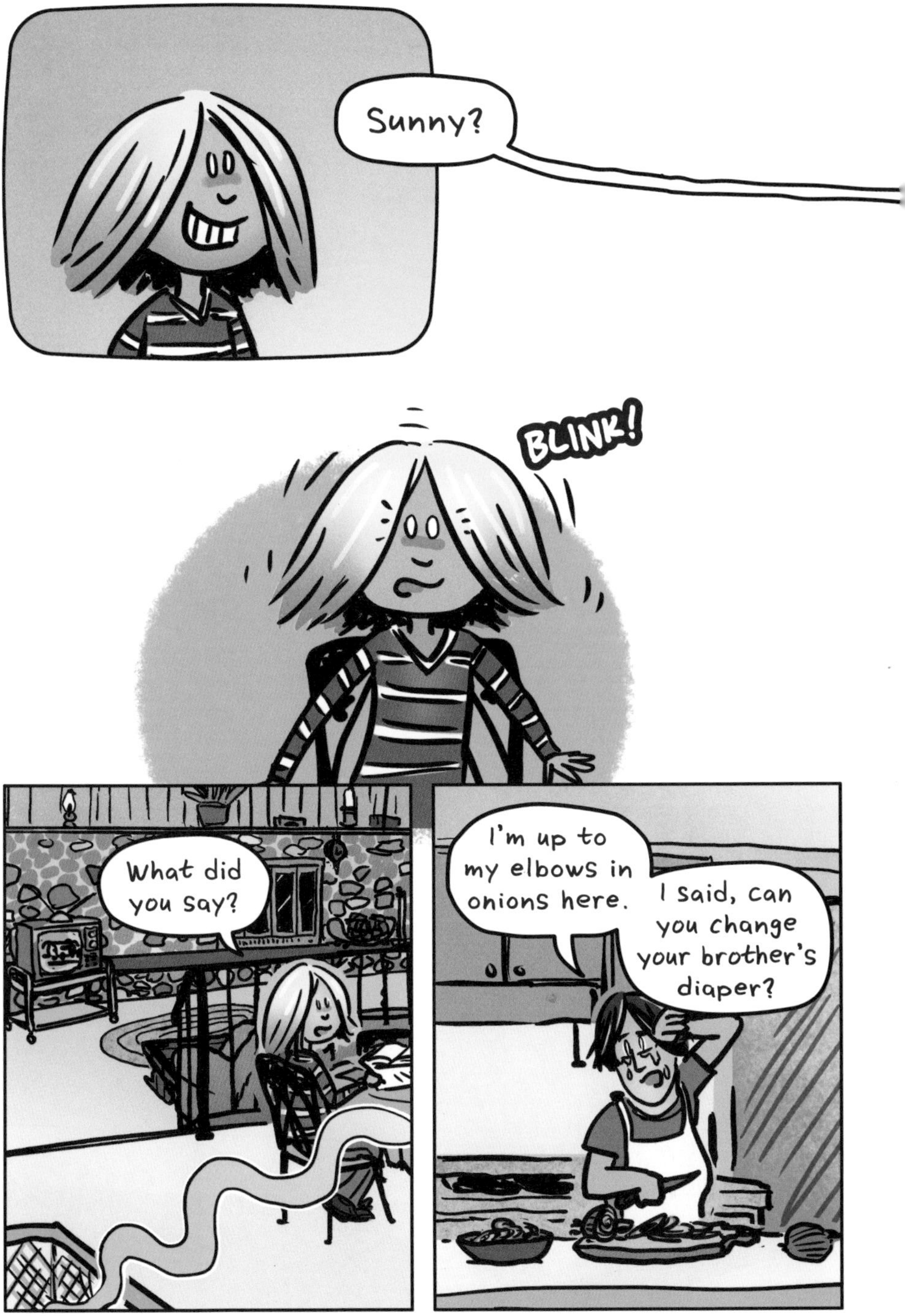
Sunny?
BLINK!
What did you say?
I'm up to my elbows in onions here.
I said, can you change your brother's diaper?

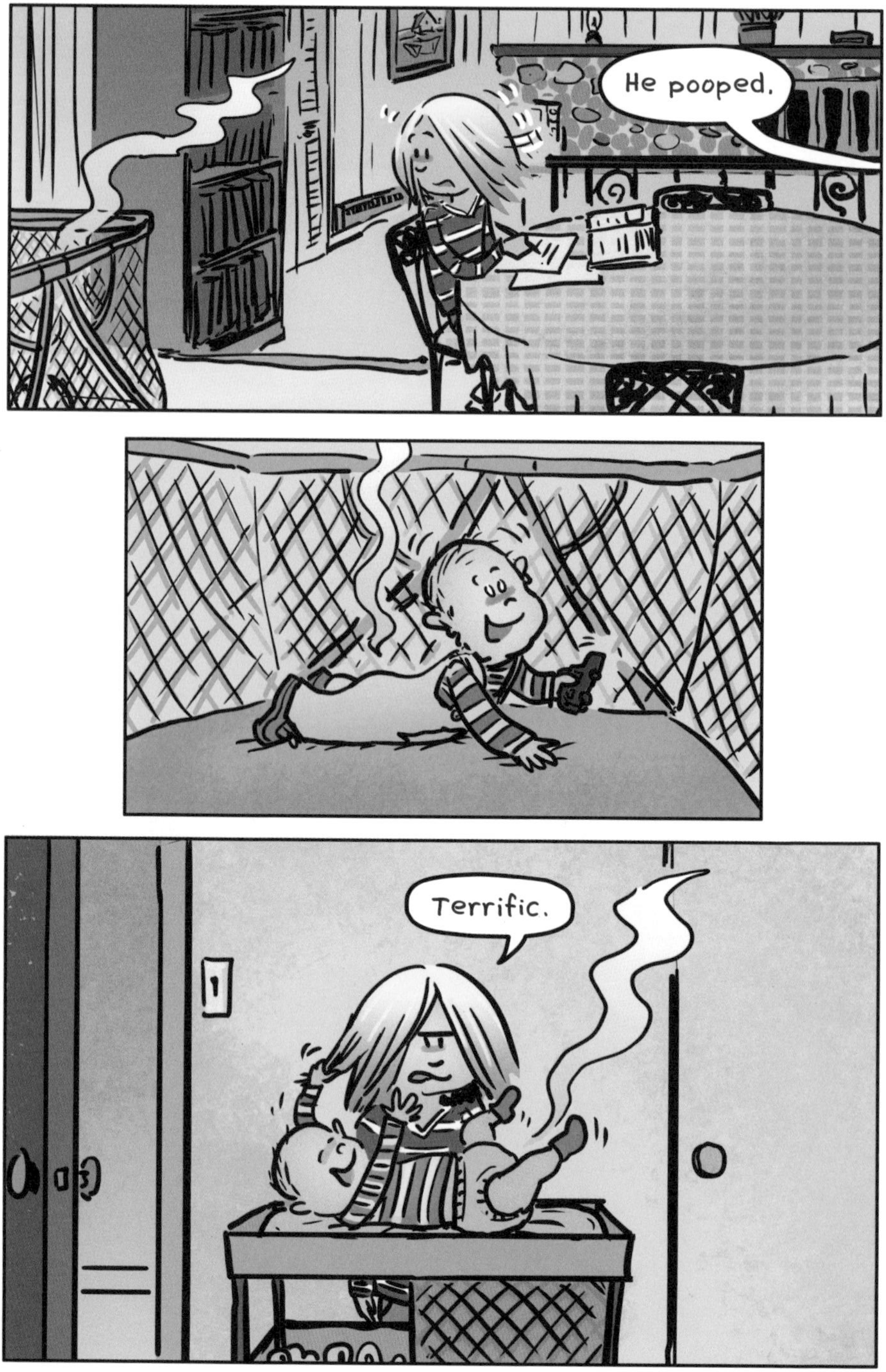
He pooped.
Terrific.

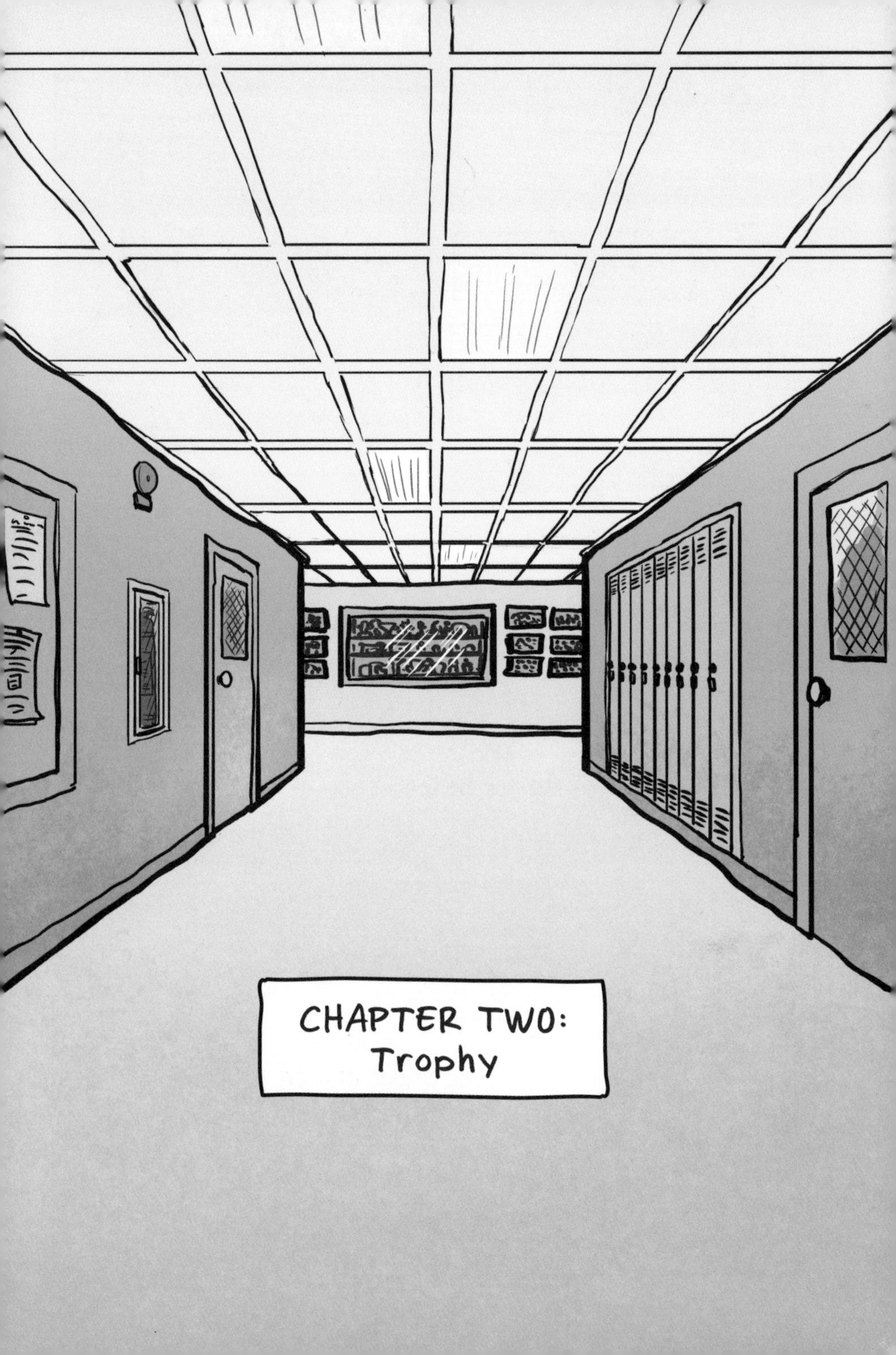
CHAPTER TWO:
Trophy

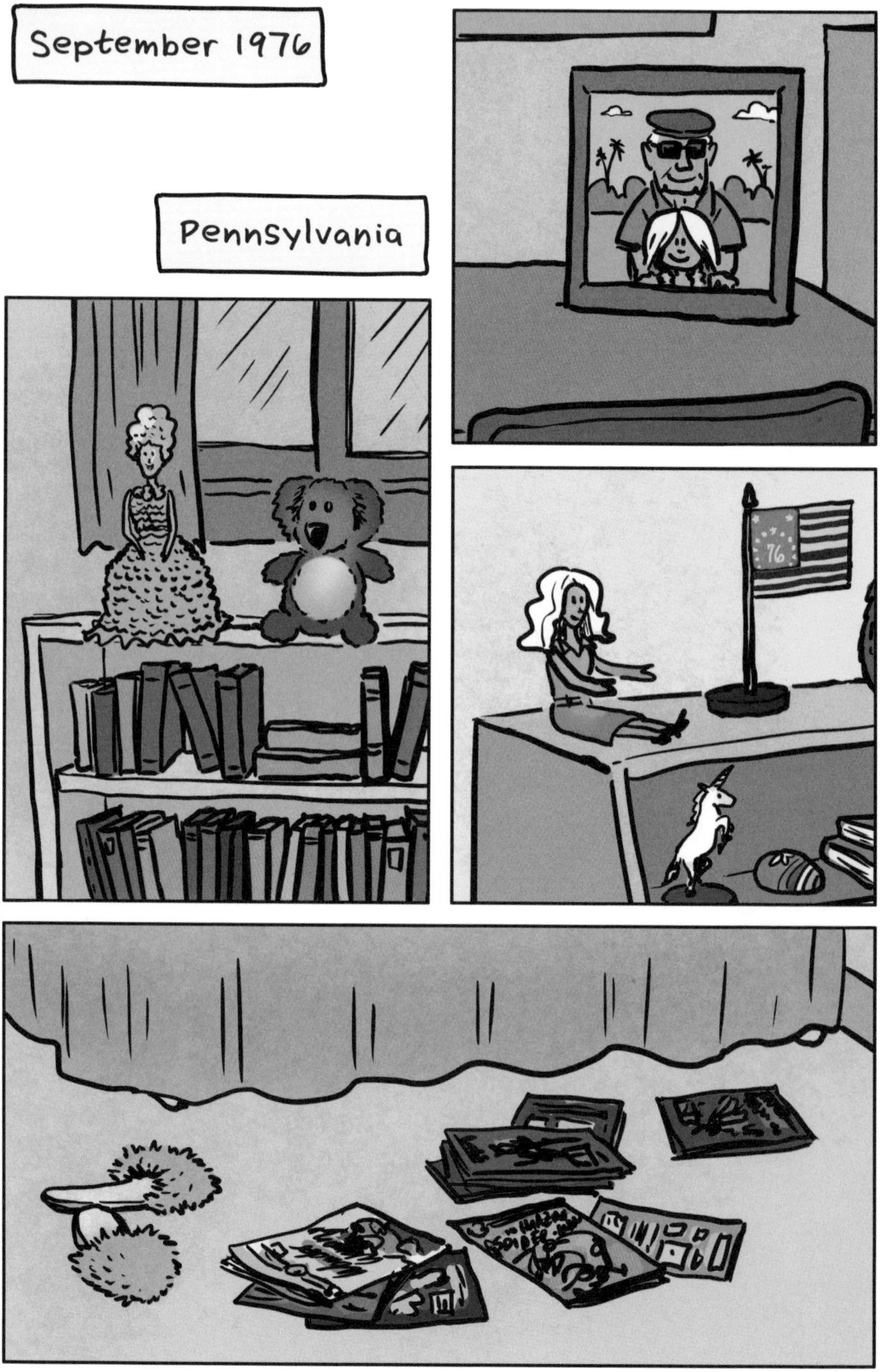
September 1976
Pennsylvania
76

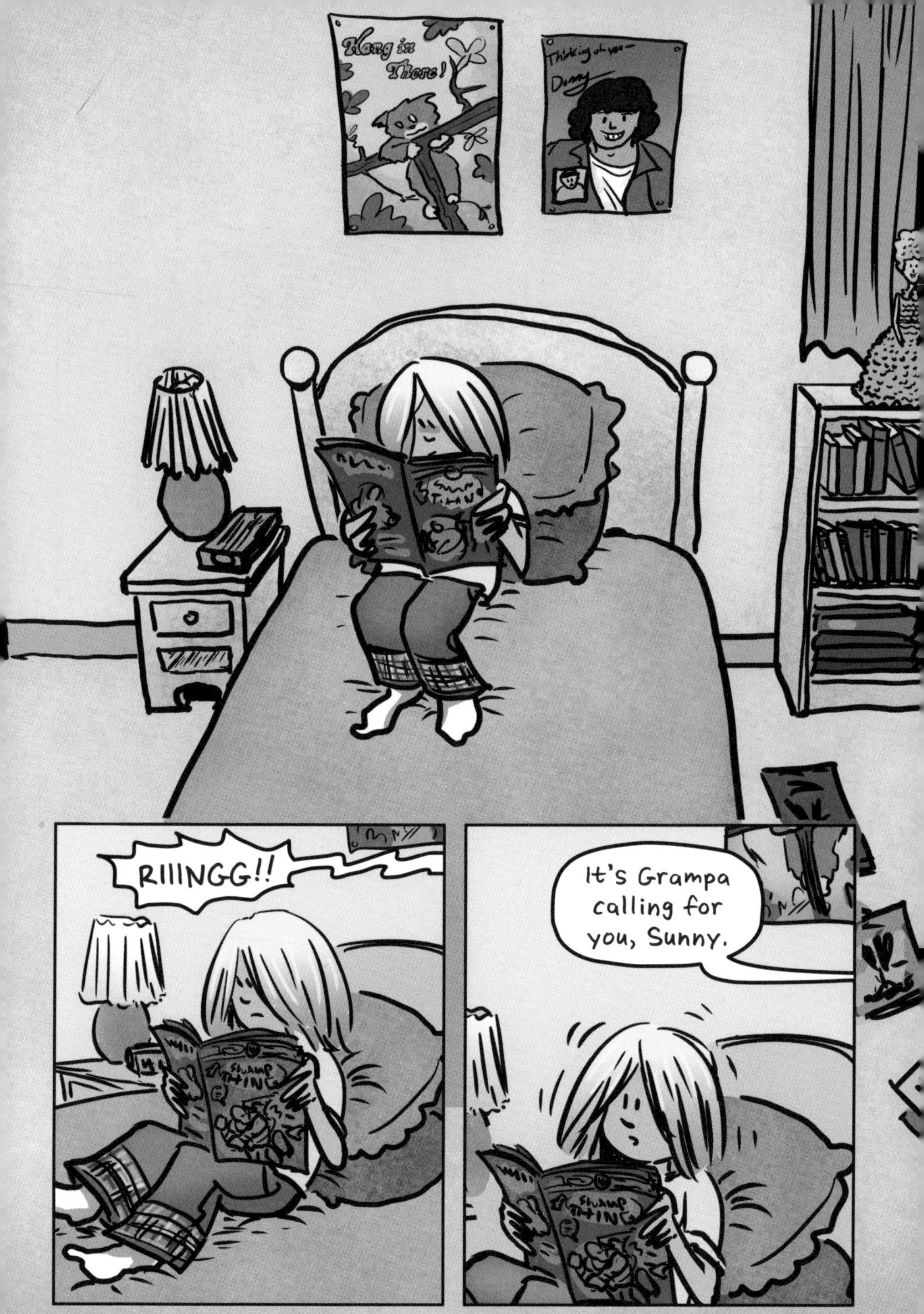
Hang in There!
RIIINGG!!
It's Grampa calling for you, Sunny.

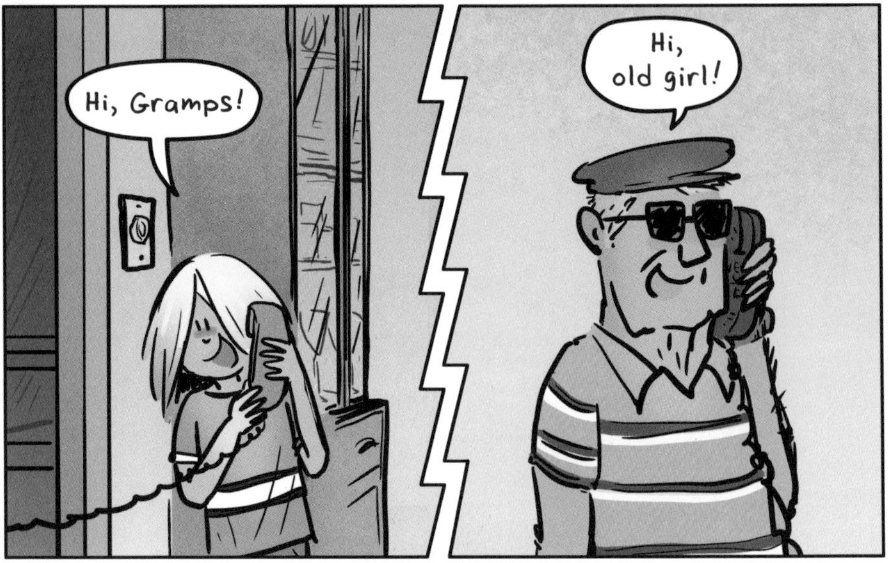
Hi, Gramps!
Hi, old girl!

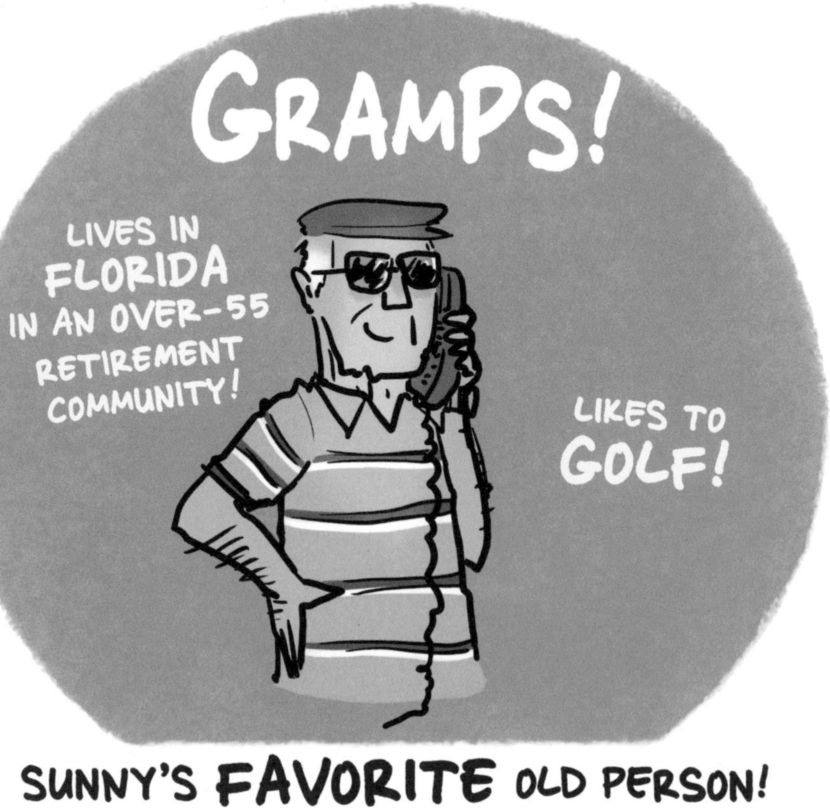
GRAMPS!
LIVES IN FLORIDA IN AN OVER-55 RETIREMENT COMMUNITY!
LIKES TO GOLF!

SUNNY'S **FAVORITE** OLD PERSON!

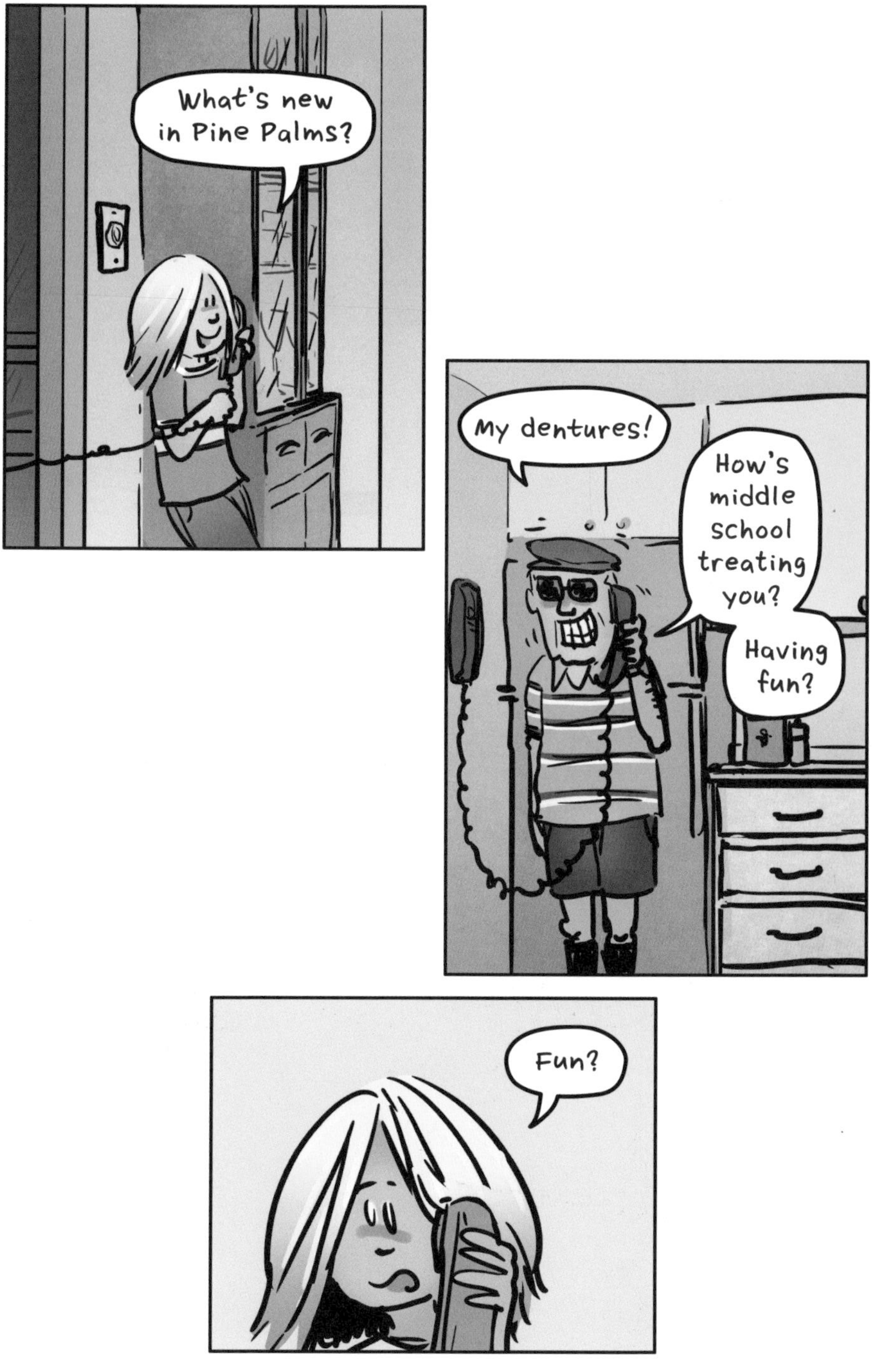
What's new in Pine Palms?
My dentures!
How's middle school treating you?
Having fun?
Fun?

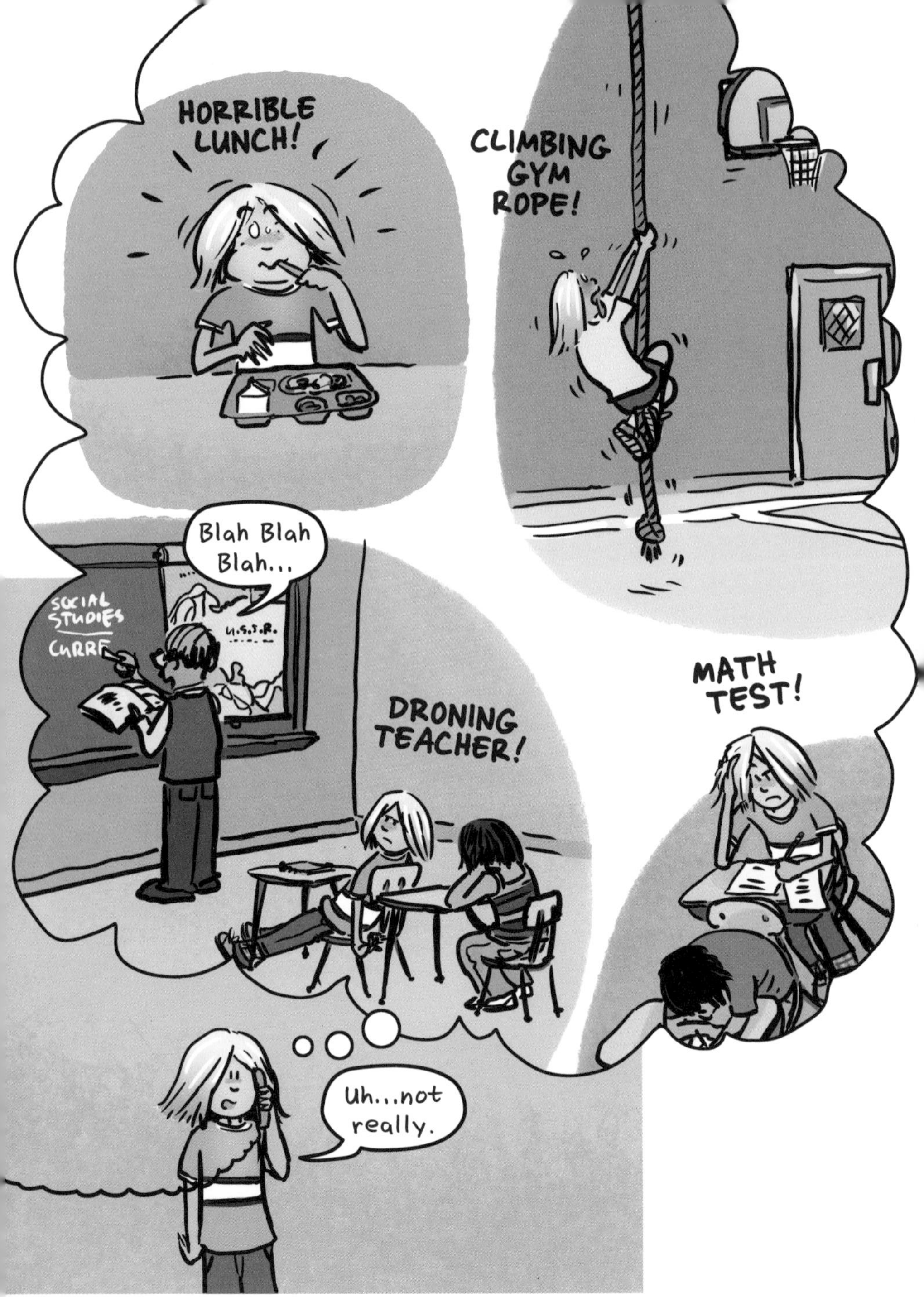
HORRIBLE LUNCH!
CLIMBING GYM ROPE!
SOCIAL STUDIES
CURRE
U.S.S.R.
Blah Blah Blah...
DRONING TEACHER!
MATH TEST!
Uh...not really.

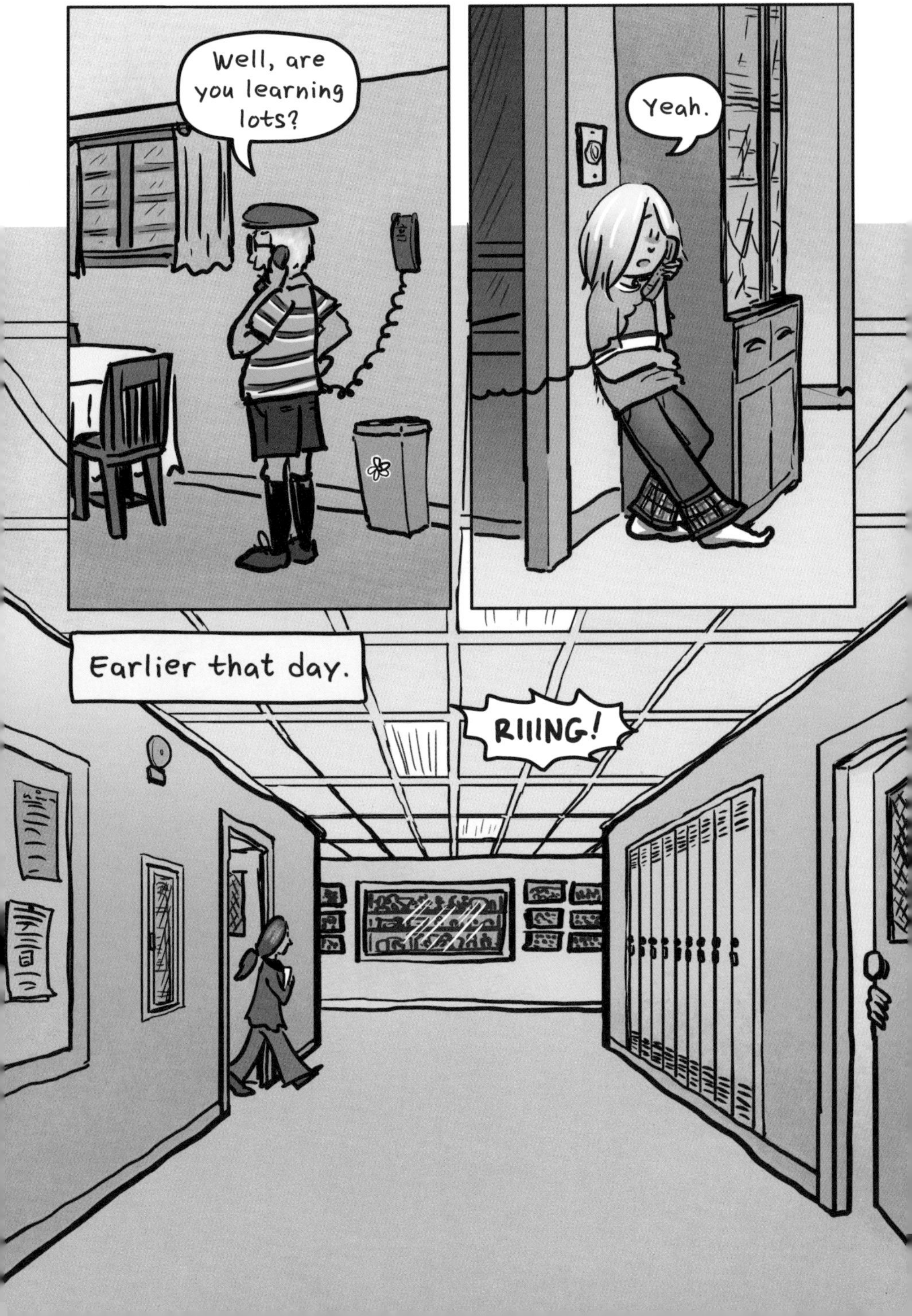
Well, are you learning lots?
Yeah.
Earlier that day.
RIIING!

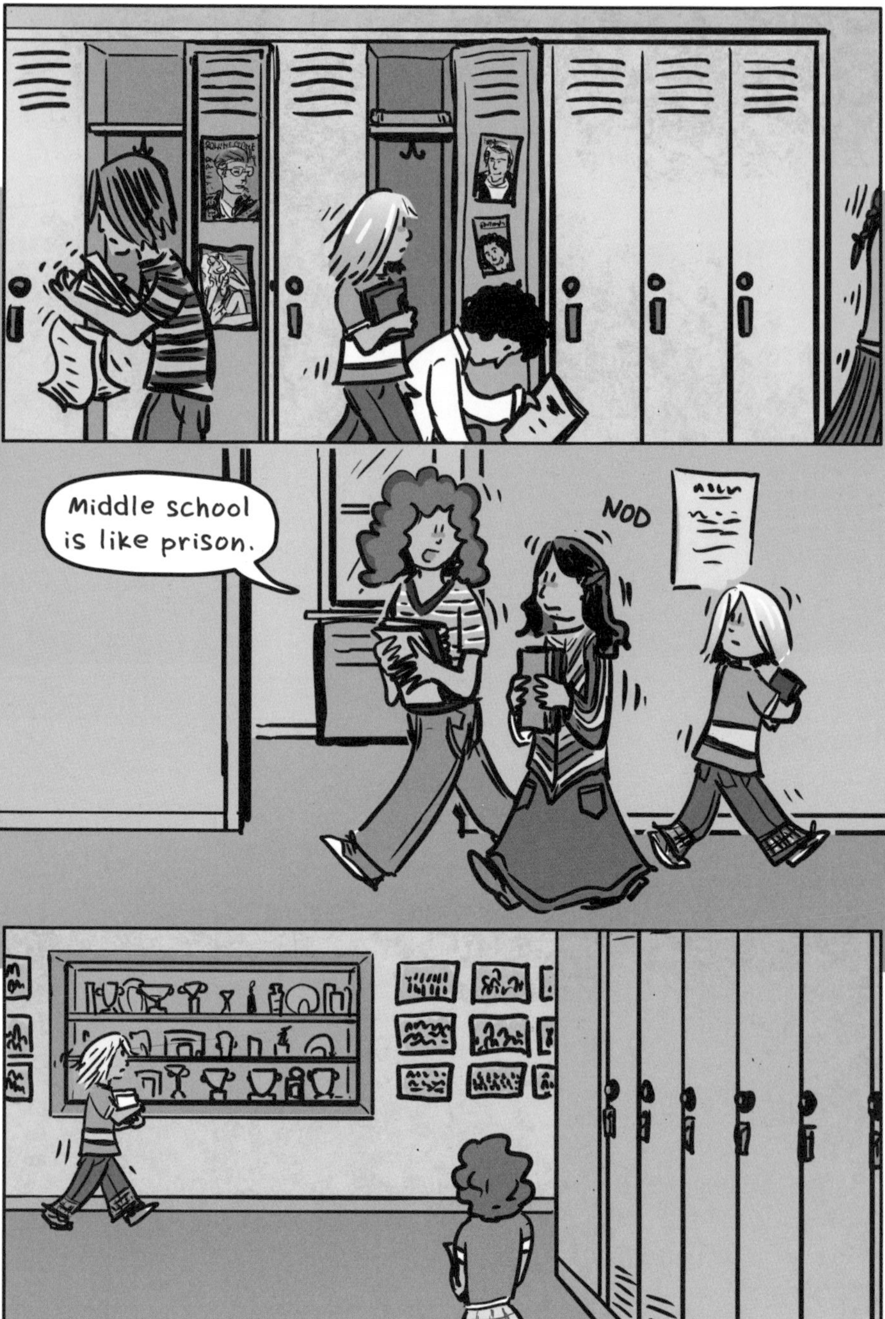
Middle school is like prison.
NOD

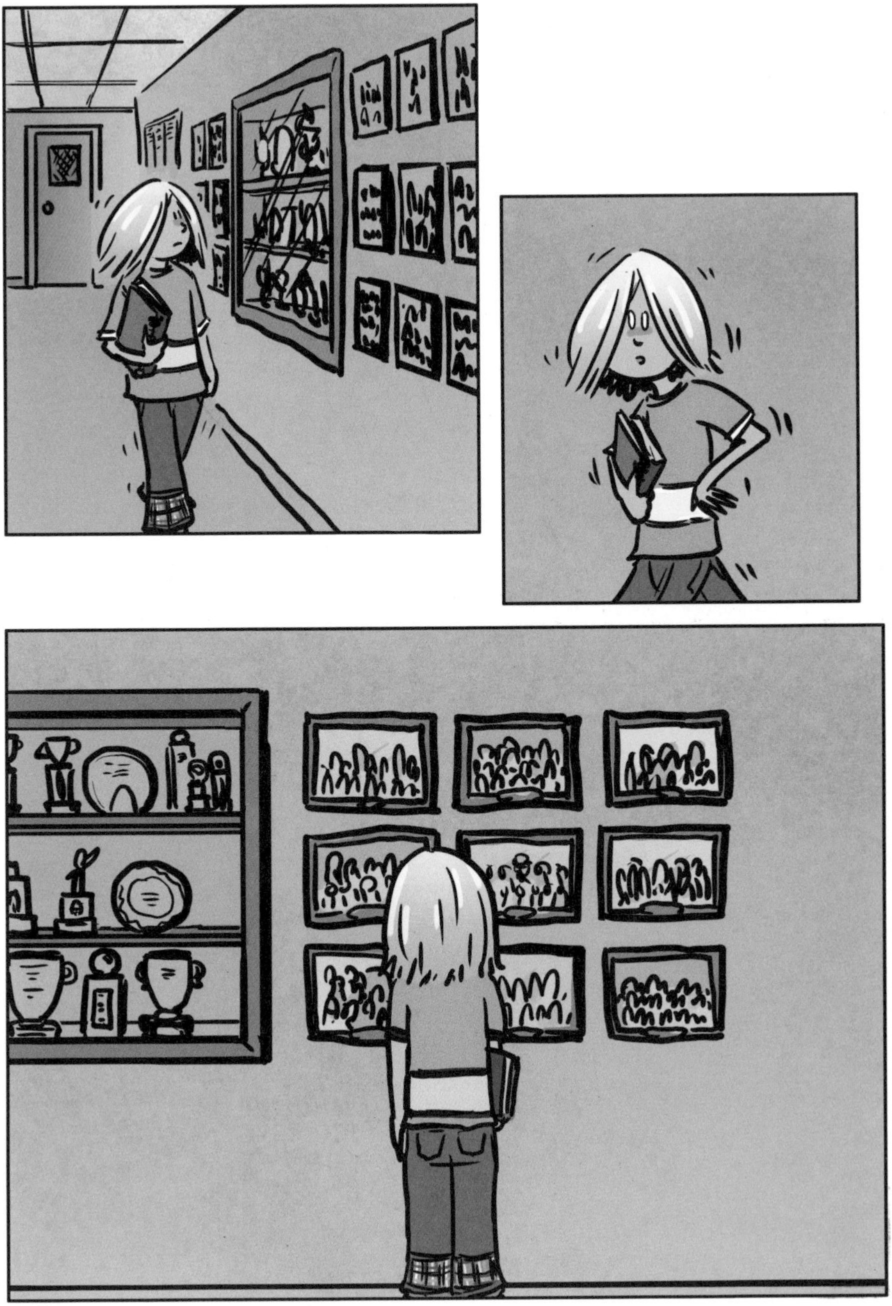

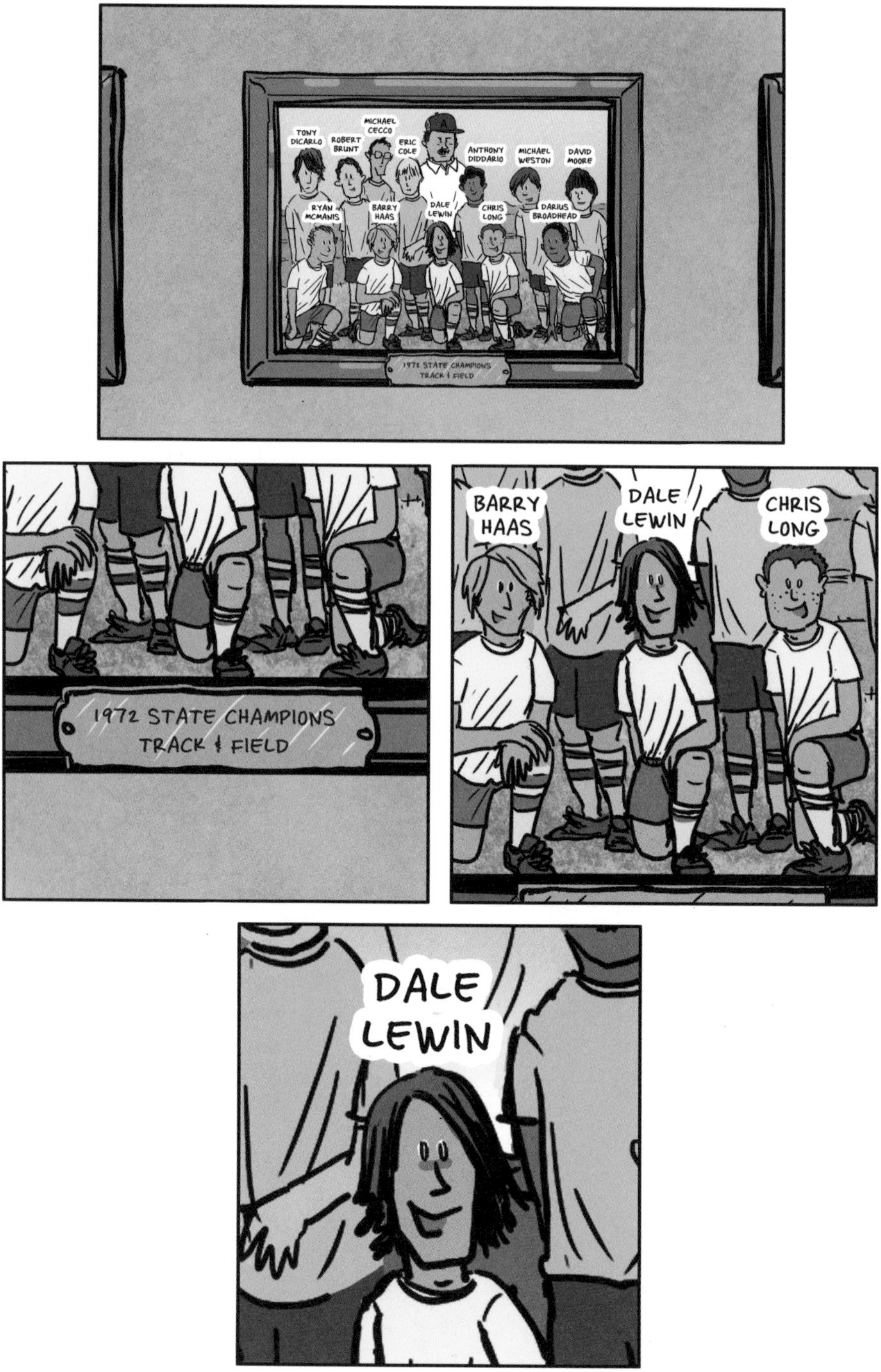
TONY DICARLO
ROBERT BRUNT
MICHAEL CECCO
ERIC COLE
ANTHONY DIDDARIO
MICHAEL WESTON
DAVID MOORE
RYAN MCMANIS
BARRY HAAS
DALE LEWIN
CHRIS LONG
DARIUS BROADHEAD
1972 STATE CHAMPIONS
TRACK & FIELD
1972 STATE CHAMPIONS
TRACK & FIELD
BARRY HAAS
DALE LEWIN
CHRIS LONG
DALE LEWIN

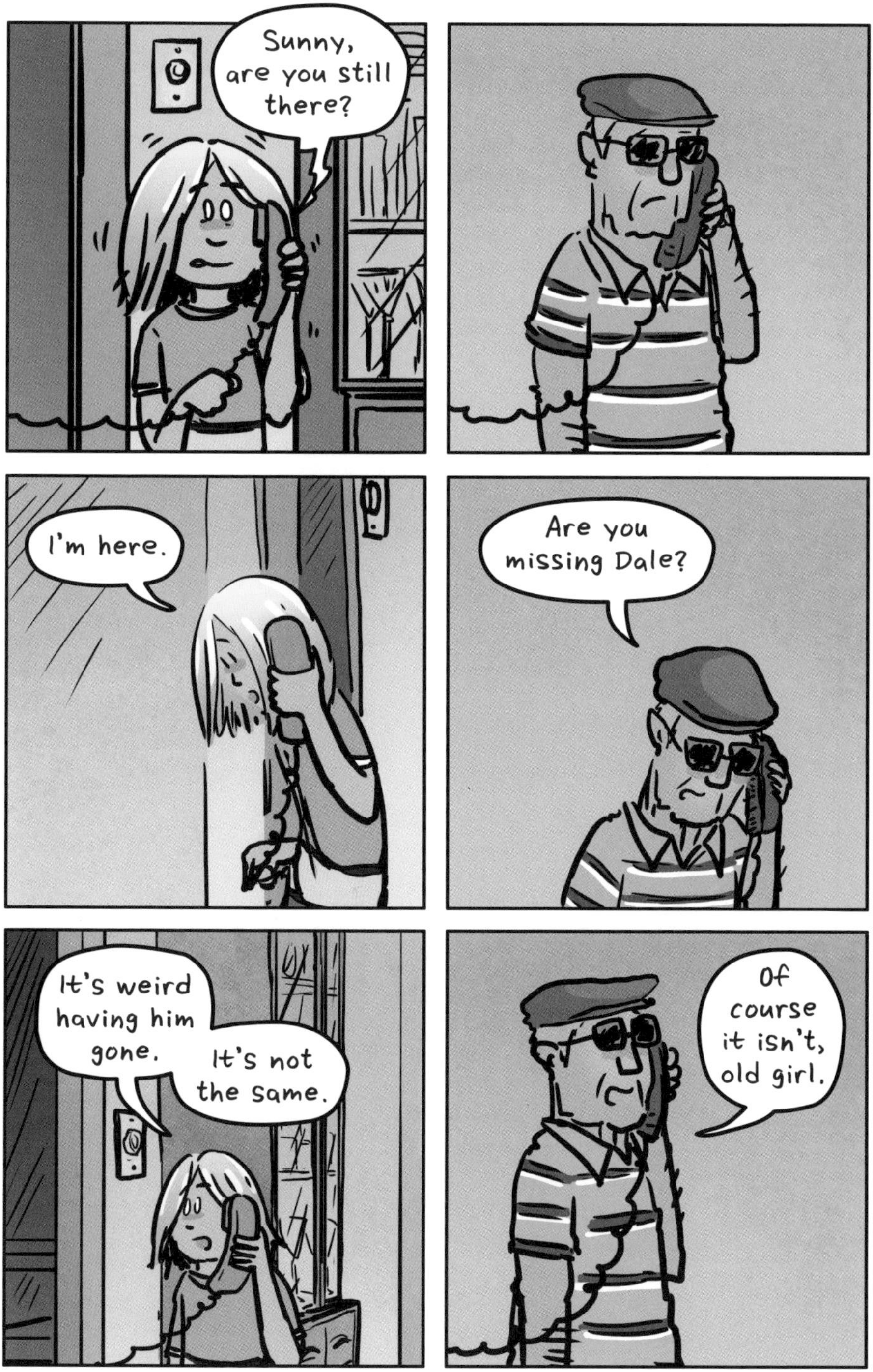
Sunny, are you still there?
I'm here.
Are you missing Dale?
It's weird having him gone.
It's not the same.
Of course it isn't, old girl.

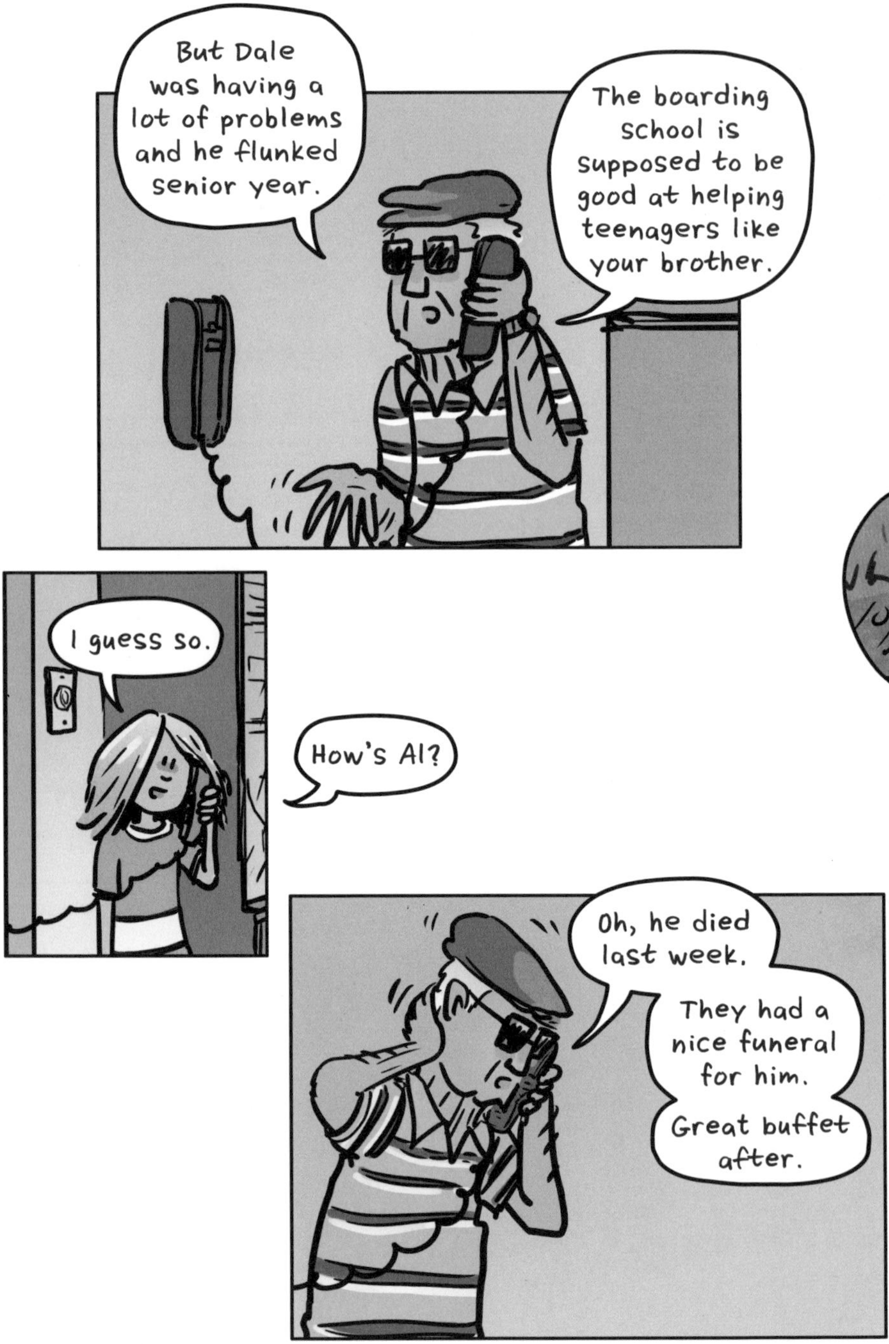

But Dale was having a lot of problems and he flunked senior year.
The boarding school is supposed to be good at helping teenagers like your brother.
I guess so.
How's Al?
Oh, he died last week.
They had a nice funeral for him.
Great buffet after.

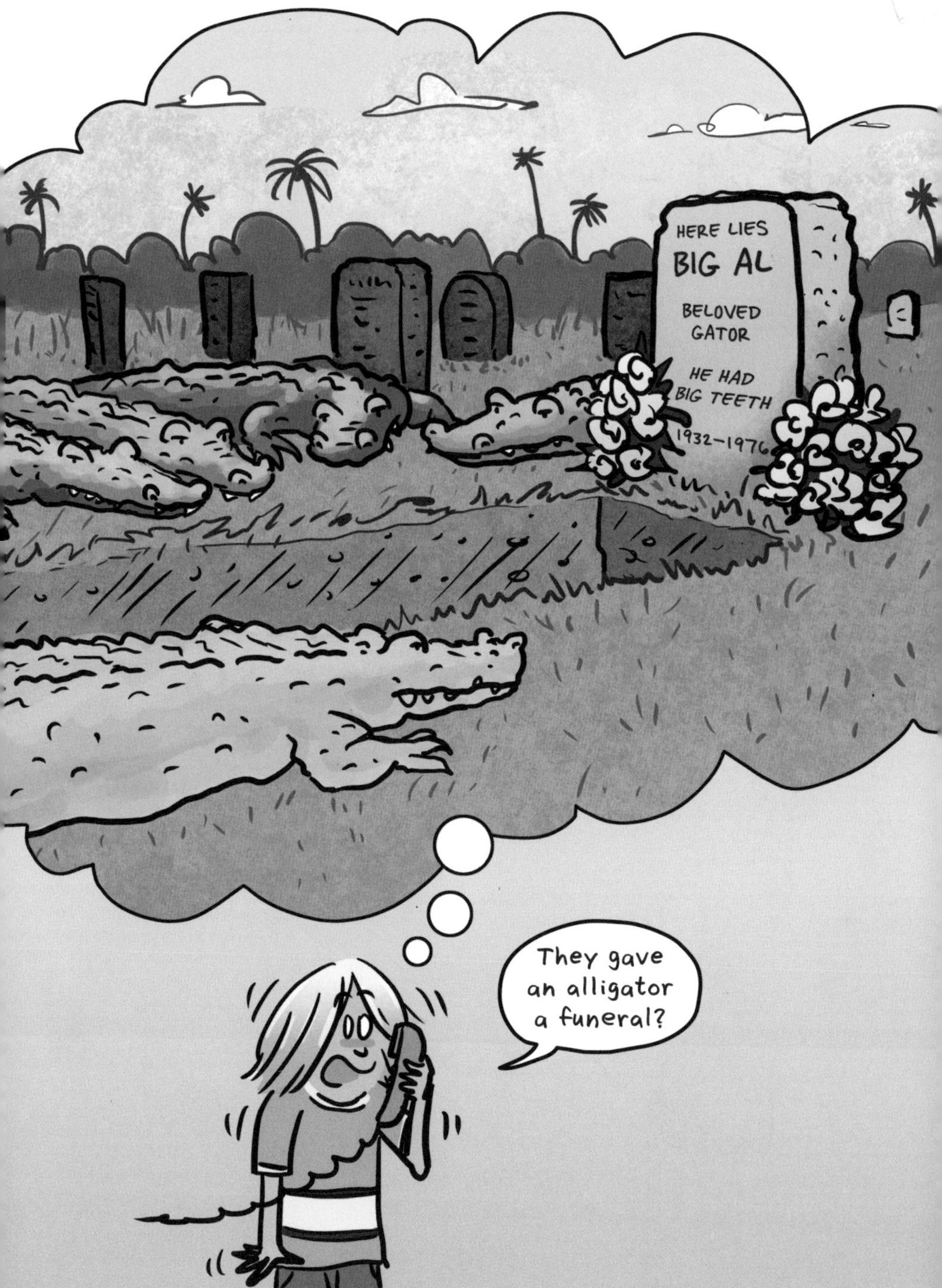
HERE LIES
BIG AL
BELOVED
GATOR
HE HAD
BIG TEETH
1932–1976
They gave an alligator a funeral?

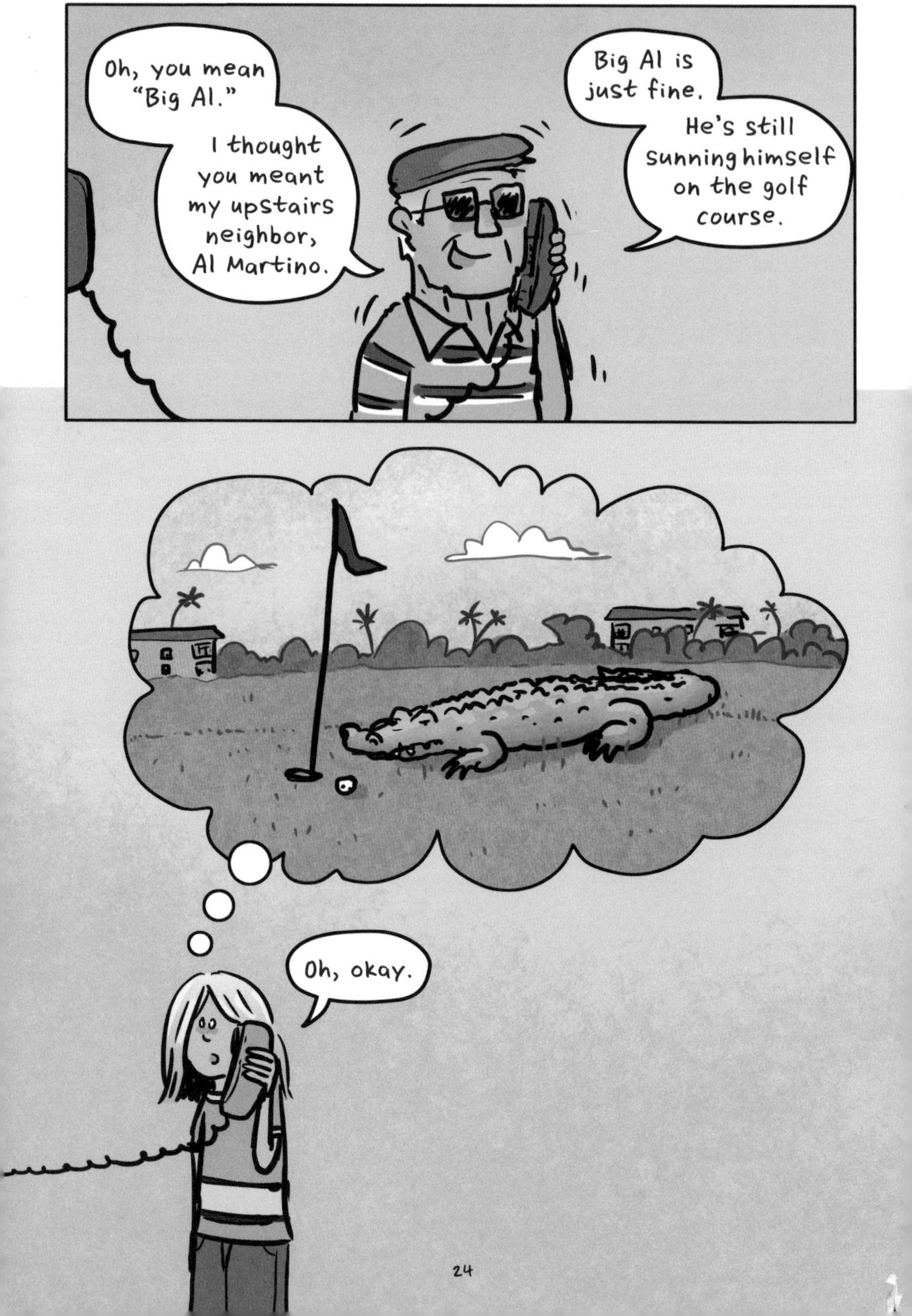
Oh, you mean "Big Al."
I thought you meant my upstairs neighbor, Al Martino.
Big Al is just fine.
He's still sunning himself on the golf course.
Oh, okay.

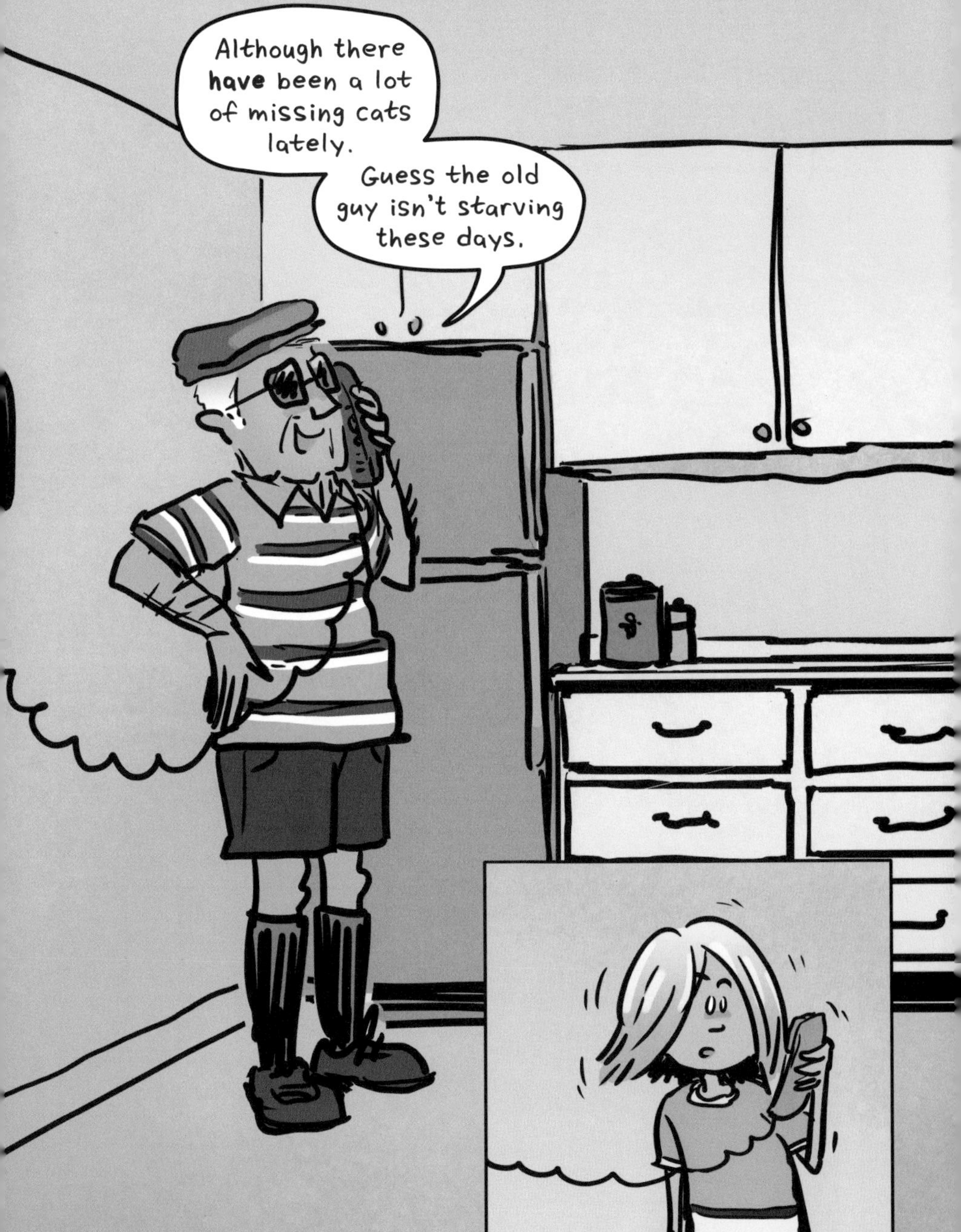
Although there **have** been a lot of missing cats lately.
Guess the old guy isn't starving these days.

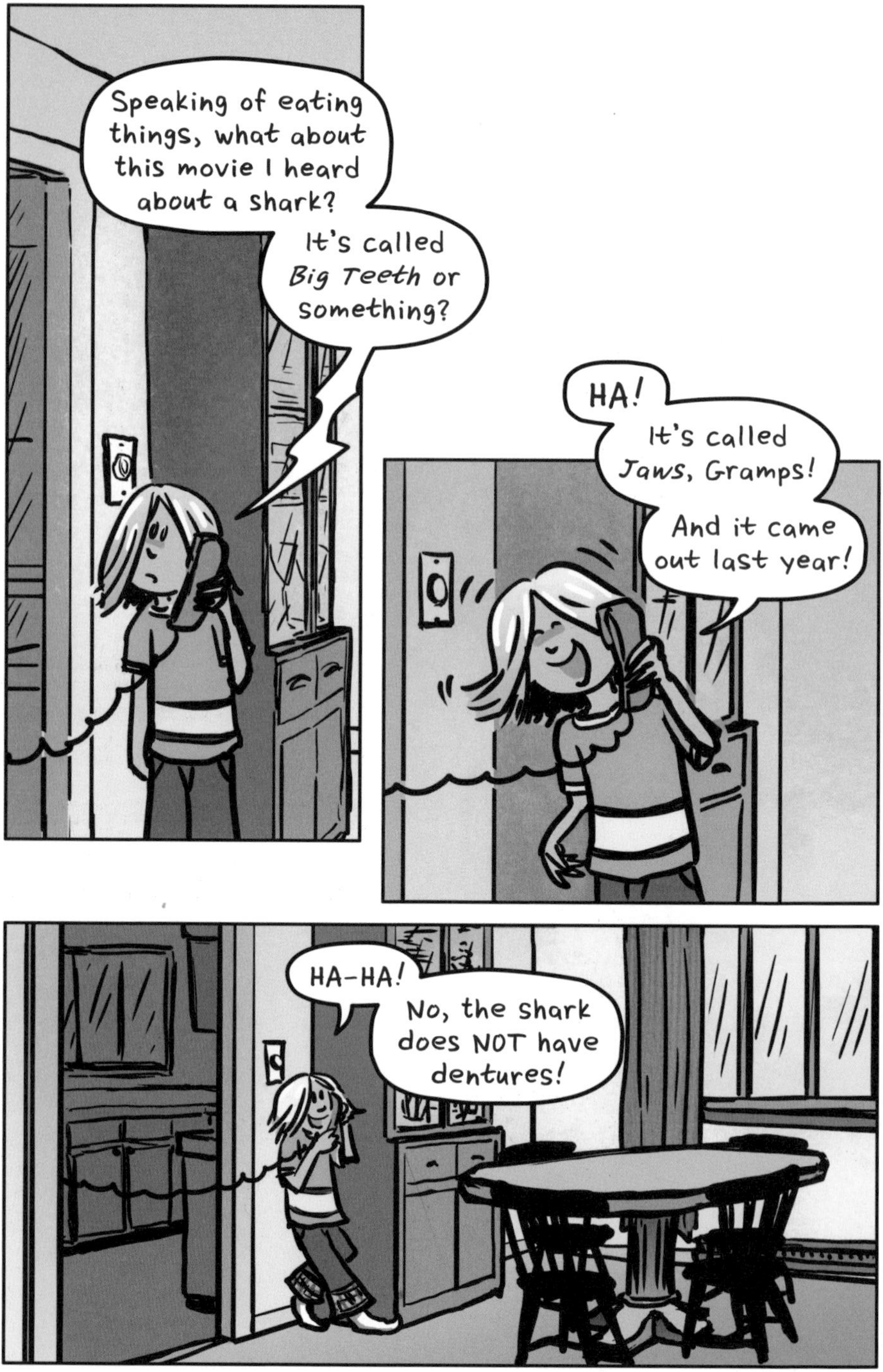
Speaking of eating things, what about this movie I heard about a shark?
It's called *Big Teeth* or something?
HA!
It's called *Jaws*, Gramps!
And it came out last year!
HA-HA!
No, the shark does NOT have dentures!

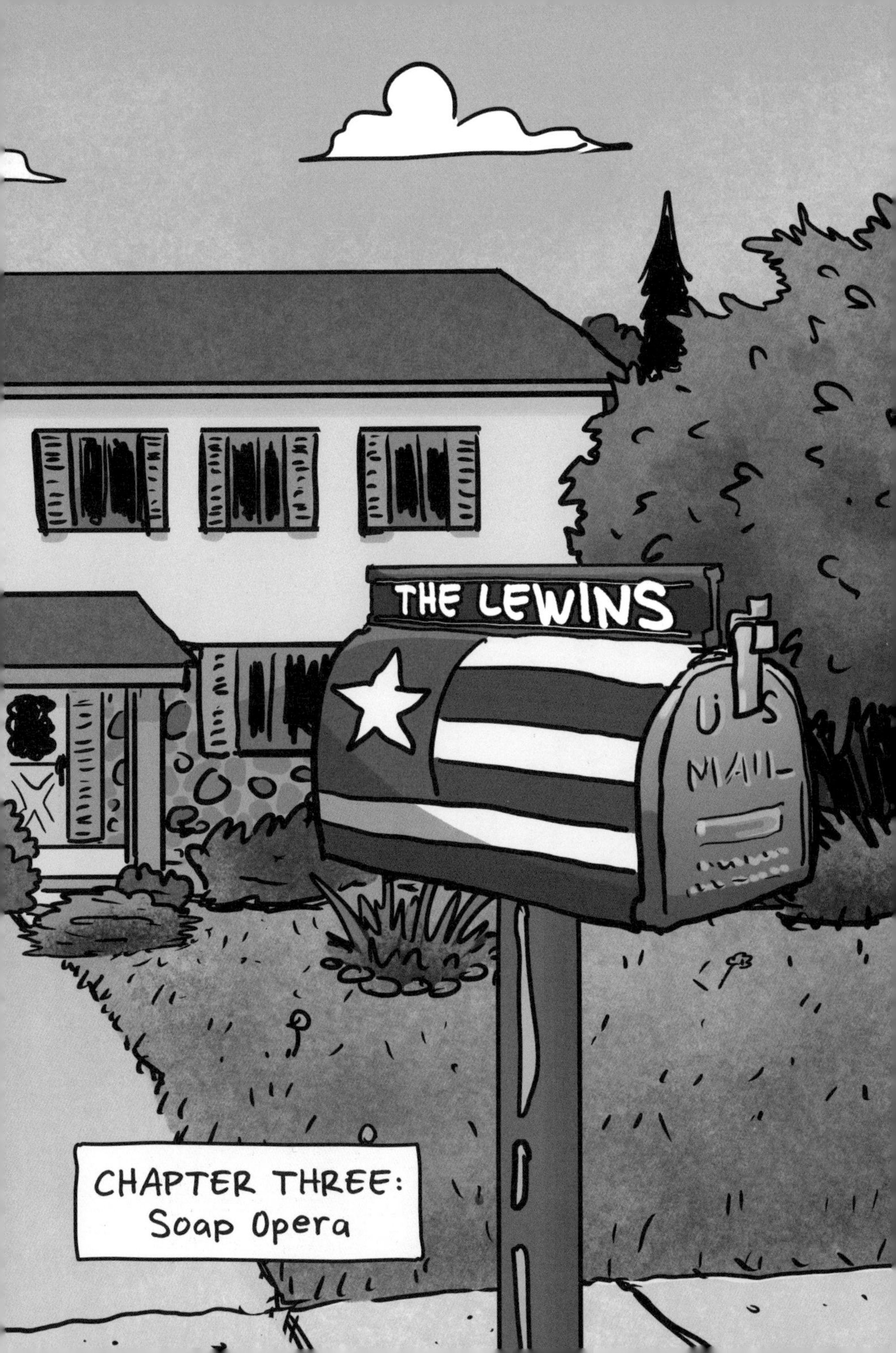
THE LEWINS
U.S. MAIL
CHAPTER THREE:
Soap Opera

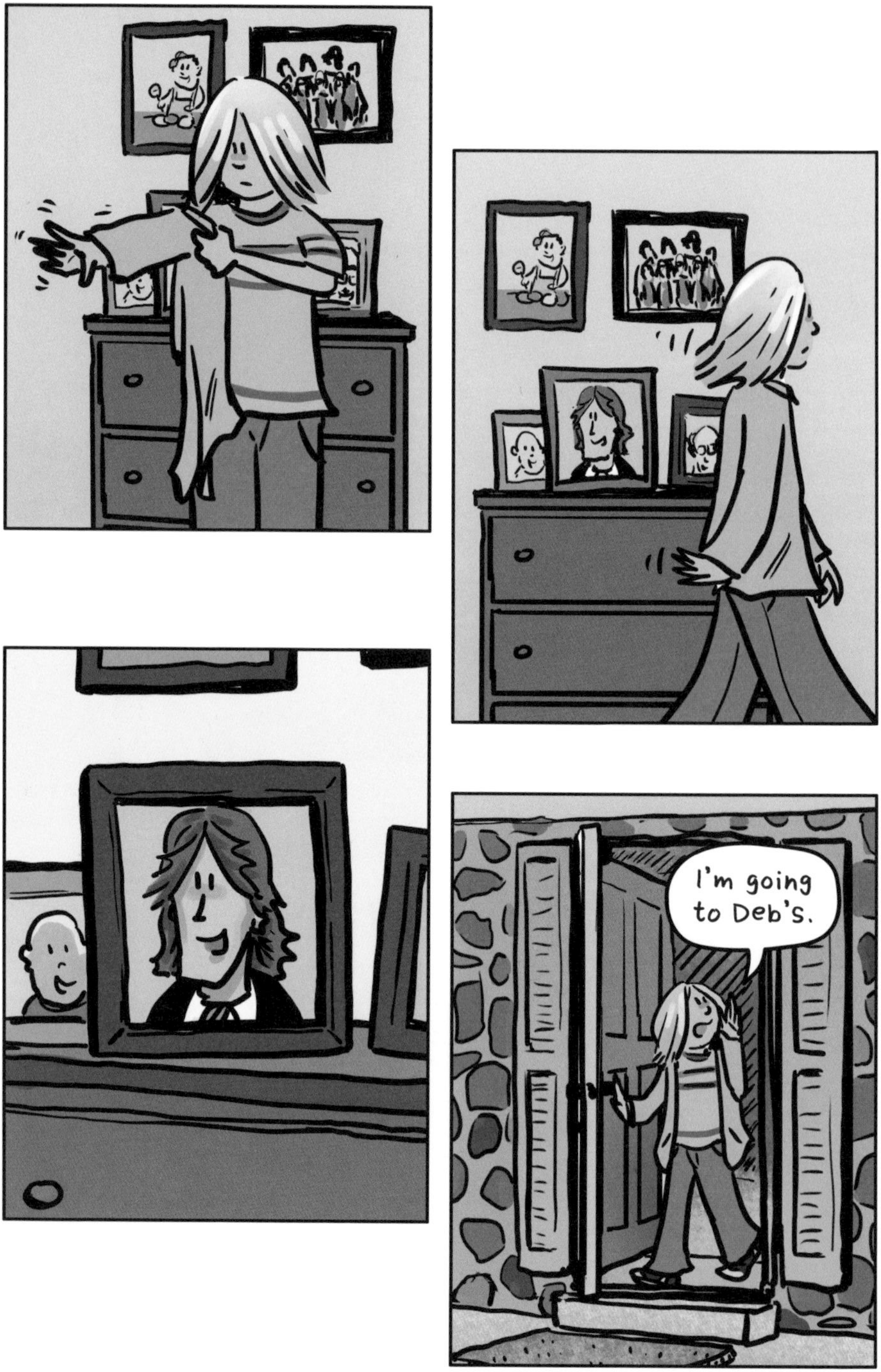
I'm going to Deb's.

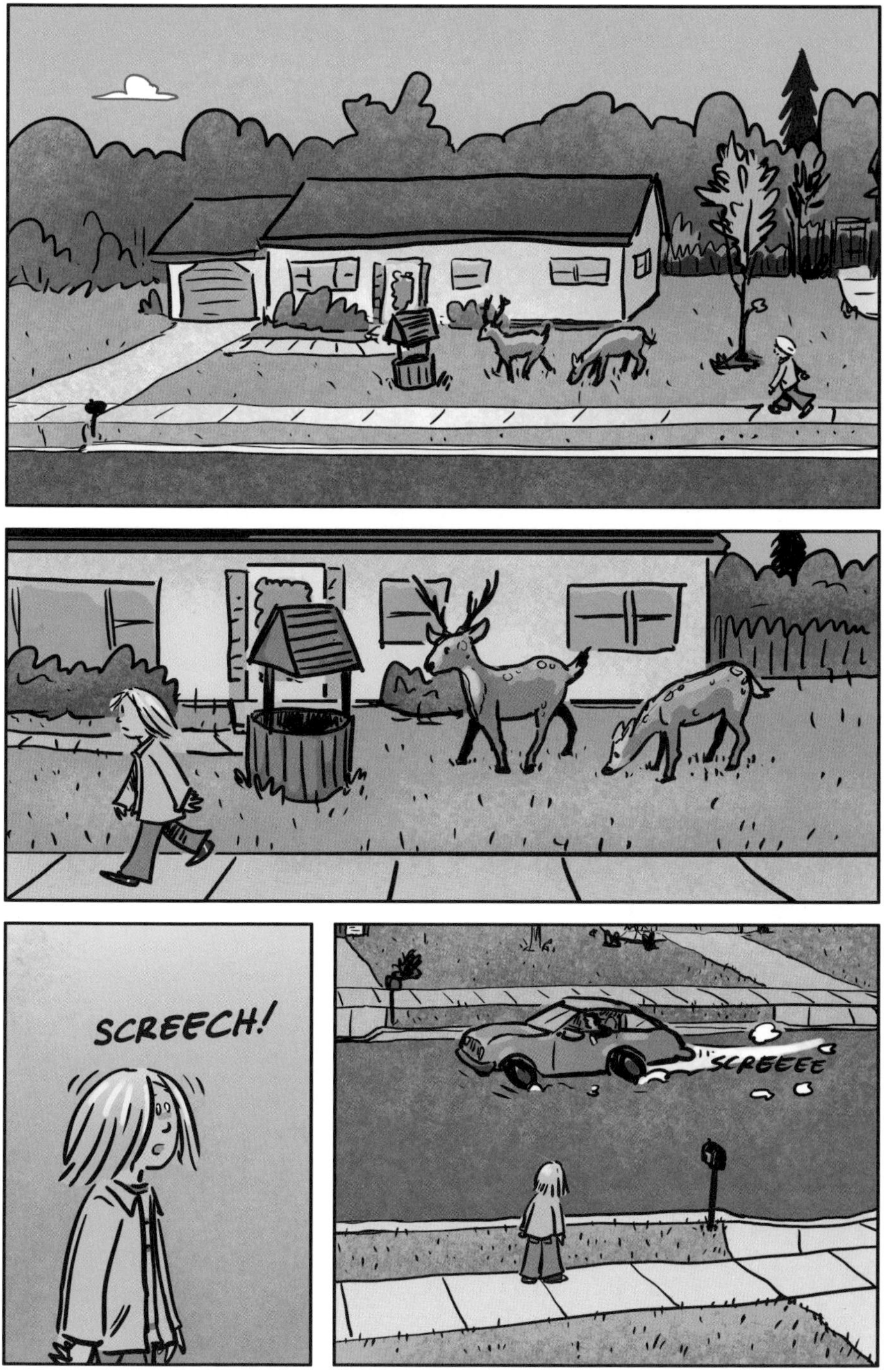
SCREECH!
SCREEEE

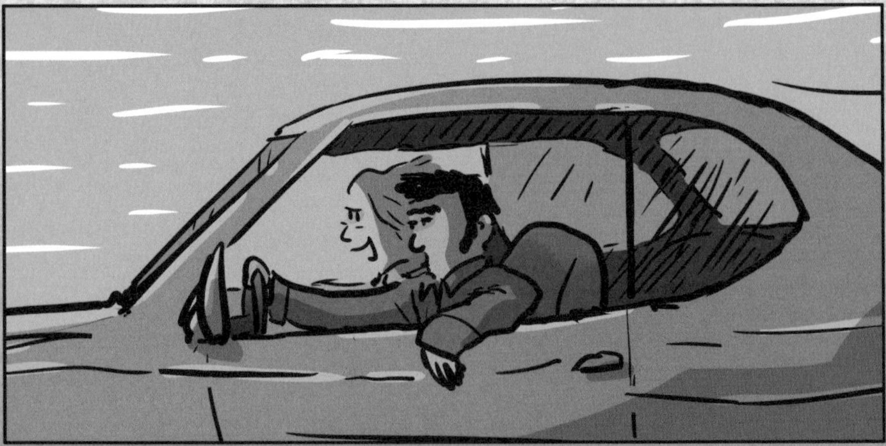

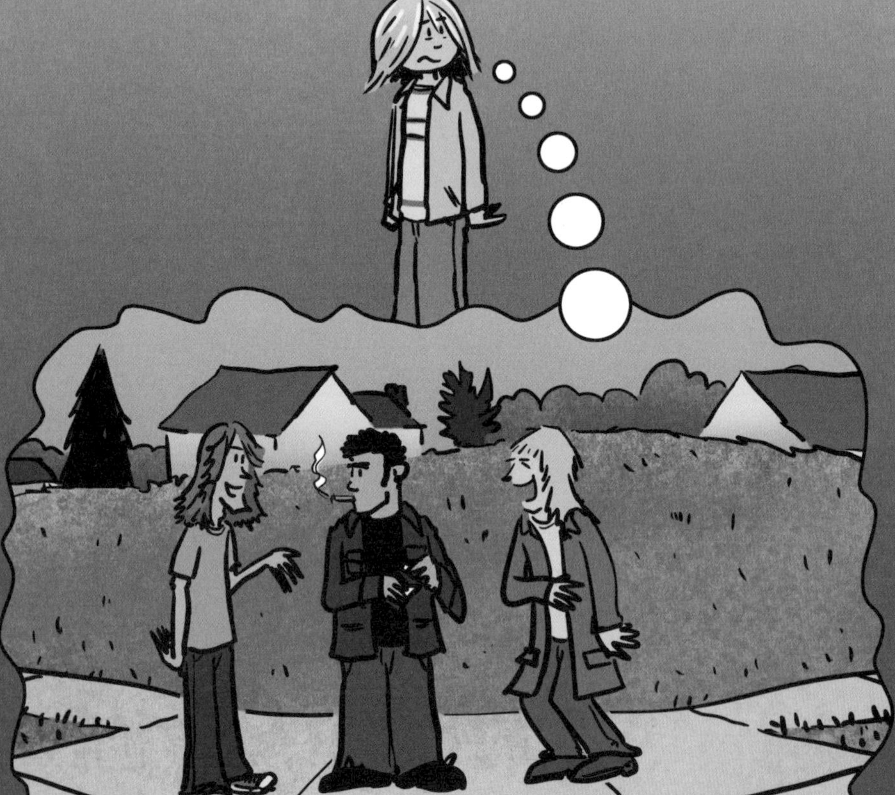

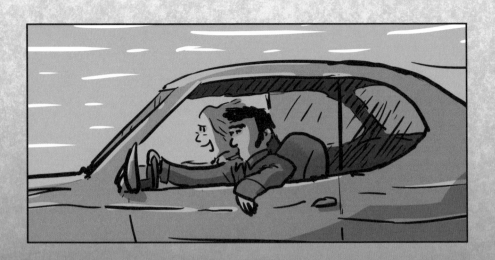

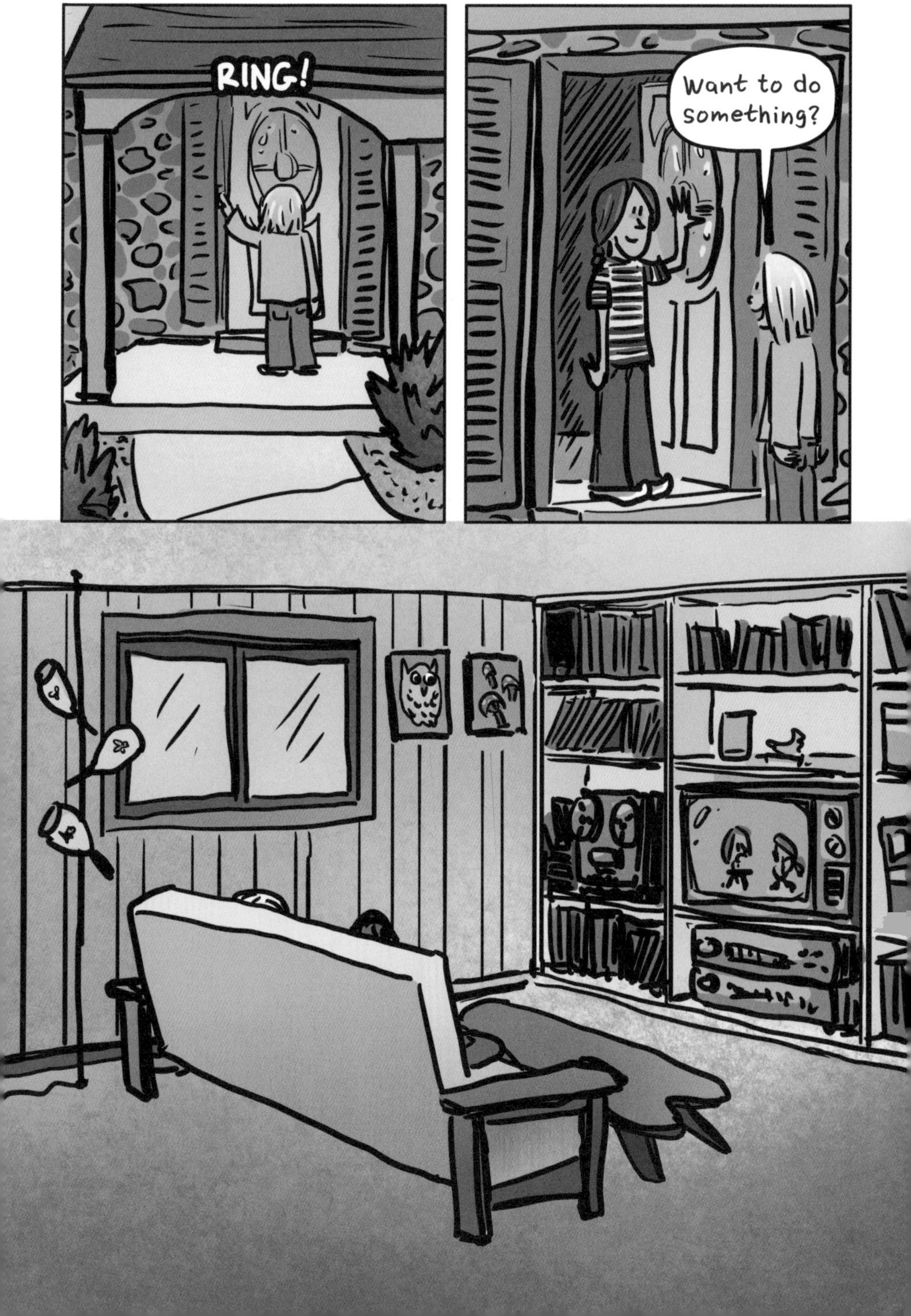
RING!
Want to do something?

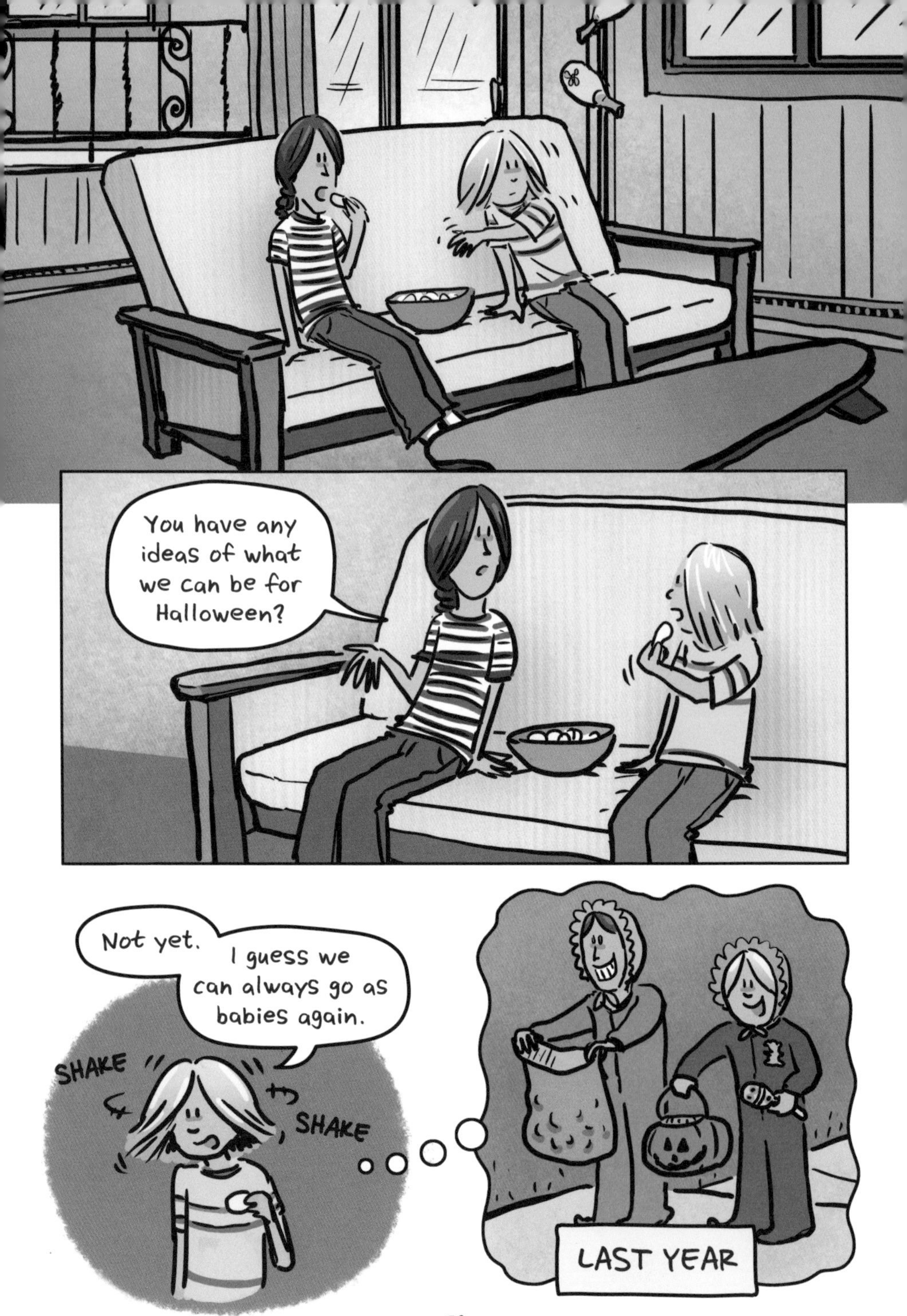

You have any ideas of what we can be for Halloween?
Not yet.
I guess we can always go as babies again.
SHAKE
SHAKE
LAST YEAR

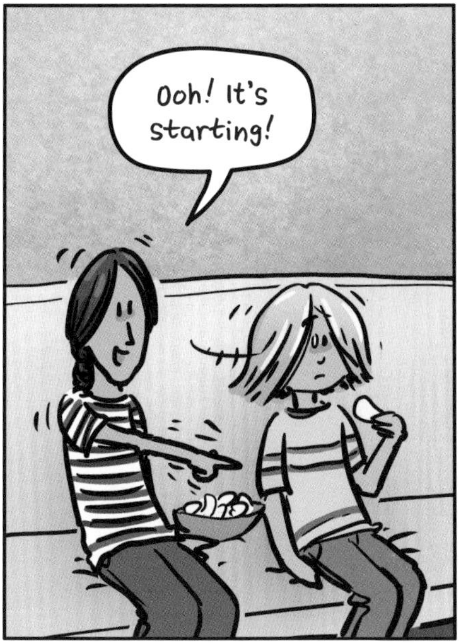
Ooh! It's starting!

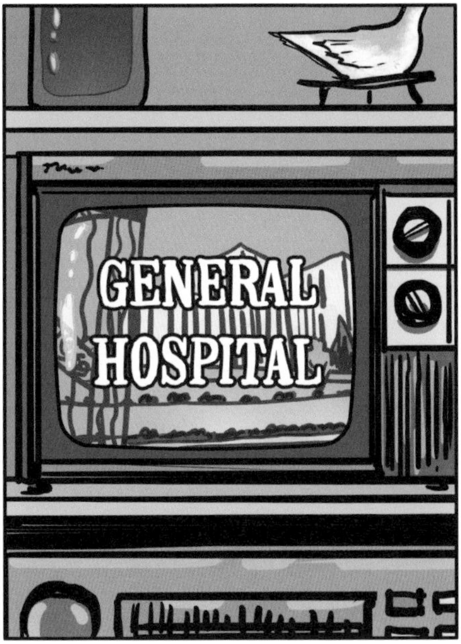
GENERAL HOSPITAL

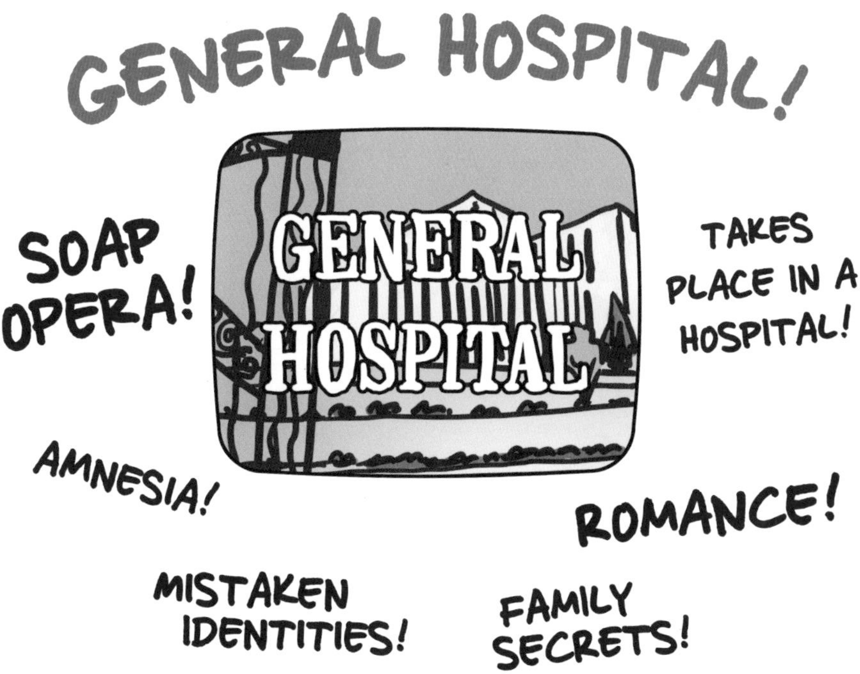
GENERAL HOSPITAL!
SOAP OPERA!
GENERAL HOSPITAL
TAKES PLACE IN A HOSPITAL!
AMNESIA!
ROMANCE!
MISTAKEN IDENTITIES!
FAMILY SECRETS!

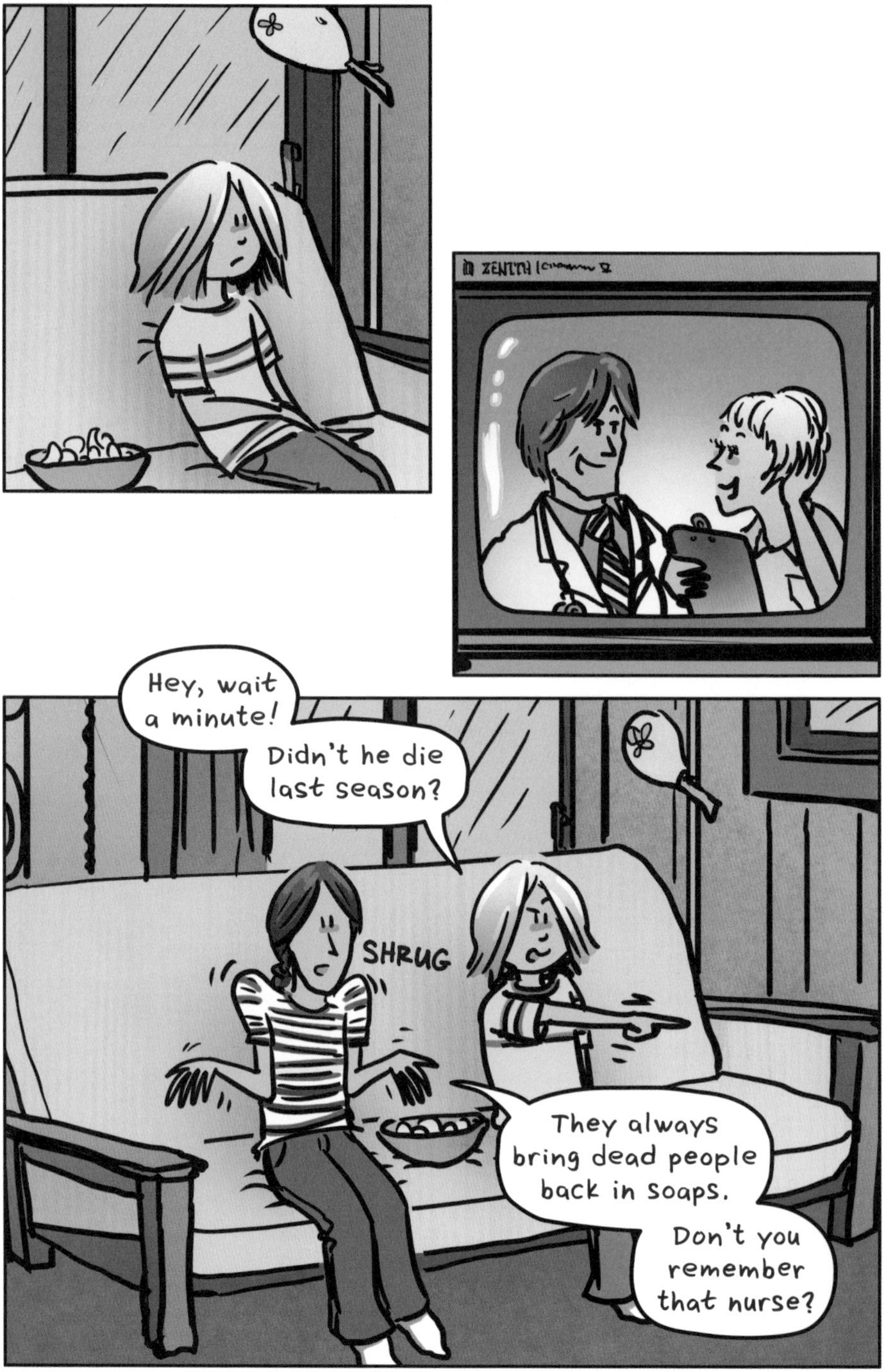
ZENITH
Hey, wait a minute!
Didn't he die last season?
SHRUG
They always bring dead people back in soaps.
Don't you remember that nurse?

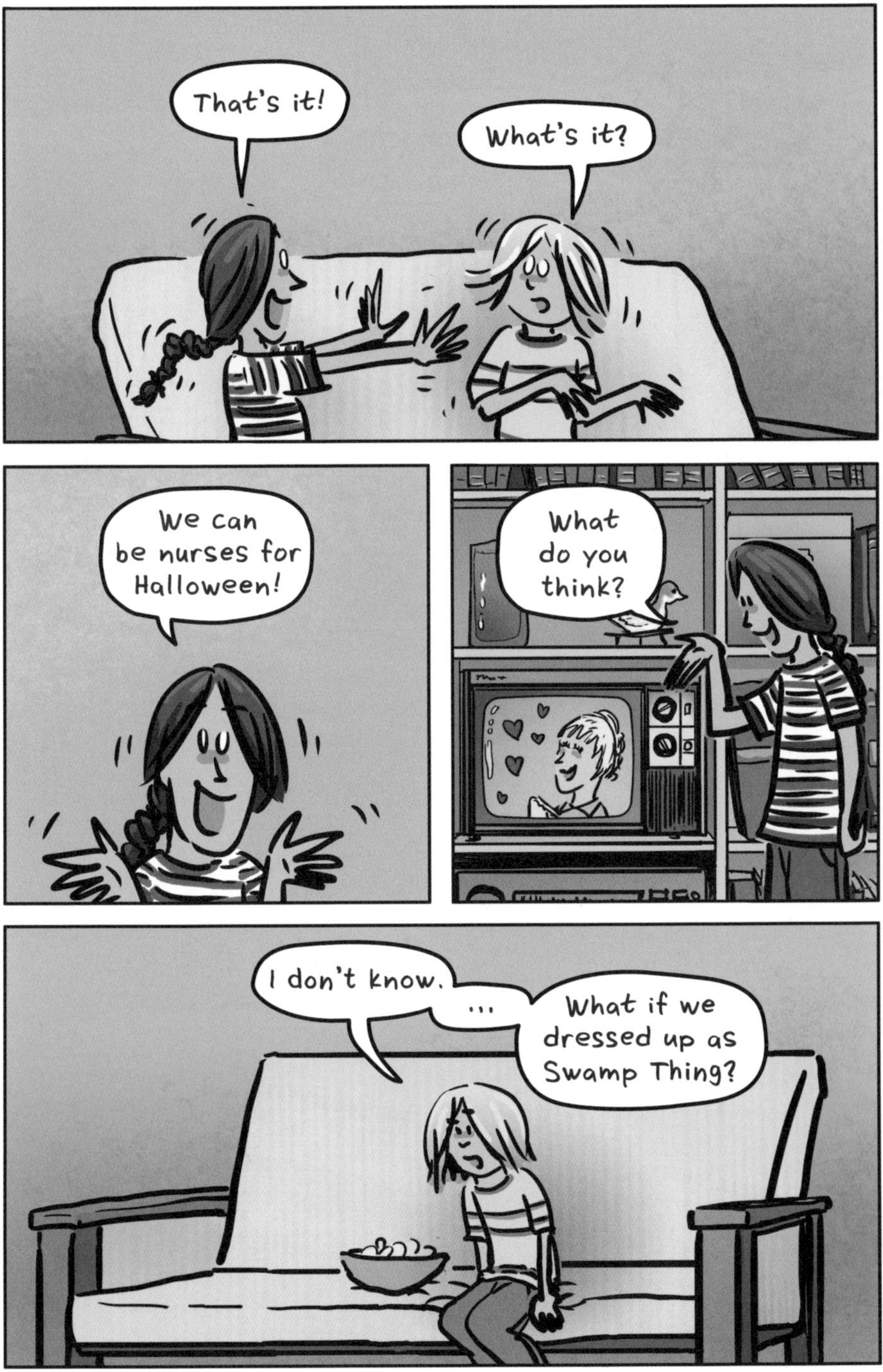
That's it!
What's it?
We can be nurses for Halloween!
What do you think?
I don't know.
...
What if we dressed up as Swamp Thing?

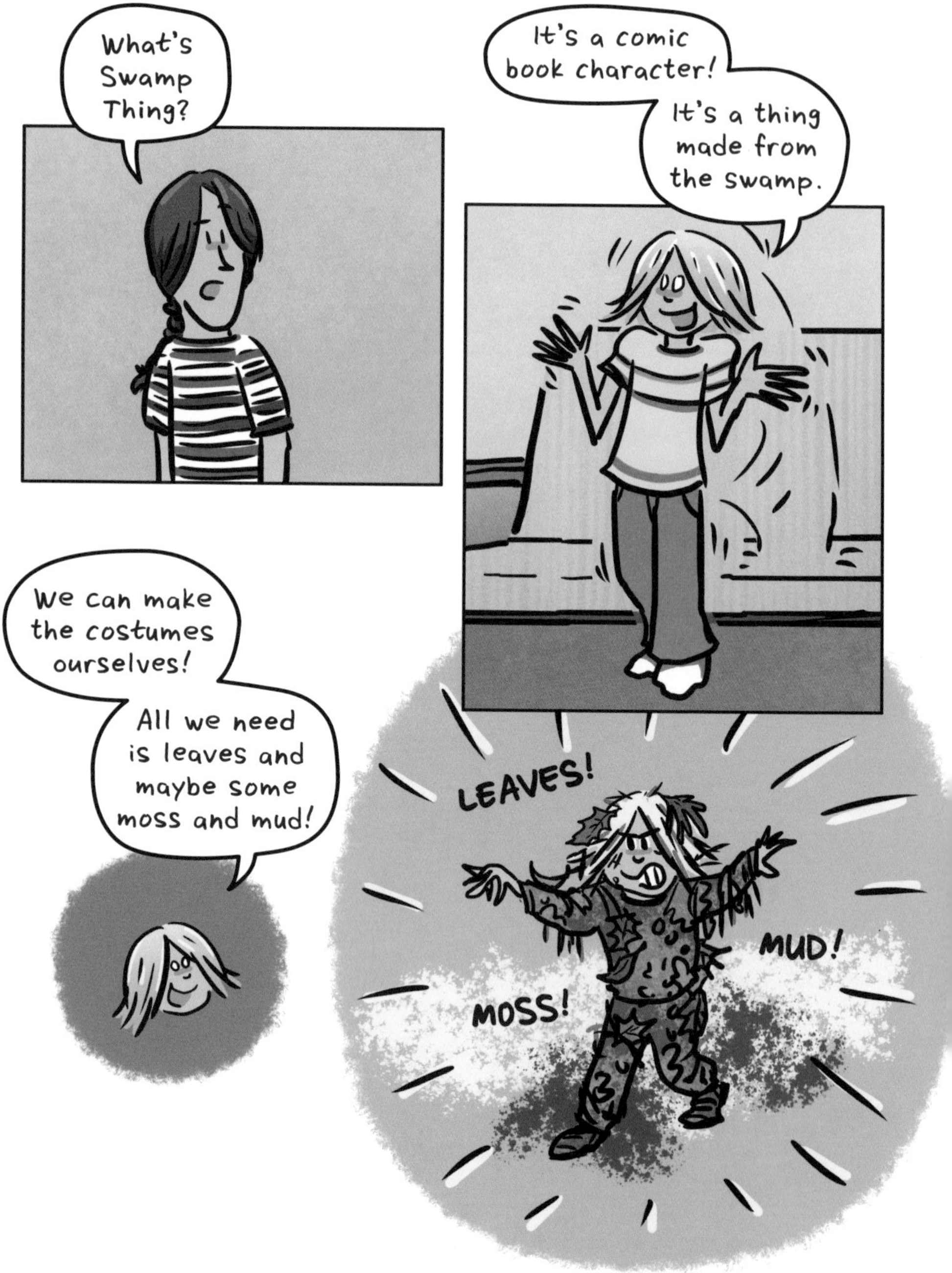
What's Swamp Thing?
It's a comic book character!
It's a thing made from the swamp.
We can make the costumes ourselves!
All we need is leaves and maybe some moss and mud!
LEAVES!
MUD!
MOSS!

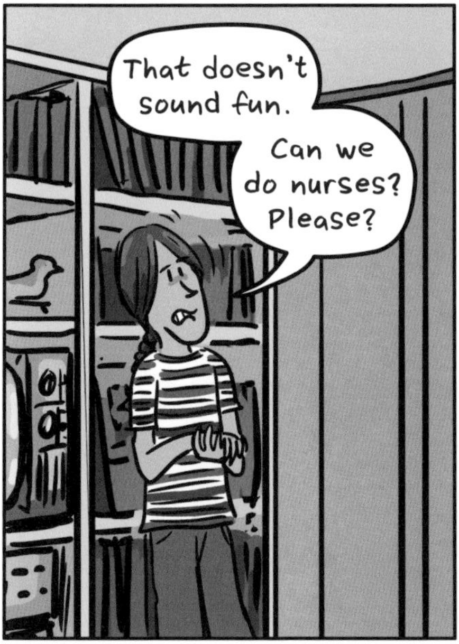
That doesn't sound fun.
Can we do nurses? Please?

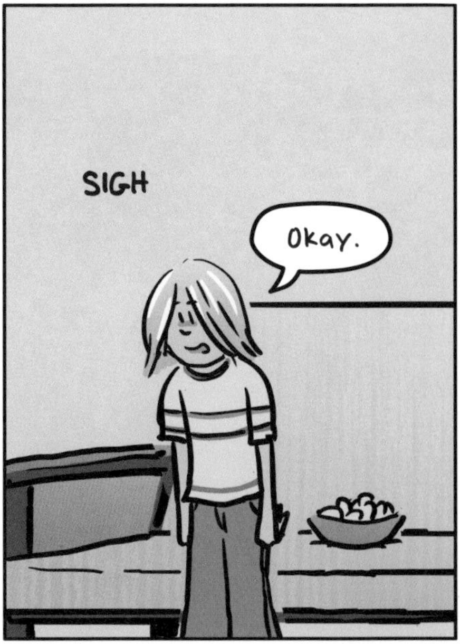
SIGH
Okay.

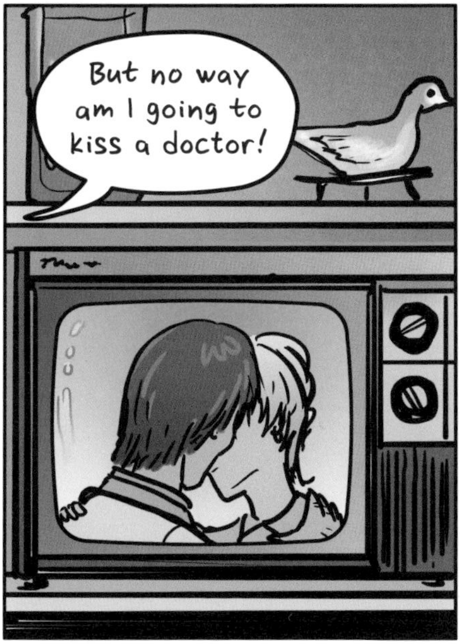
But no way am I going to kiss a doctor!

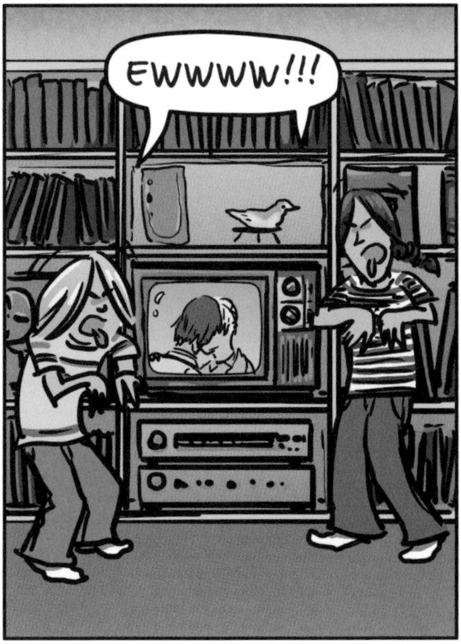
EWWWW!!!

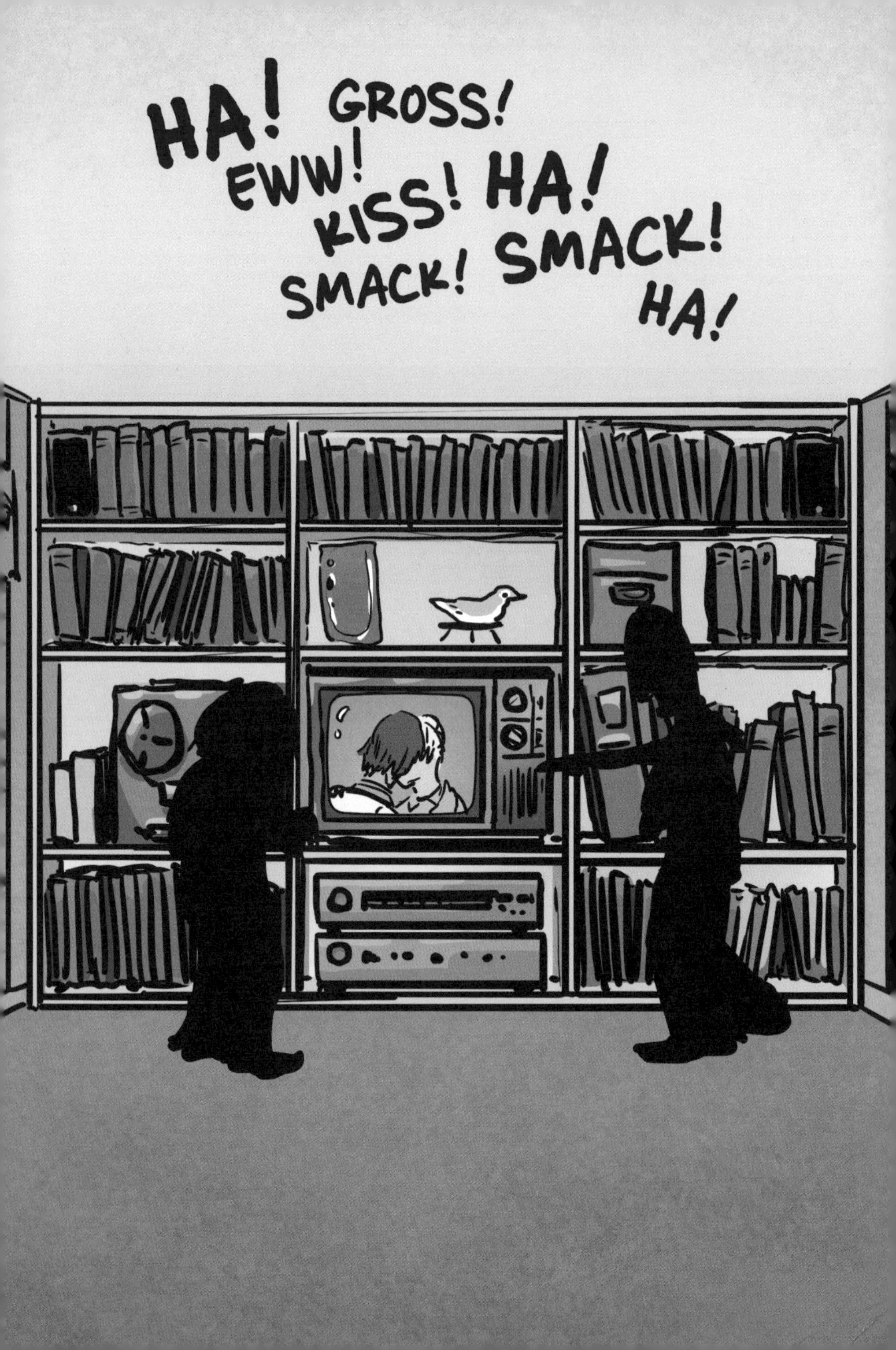
HA!
GROSS!
EWW!
KISS!
HA!
SMACK!
SMACK!
HA!

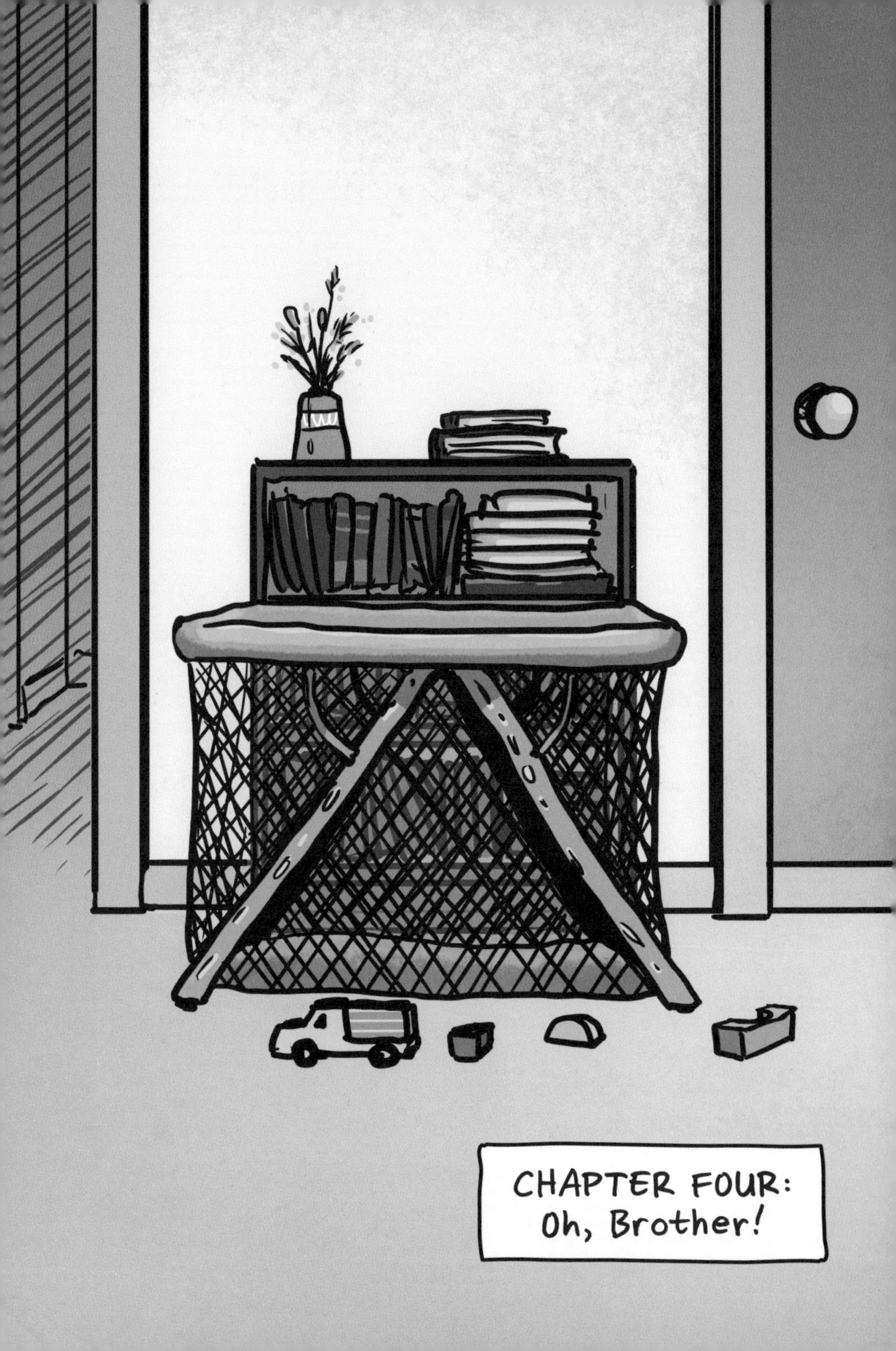
CHAPTER FOUR:
Oh, Brother!

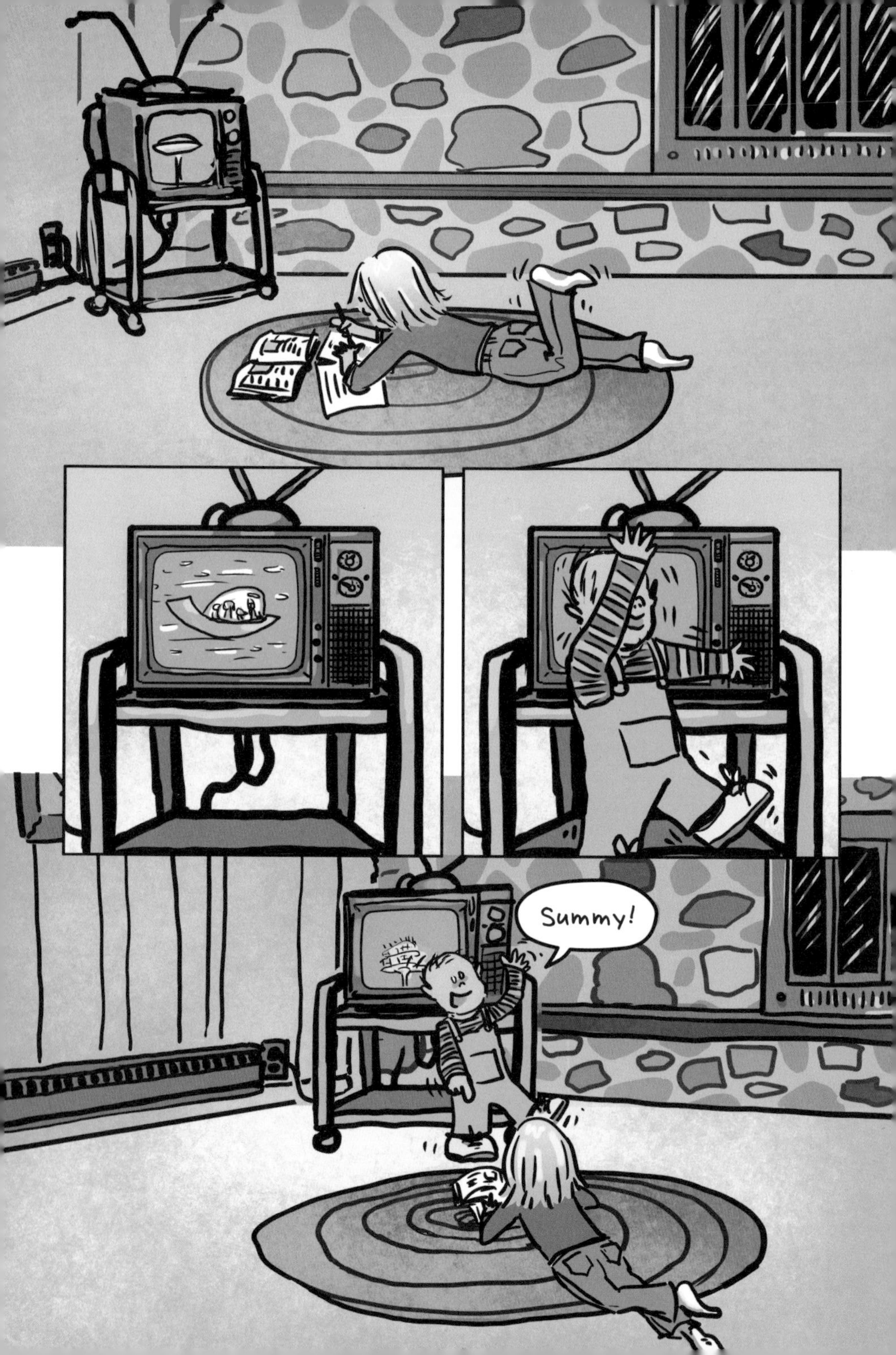
Summy!

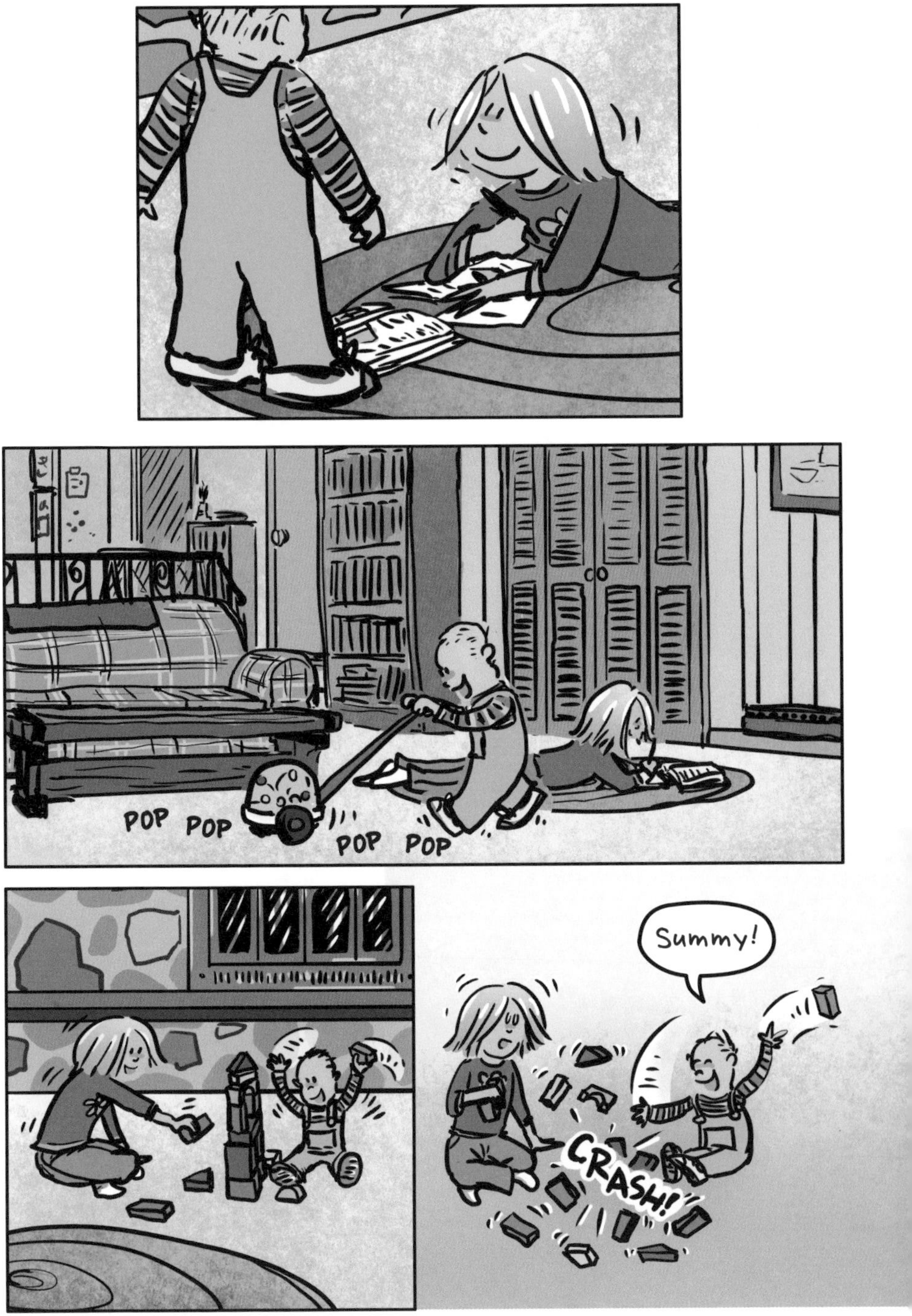
POP POP
POP POP
Summy!
CRASH!

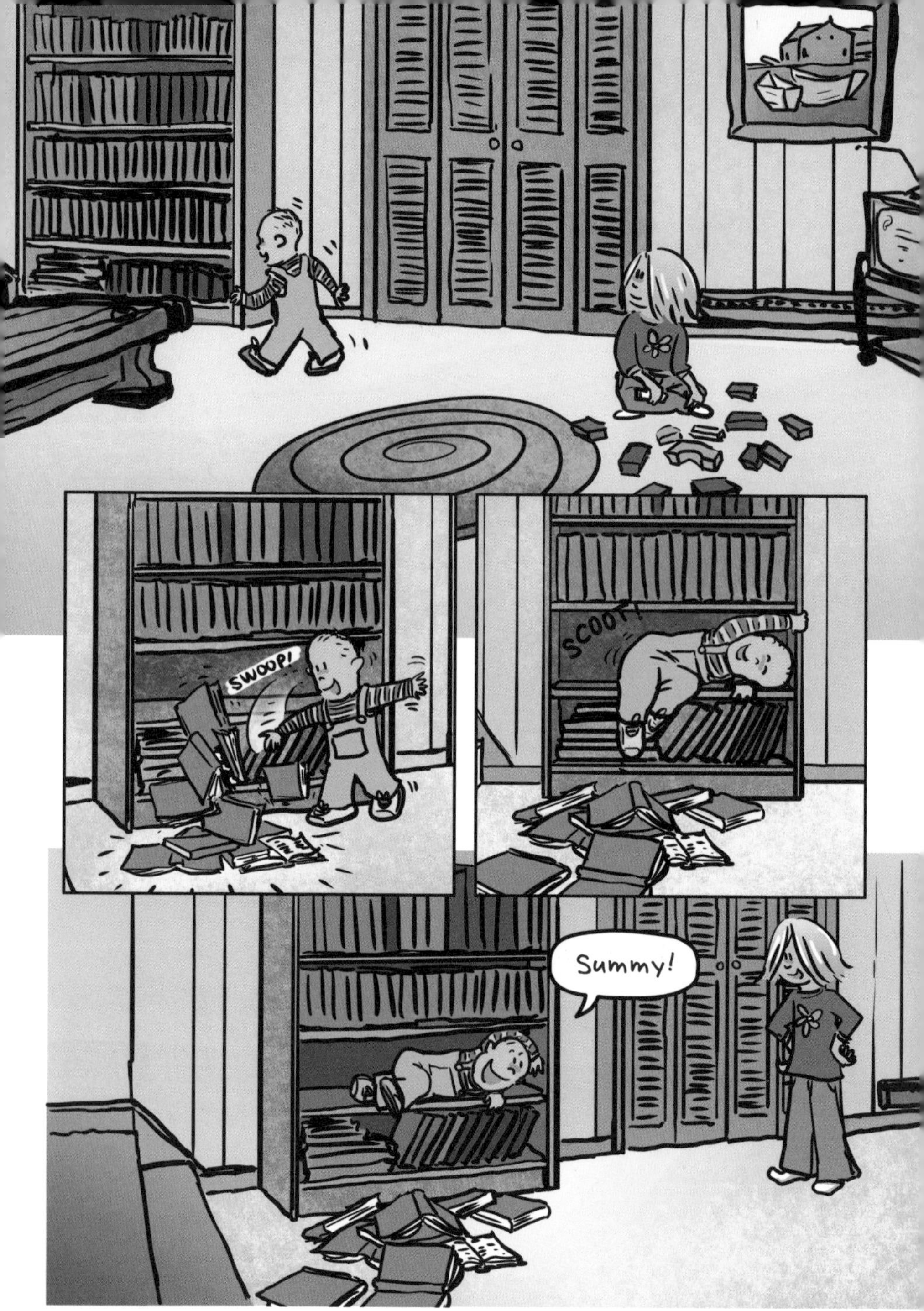
SWOOP!
SCOOT!
Summy!

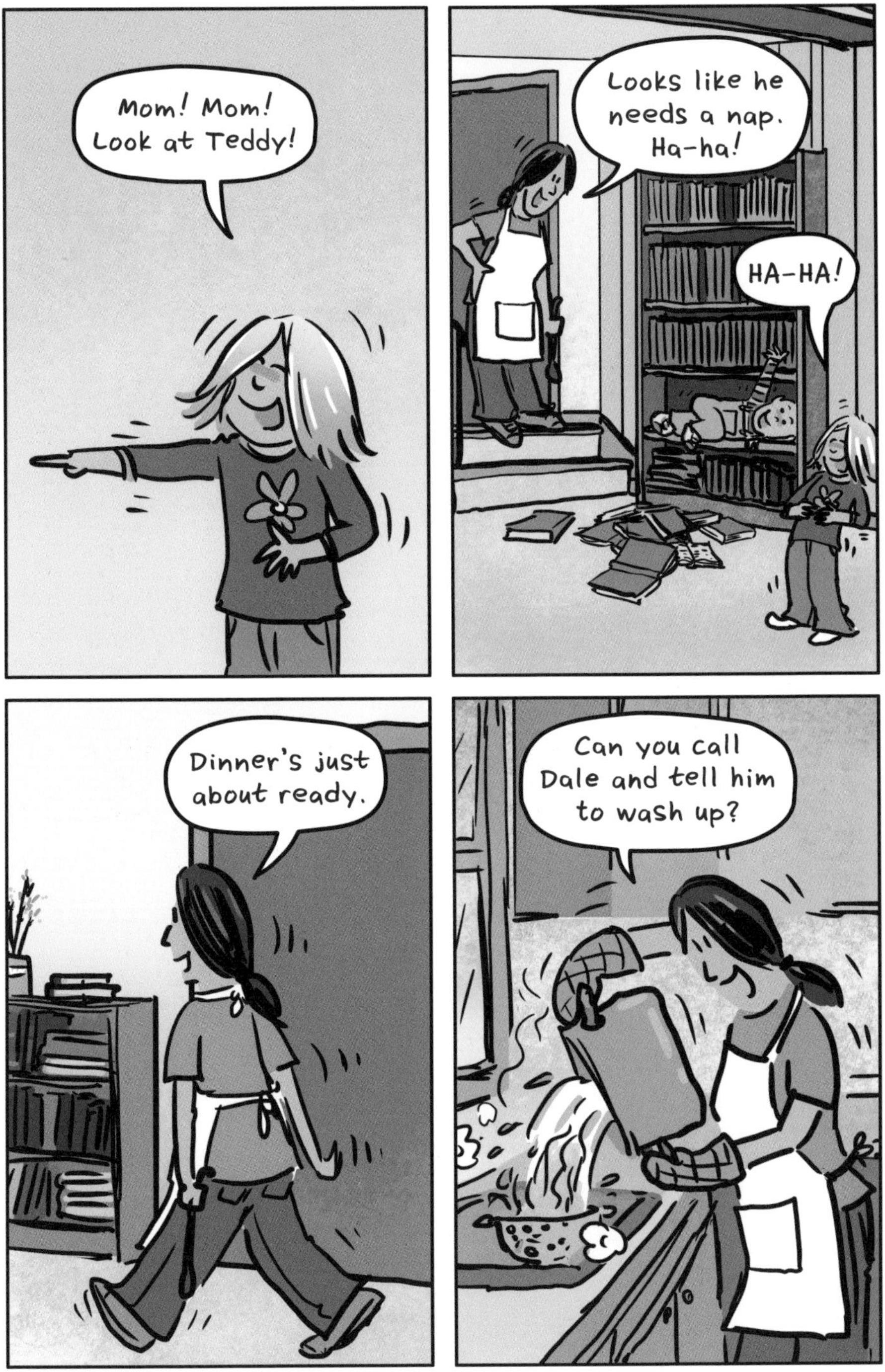
Mom! Mom! Look at Teddy!
Looks like he needs a nap. Ha-ha!
HA-HA!
Dinner's just about ready.
Can you call Dale and tell him to wash up?

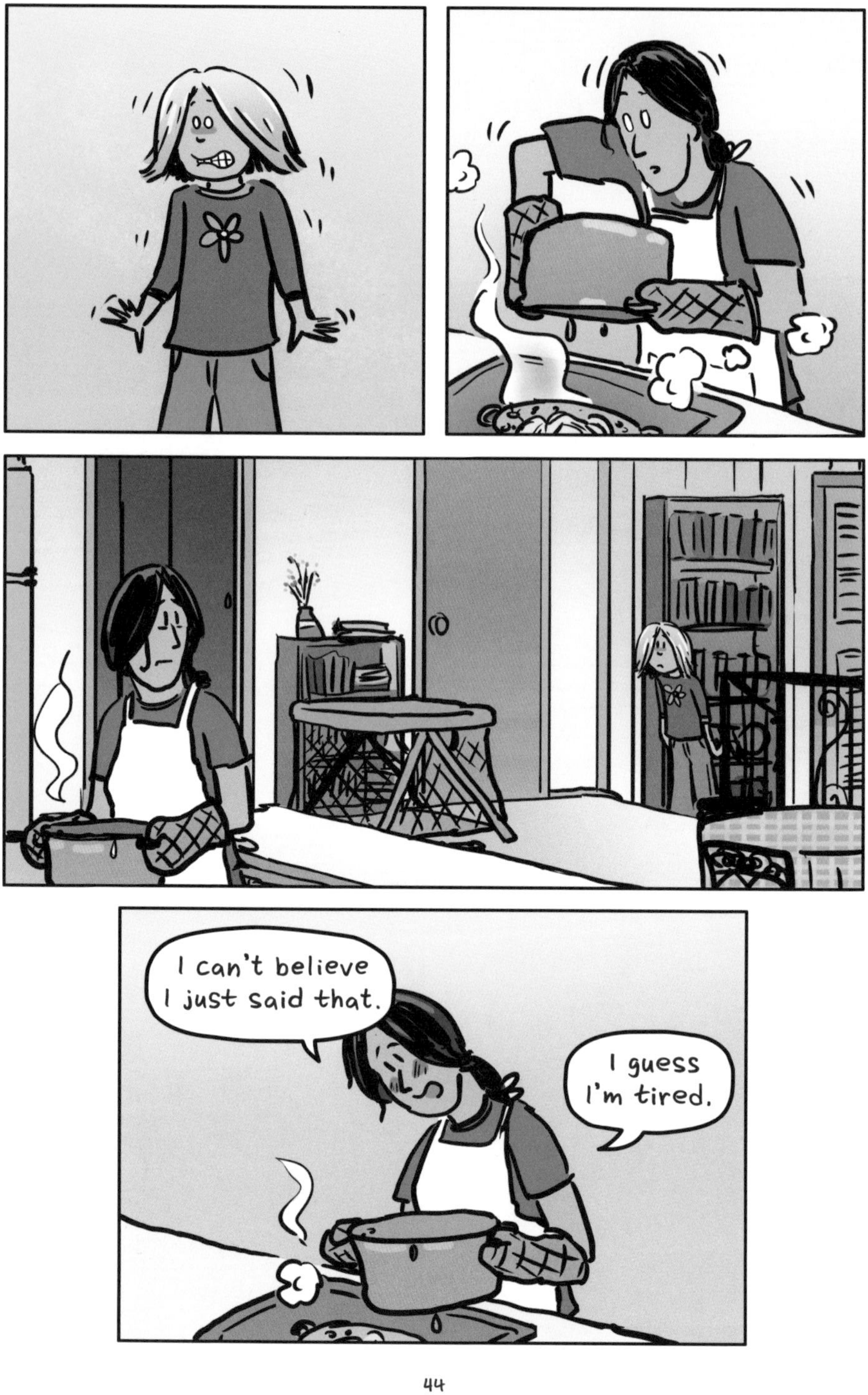
I can't believe I just said that.
I guess I'm tired.

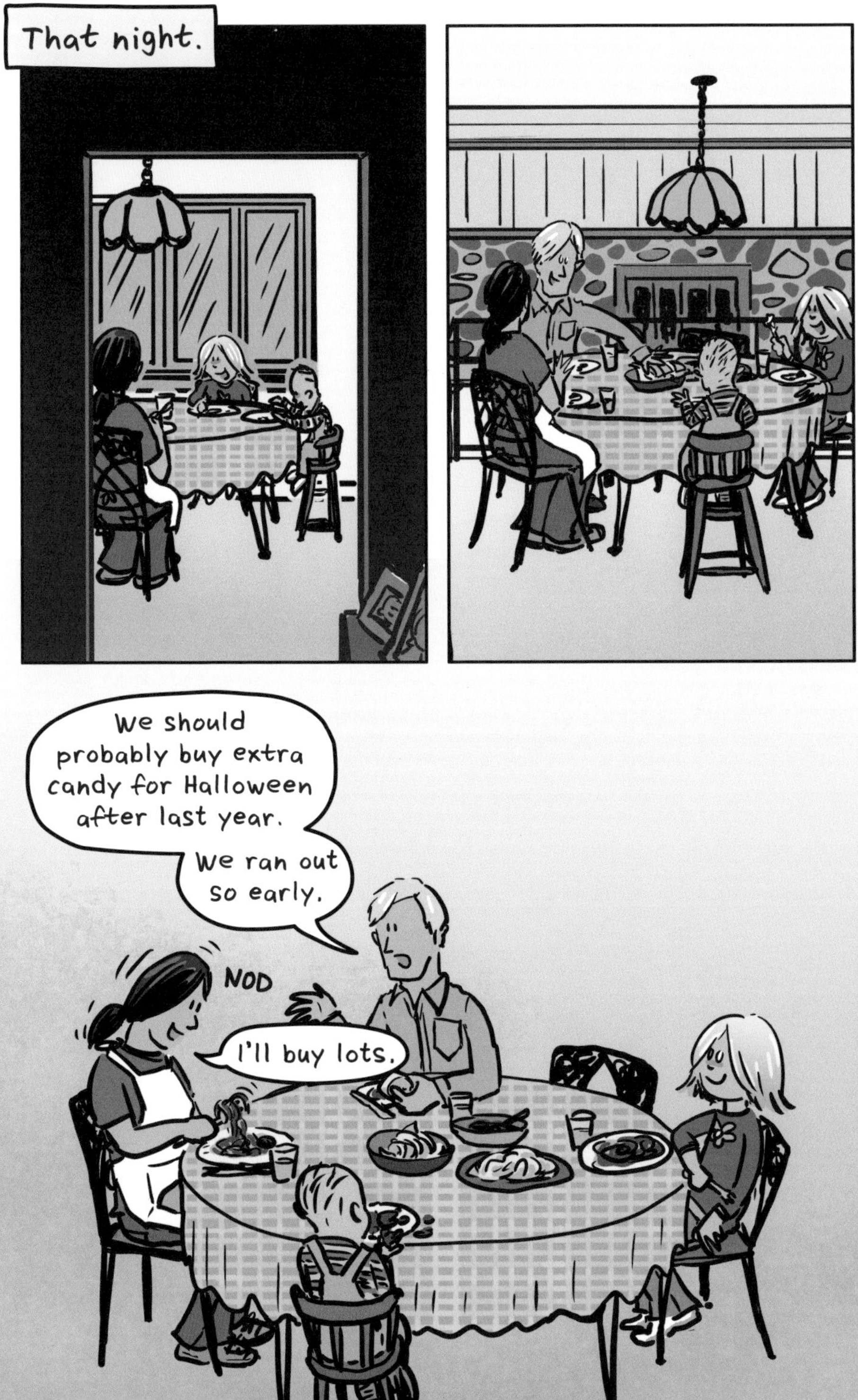
That night.
We should probably buy extra candy for Halloween after last year.
We ran out so early.
NOD
I'll buy lots.

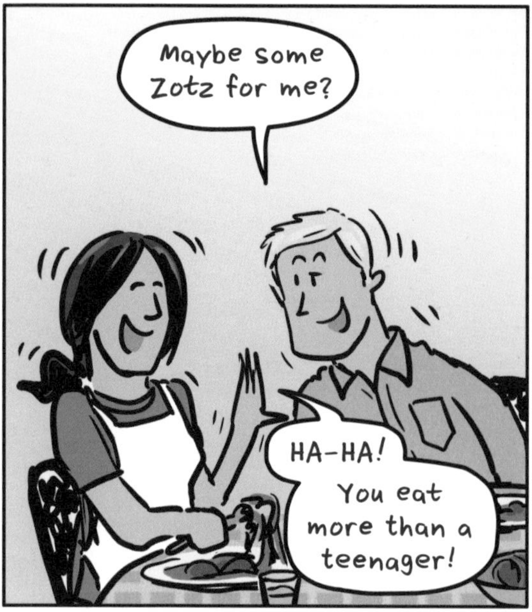
Maybe some Zotz for me?
HA-HA! You eat more than a teenager!

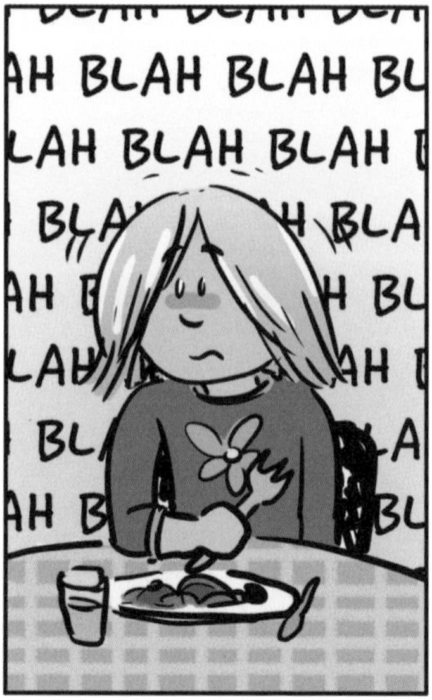
AH BLAH BLAH BL
LAH BLAH BLAH B

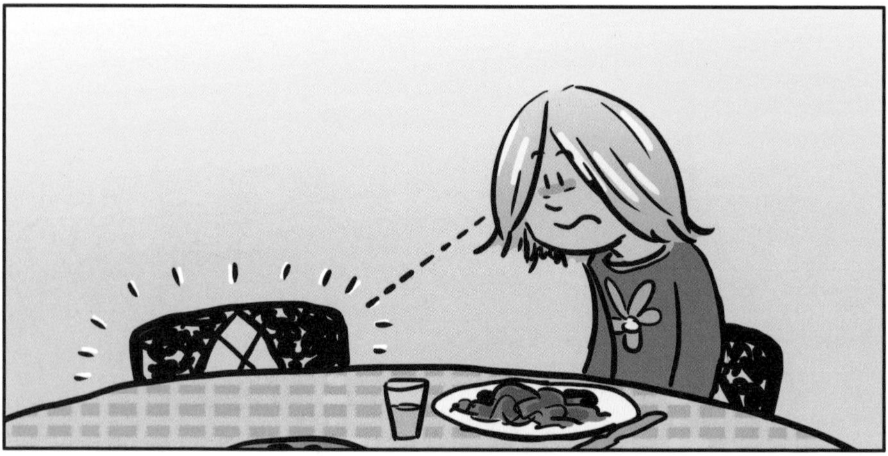

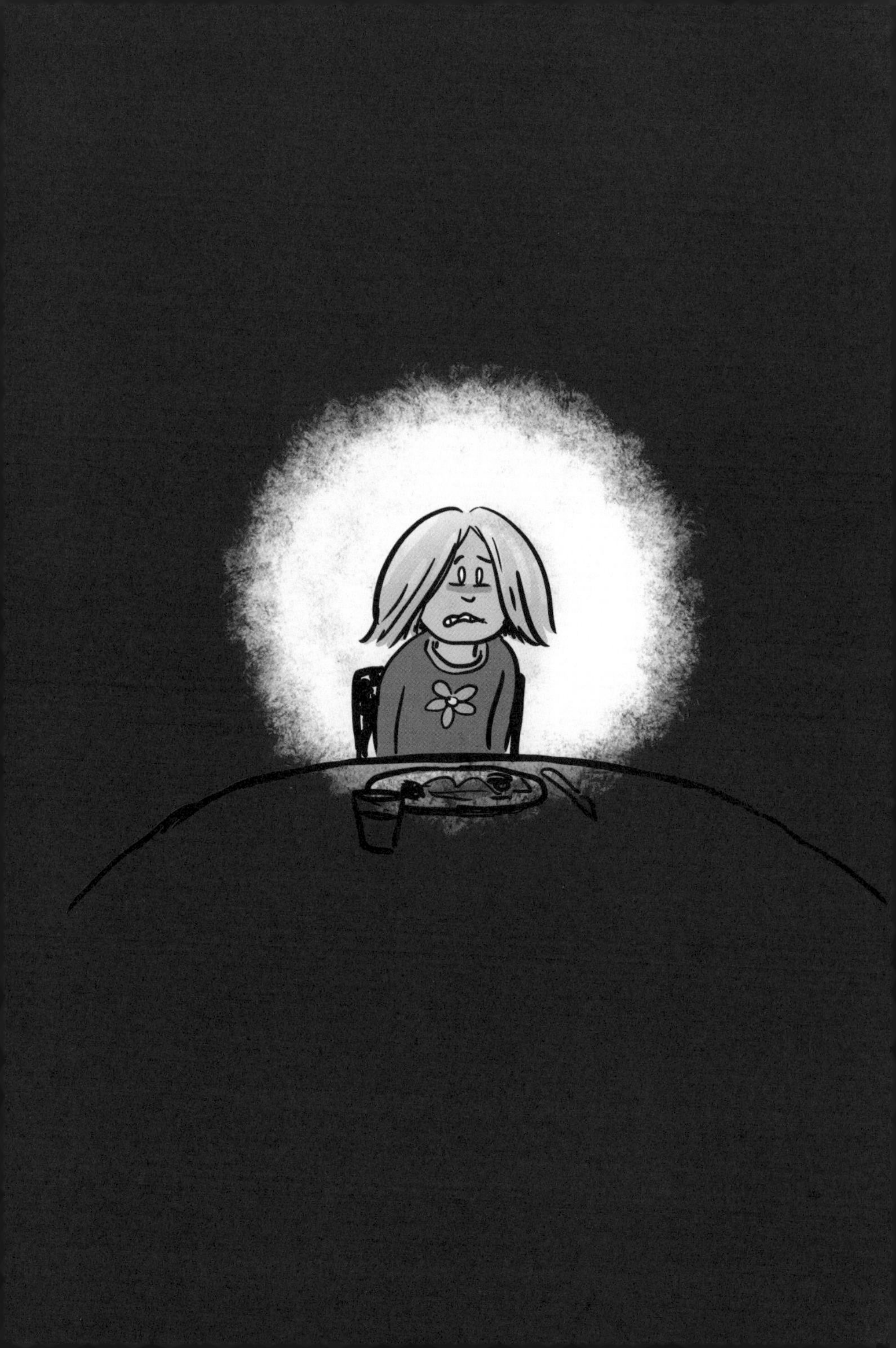

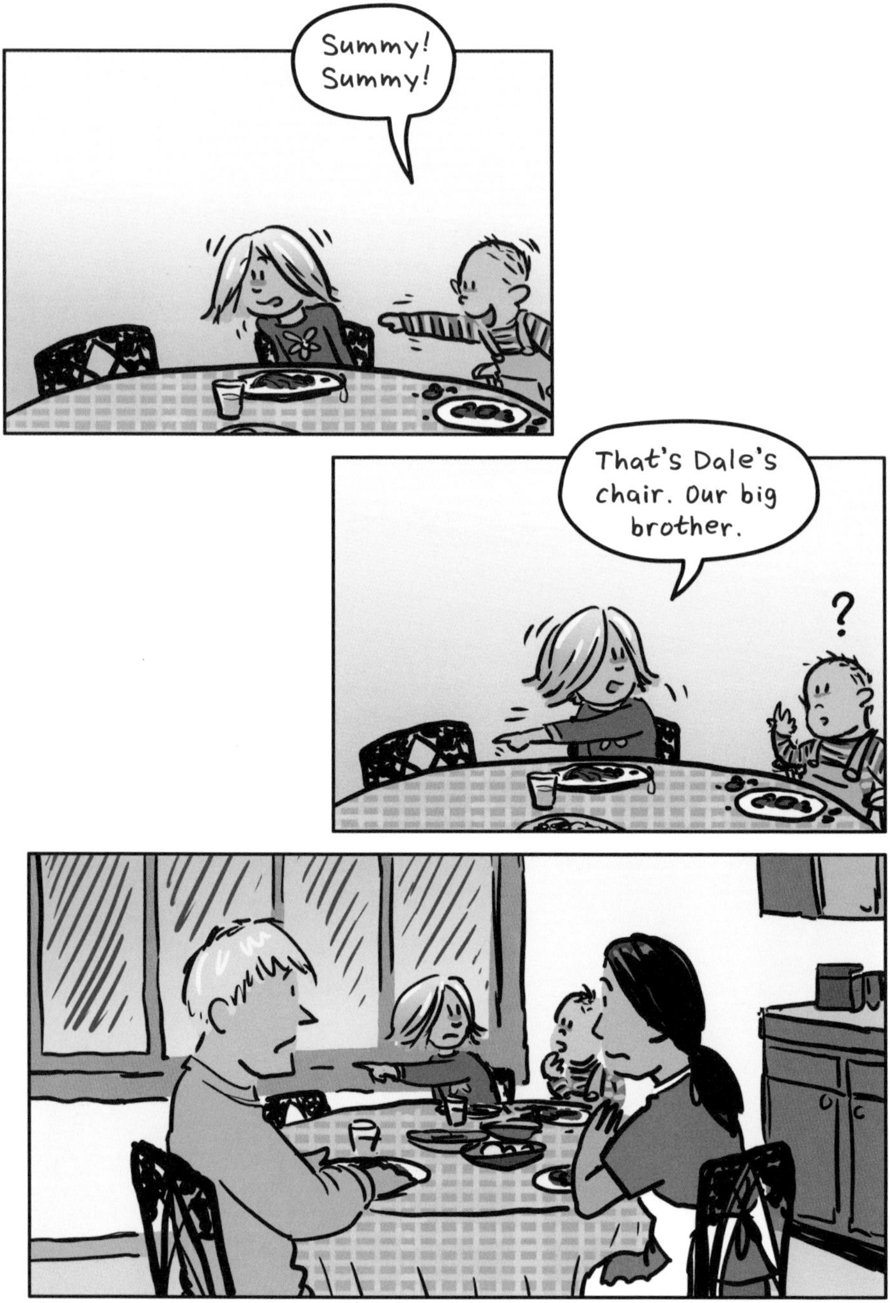
Summy! Summy!
That's Dale's chair. Our big brother.
?

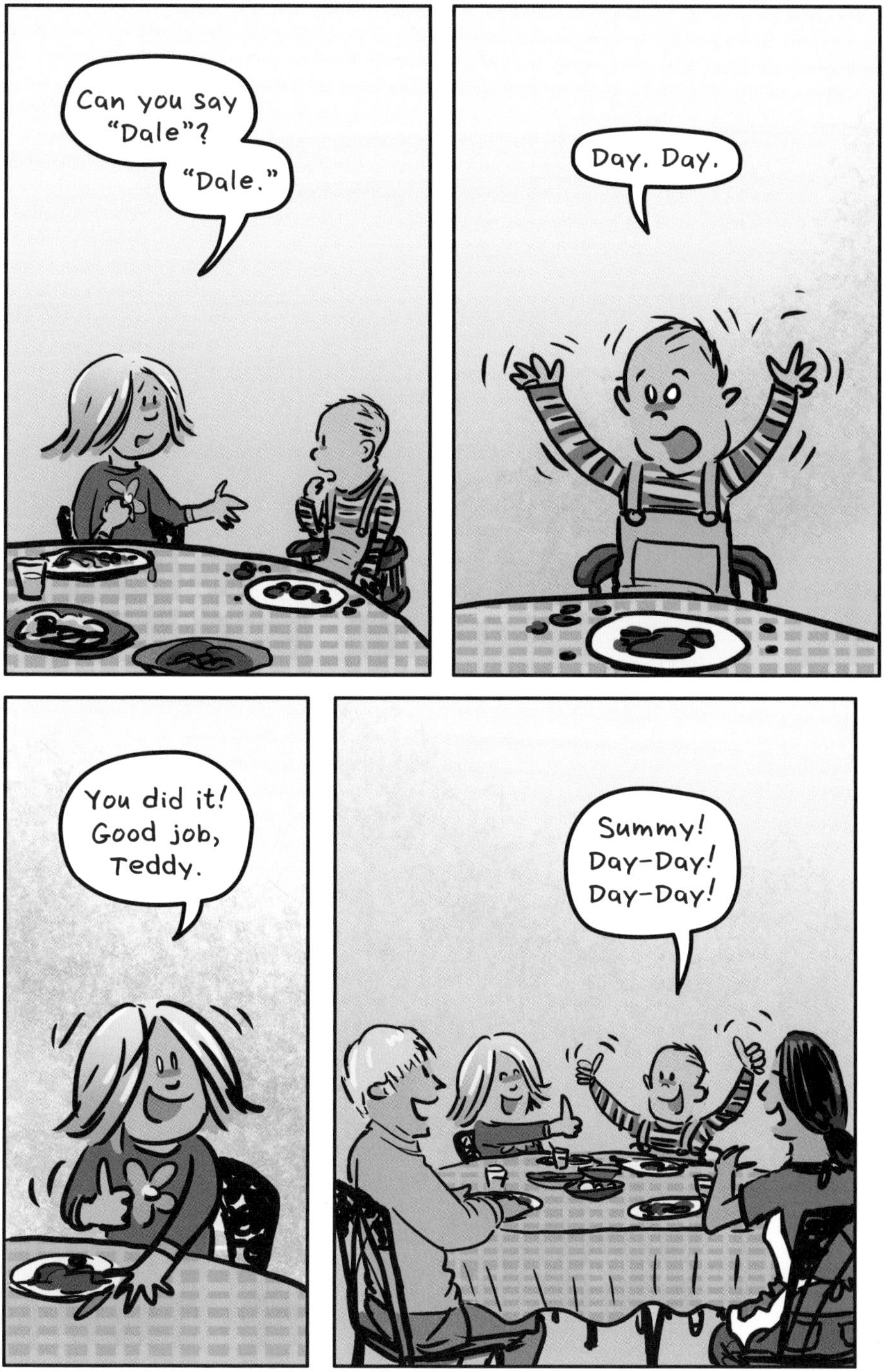
Can you say "Dale"?
"Dale."
Day. Day.
You did it! Good job, Teddy.
Summy! Day-Day! Day-Day!

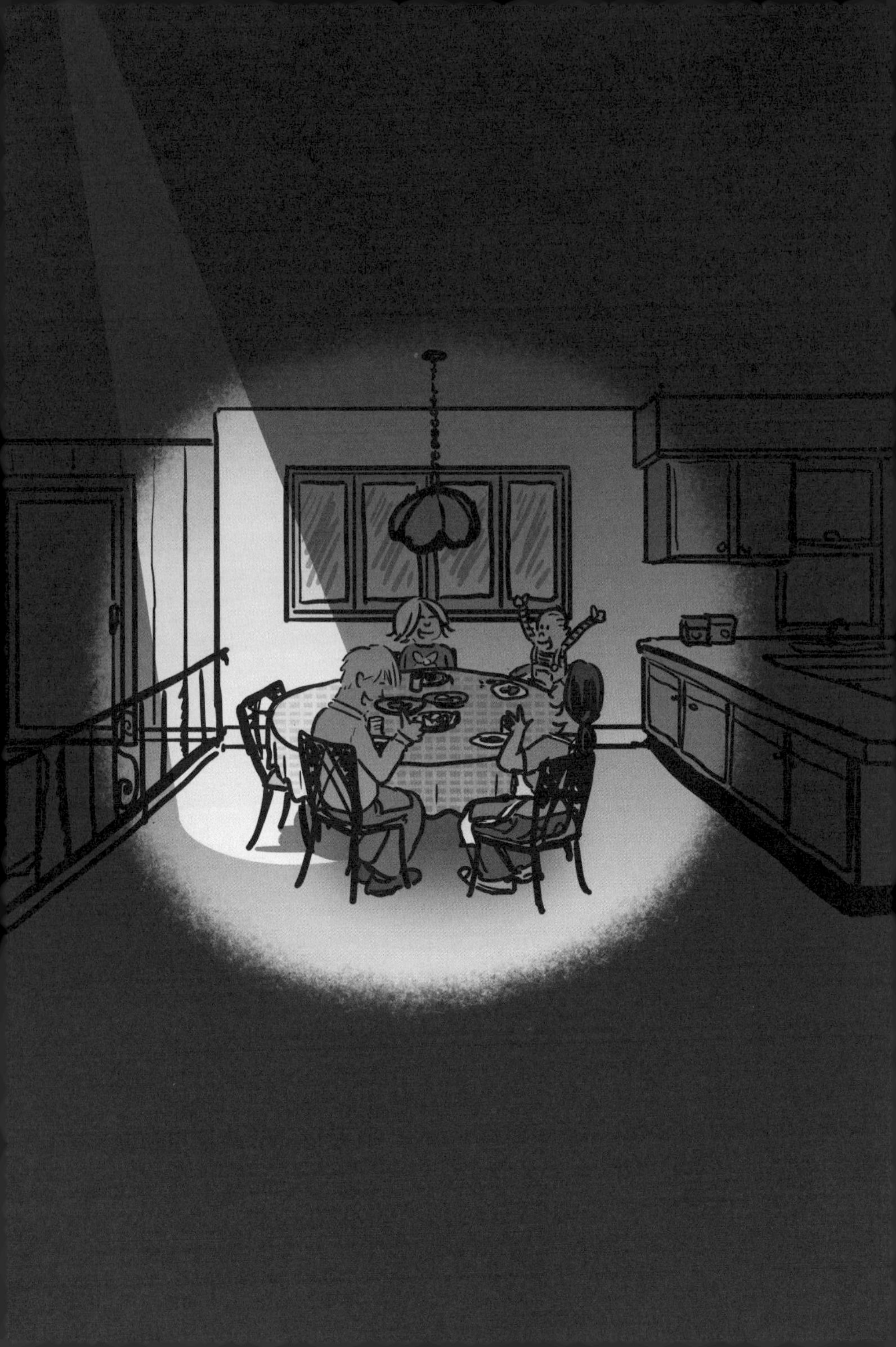

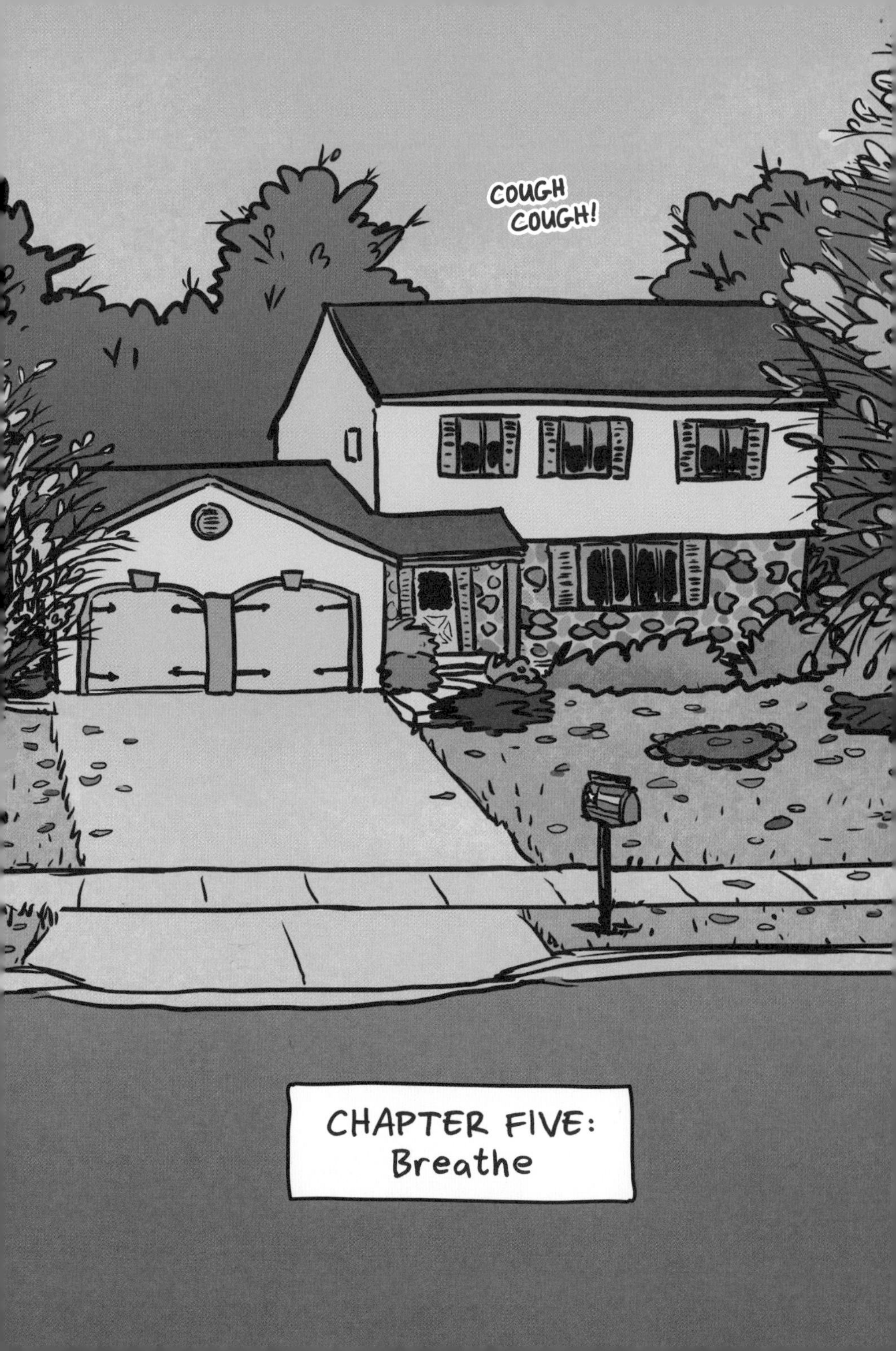
COUGH
COUGH!

CHAPTER FIVE: Breathe

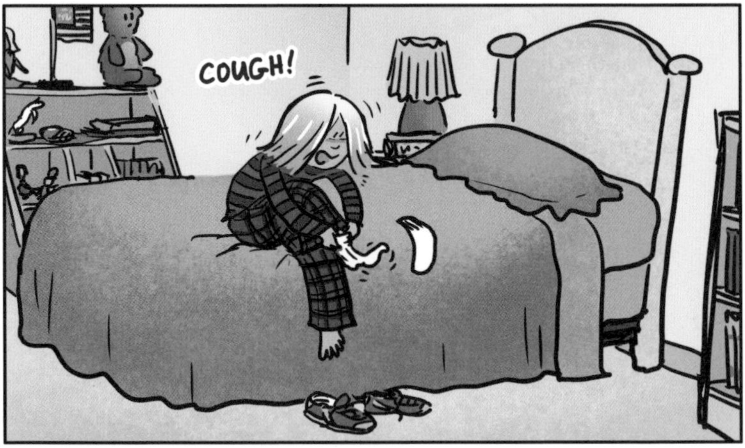
COUGH!

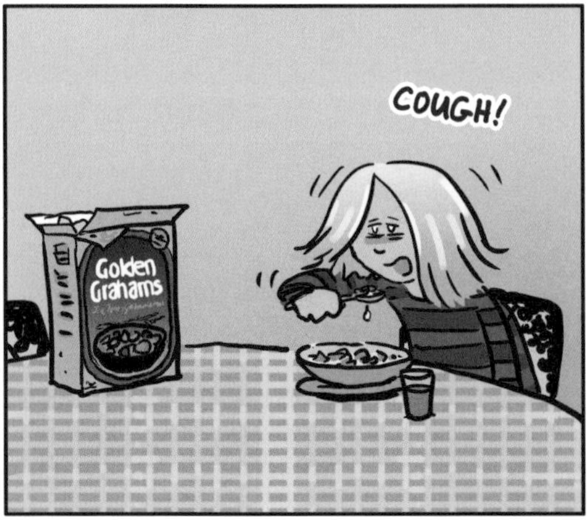
COUGH!
Golden Grahams

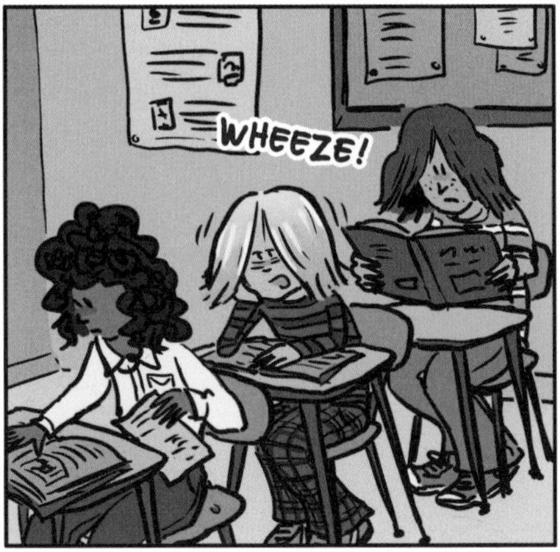
WHEEZE!

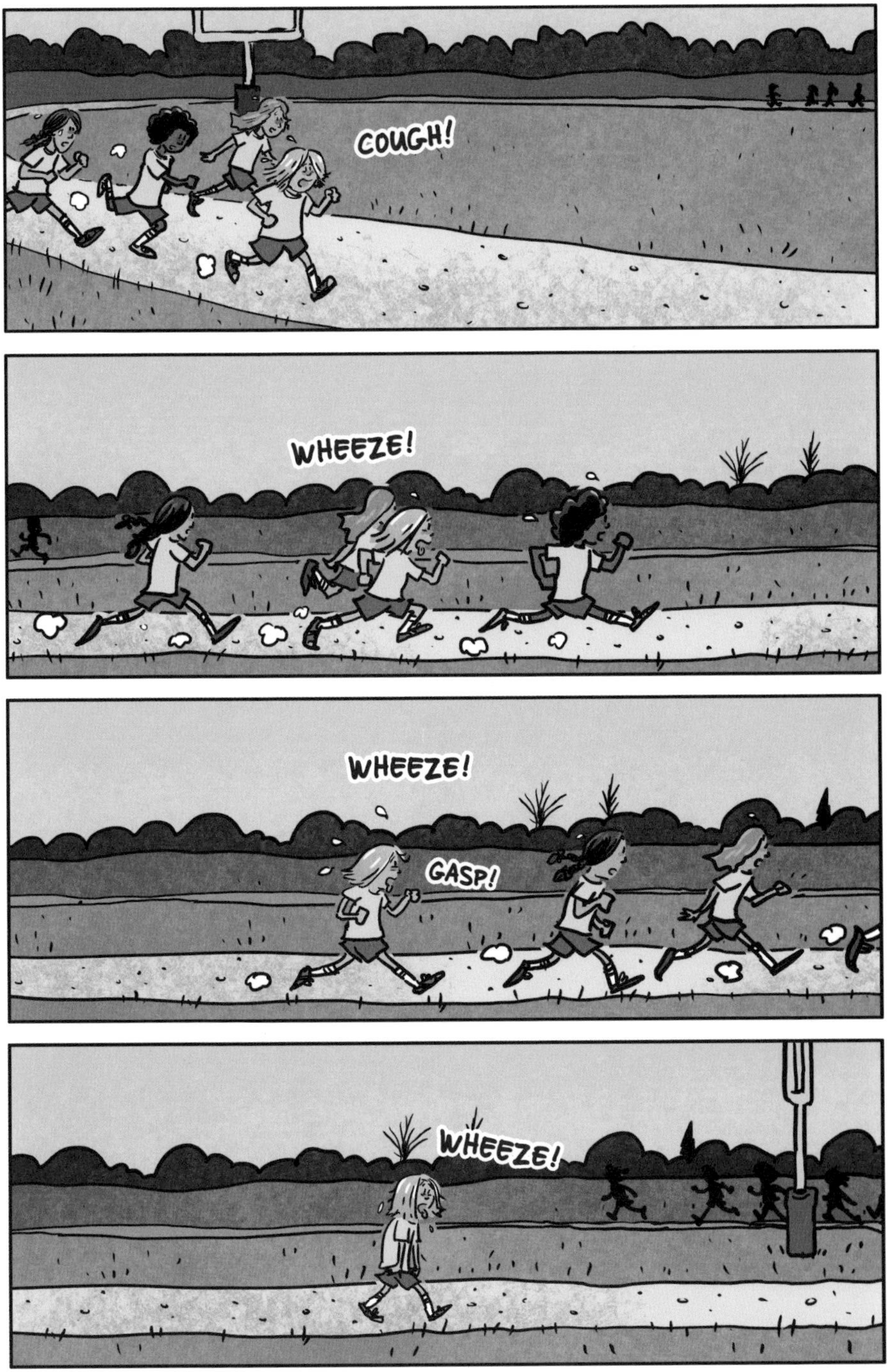
COUGH!
WHEEZE!
WHEEZE!
GASP!
WHEEZE!

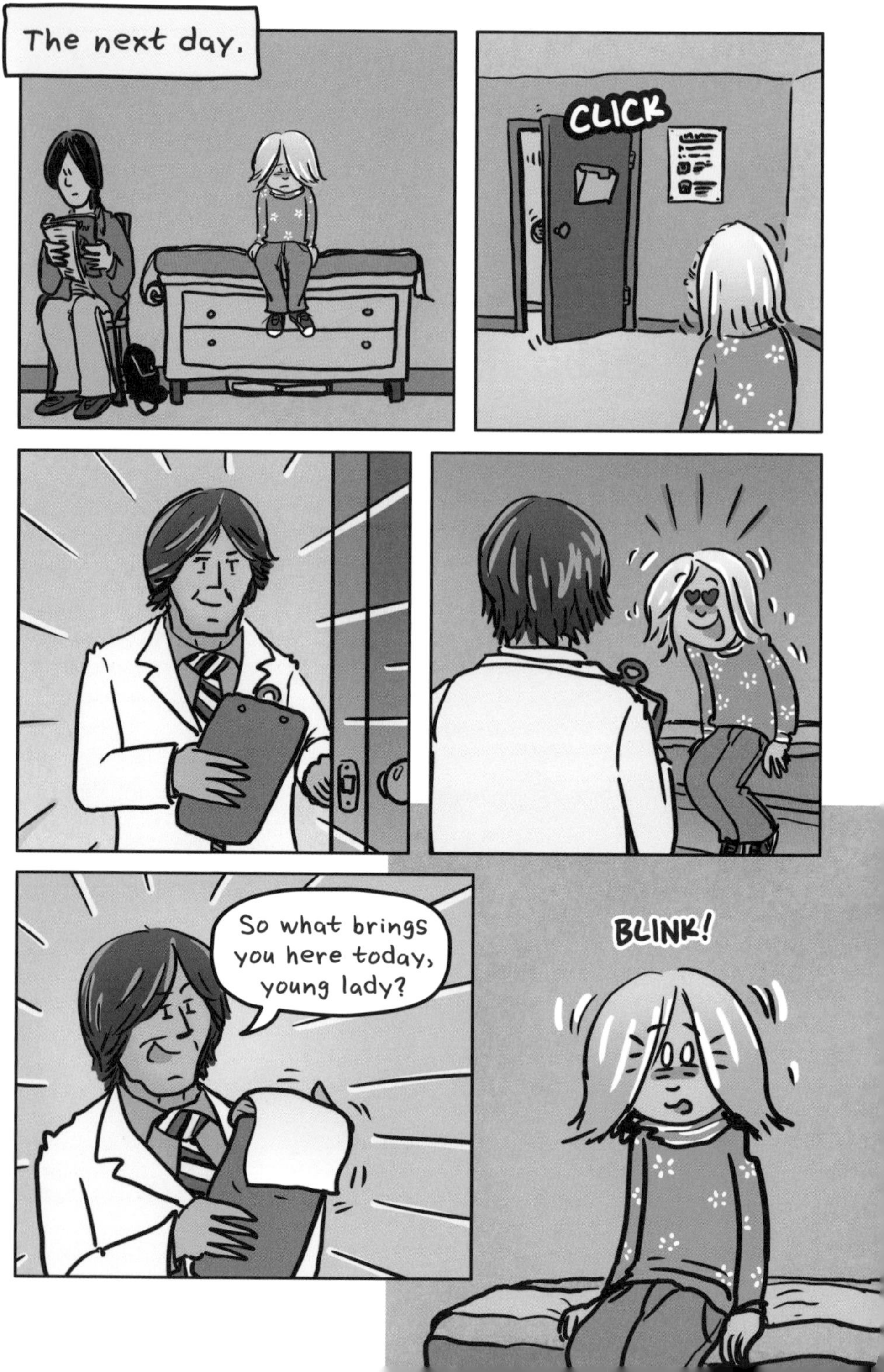
The next day.
CLICK
So what brings you here today, young lady?
BLINK!

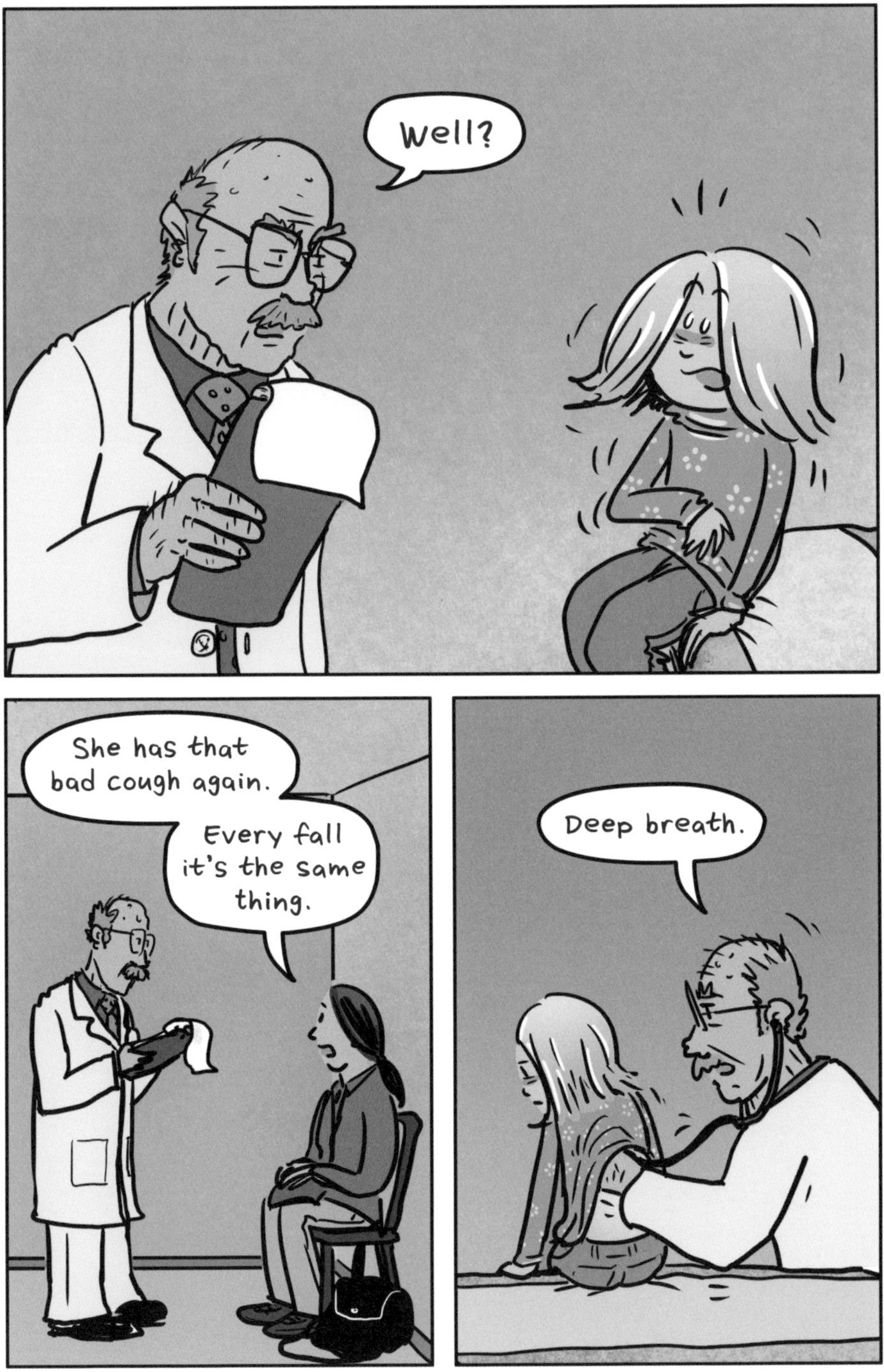
Well?
She has that bad cough again.
Every fall it's the same thing.
Deep breath.

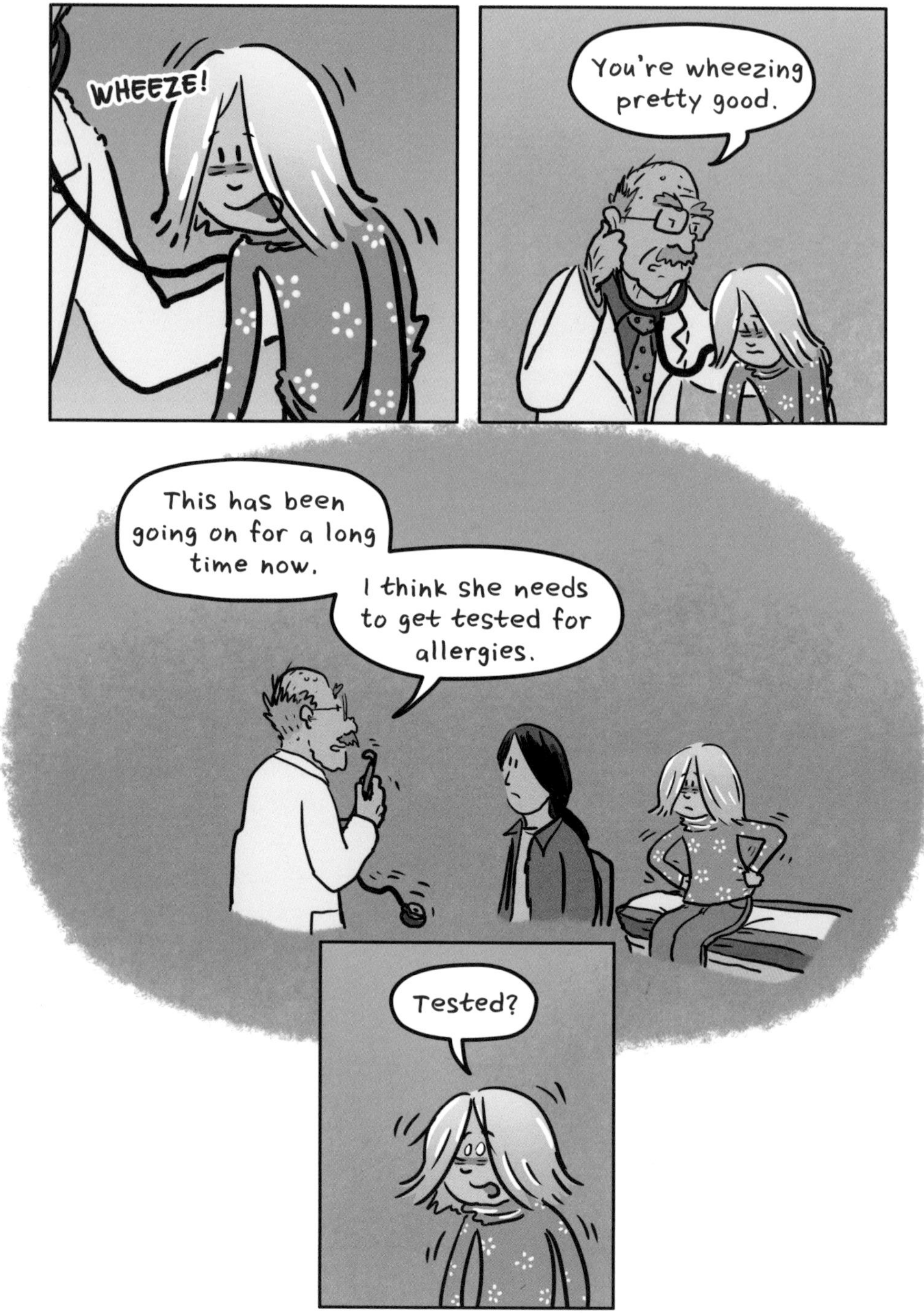
WHEEZE!
You're wheezing pretty good.
This has been going on for a long time now.
I think she needs to get tested for allergies.
Tested?

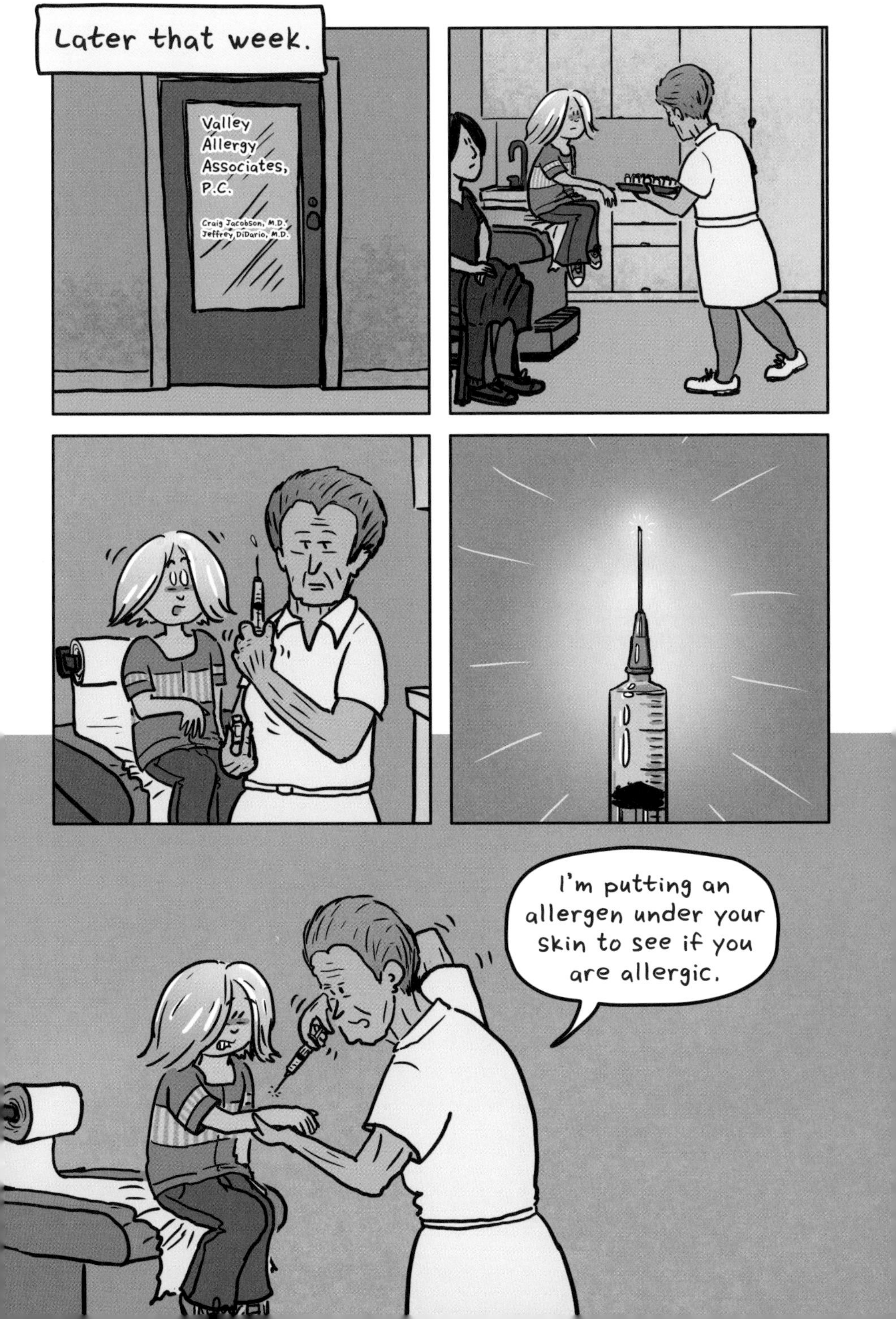
Later that week.
Valley Allergy Associates, P.C.
Craig Jacobson, M.D.
Jeffrey DiDario, M.D.
I'm putting an allergen under your skin to see if you are allergic.

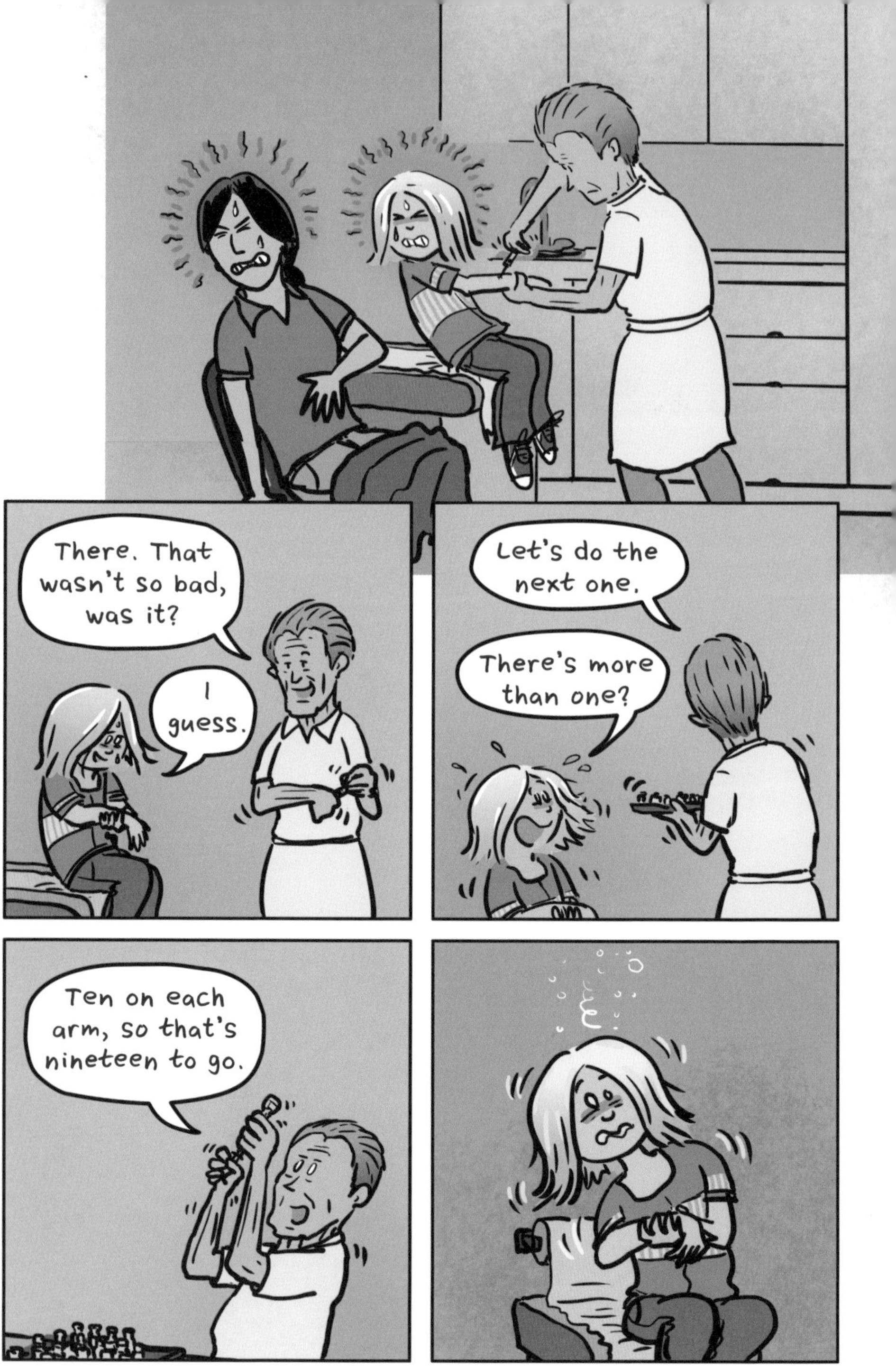
There. That wasn't so bad, was it?
I guess.
Let's do the next one.
There's more than one?
Ten on each arm, so that's nineteen to go.

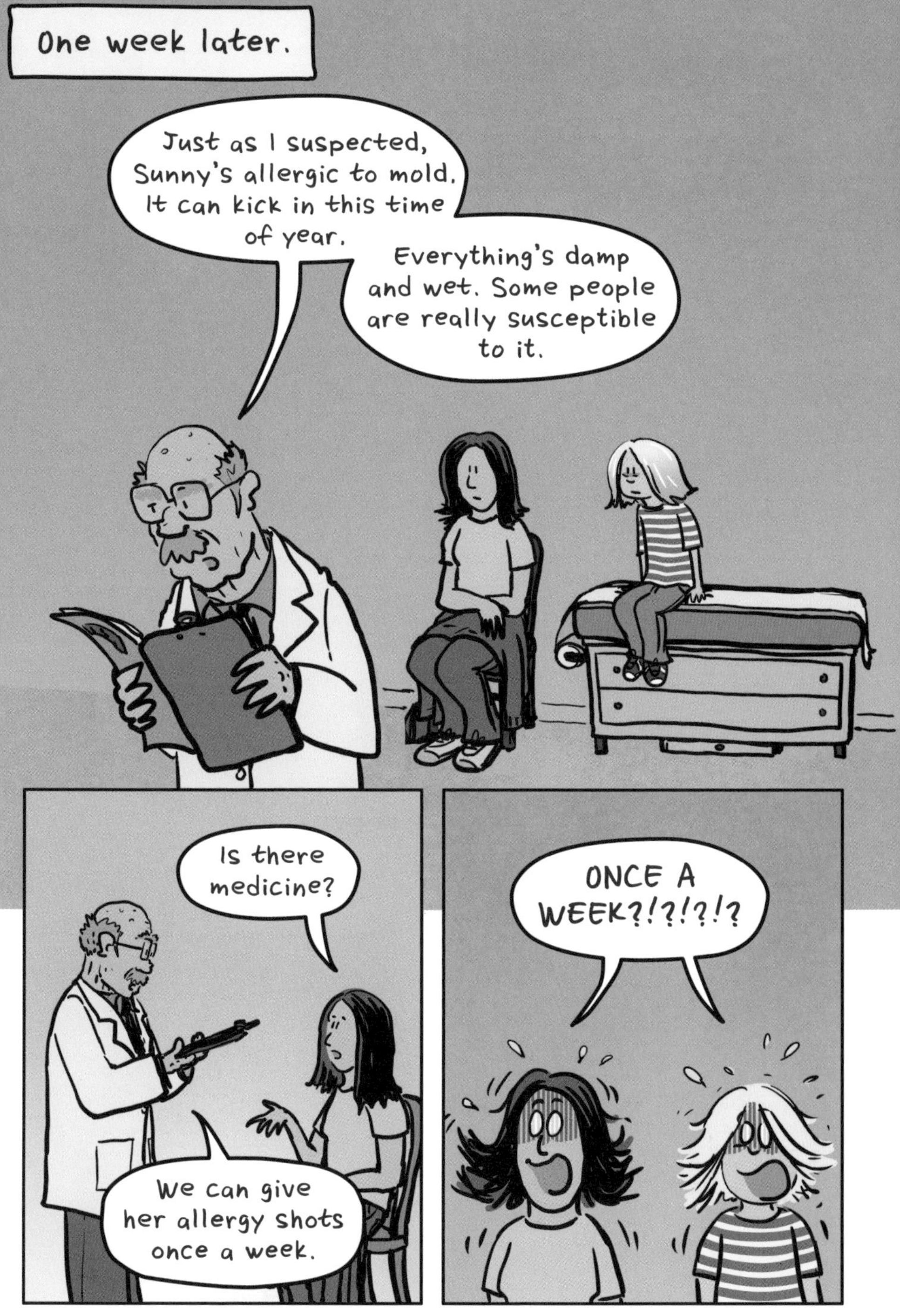
One week later.
Just as I suspected, Sunny's allergic to mold. It can kick in this time of year.
Everything's damp and wet. Some people are really susceptible to it.
Is there medicine?
We can give her allergy shots once a week.
ONCE A WEEK?!?!?!?

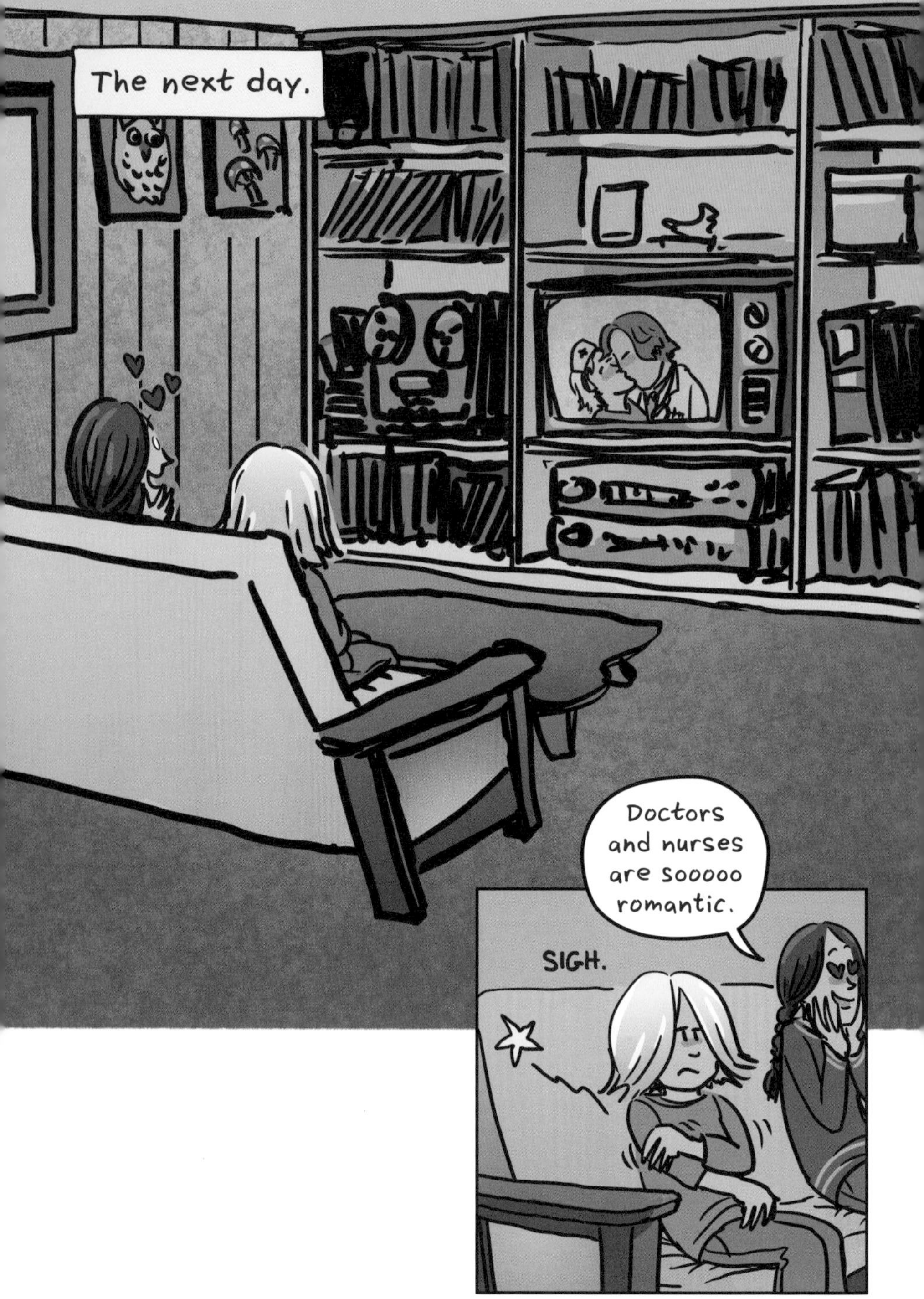
The next day.
Doctors and nurses are sooooo romantic.
SIGH.

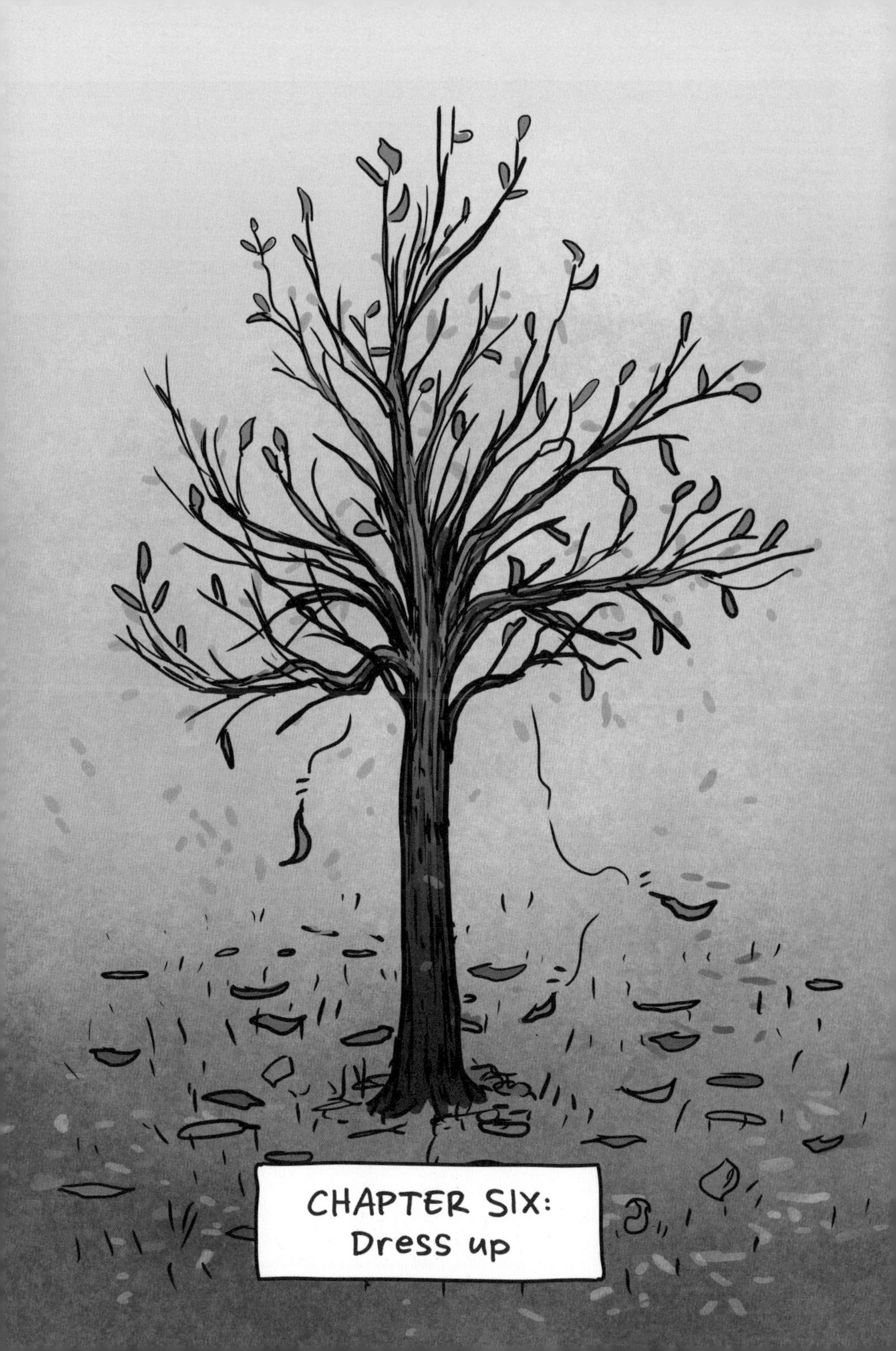

CHAPTER SIX: Dress up

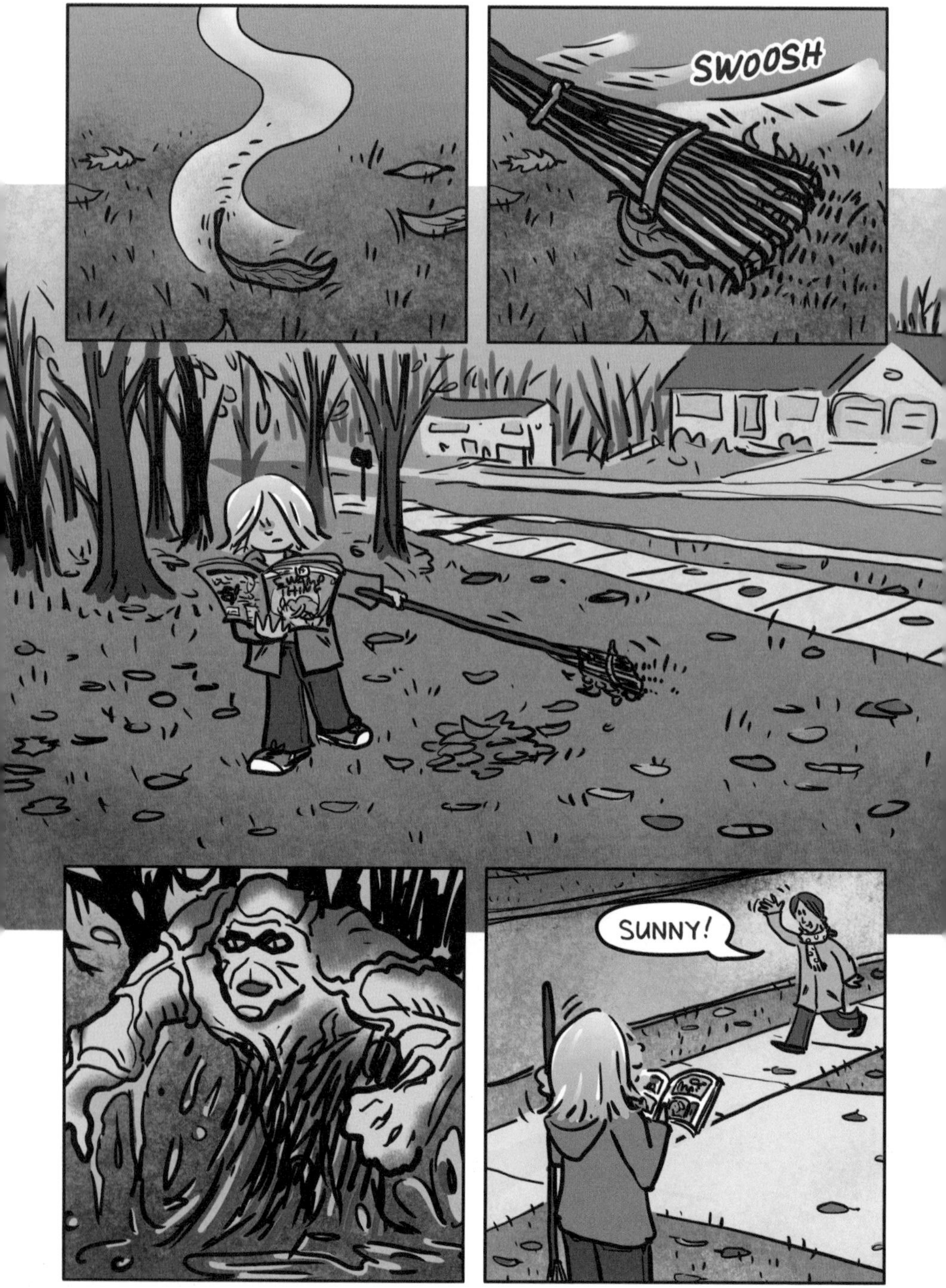
SWOOSH
SUNNY!

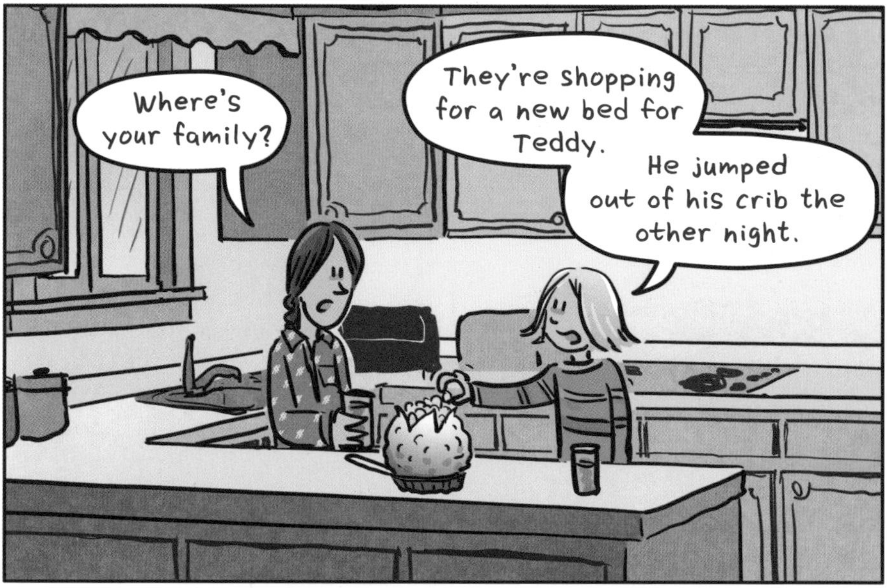
Where's your family?
They're shopping for a new bed for Teddy.
He jumped out of his crib the other night.

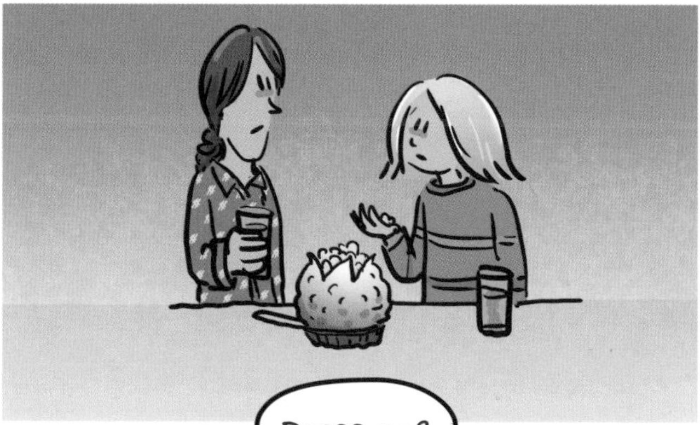

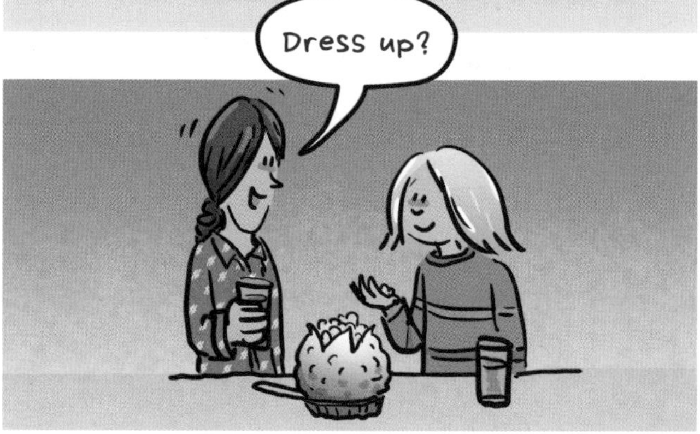
Dress up?

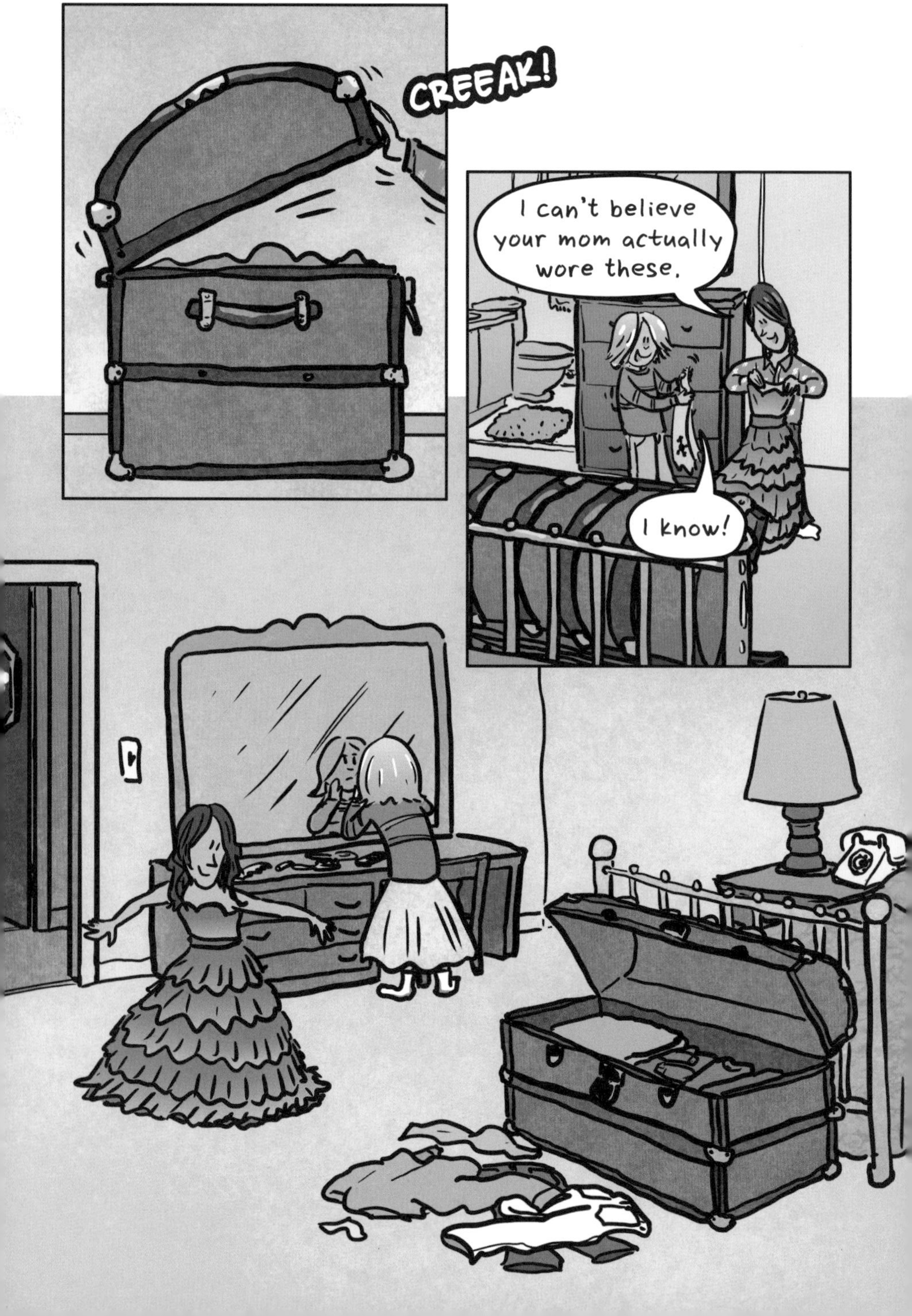
CREEAK!
I can't believe your mom actually wore these.
I know!

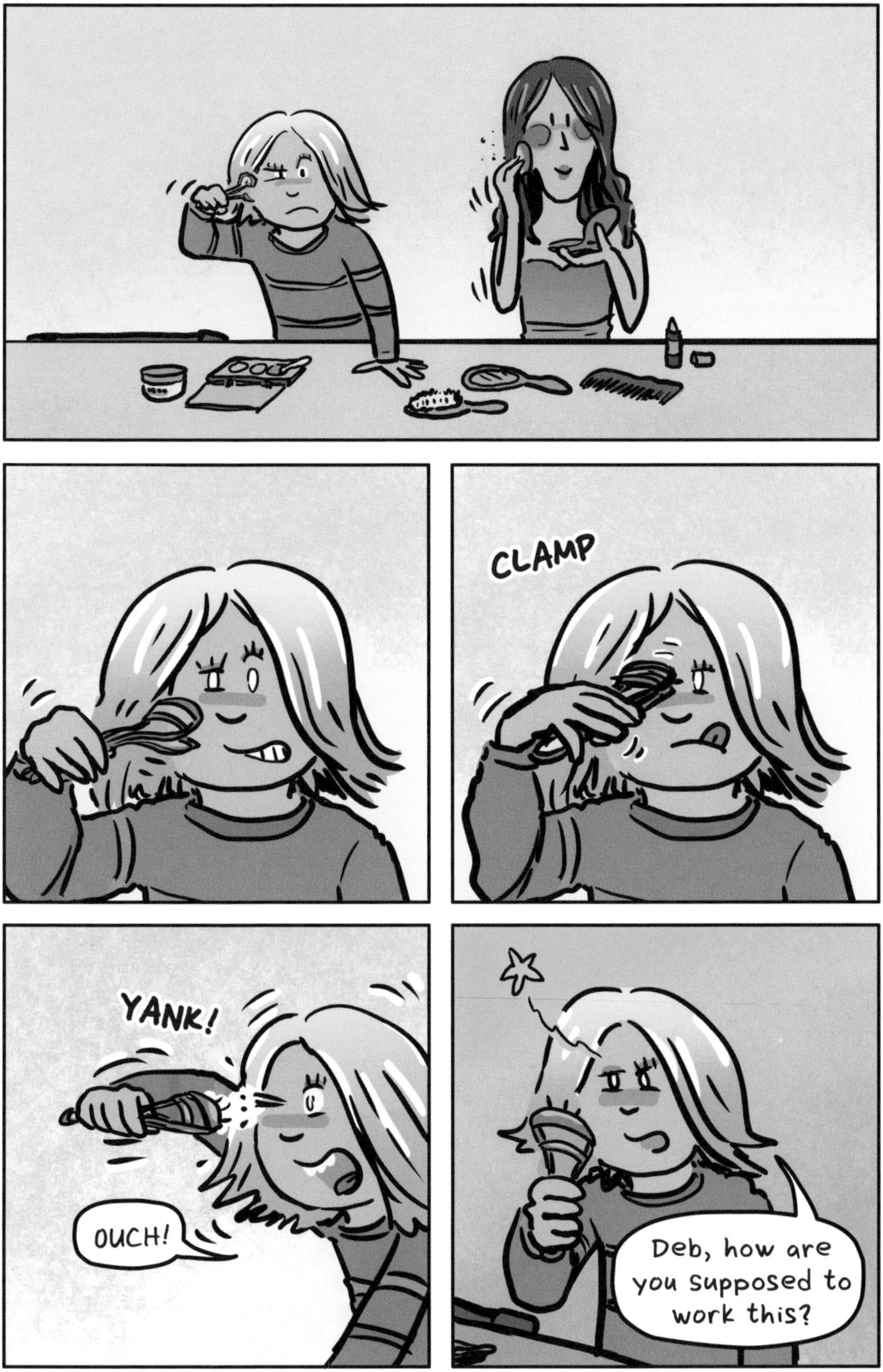
CLAMP
YANK!
OUCH!
Deb, how are you supposed to work this?

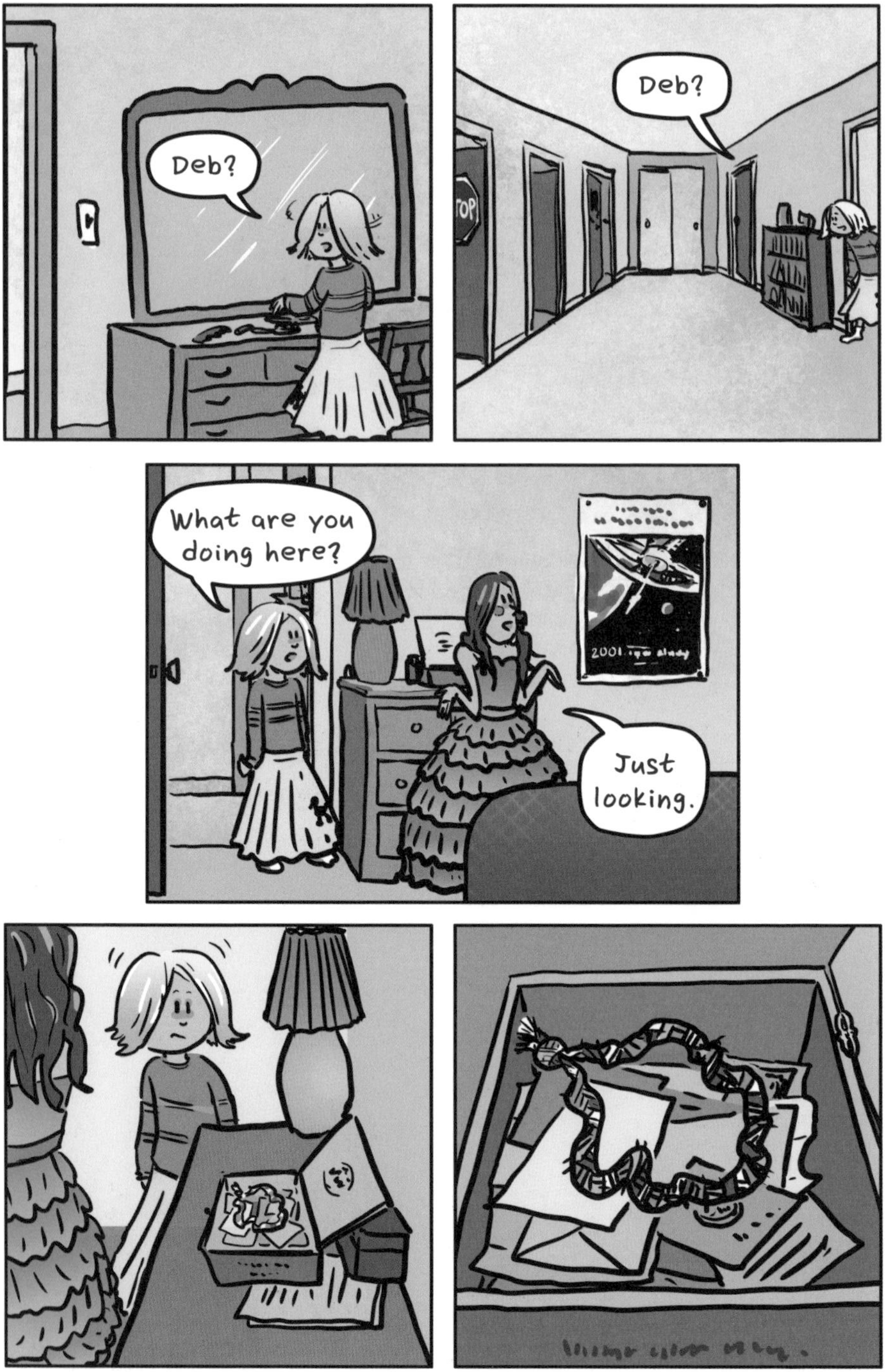
Deb?
Deb?
What are you doing here?
Just looking.

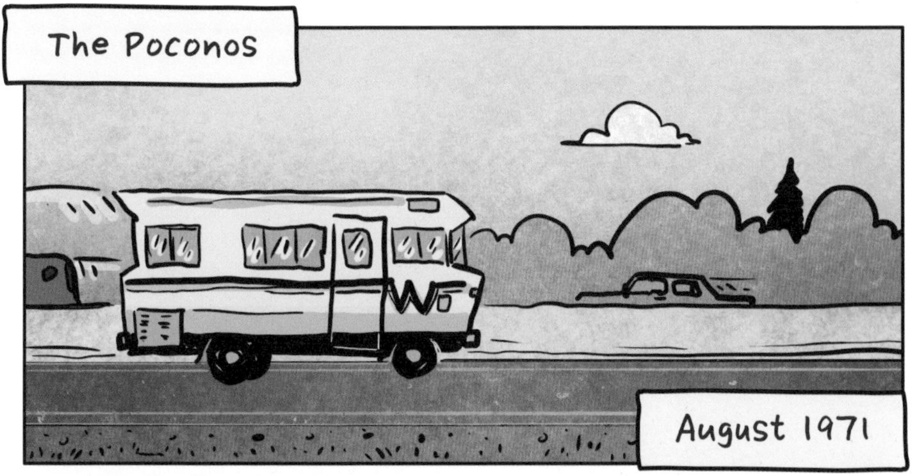
The Poconos
August 1971

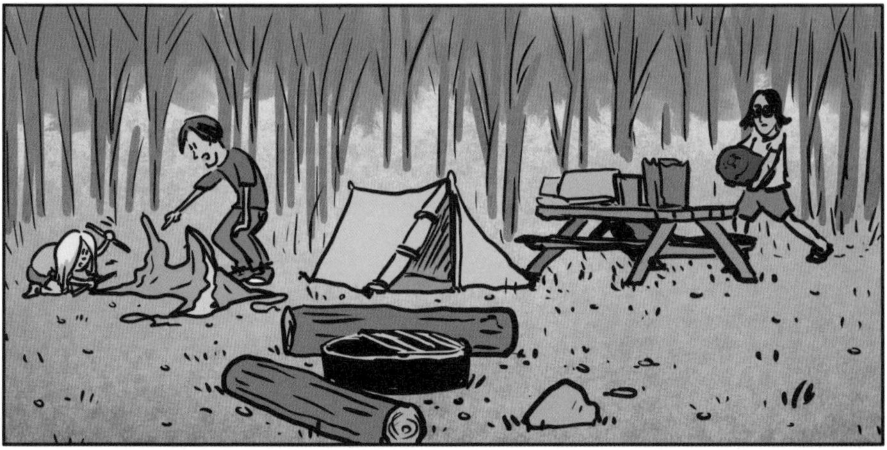

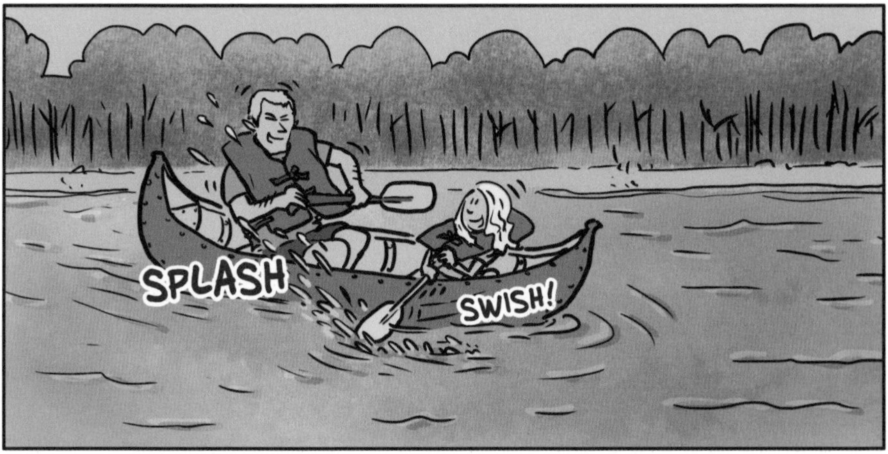
SPLASH
SWISH!

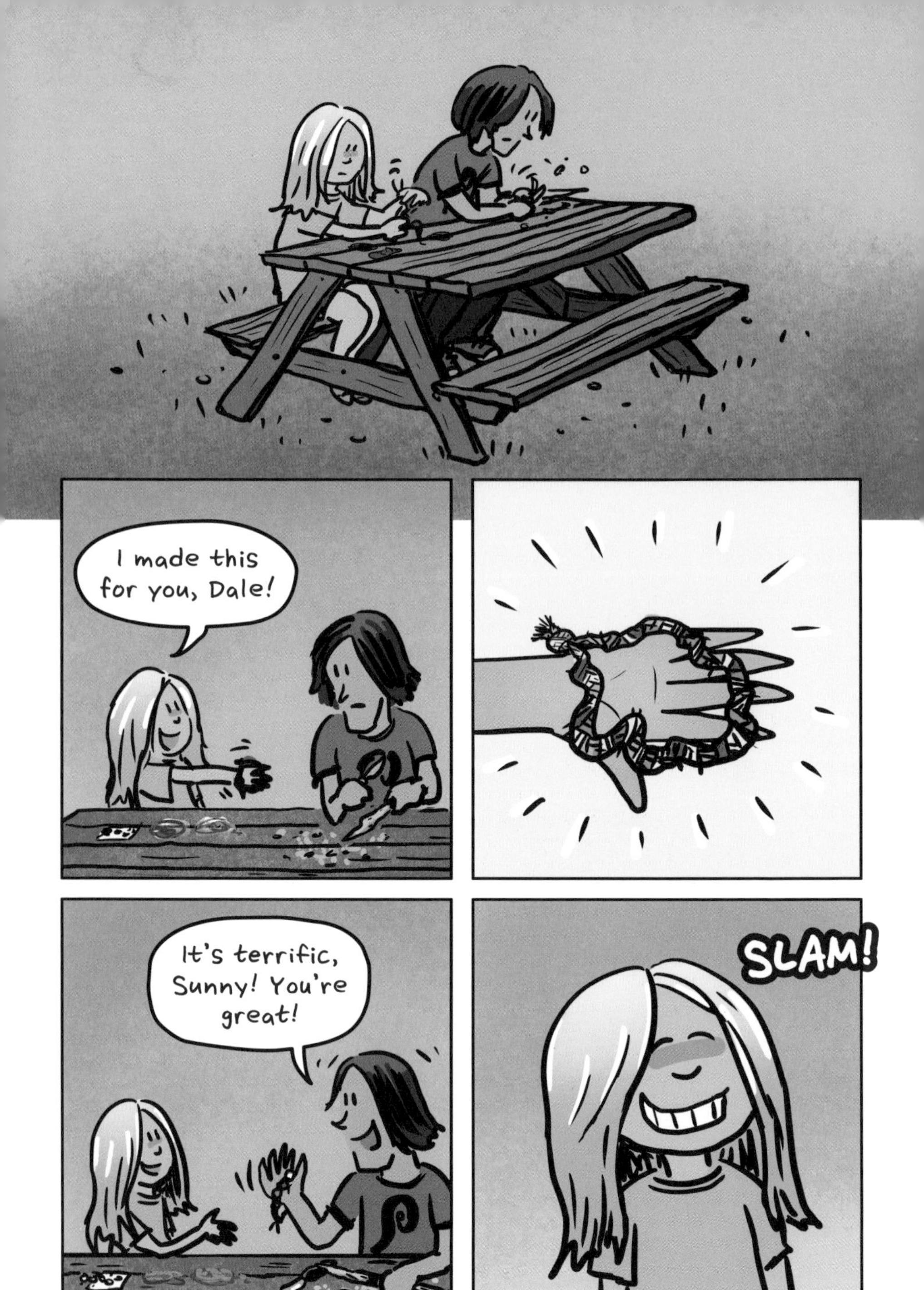
I made this for you, Dale!
It's terrific, Sunny! You're great!
SLAM!

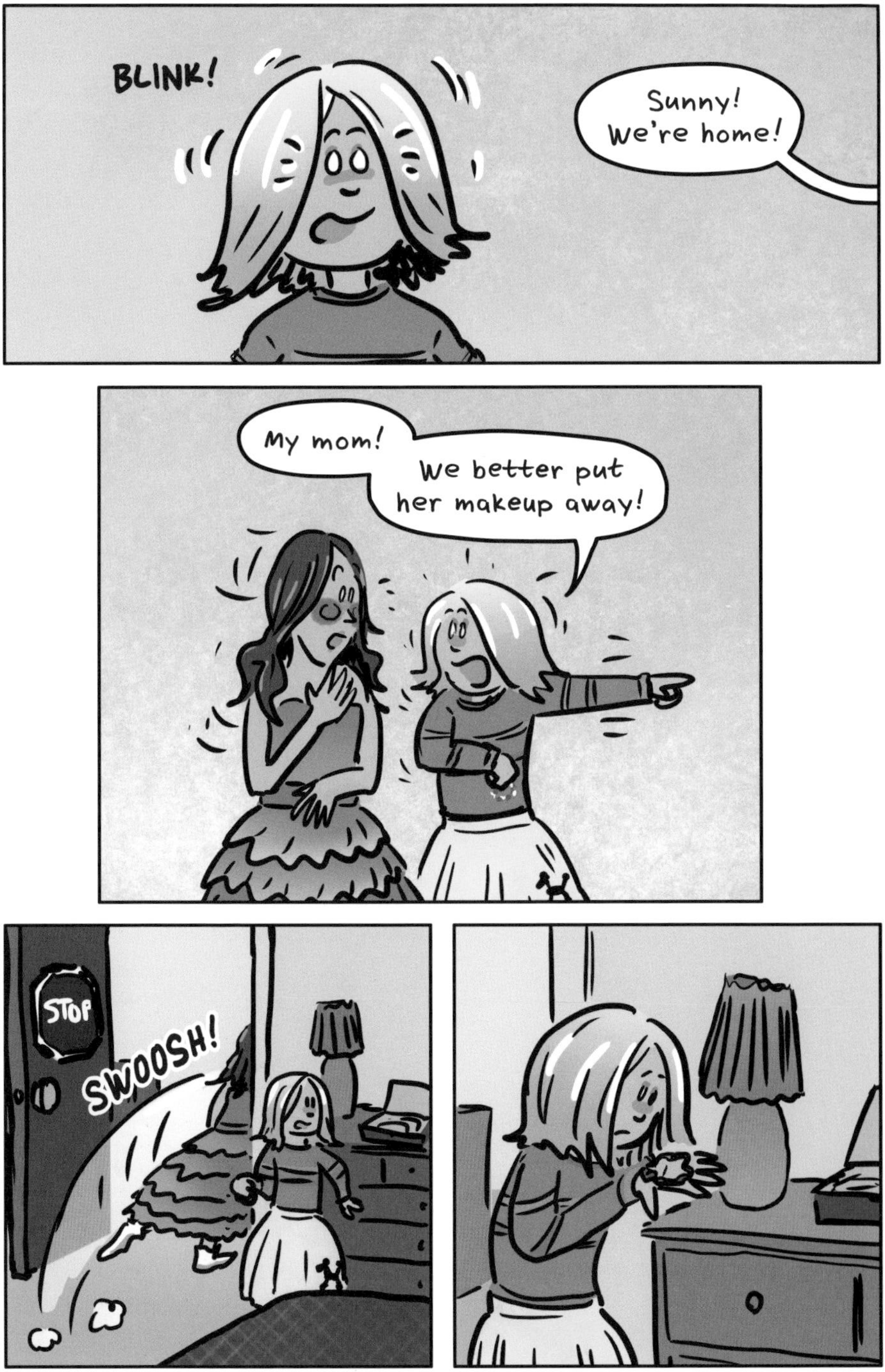
BLINK!
Sunny! We're home!
My mom!
We better put her makeup away!
STOP
SWOOSH!

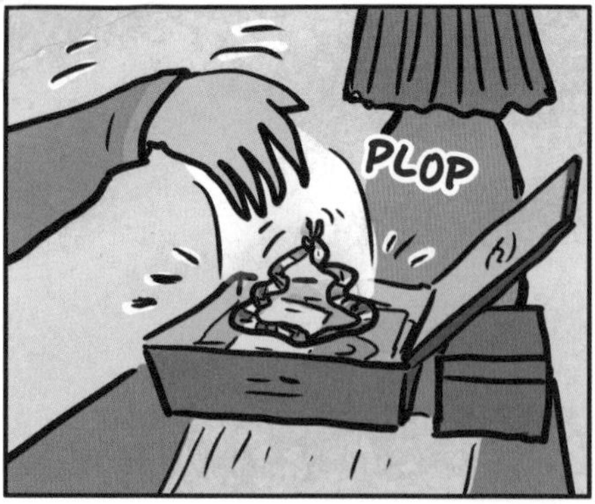
PLOP

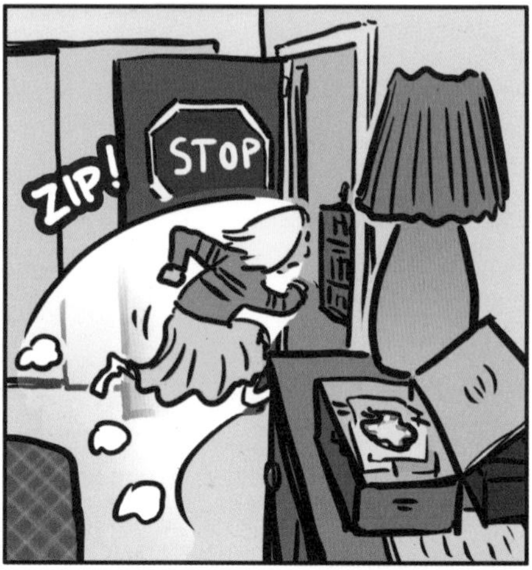
ZIP!
STOP

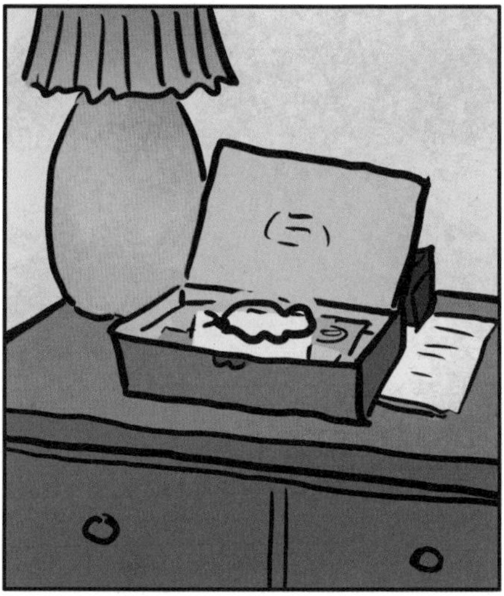

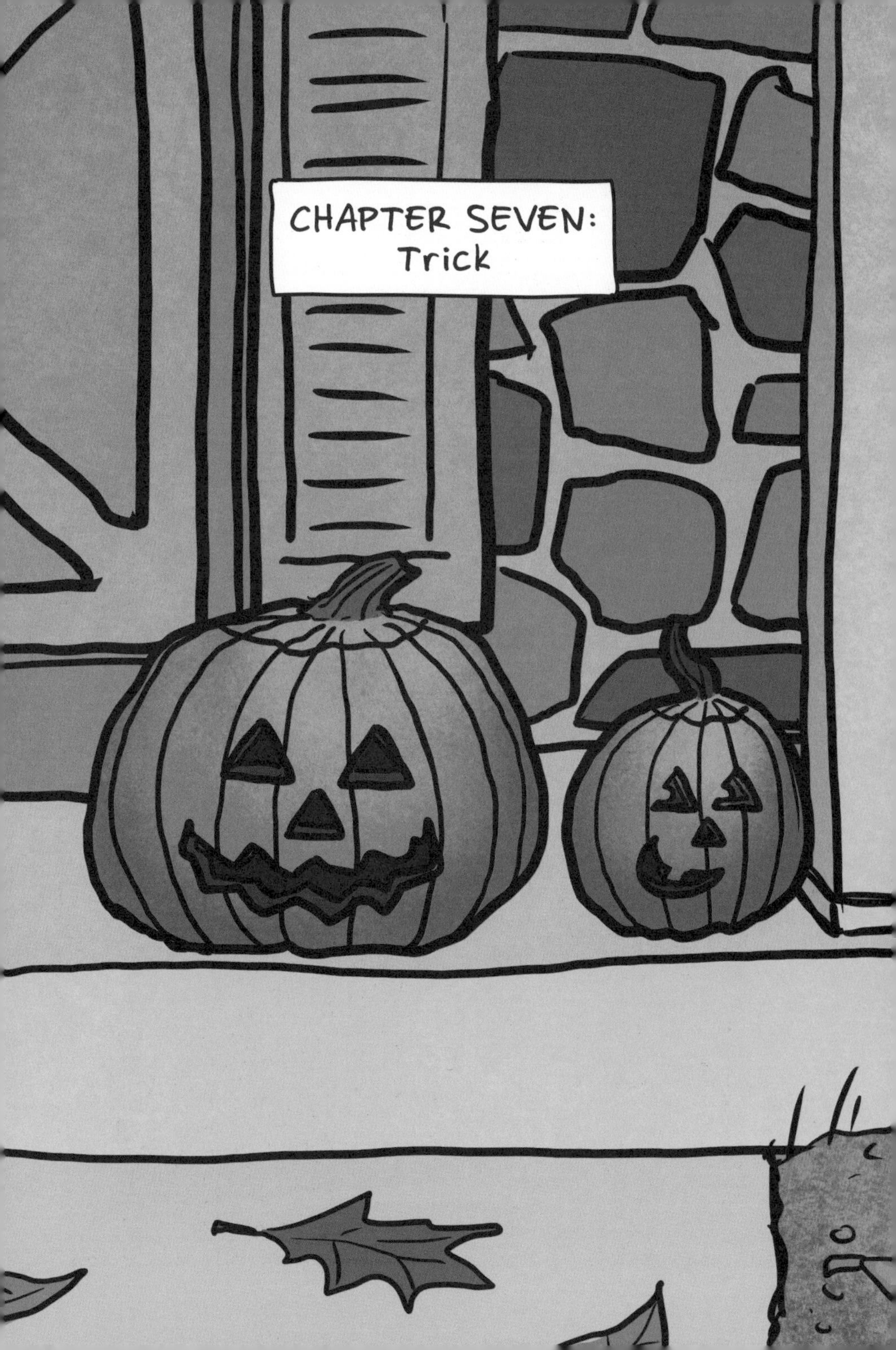
CHAPTER SEVEN:
Trick

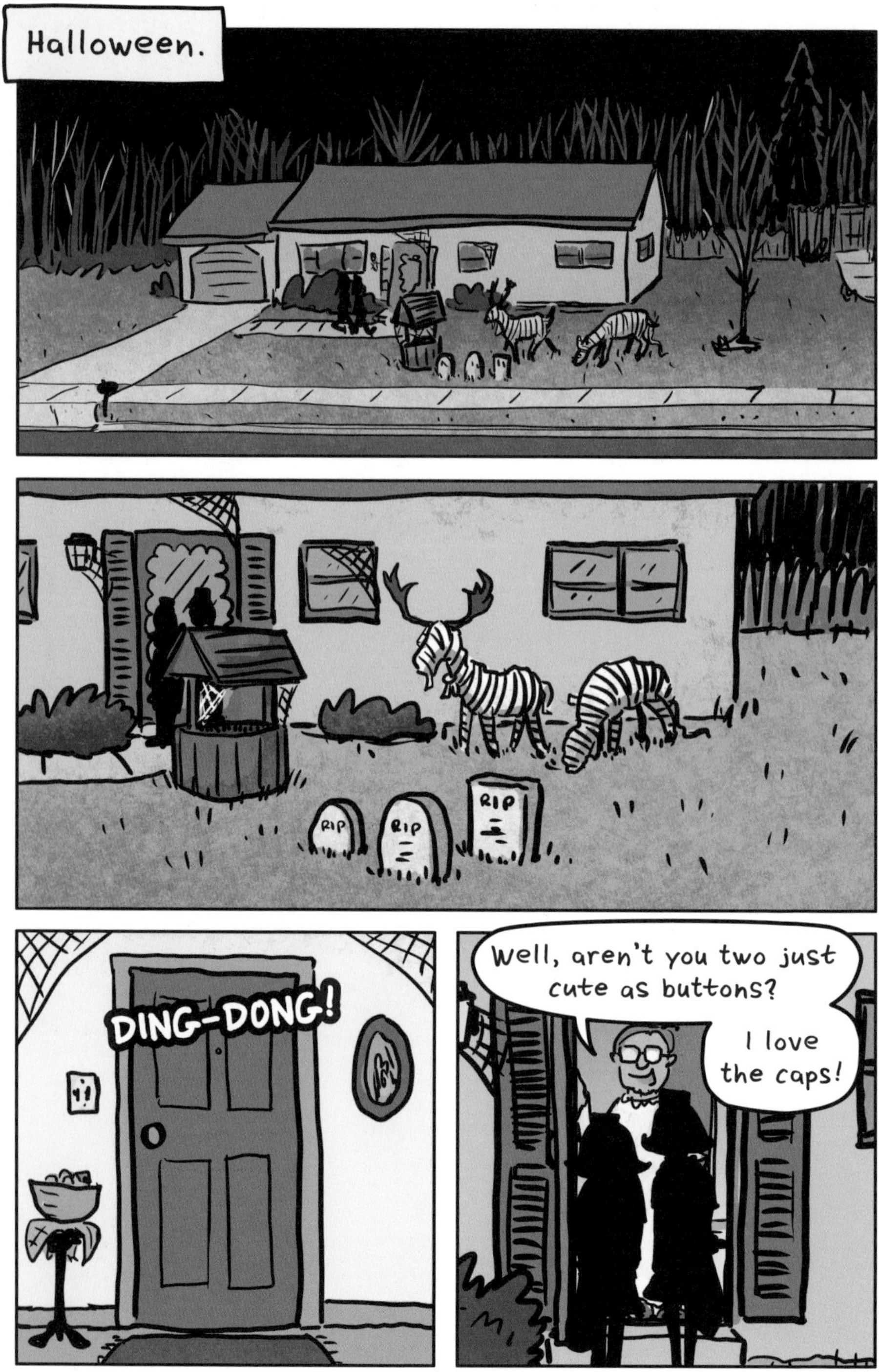
Halloween.
RIP
RIP
RIP
DING-DONG!
Well, aren't you two just cute as buttons?
I love the caps!

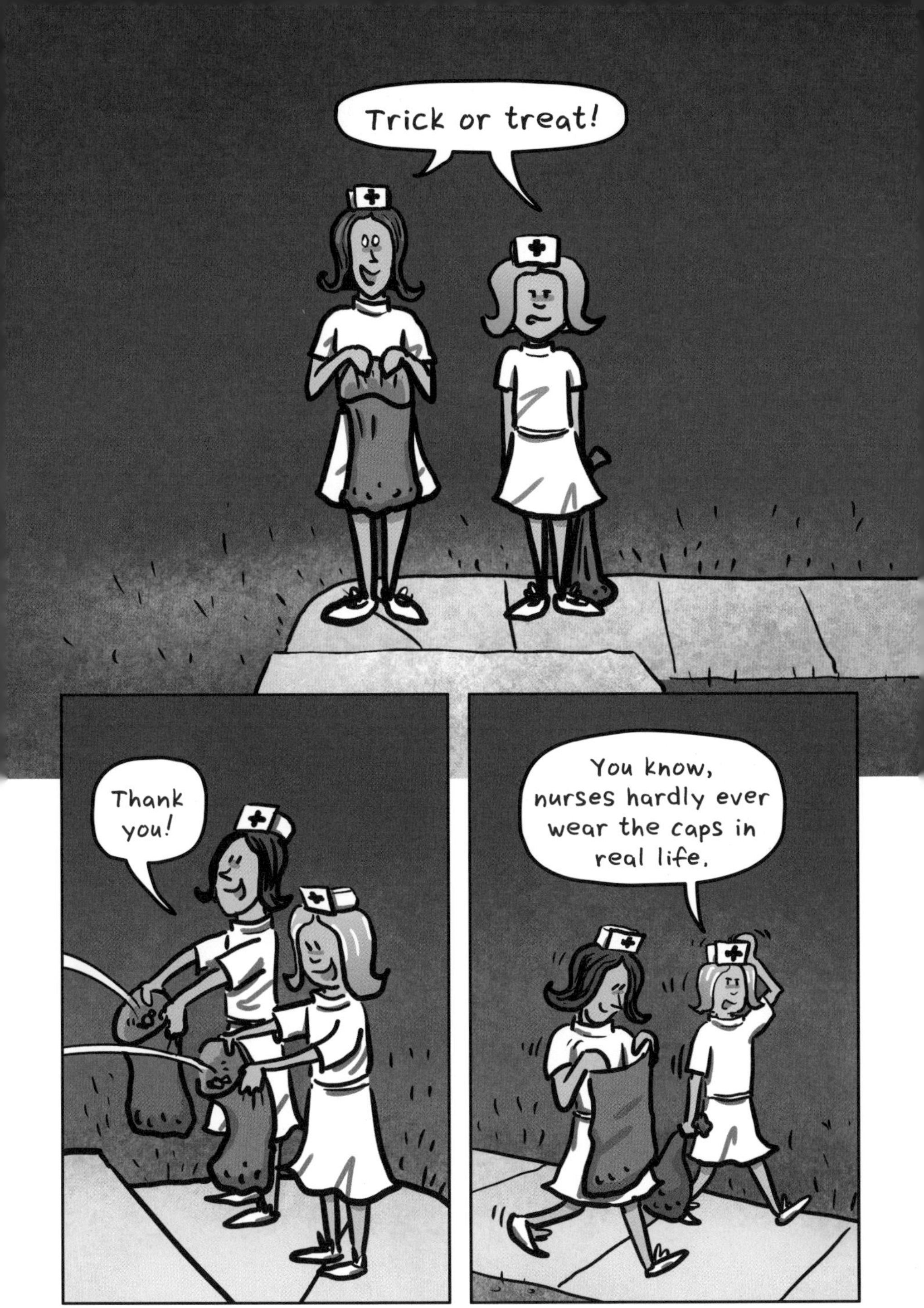
Trick or treat!
Thank you!
You know, nurses hardly ever wear the caps in real life.

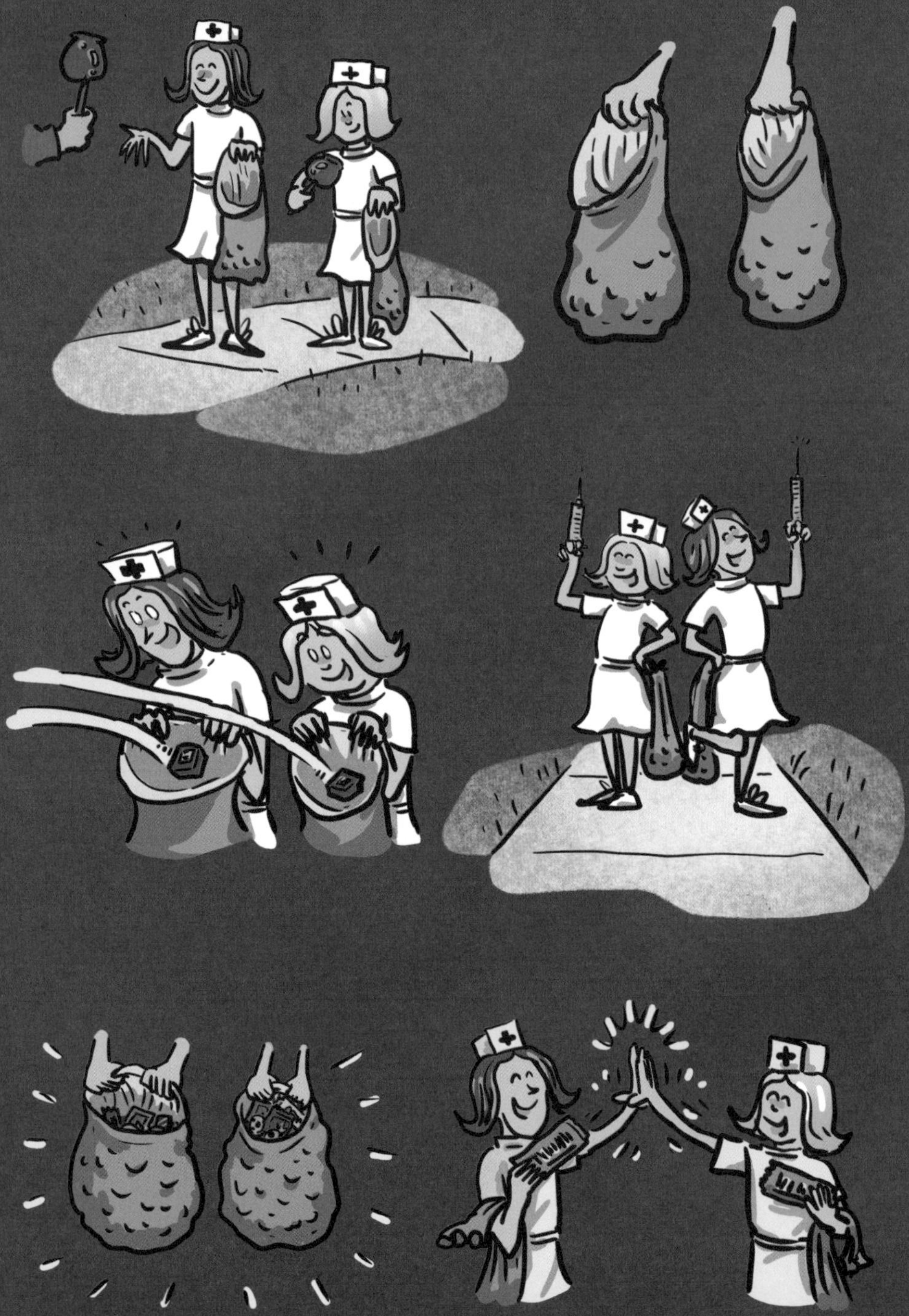

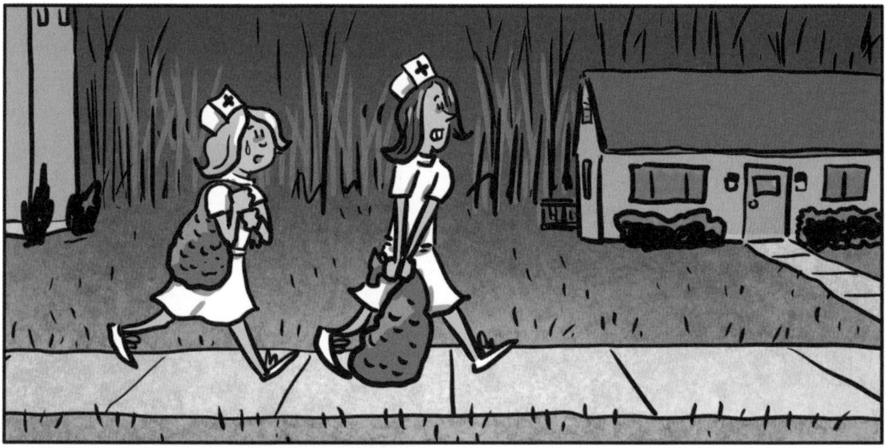

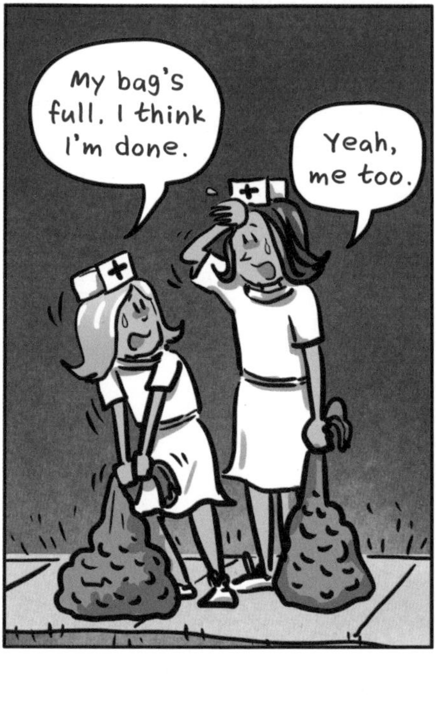
My bag's full. I think I'm done.
Yeah, me too.

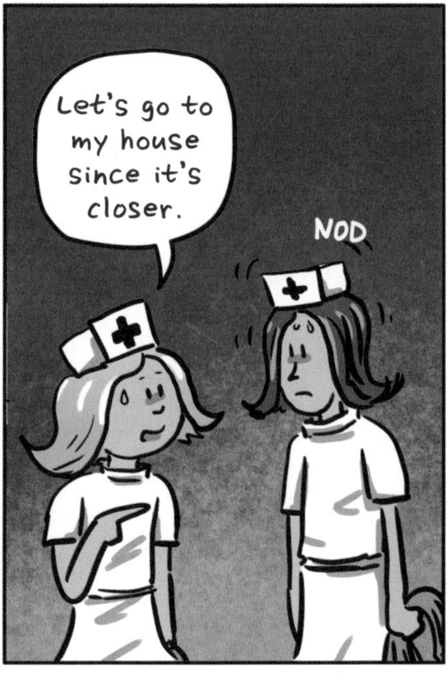
Let's go to my house since it's closer.
NOD

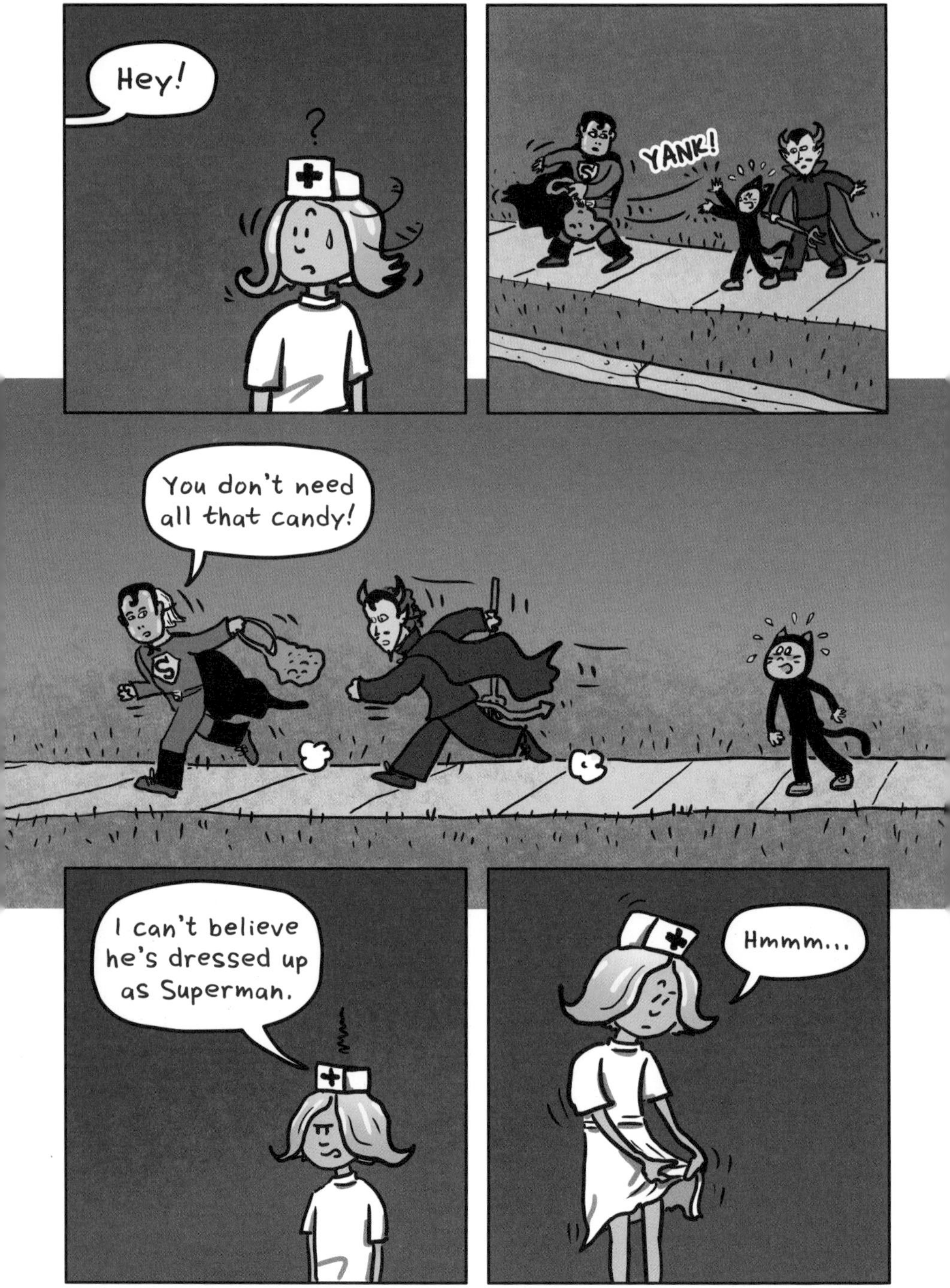
Hey!
YANK!
You don't need all that candy!
I can't believe he's dressed up as Superman.
Hmmm...

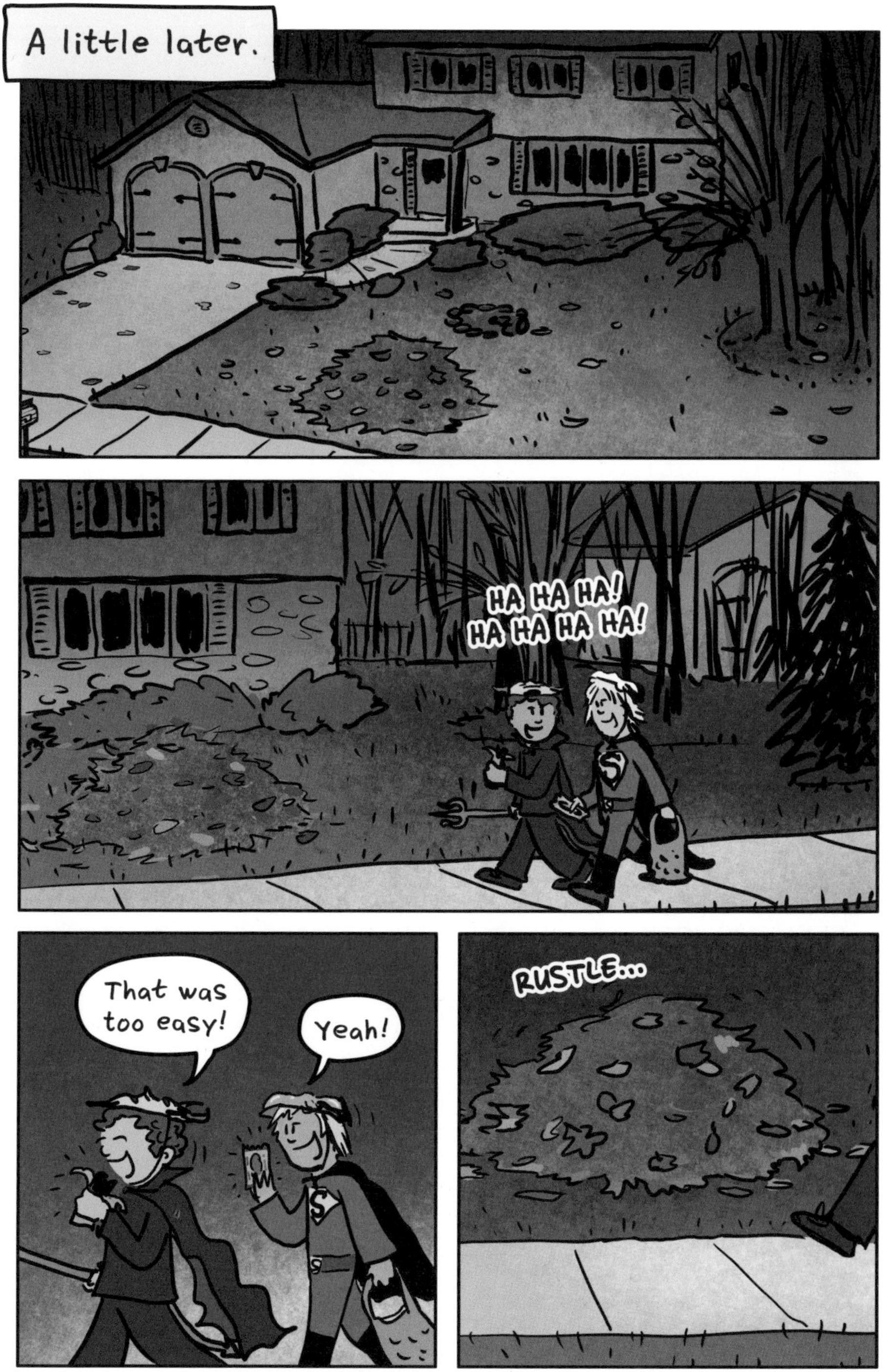
A little later.
HA HA HA! HA HA HA HA!
That was too easy!
Yeah!
RUSTLE...

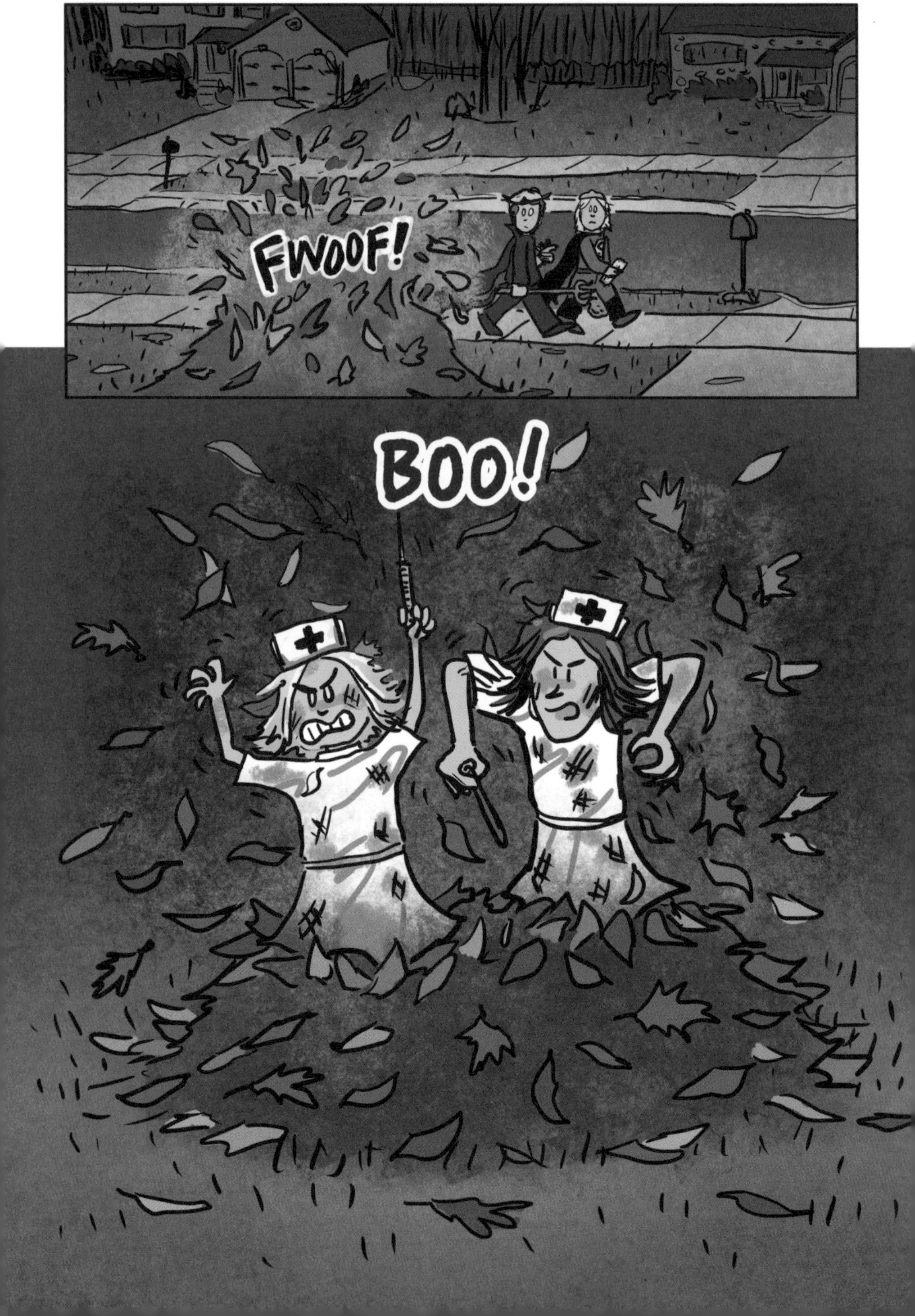
FWOOF!
BOO!

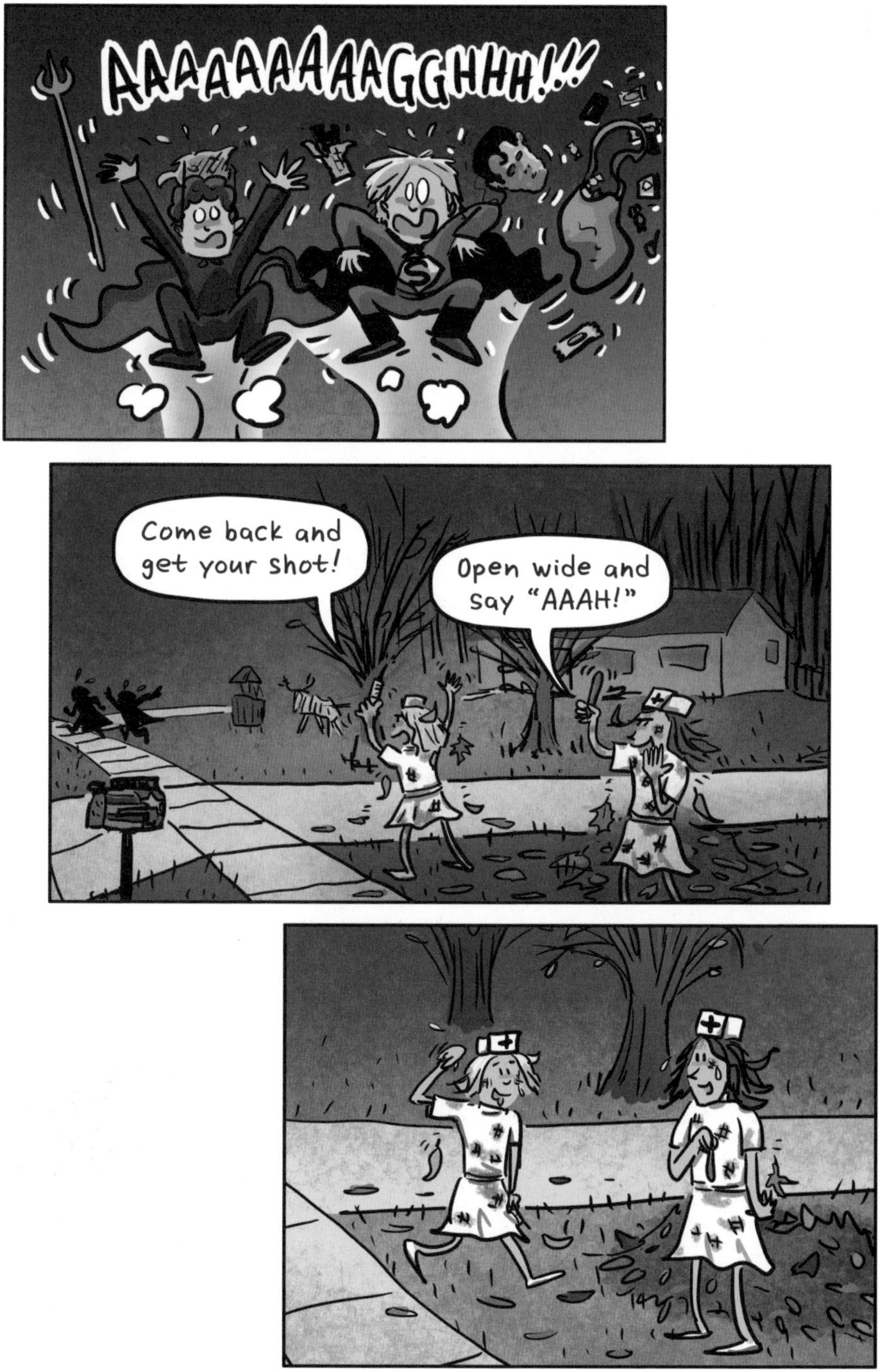
AAAAAAAAAGGHHH!!!
Come back and get your shot!
Open wide and say "AAAH!"

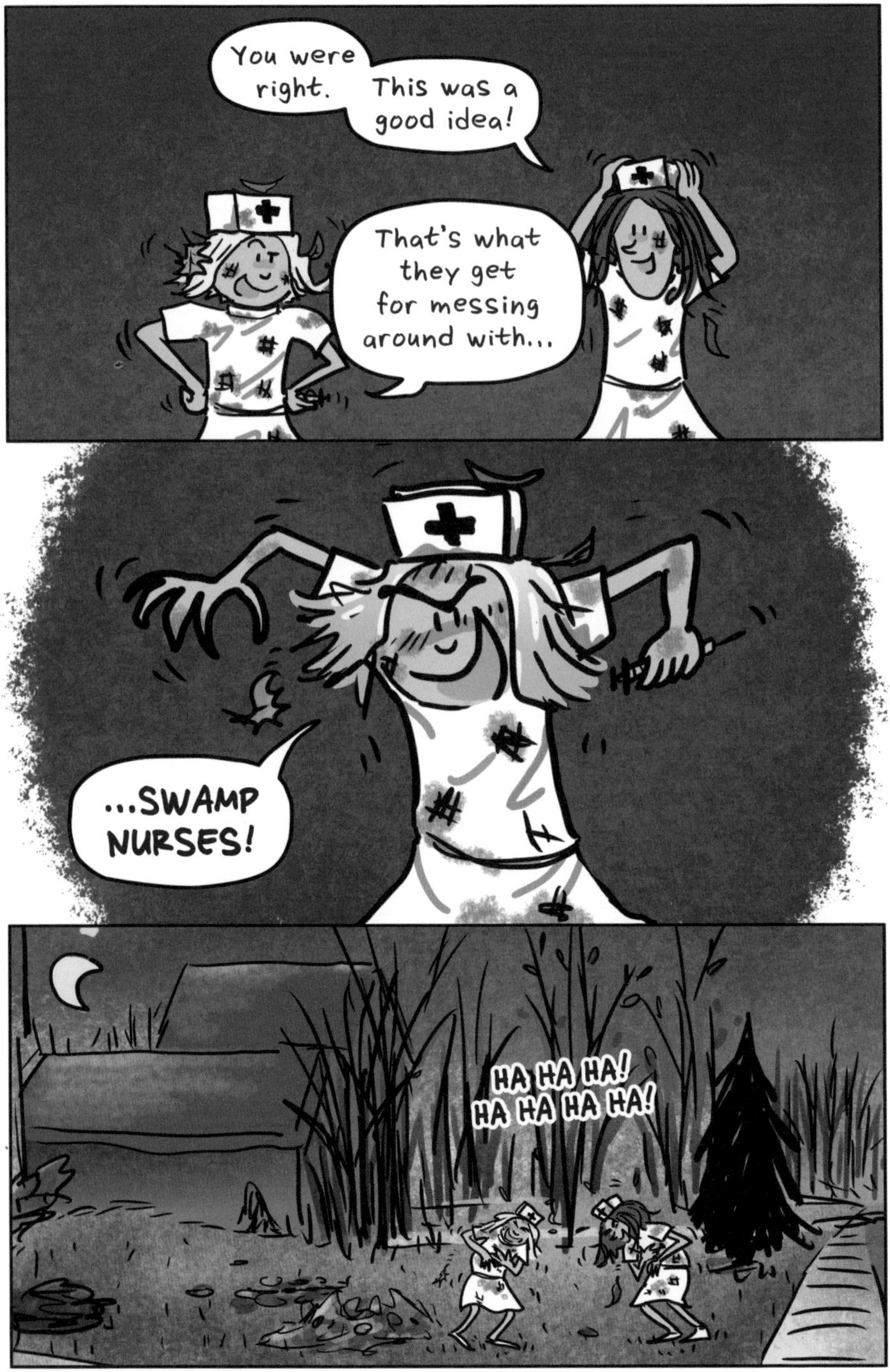
You were right.
This was a good idea!
That's what they get for messing around with...
...SWAMP NURSES!
HA HA HA!
HA HA HA HA!

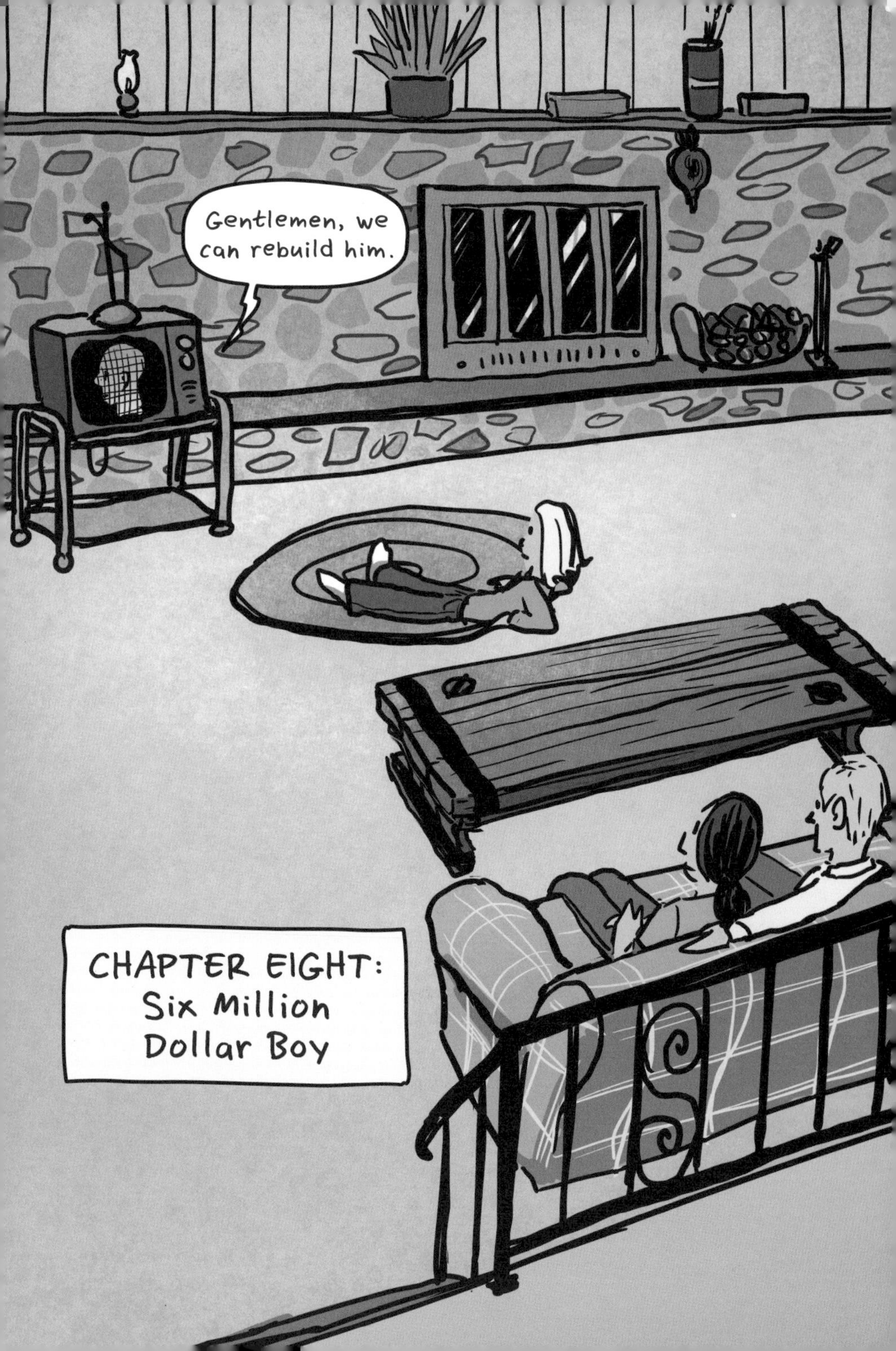
Gentlemen, we can rebuild him.

CHAPTER EIGHT: Six Million Dollar Boy

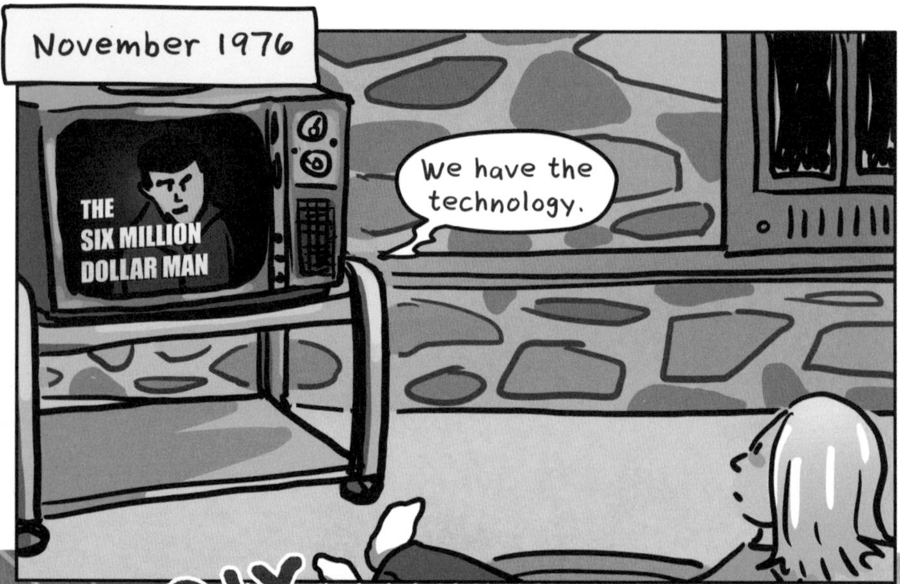
November 1976
THE SIX MILLION DOLLAR MAN
We have the technology.

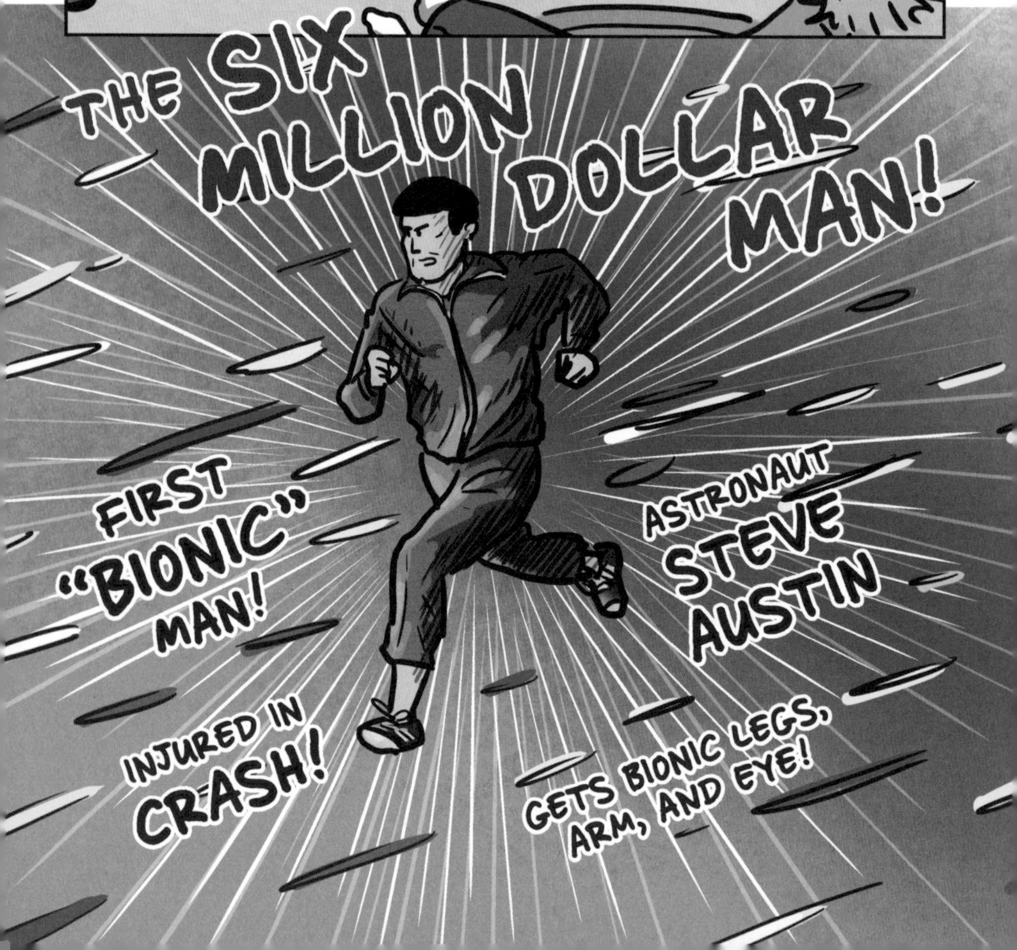
THE SIX MILLION DOLLAR MAN!
FIRST "BIONIC" MAN!
ASTRONAUT STEVE AUSTIN
INJURED IN CRASH!
GETS BIONIC LEGS, ARM, AND EYE!

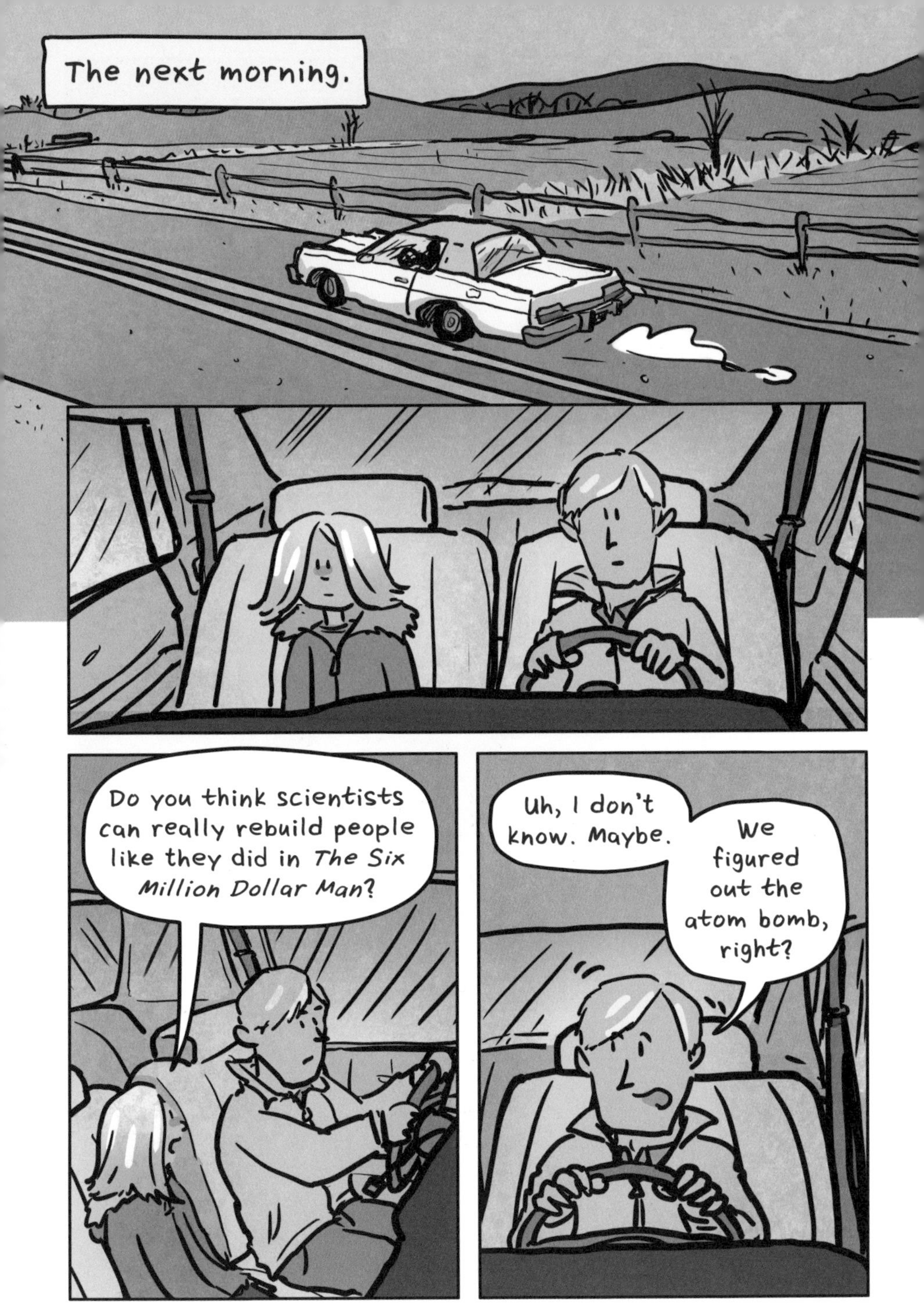
The next morning.
Do you think scientists can really rebuild people like they did in *The Six Million Dollar Man*?
Uh, I don't know. Maybe.
We figured out the atom bomb, right?

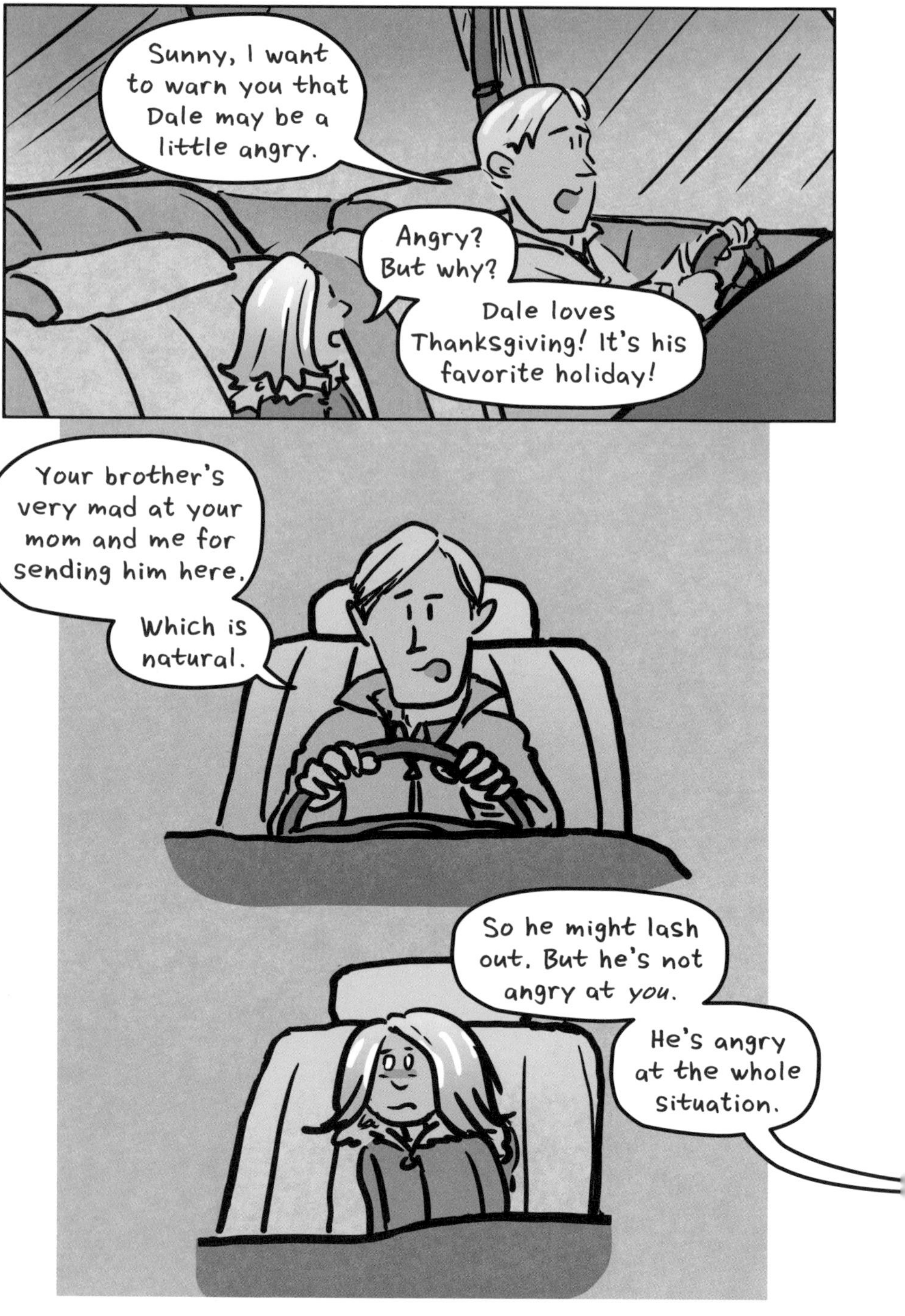
Sunny, I want to warn you that Dale may be a little angry.
Angry? But why?
Dale loves Thanksgiving! It's his favorite holiday!
Your brother's very mad at your mom and me for sending him here.
Which is natural.
So he might lash out. But he's not angry at *you*.
He's angry at the whole situation.

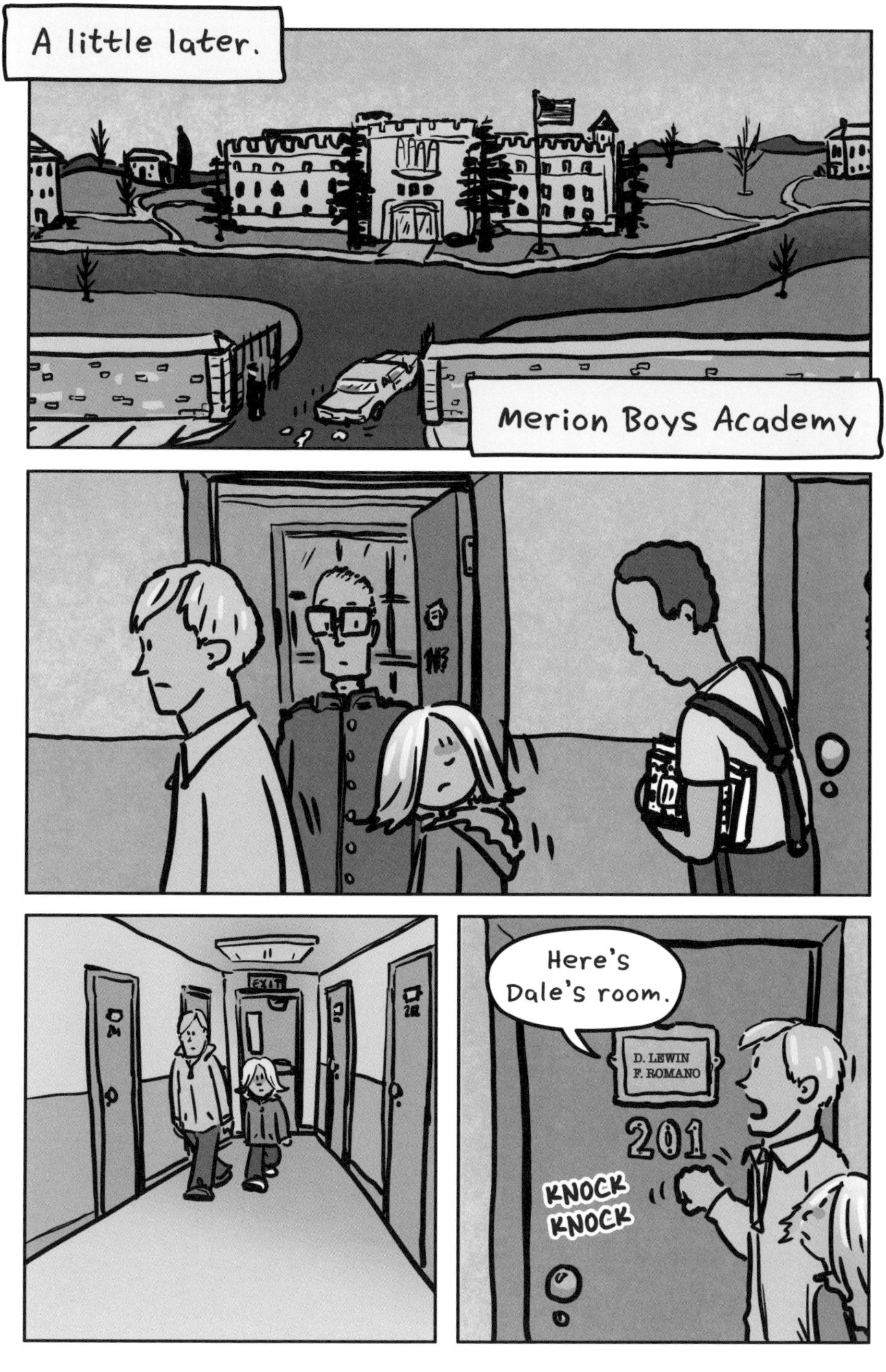
A little later.
Merion Boys Academy
Here's Dale's room.
D. LEWIN
F. ROMANO
201
KNOCK KNOCK

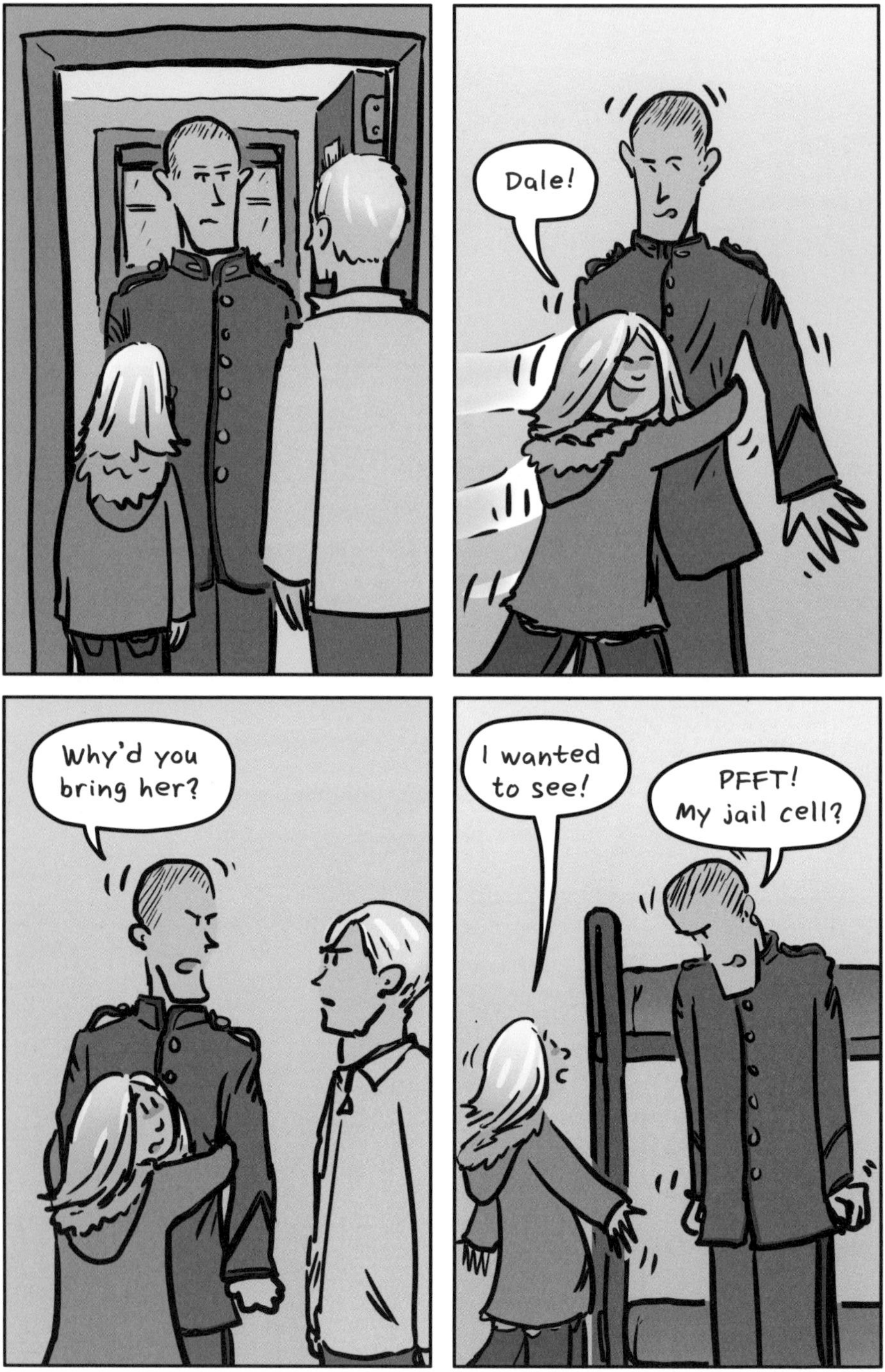
Dale!
Why'd you bring her?
I wanted to see!
PFFT! My jail cell?

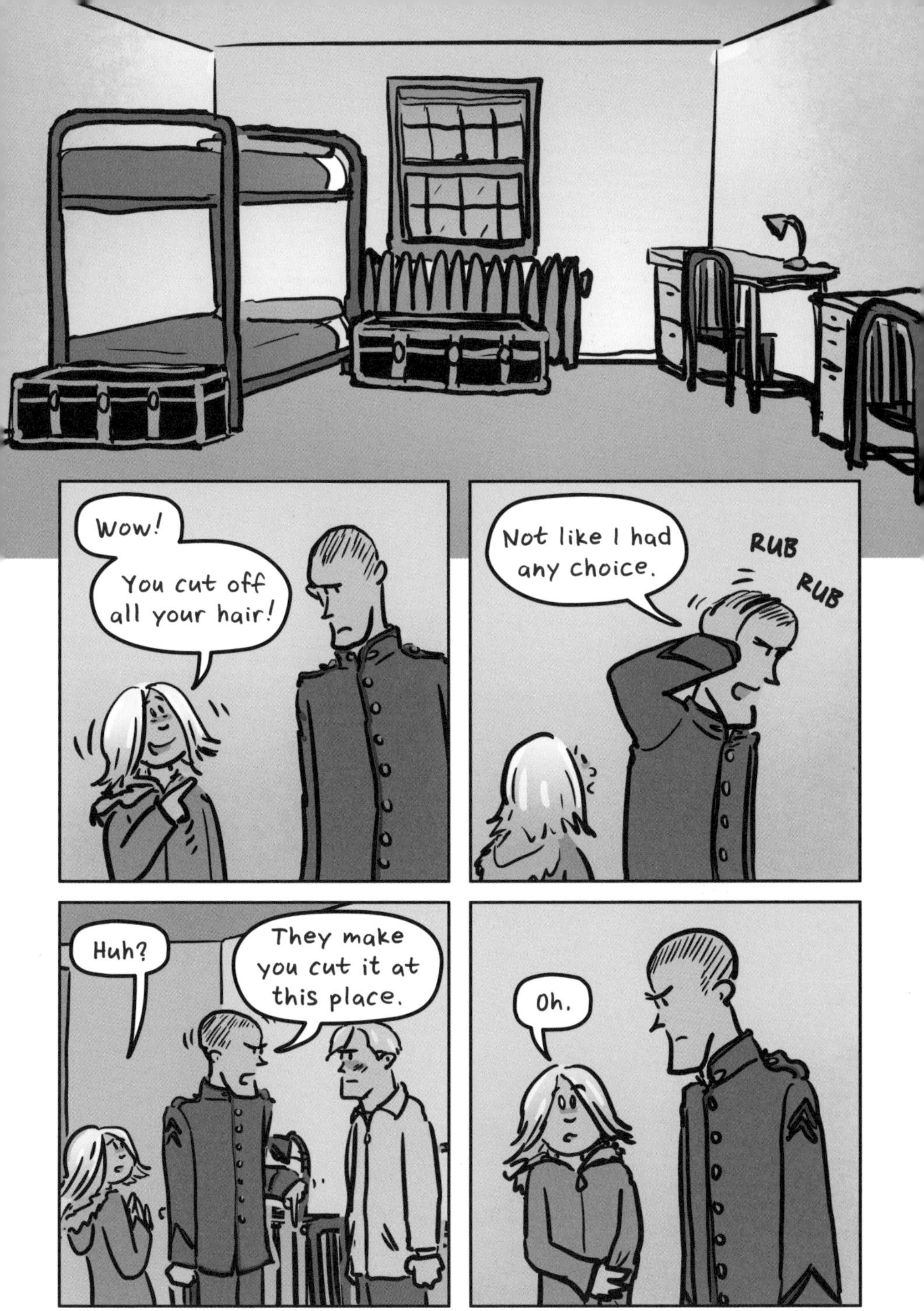
Wow!
You cut off all your hair!
Not like I had any choice.
RUB RUB
Huh?
They make you cut it at this place.
Oh.

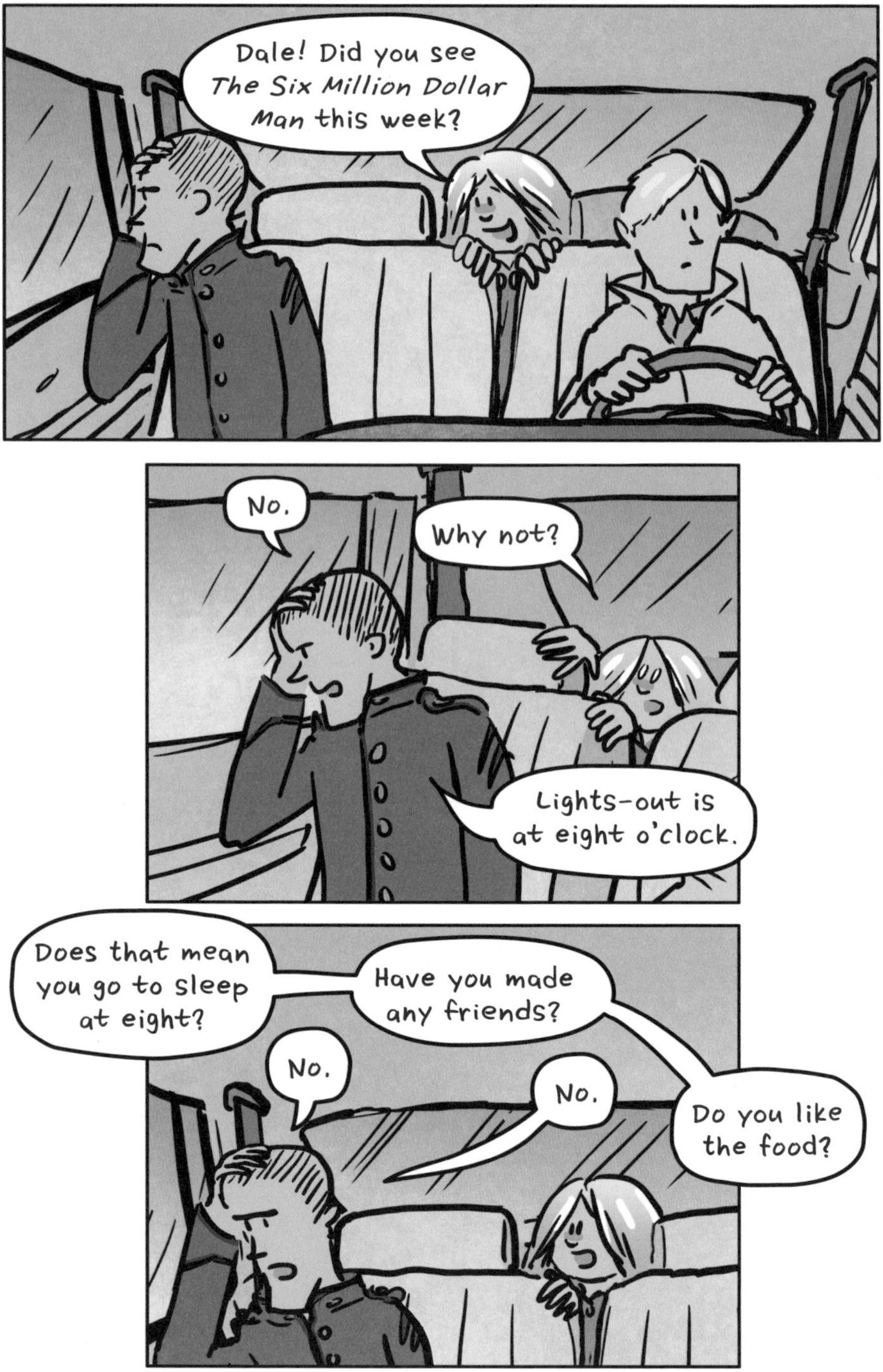
Dale! Did you see *The Six Million Dollar Man* this week?
No.
Why not?
Lights-out is at eight o'clock.
Does that mean you go to sleep at eight?
Have you made any friends?
Do you like the food?
No.
No.

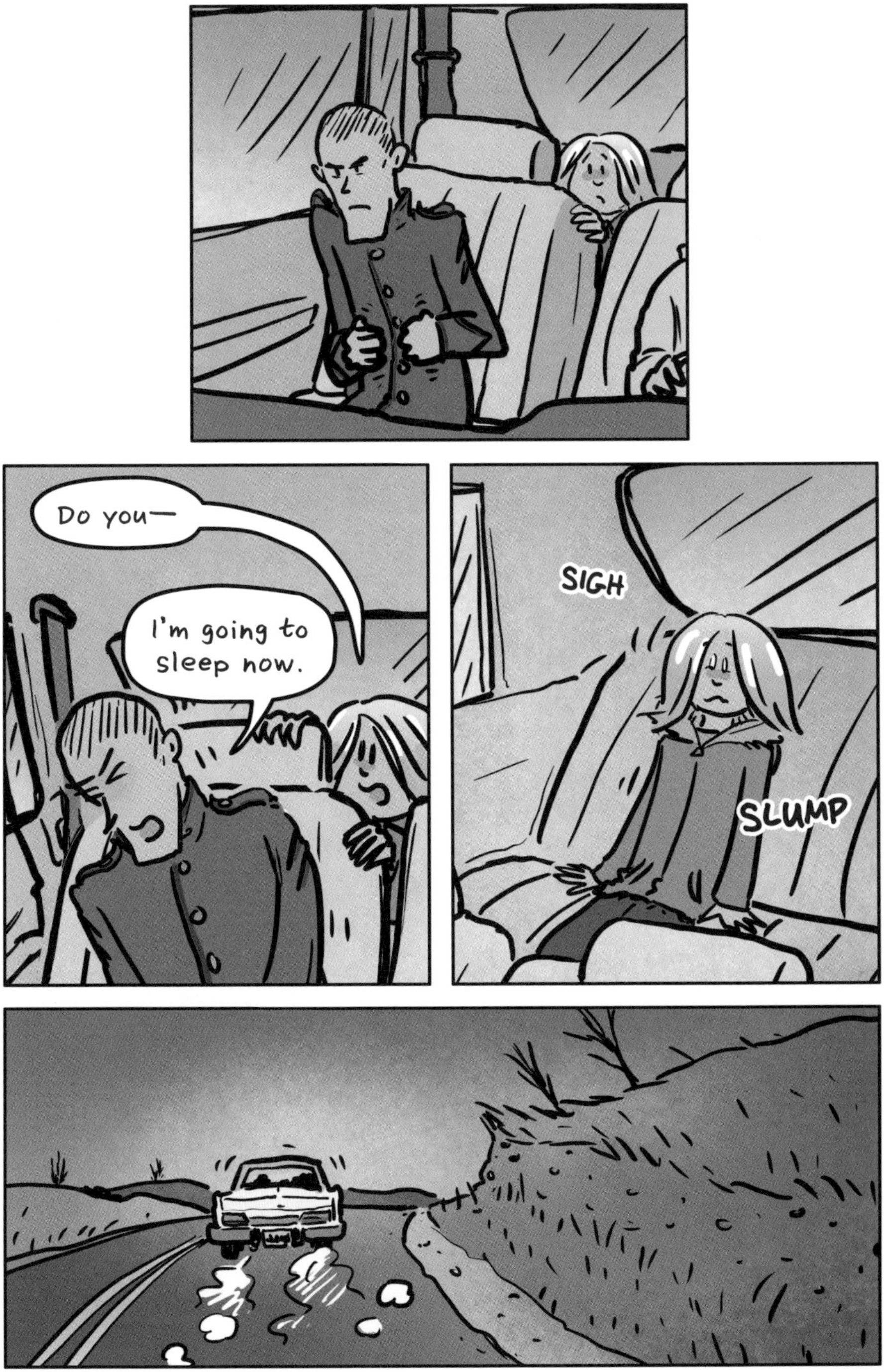
Do you—
I'm going to sleep now.
SIGH
SLUMP

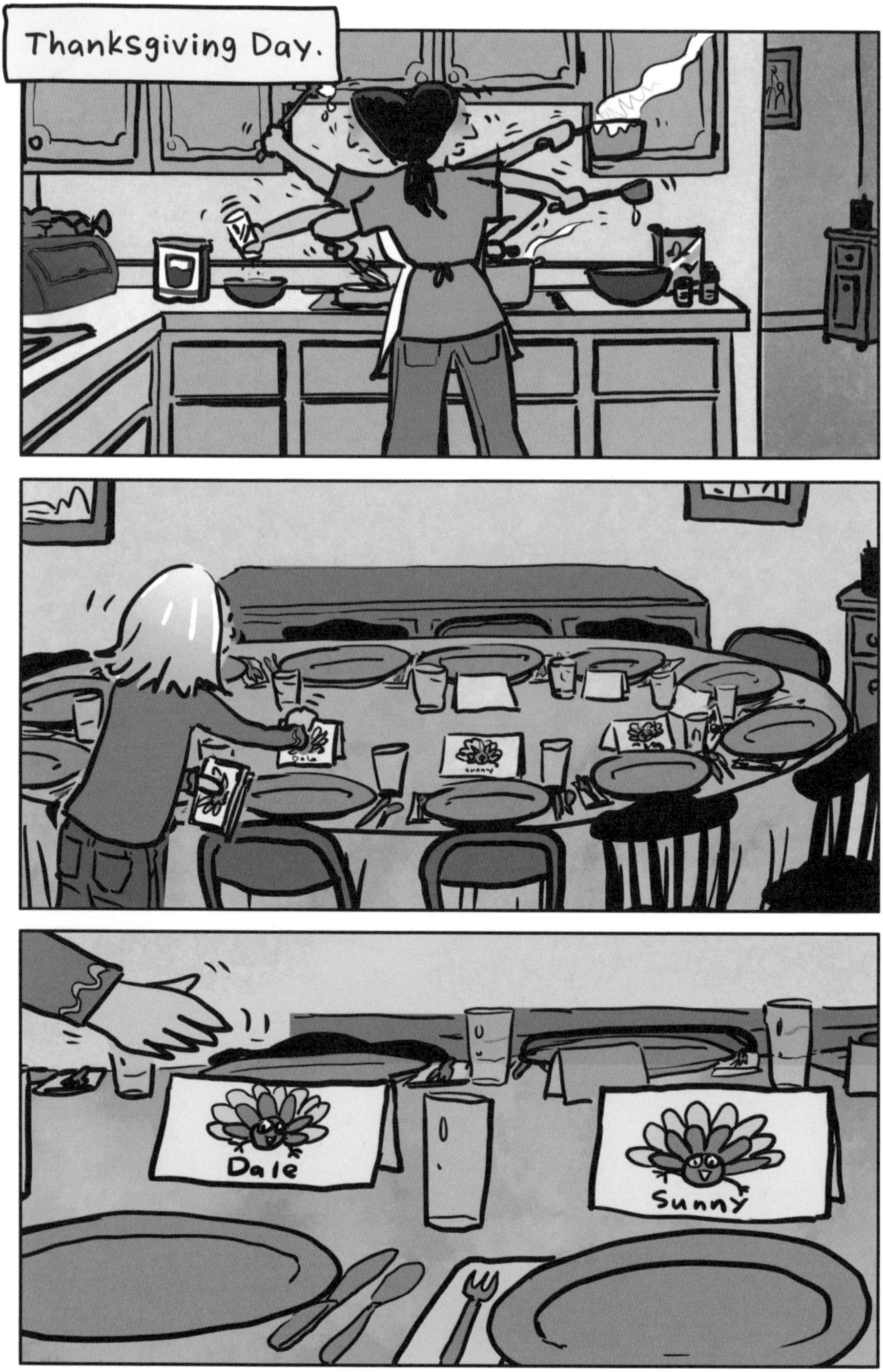
Thanksgiving Day.
Dale
Sunny
Dale
Sunny

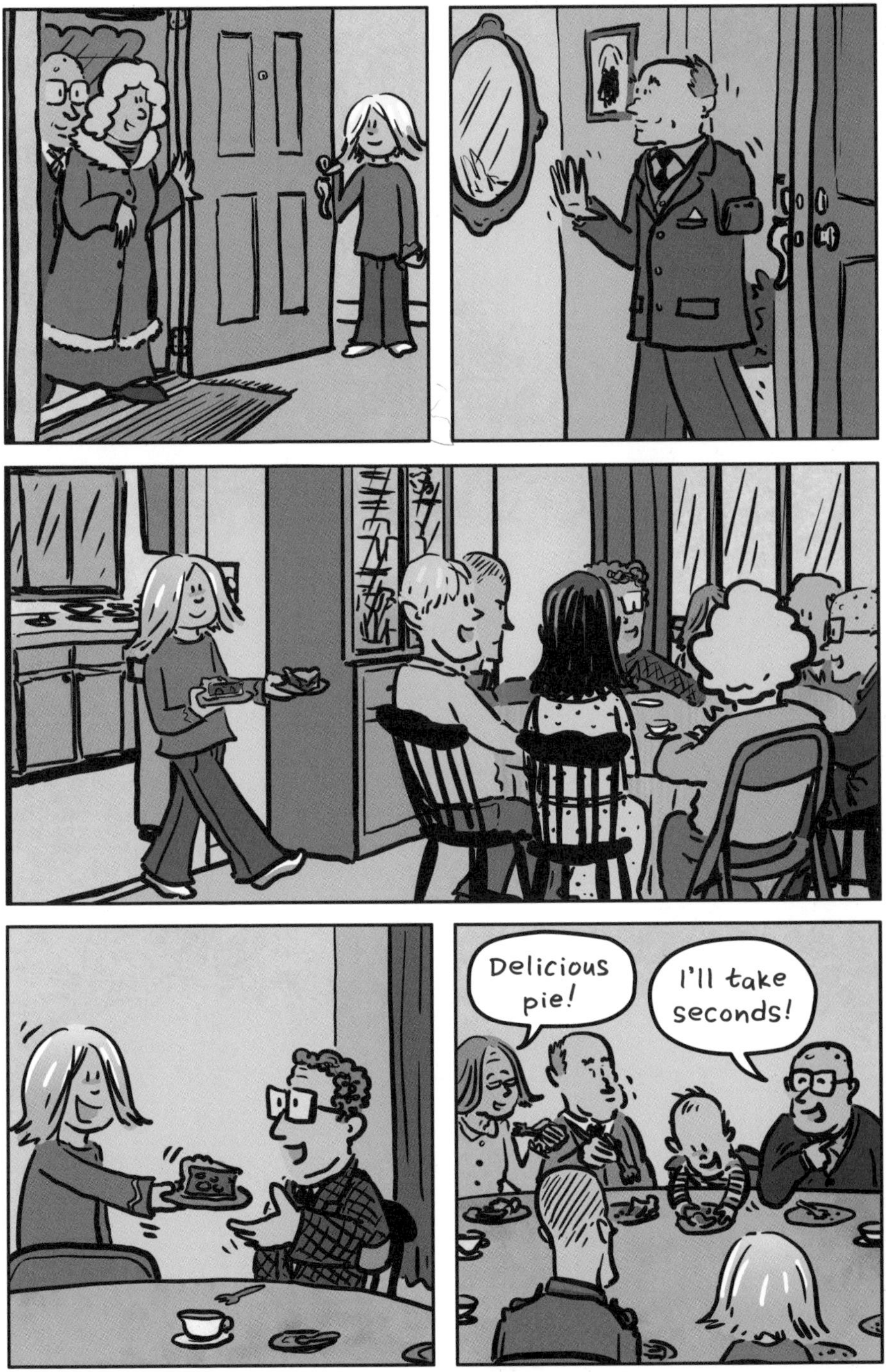
Delicious pie!
I'll take seconds!

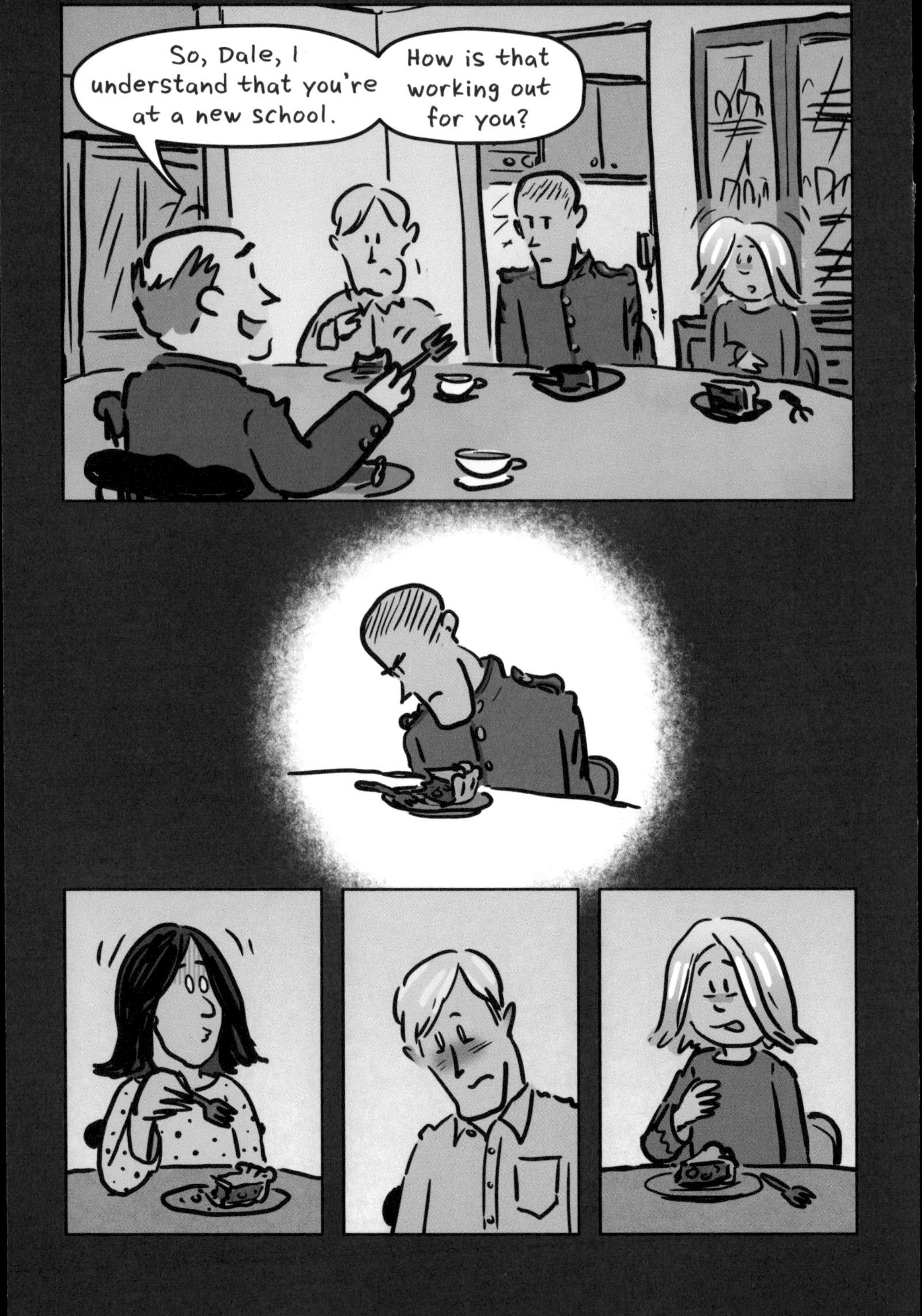
So, Dale, I understand that you're at a new school.
How is that working out for you?

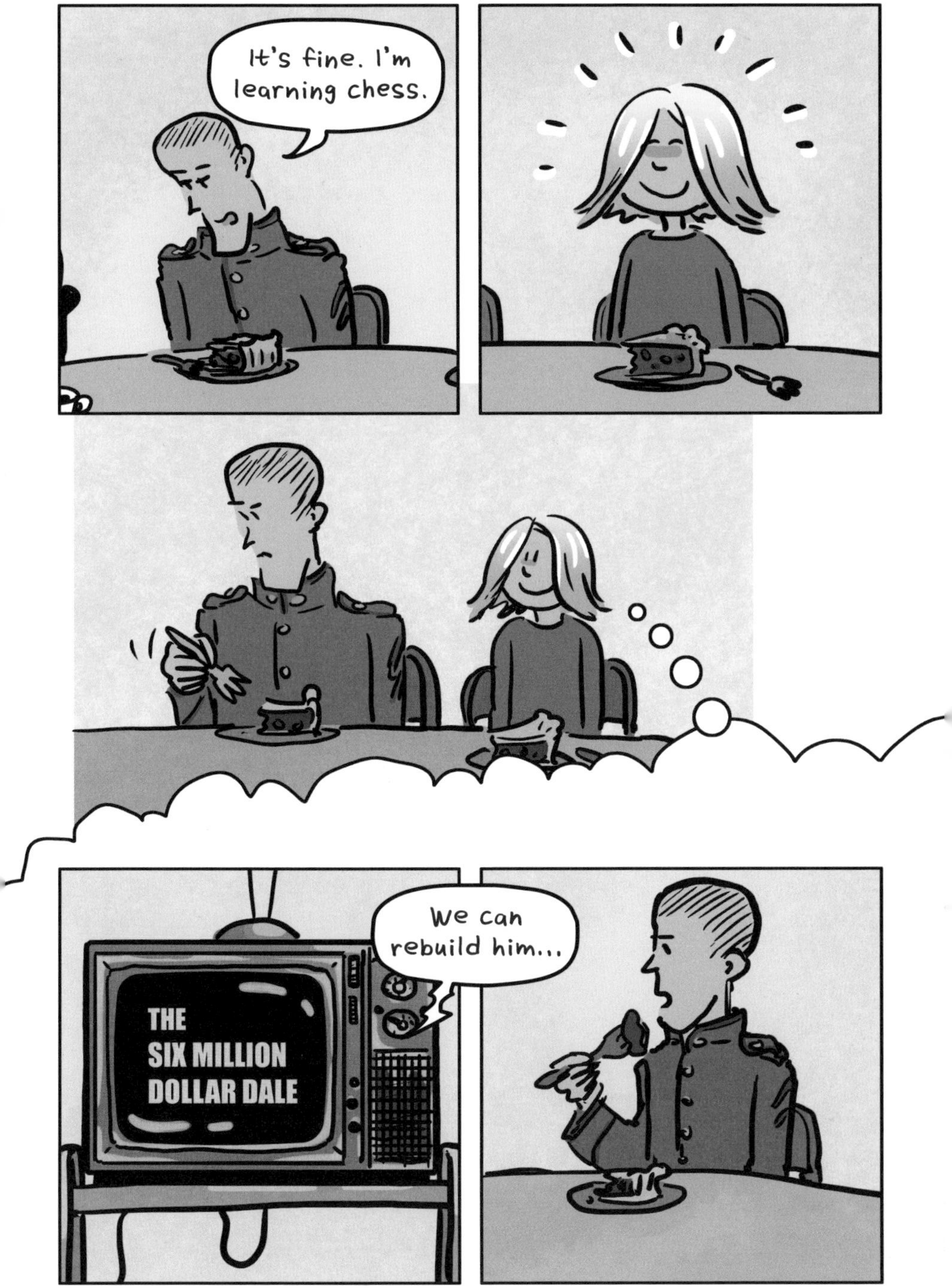
It's fine. I'm learning chess.
THE SIX MILLION DOLLAR DALE
We can rebuild him...

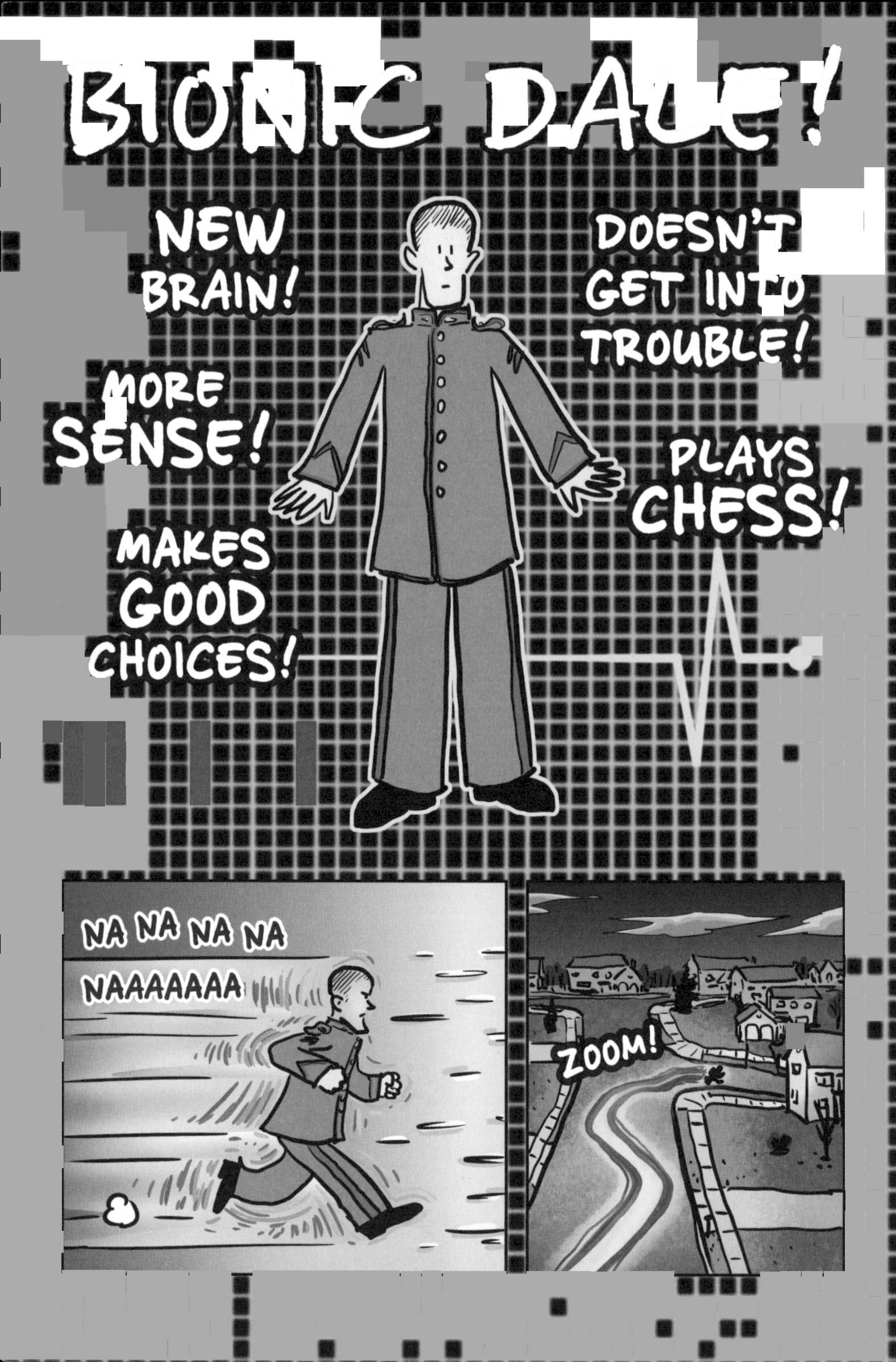

BIONIC DALE!
NEW BRAIN!
DOESN'T GET INTO TROUBLE!
MORE SENSE!
PLAYS CHESS!
MAKES GOOD CHOICES!
NA NA NA NA
NAAAAAAA
ZOOM!

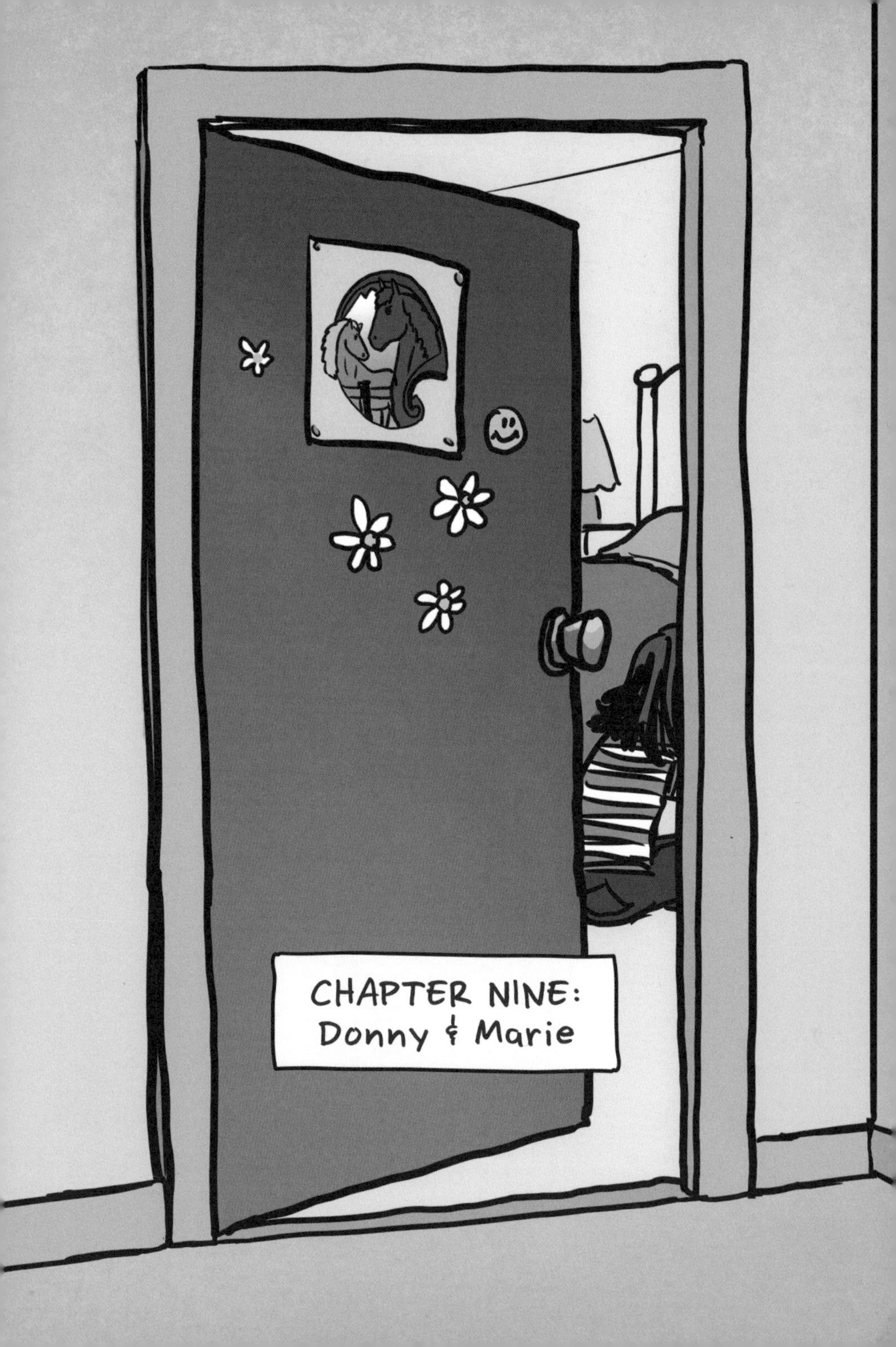
CHAPTER NINE:
Donny & Marie

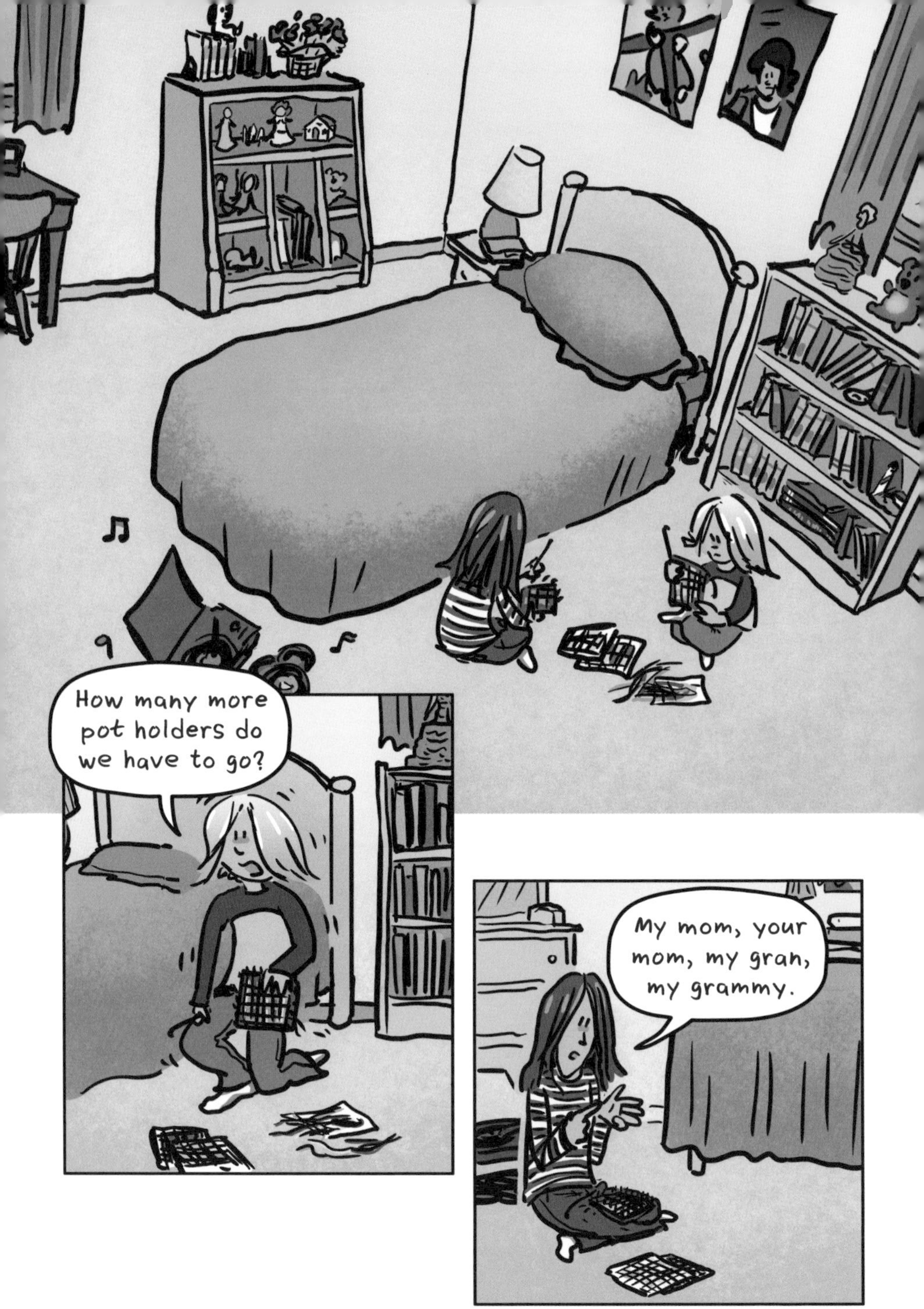
How many more pot holders do we have to go?
My mom, your mom, my gran, my grammy.

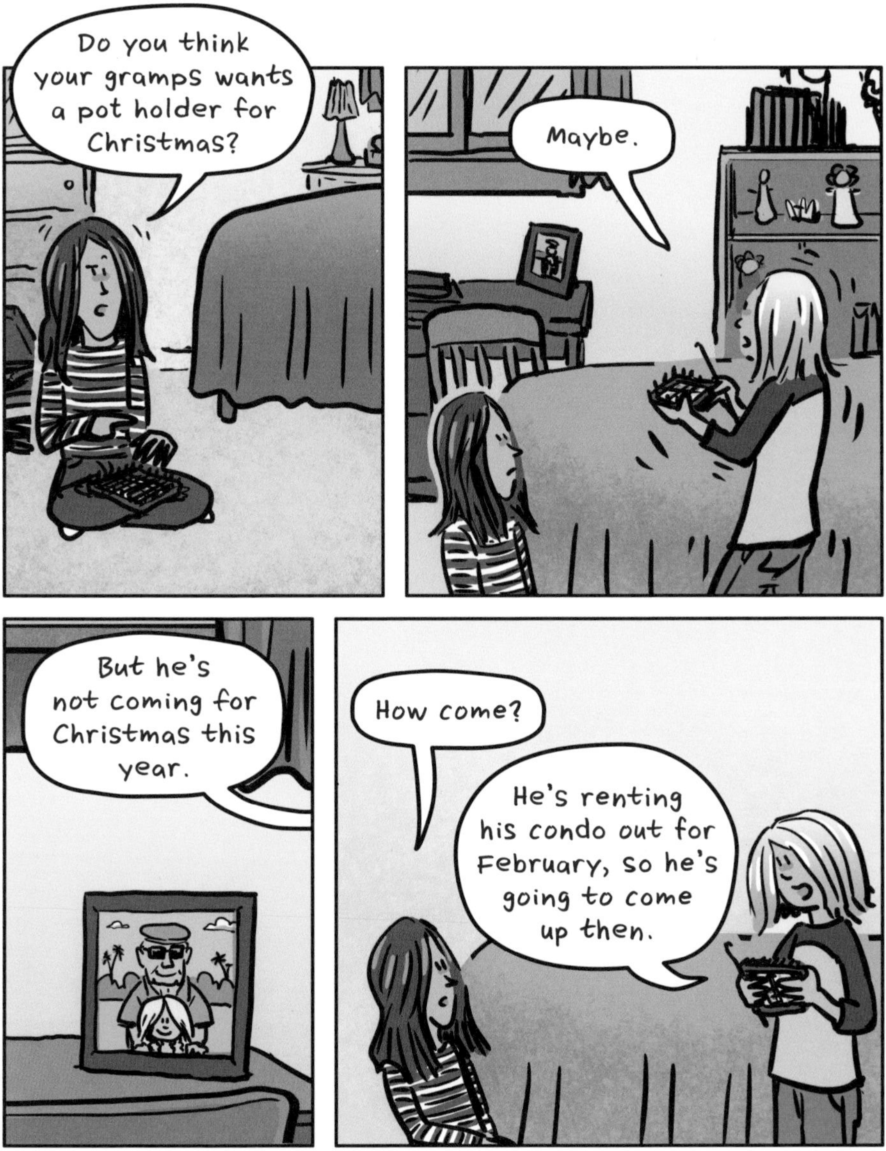
Do you think your gramps wants a pot holder for Christmas?
Maybe.
But he's not coming for Christmas this year.
How come?
He's renting his condo out for February, so he's going to come up then.

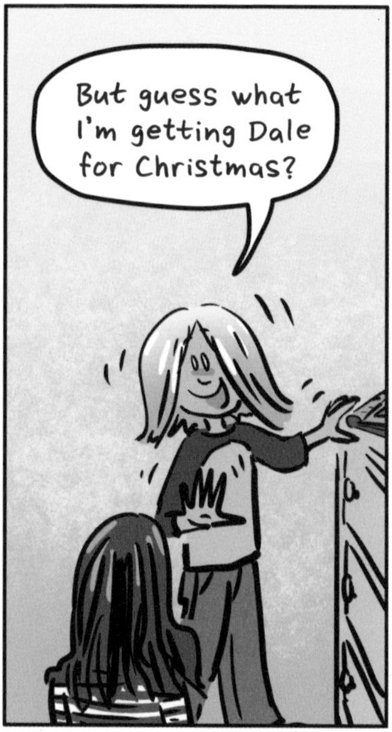
But guess what I'm getting Dale for Christmas?

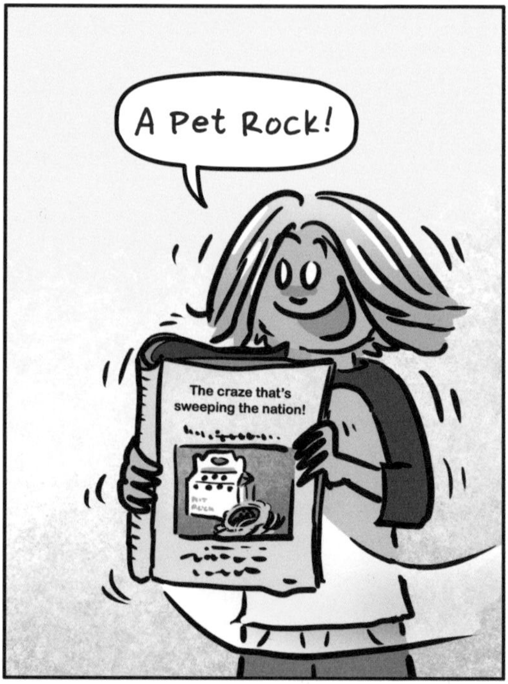
A Pet Rock!
The craze that's sweeping the nation!

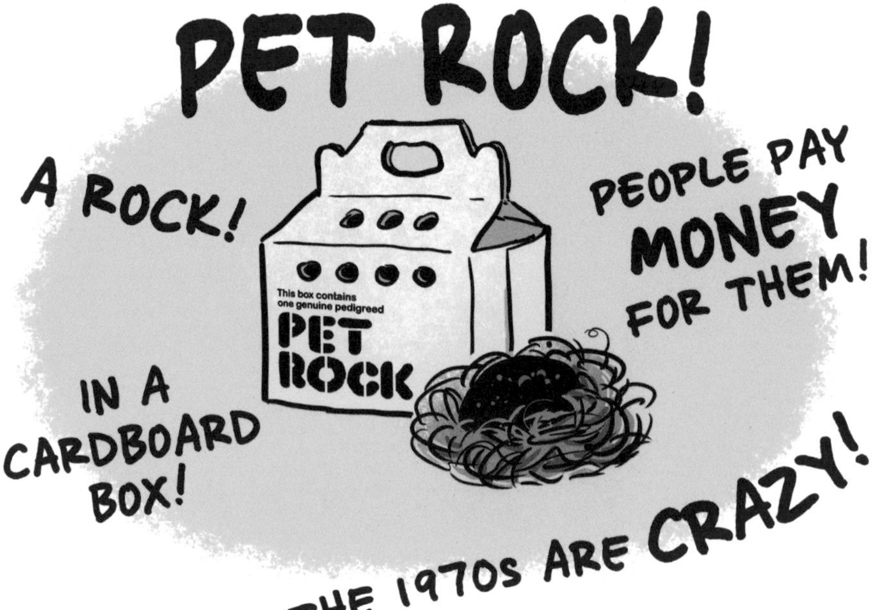
PET ROCK!
A ROCK!
IN A CARDBOARD BOX!
This box contains one genuine pedigreed
PET ROCK
PEOPLE PAY MONEY FOR THEM!
THE 1970S ARE CRAZY!

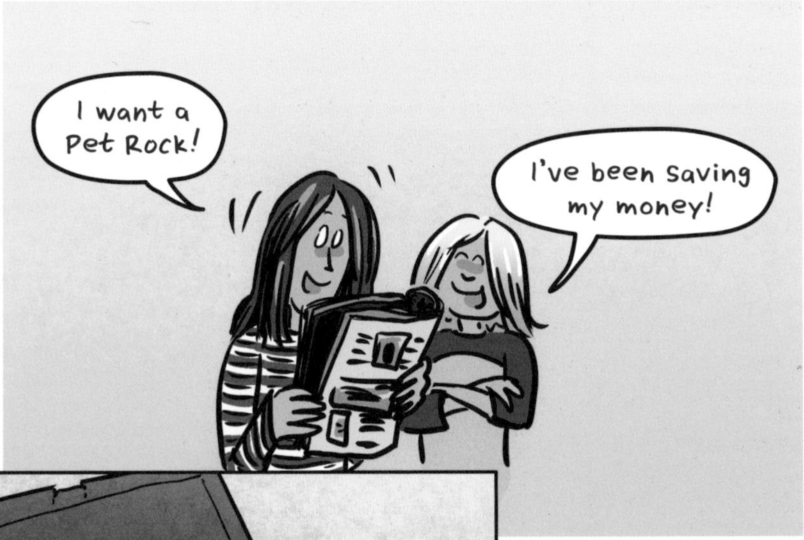
I want a Pet Rock!
I've been saving my money!

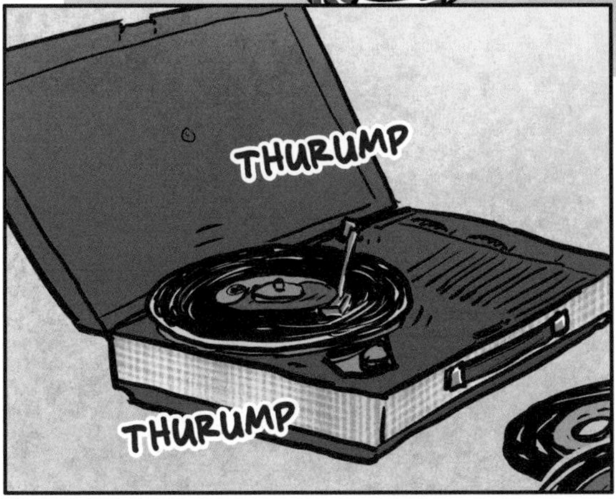
THURUMP
THURUMP

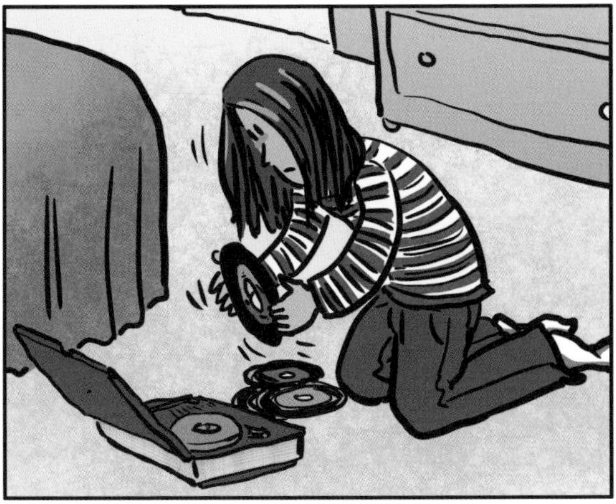

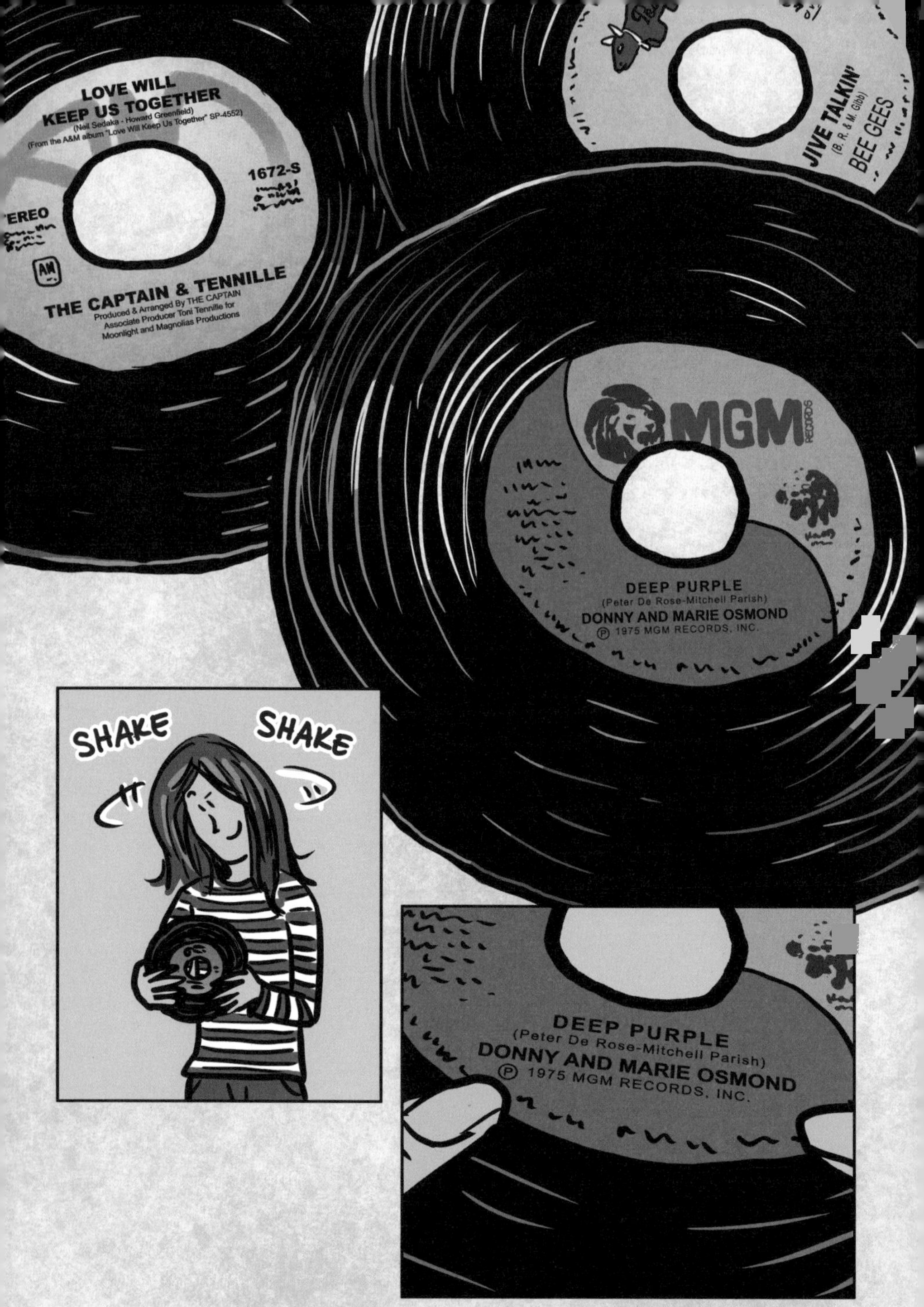
LOVE WILL
KEEP US TOGETHER
(Neil Sedaka - Howard Greenfield)
(From the A&M album "Love Will Keep Us Together" SP-4552)
1672-S
'EREO
THE CAPTAIN & TENNILLE
Produced & Arranged By THE CAPTAIN
Associate Producer Toni Tennille for
Moonlight and Magnolias Productions
JIVE TALKIN'
(B. R. & M. Gibb)
BEE GEES
MGM
RECORDS
DEEP PURPLE
(Peter De Rose-Mitchell Parish)
DONNY AND MARIE OSMOND
℗ 1975 MGM RECORDS, INC.
SHAKE
SHAKE
DEEP PURPLE
(Peter De Rose-Mitchell Parish)
DONNY AND MARIE OSMOND
℗ 1975 MGM RECORDS, INC.

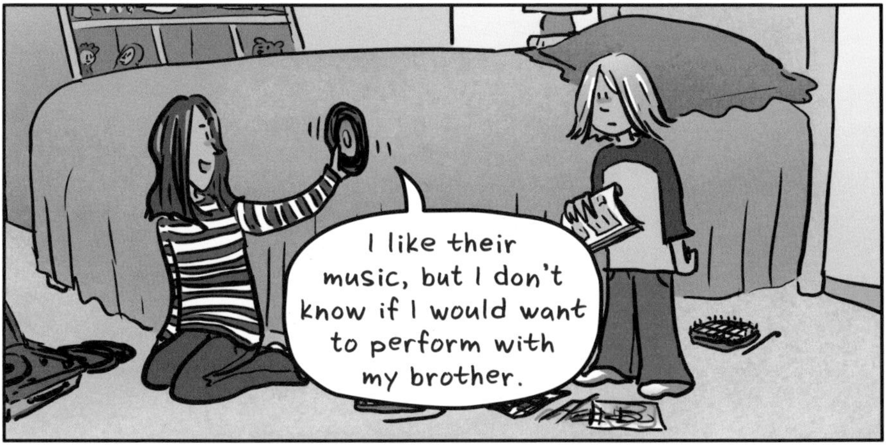
I like their music, but I don't know if I would want to perform with my brother.

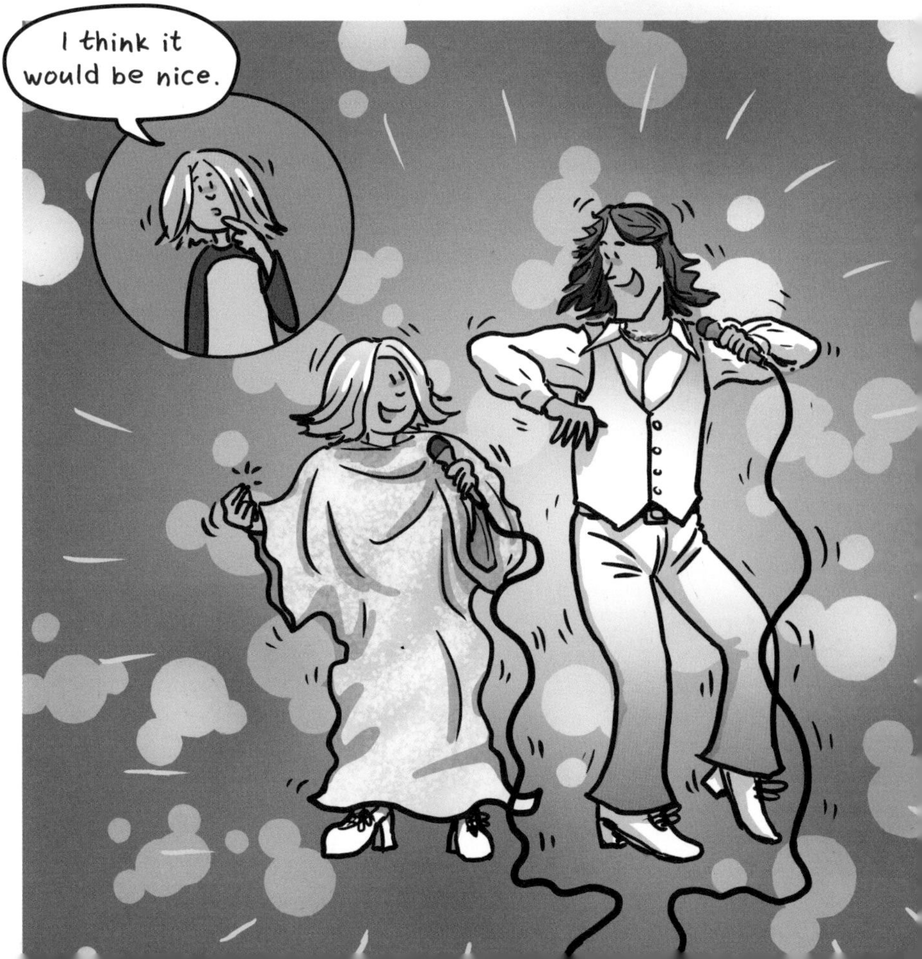
I think it would be nice.

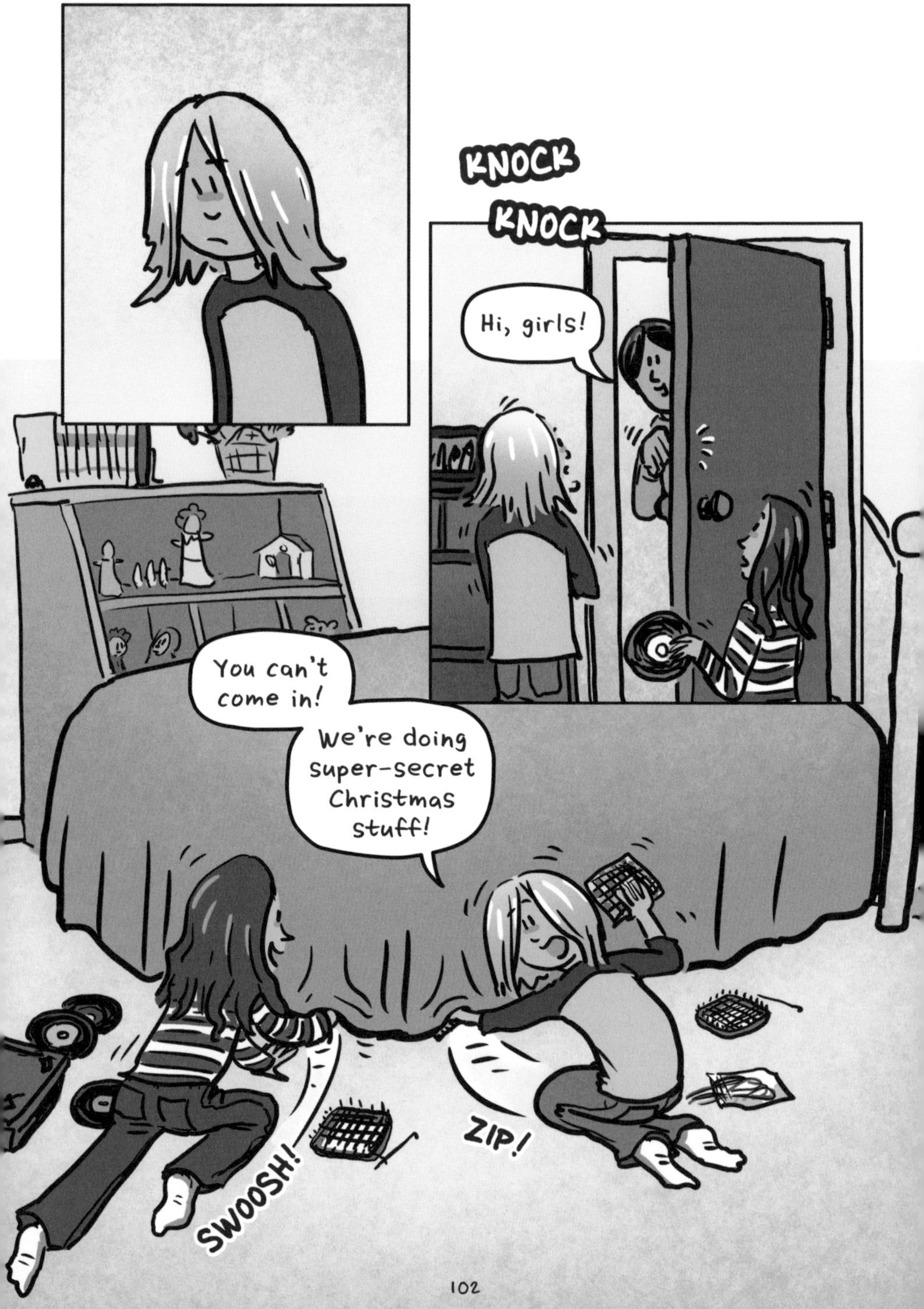
KNOCK
KNOCK
Hi, girls!
You can't come in!
We're doing super-secret Christmas stuff!
SWOOSH!
ZIP!

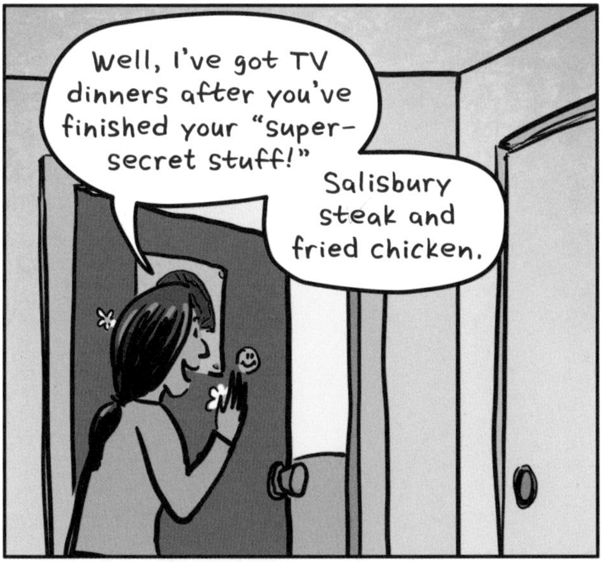
Well, I've got TV dinners after you've finished your "super-secret stuff!"
Salisbury steak and fried chicken.

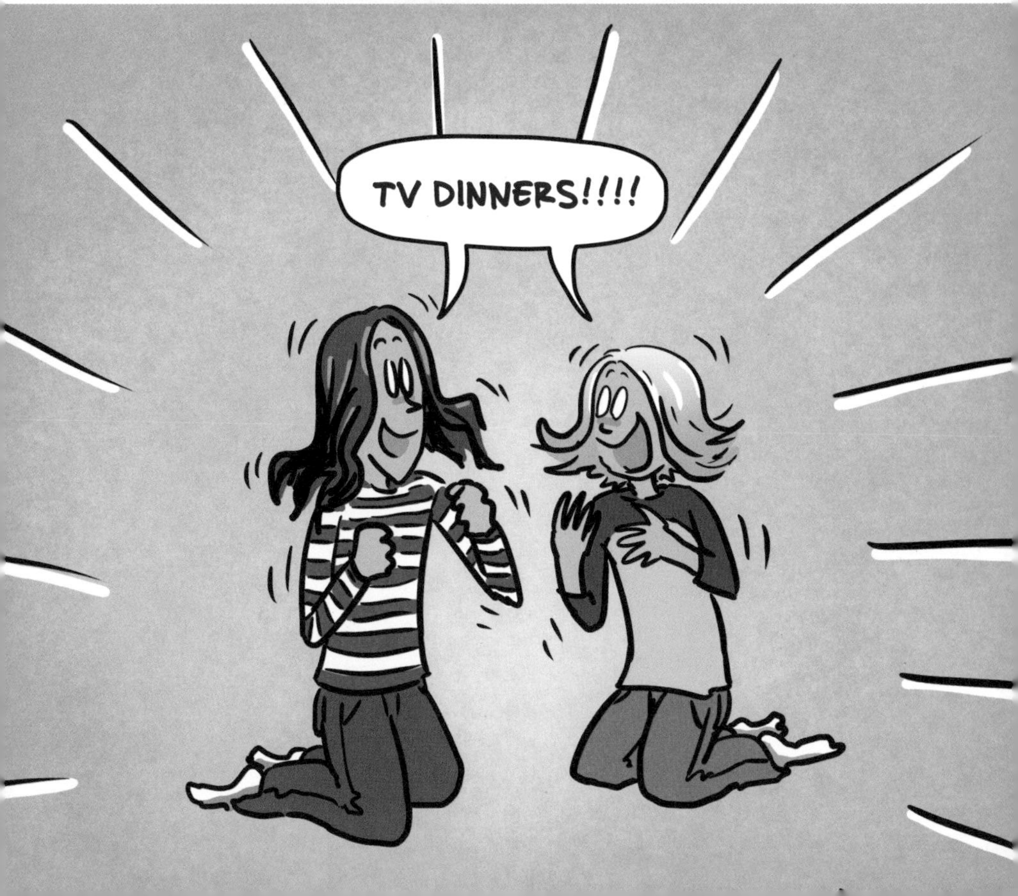
TV DINNERS!!!!

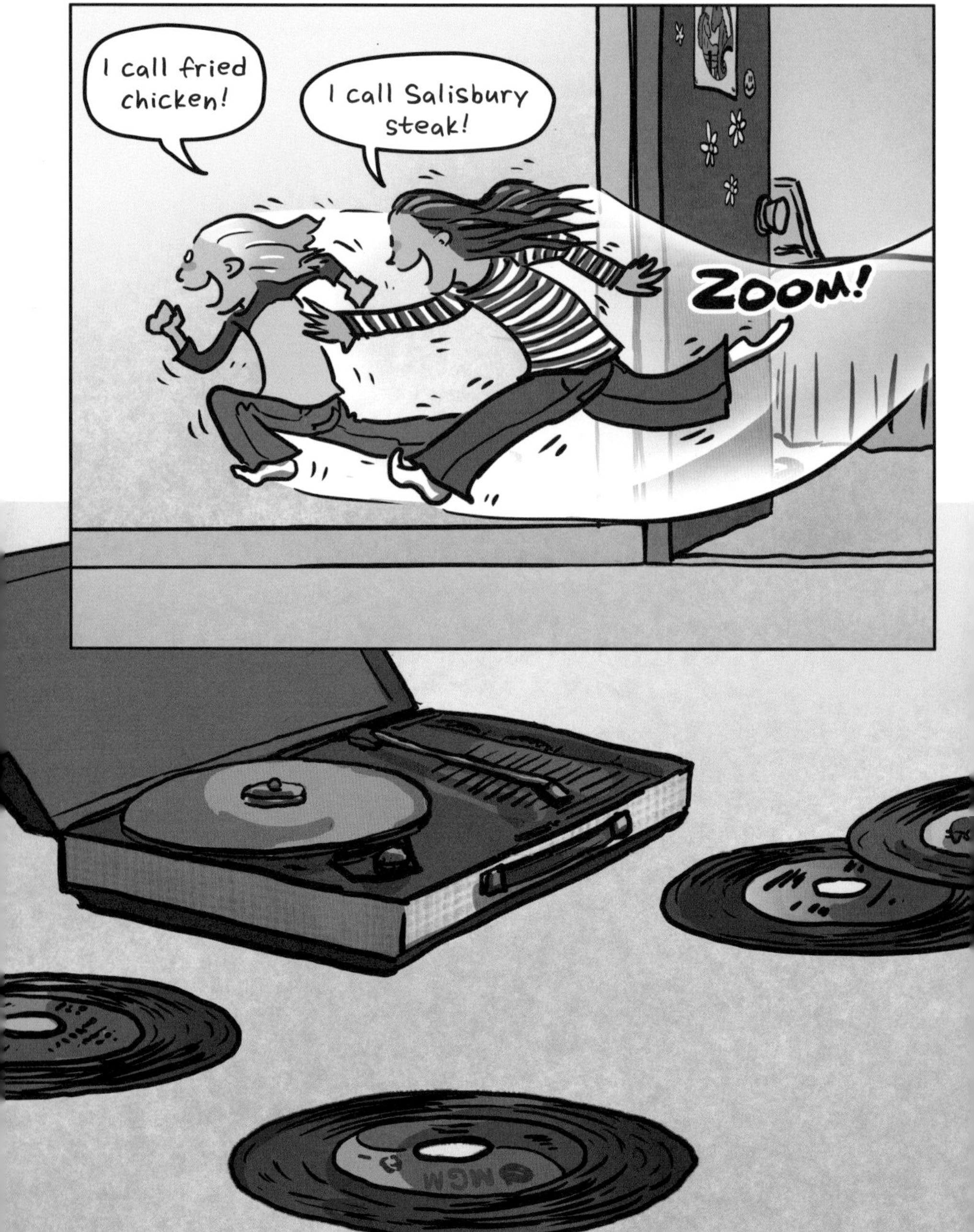
I call fried chicken!
I call Salisbury steak!
ZOOM!

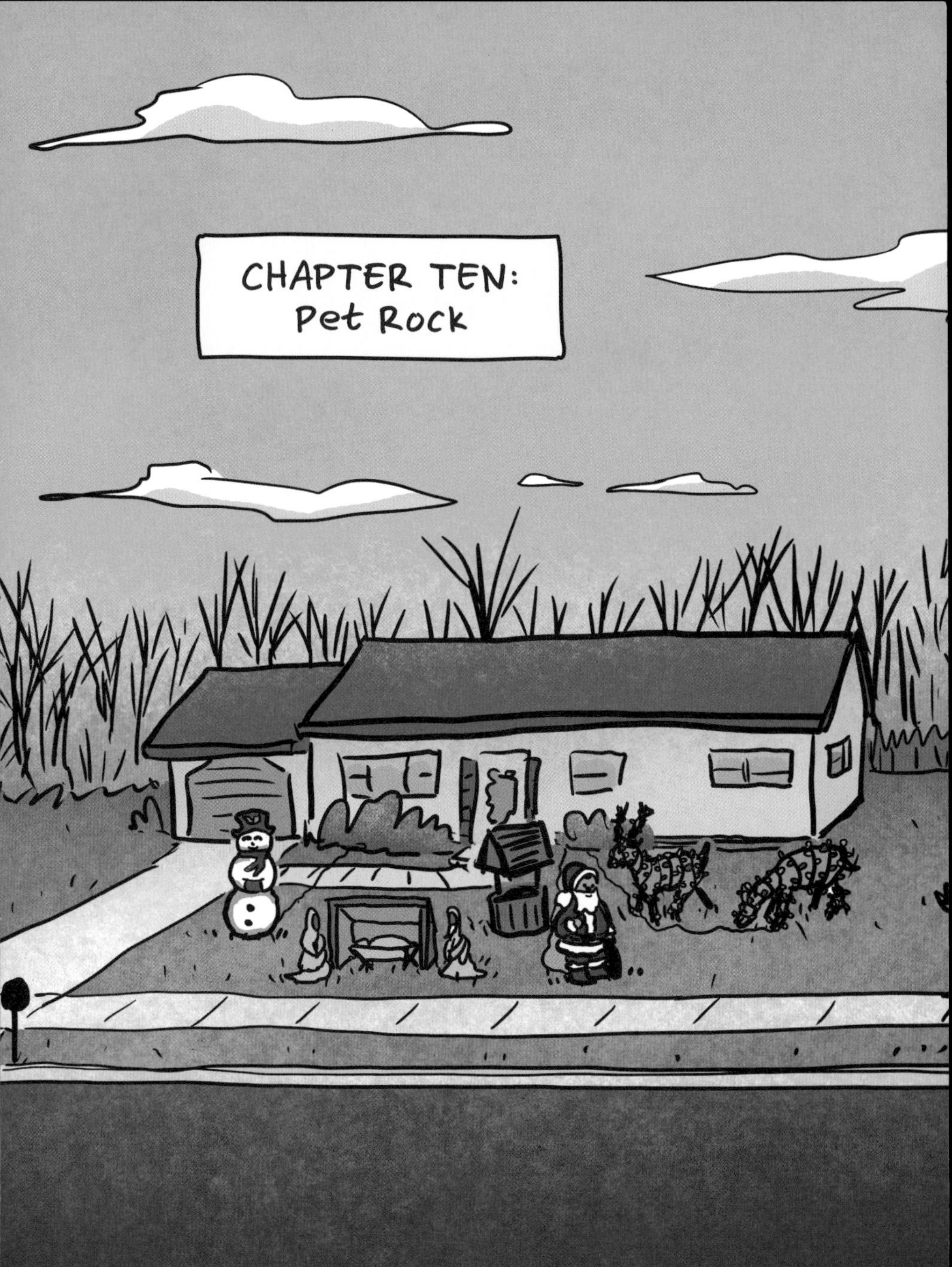
CHAPTER TEN:
Pet Rock

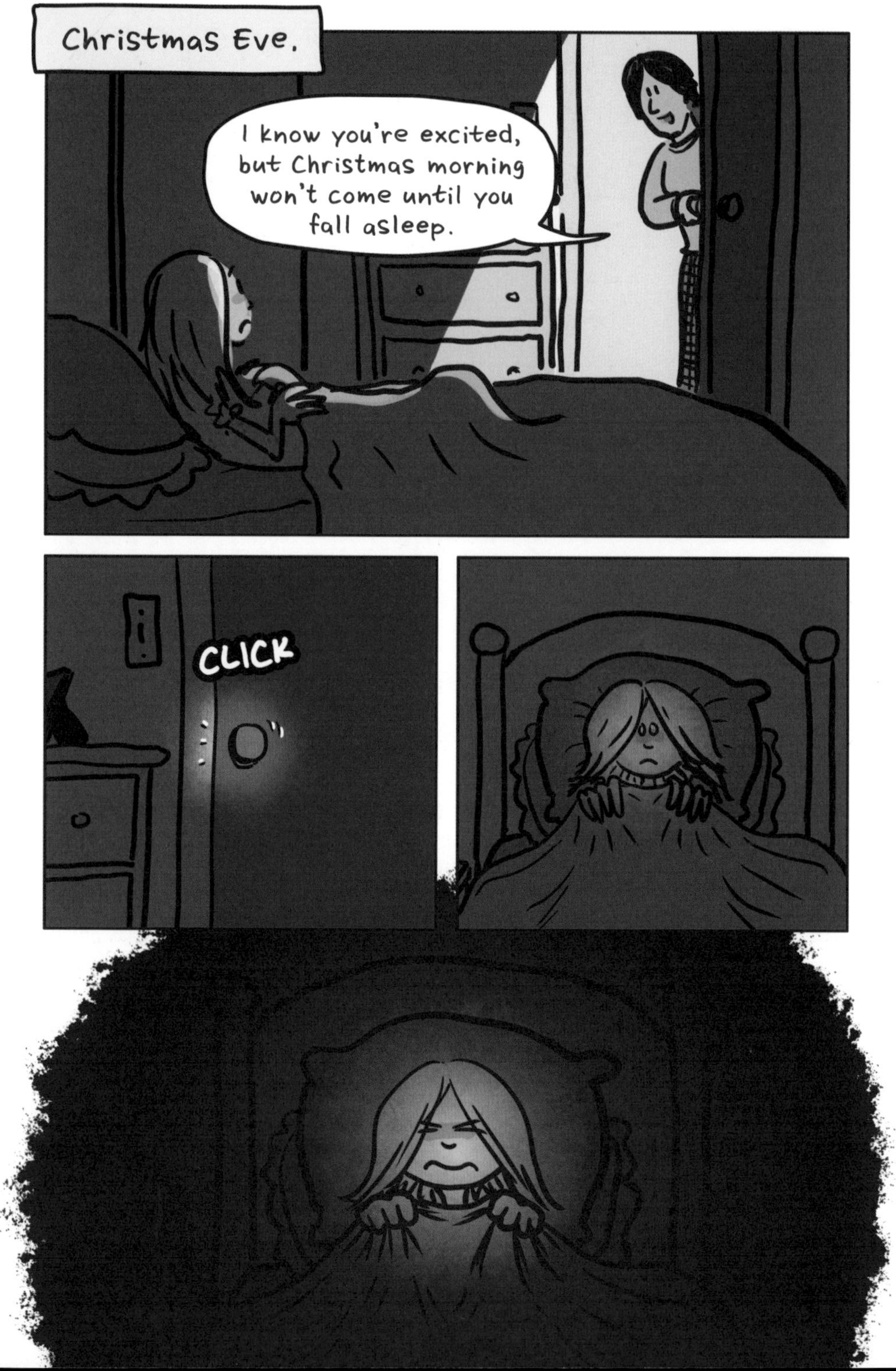
Christmas Eve.
I know you're excited, but Christmas morning won't come until you fall asleep.
CLICK

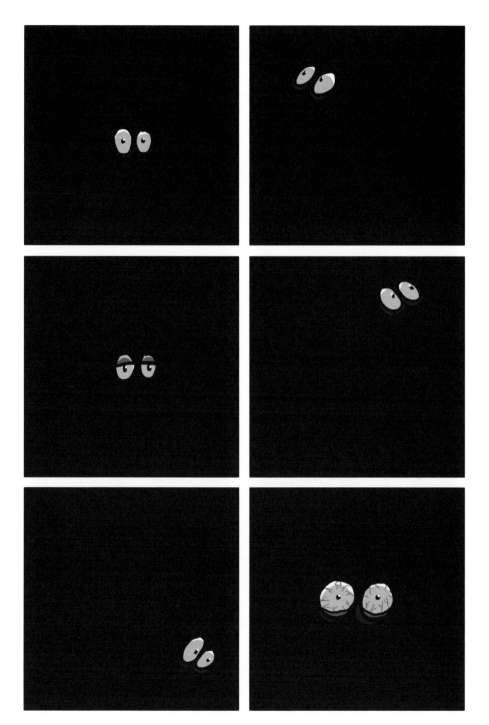

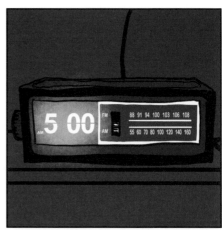

Christmas morning.

CLICK

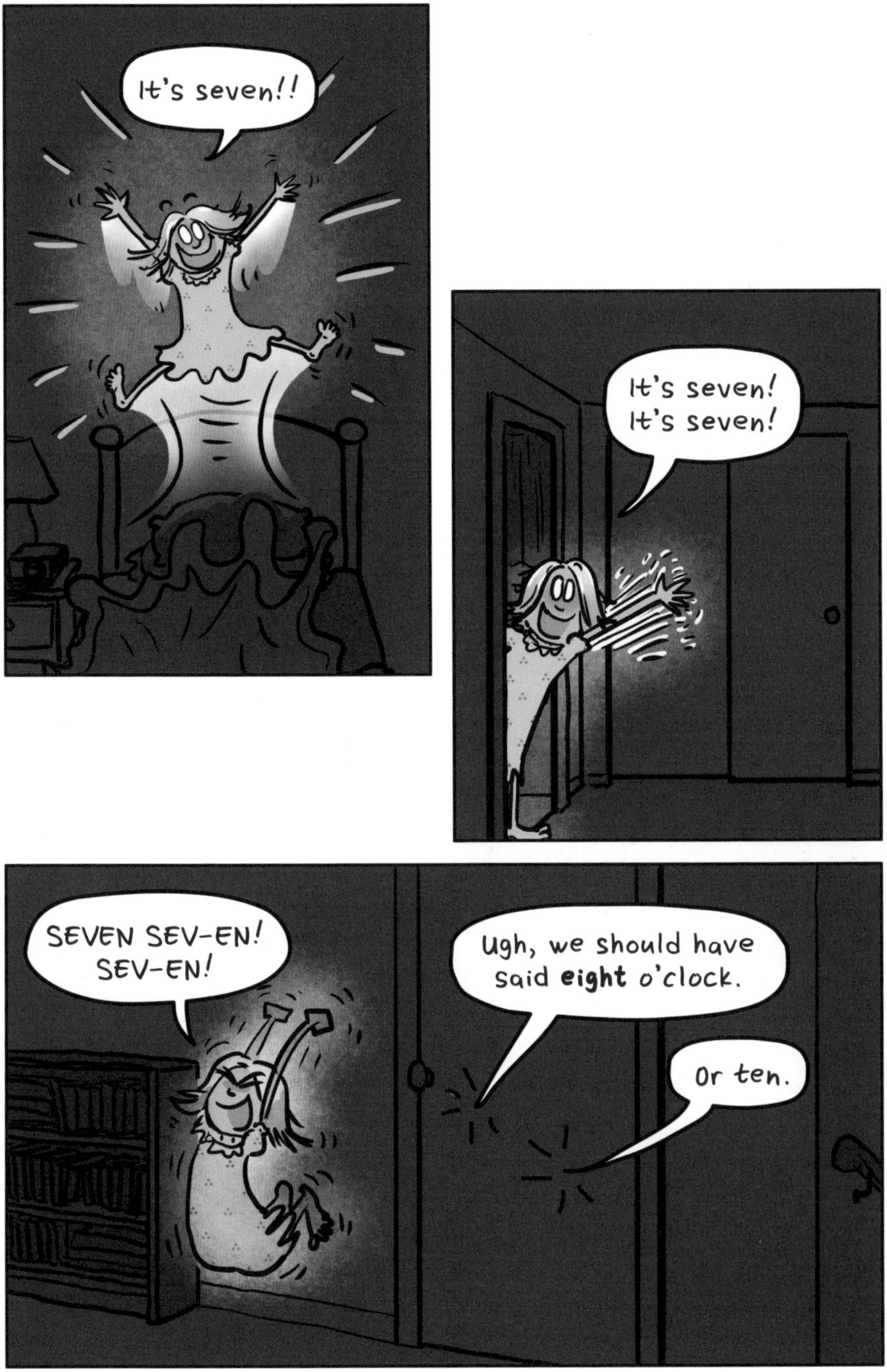
It's seven!!
It's seven!
It's seven!
SEVEN SEV-EN!
SEV-EN!
Ugh, we should have said **eight** o'clock.
Or ten.

A few minutes later.

Say "cheese."

CLICK!

SPFFT!

Wait. I have to see what it looks like.

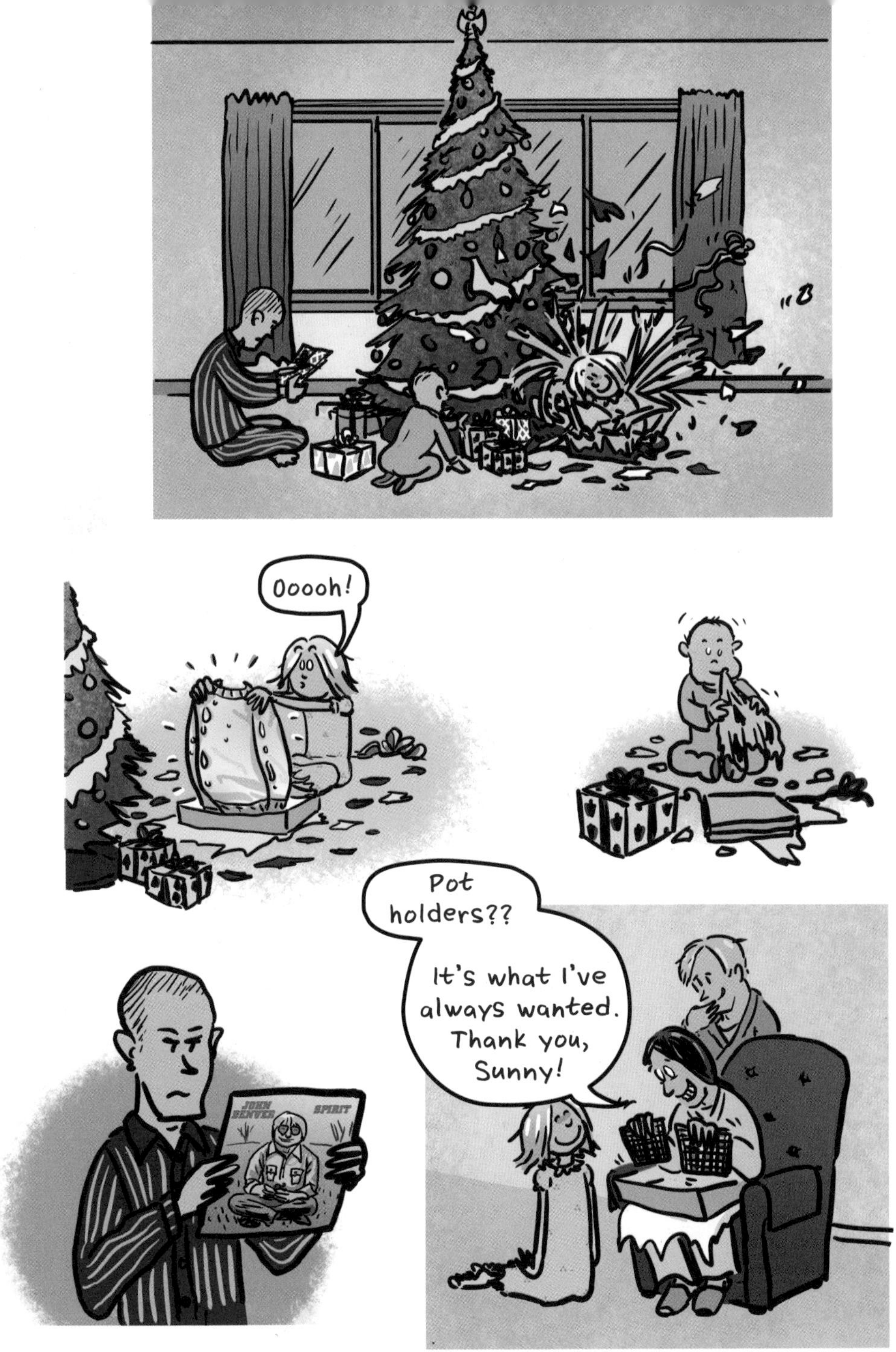
Ooooh!
Pot holders??
It's what I've always wanted. Thank you, Sunny!
JOHN DENVER
SPIRIT

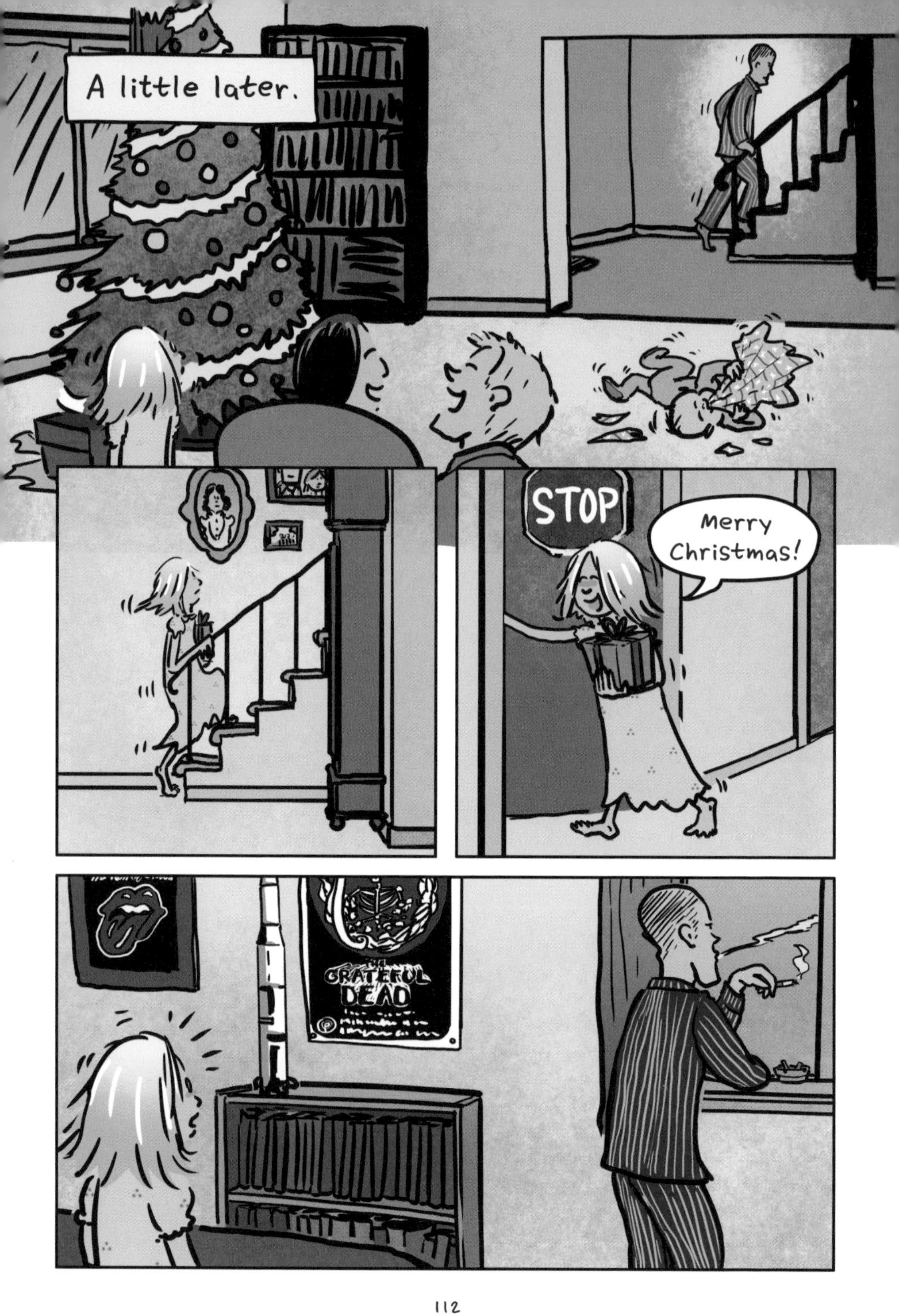
A little later.
STOP
Merry Christmas!
GRATEFUL DEAD

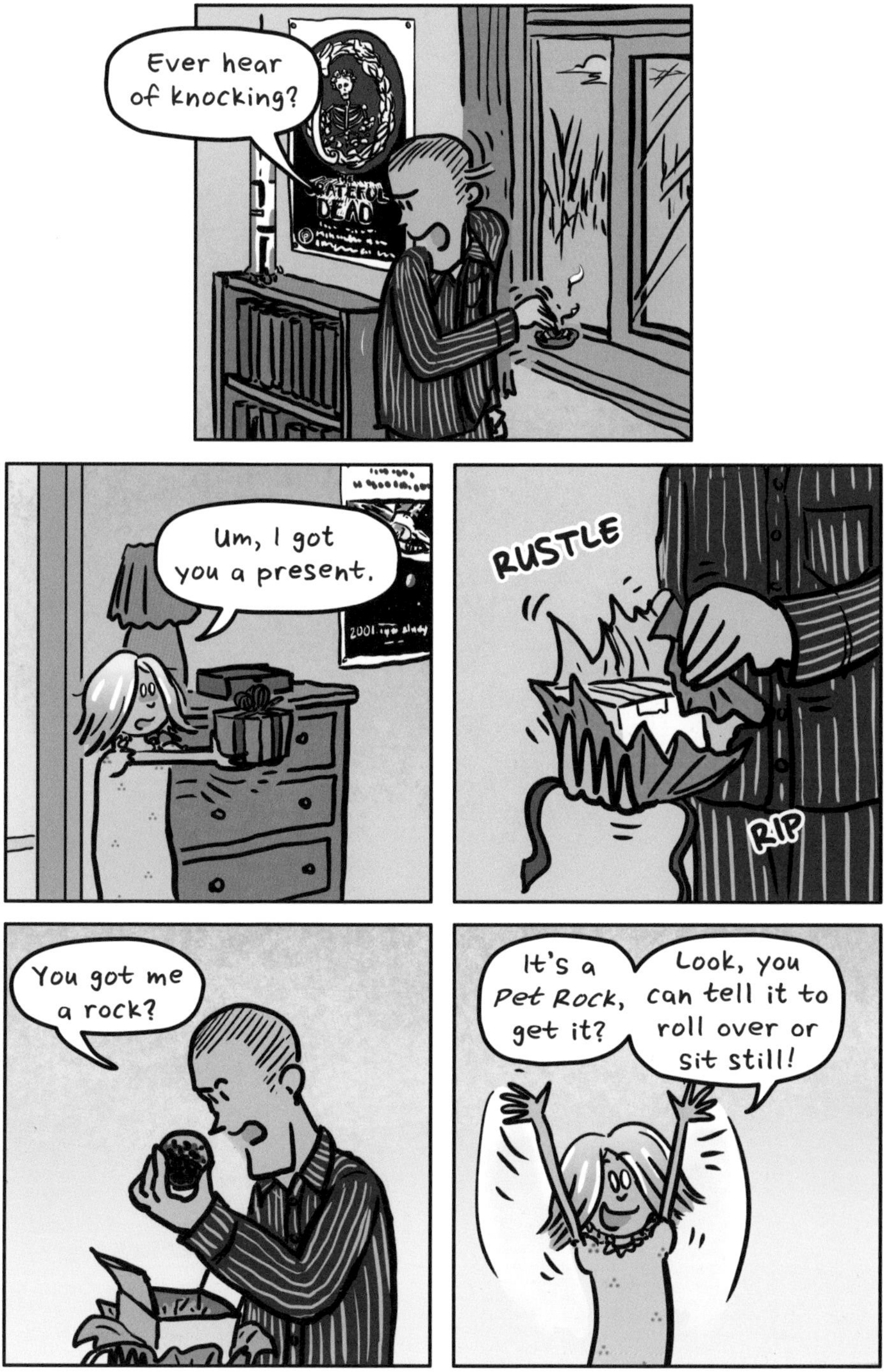

Ever hear of knocking?
Um, I got you a present.
RUSTLE
RIP
You got me a rock?
It's a *Pet Rock*, get it?
Look, you can tell it to roll over or sit still!

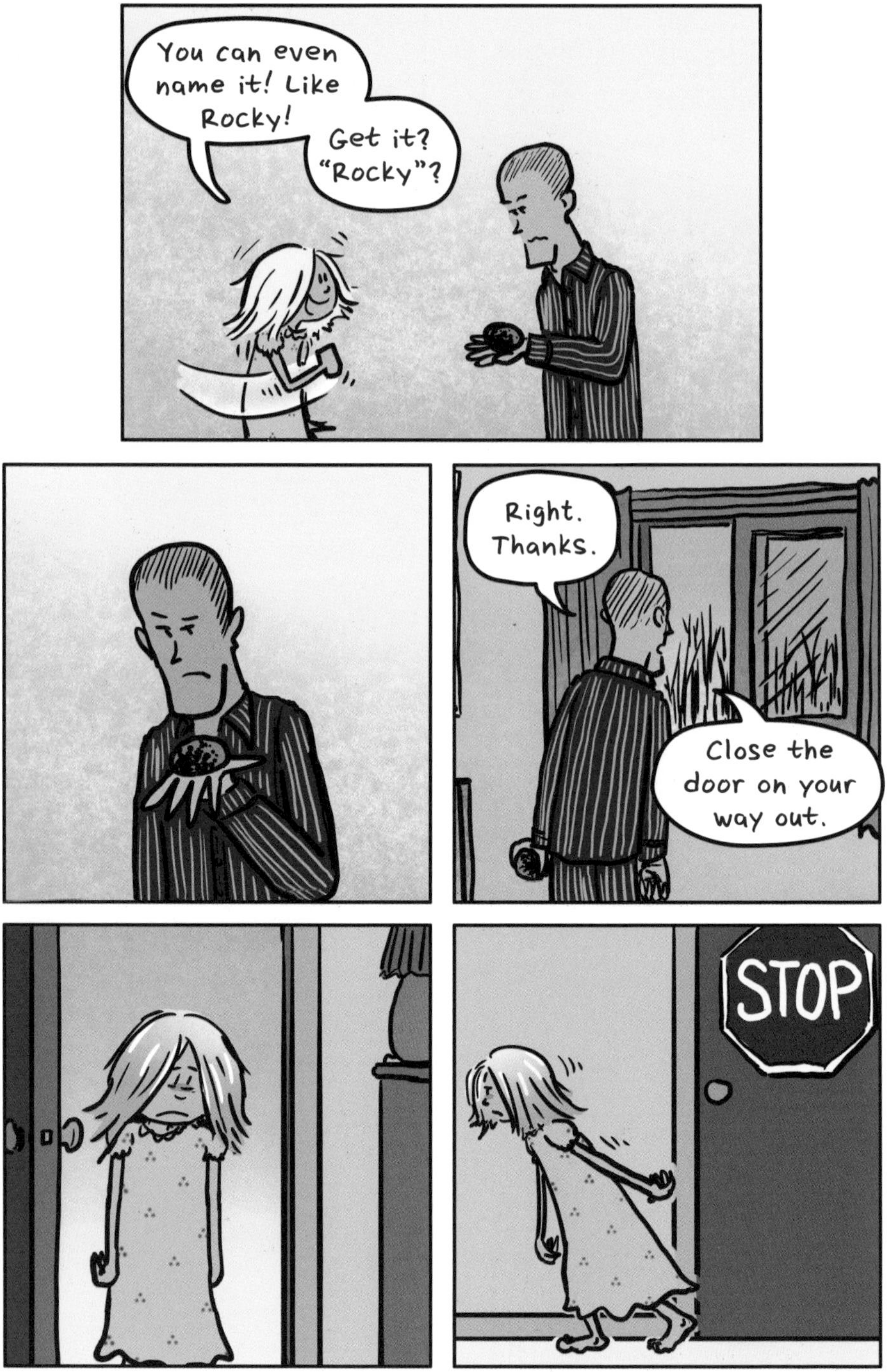
You can even name it! Like Rocky!
Get it? "Rocky"?
Right. Thanks.
Close the door on your way out.
STOP

CHAPTER ELEVEN: Ball Drop

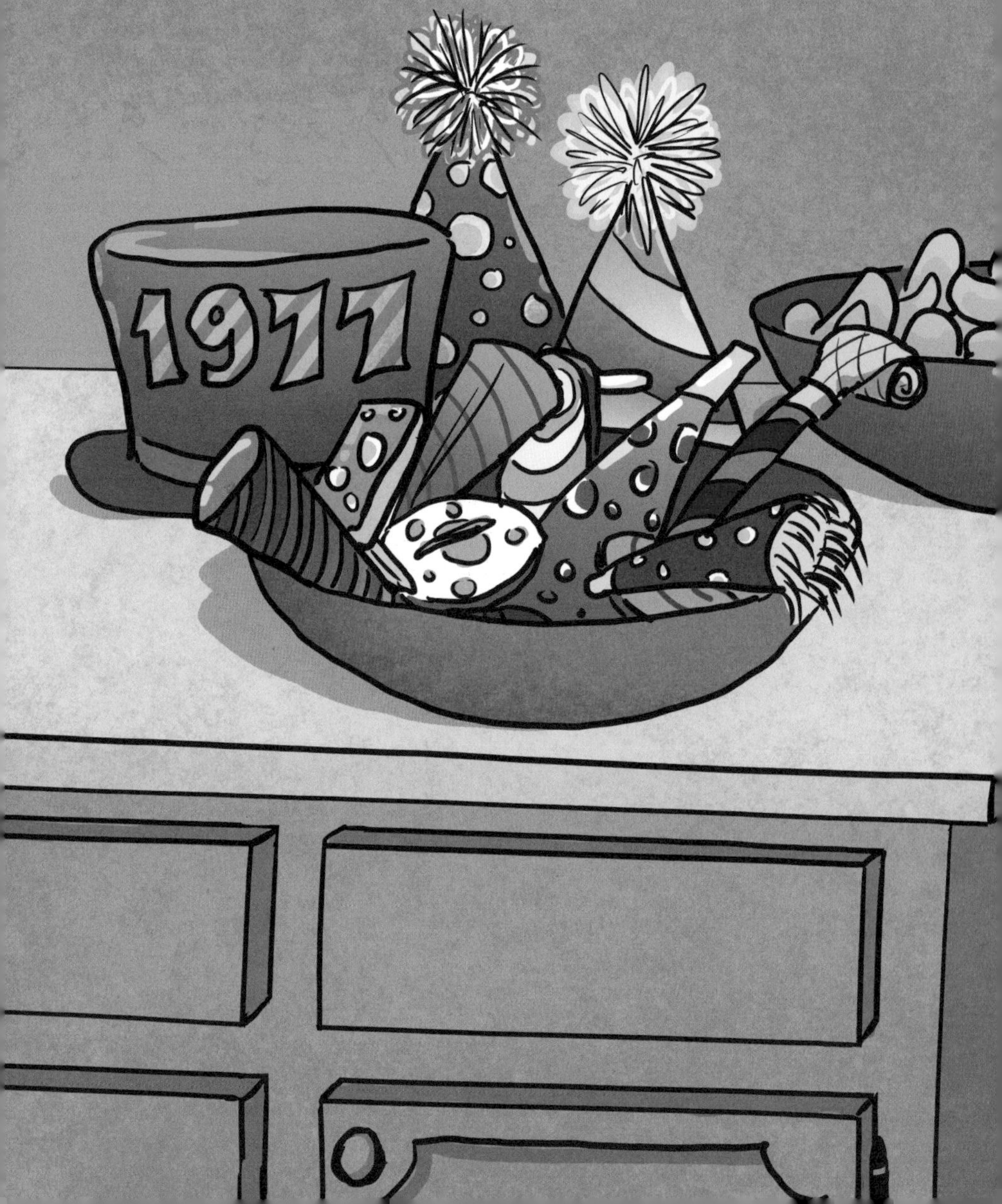
1977

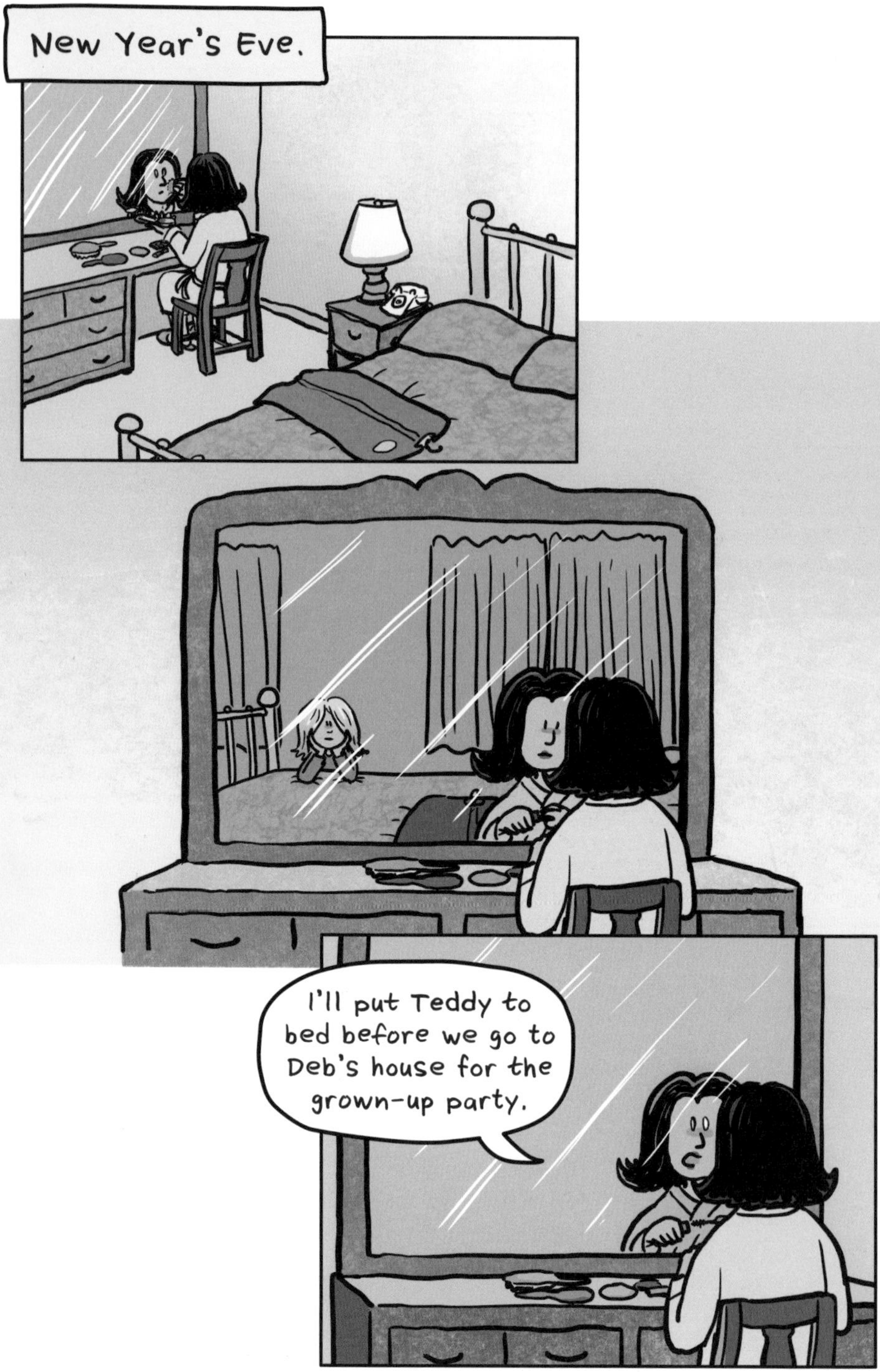
New Year's Eve.
I'll put Teddy to bed before we go to Deb's house for the grown-up party.

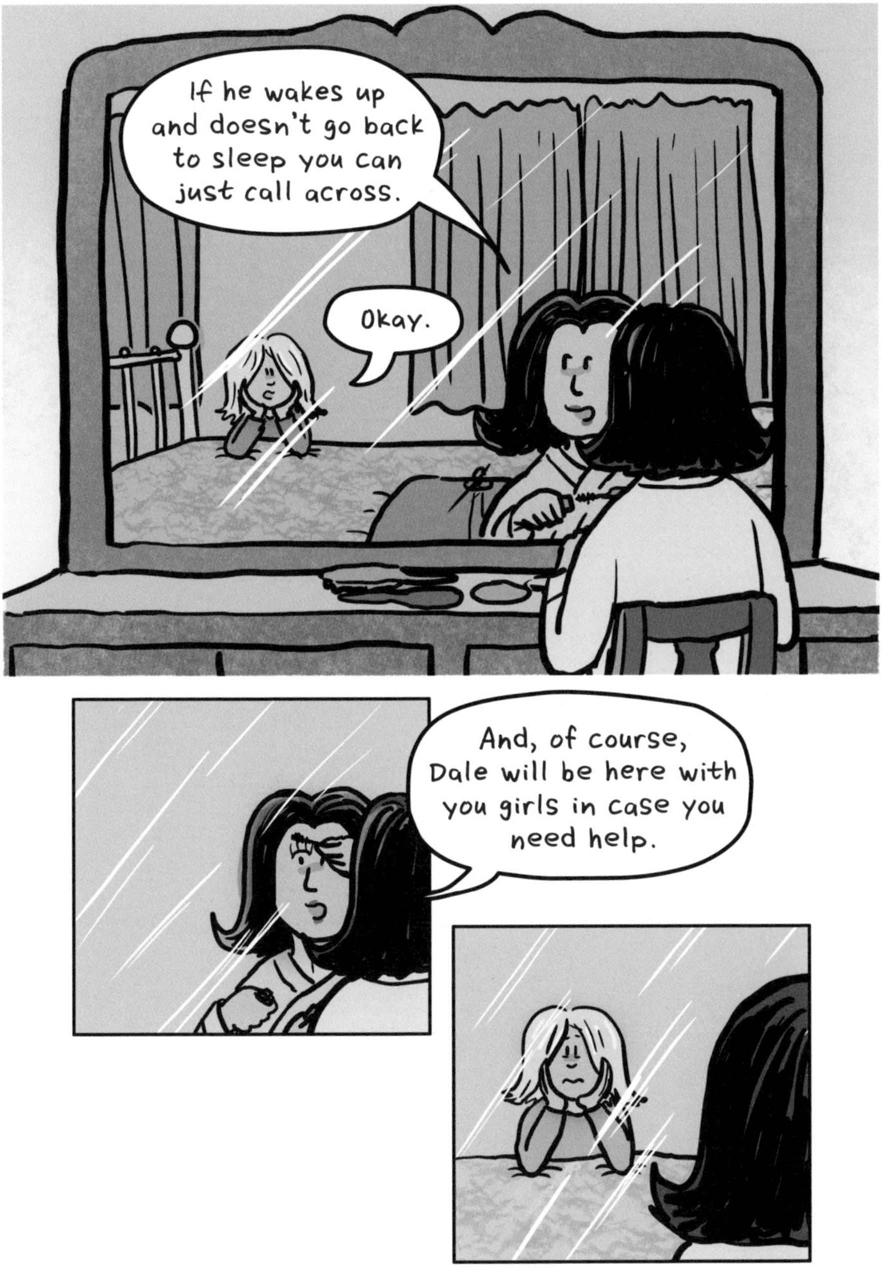
If he wakes up and doesn't go back to sleep you can just call across.
Okay.
And, of course, Dale will be here with you girls in case you need help.

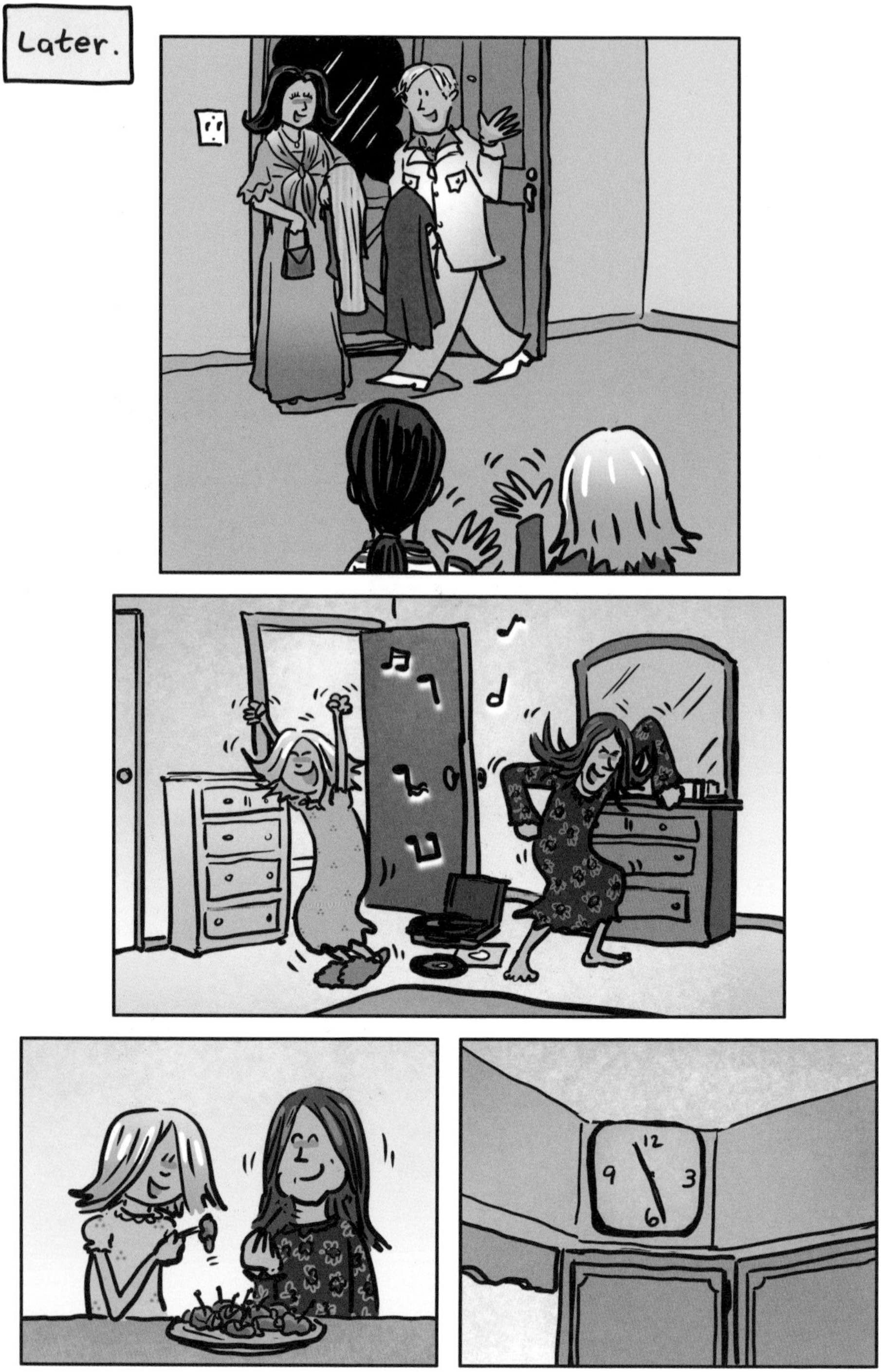
Later.

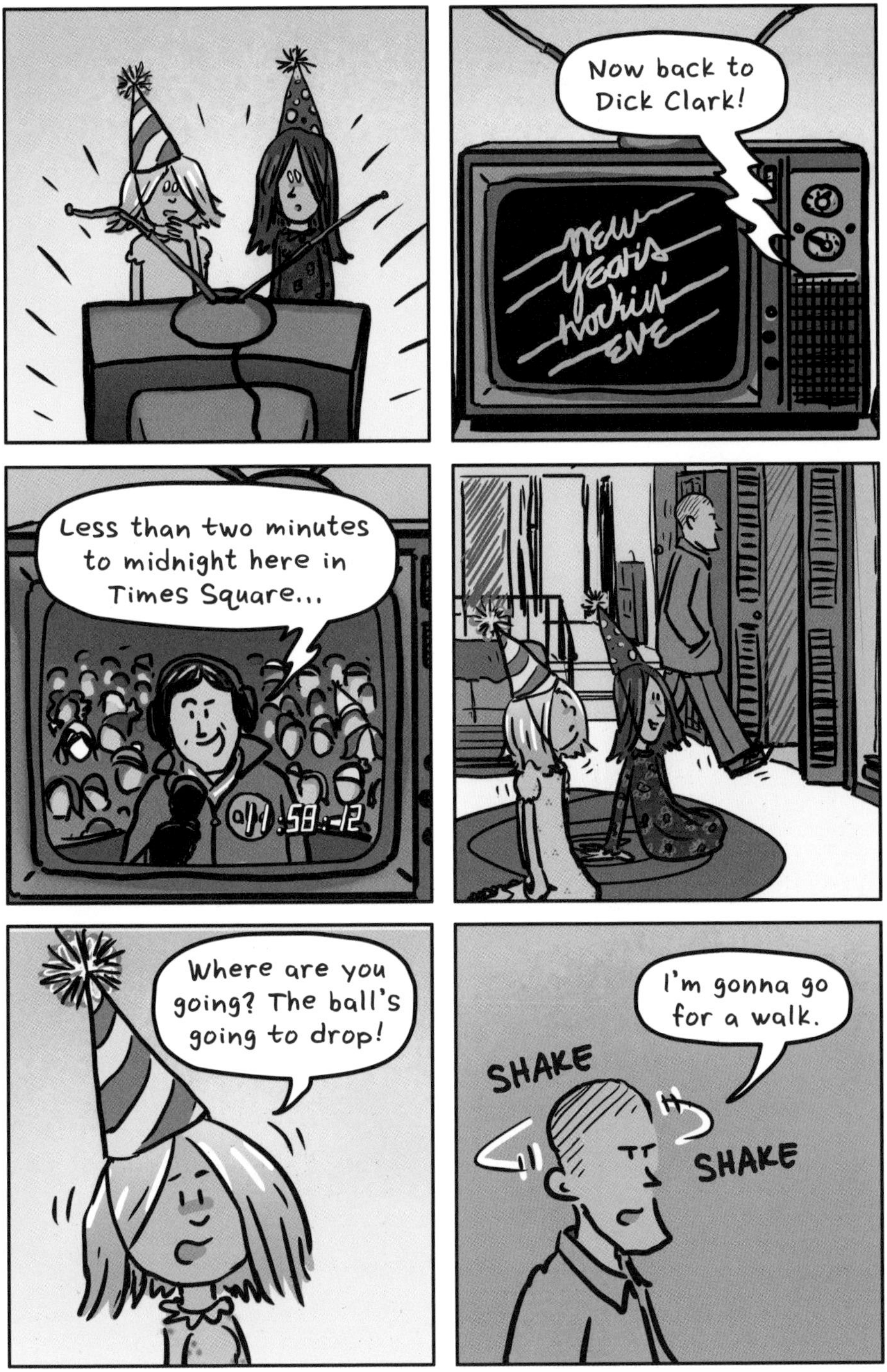
Now back to Dick Clark!
NEW YEAR'S ROCKIN' EVE
Less than two minutes to midnight here in Times Square...
11:58:12
Where are you going? The ball's going to drop!
I'm gonna go for a walk.
SHAKE
SHAKE

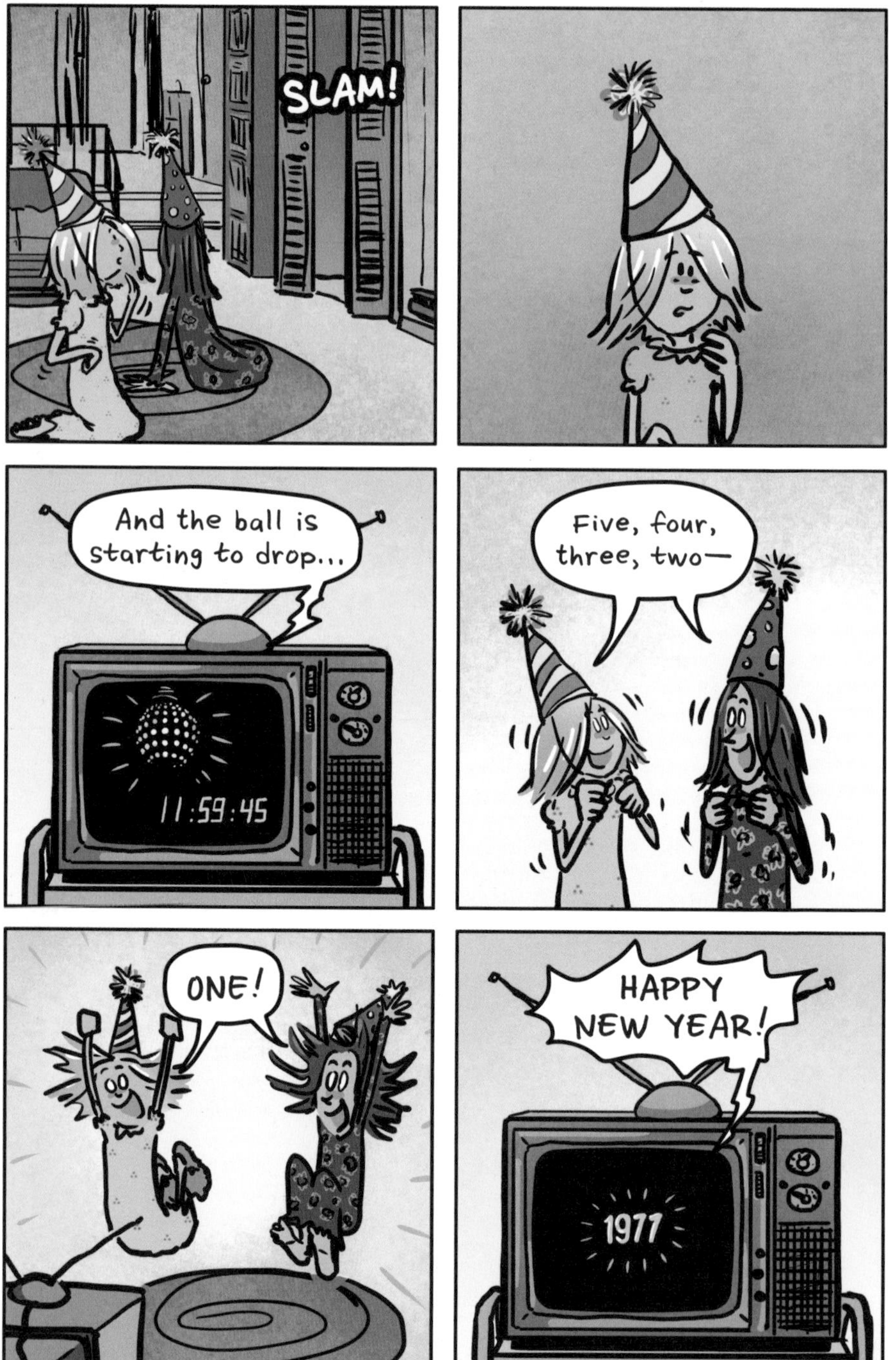
SLAM!
And the ball is starting to drop...
11:59:45
Five, four, three, two—
ONE!
HAPPY NEW YEAR!
1977

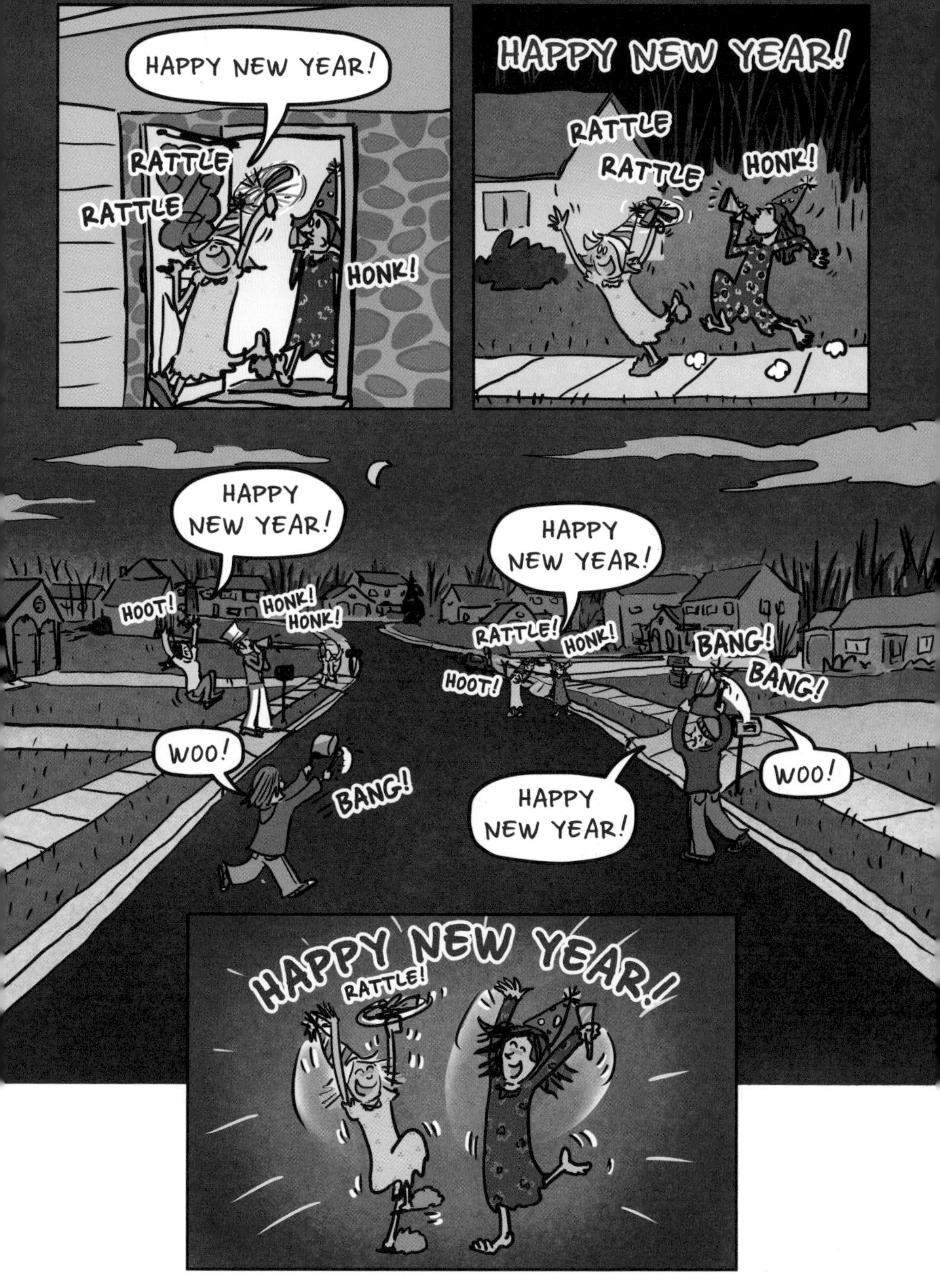
HAPPY NEW YEAR!
RATTLE
RATTLE
HONK!
HAPPY NEW YEAR!
RATTLE
RATTLE
HONK!
HAPPY NEW YEAR!
HOOT!
HONK!
HONK!
HAPPY NEW YEAR!
RATTLE!
HONK!
HOOT!
BANG!
BANG!
WOO!
BANG!
HAPPY NEW YEAR!
WOO!
HAPPY NEW YEAR!
RATTLE!

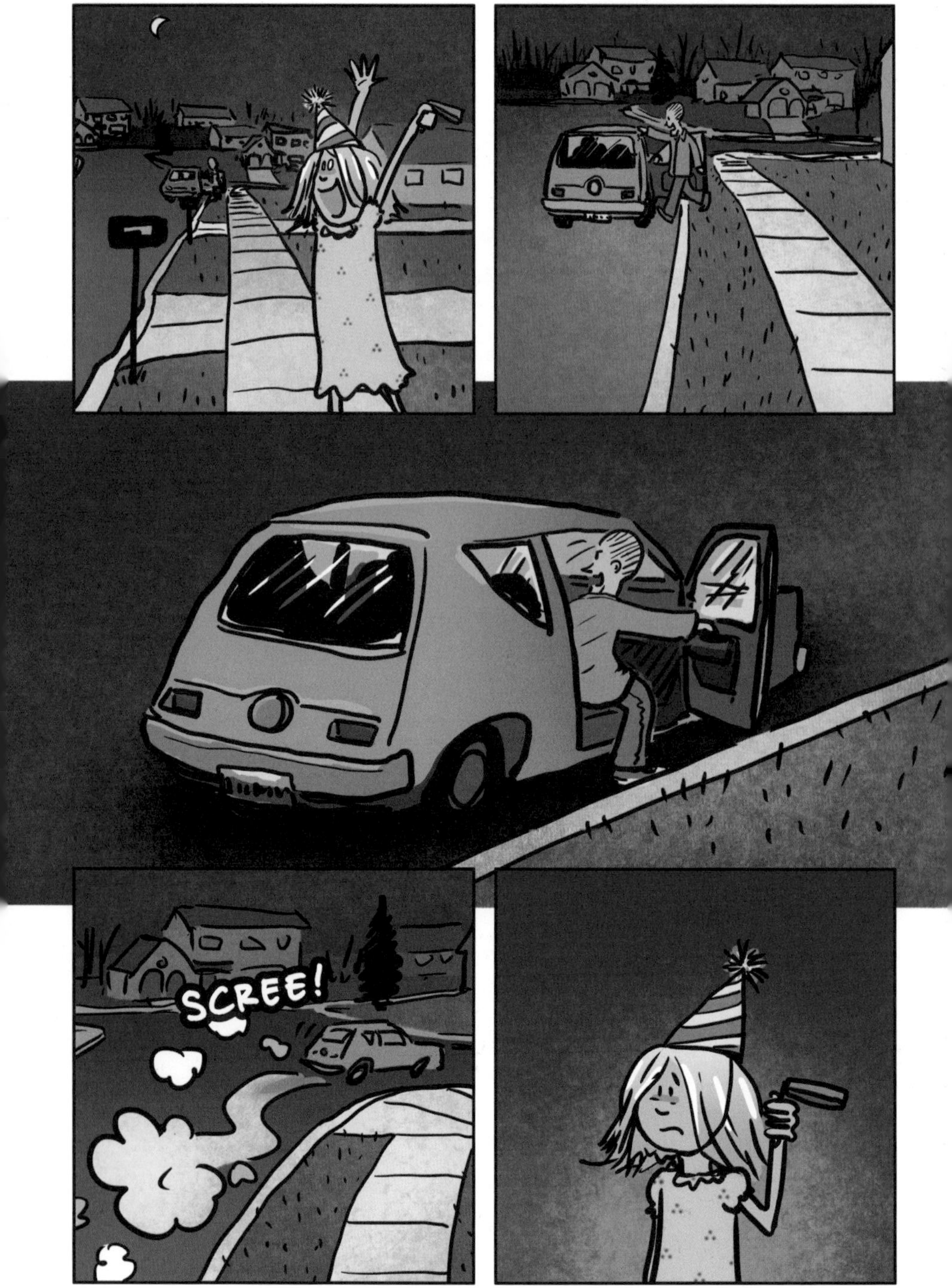
SCREE!

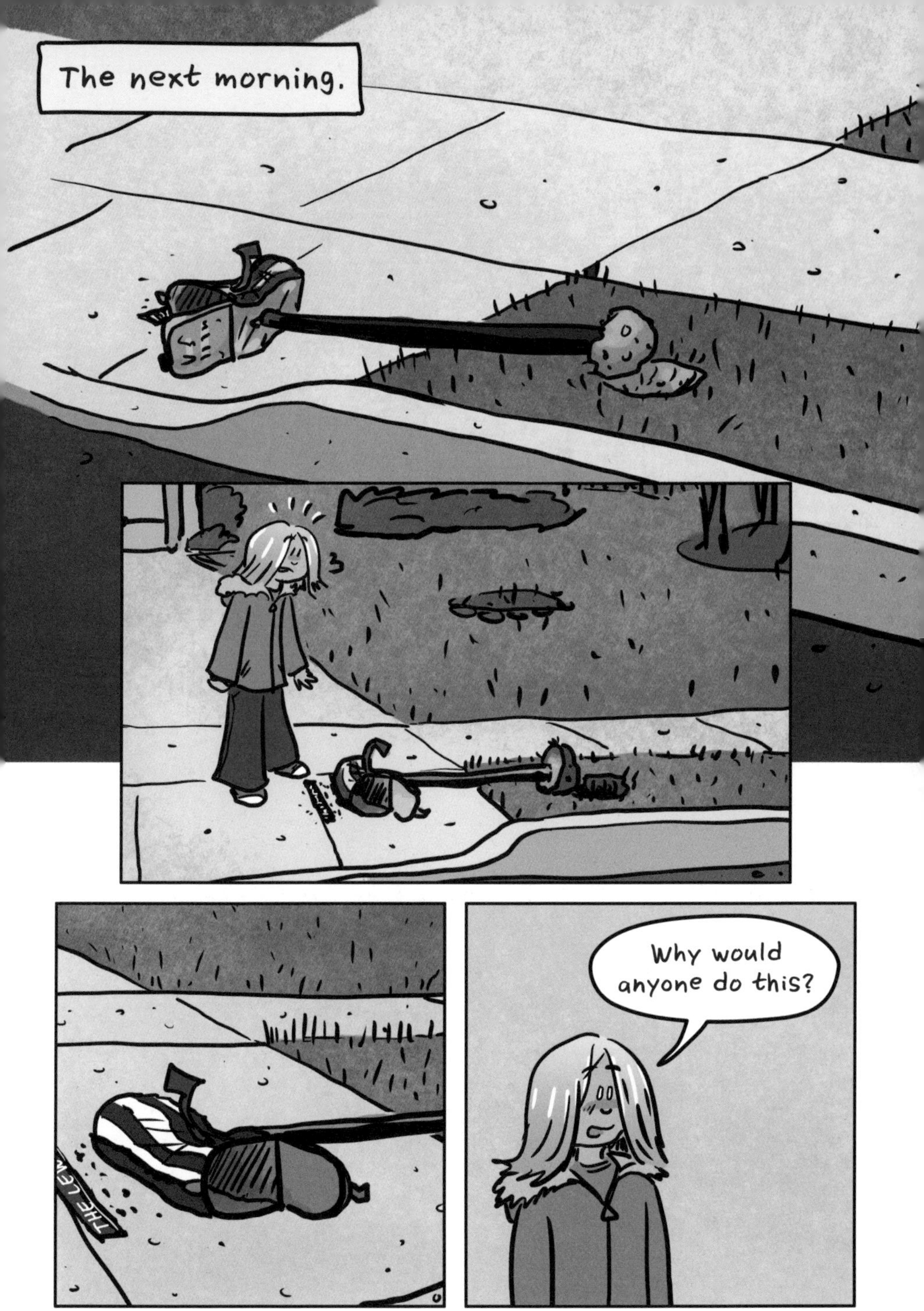
The next morning.
THE LEW
Why would anyone do this?

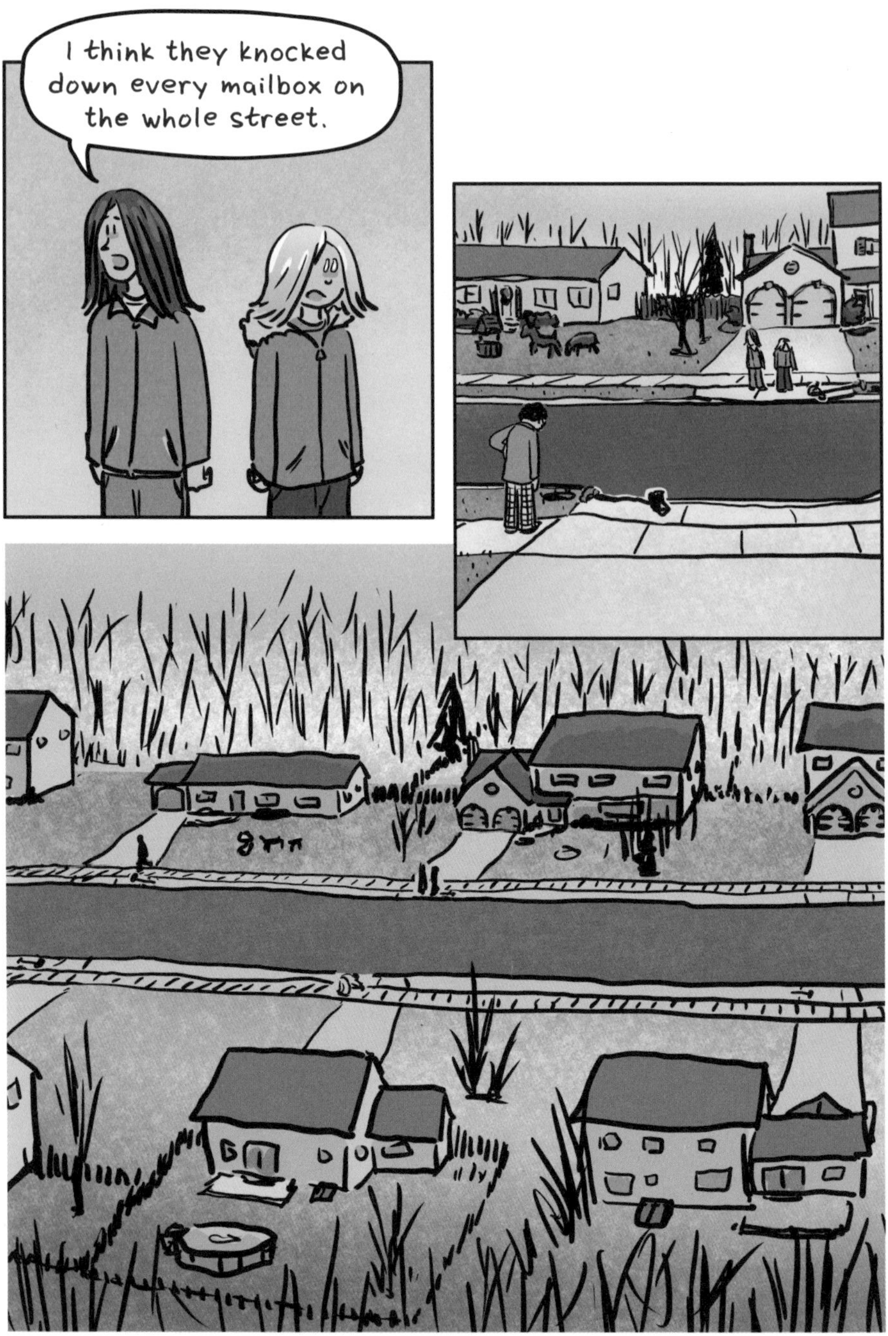
I think they knocked down every mailbox on the whole street.

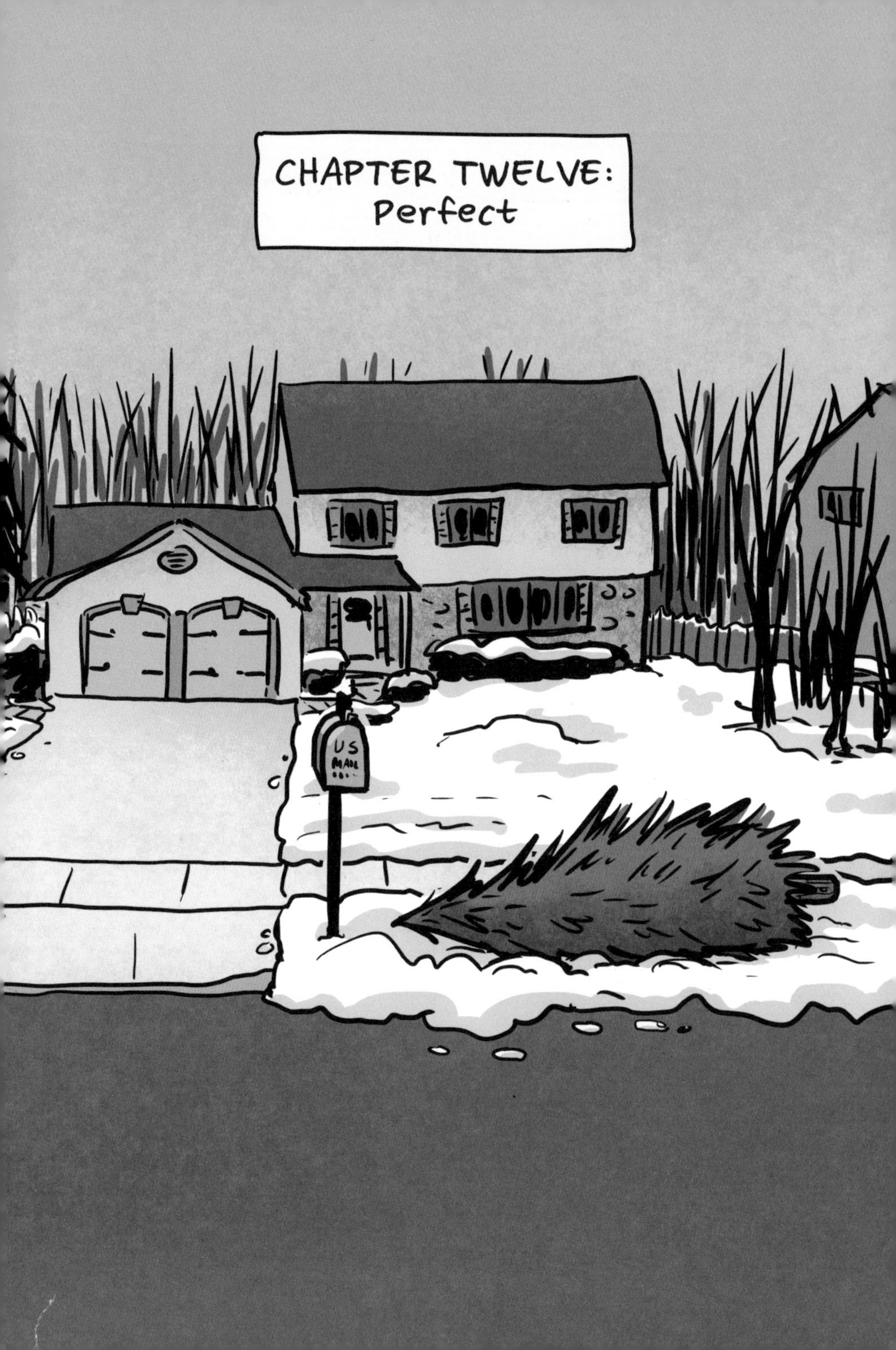
CHAPTER TWELVE:
Perfect
US

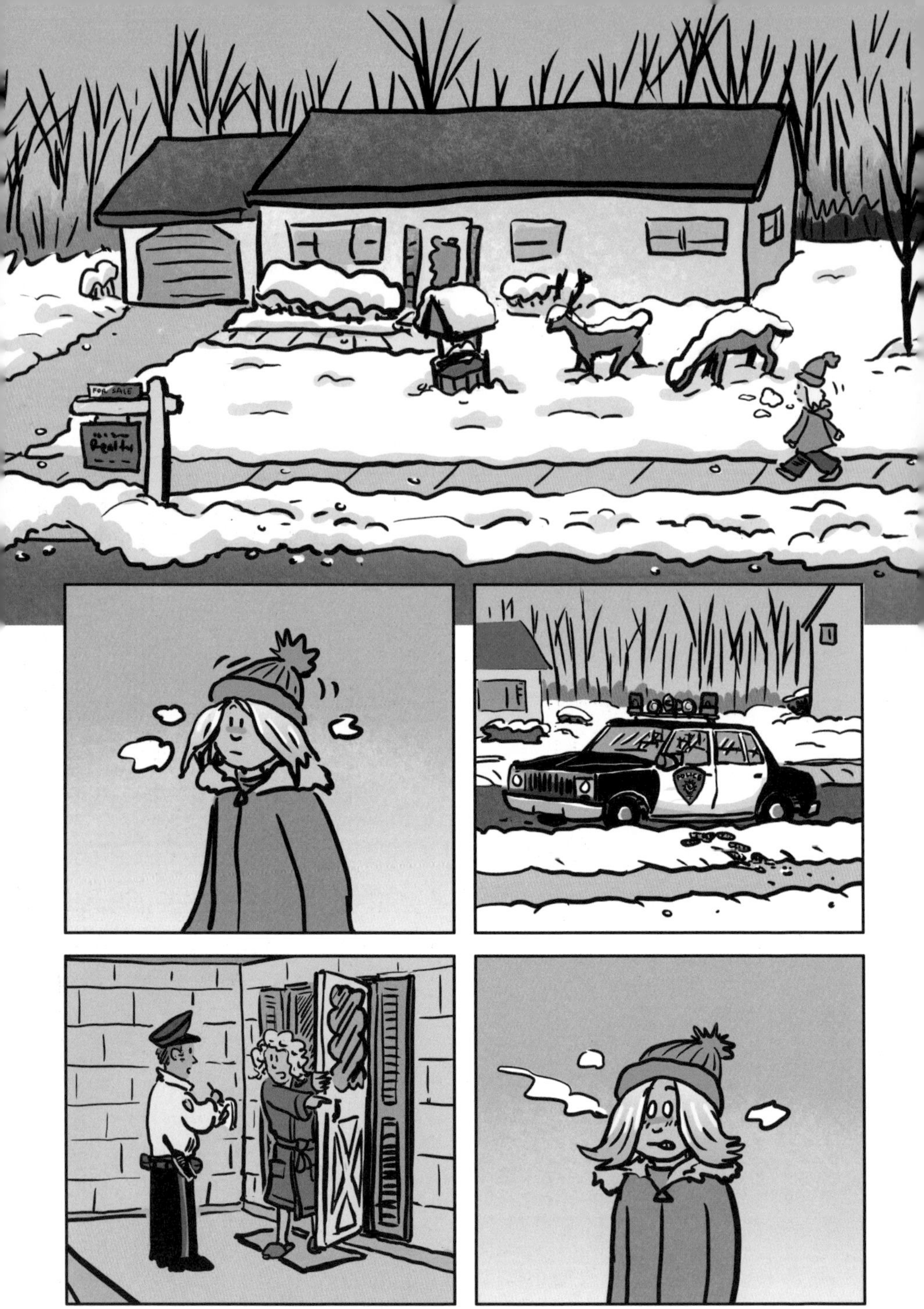
FOR SALE
POLICE

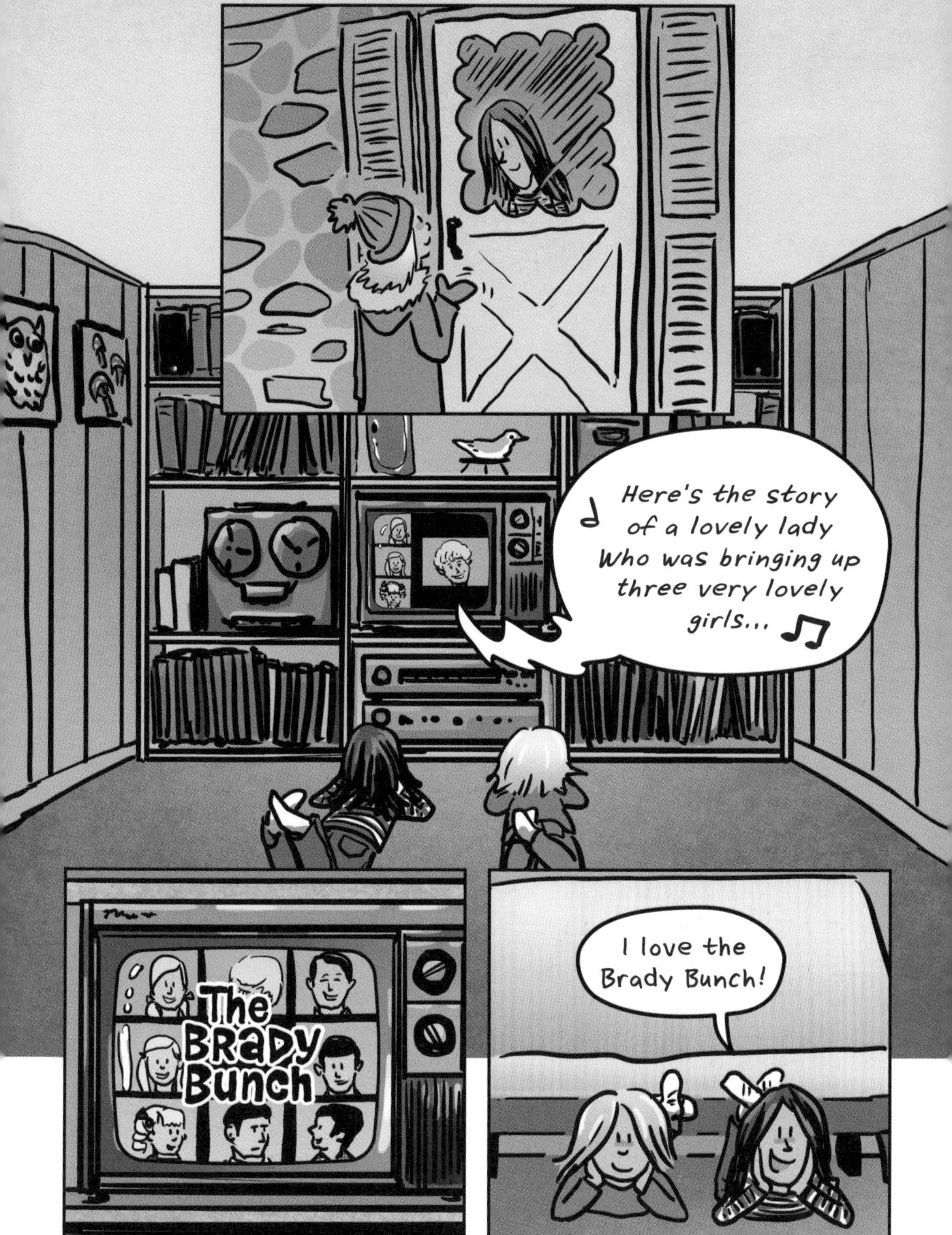
Here's the story of a lovely lady Who was bringing up three very lovely girls...
The Brady Bunch
I love the Brady Bunch!

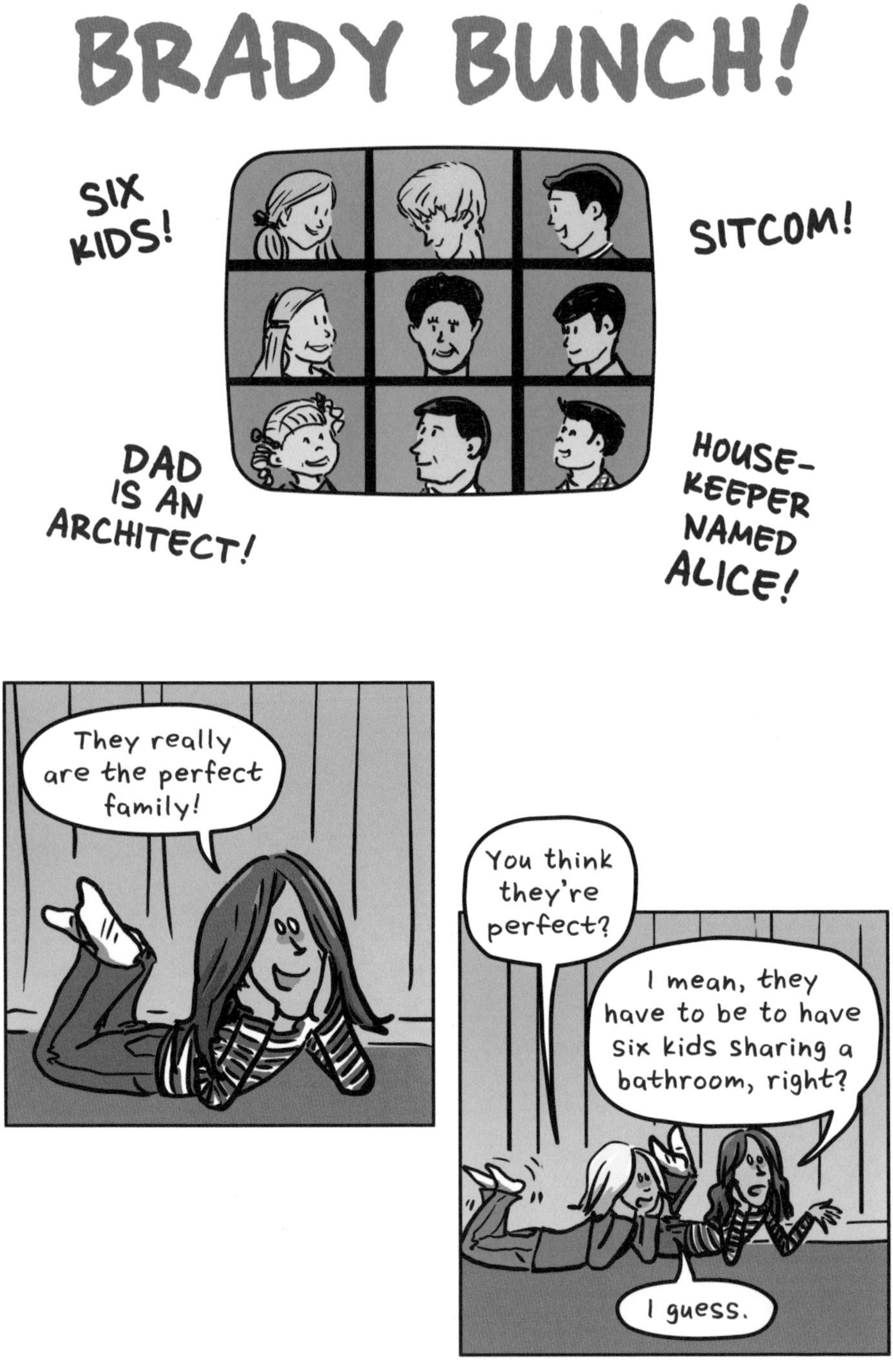
BRADY BUNCH!
SIX KIDS!
SITCOM!
DAD IS AN ARCHITECT!
HOUSE-KEEPER NAMED ALICE!
They really are the perfect family!
You think they're perfect?
I mean, they have to be to have six kids sharing a bathroom, right?
I guess.

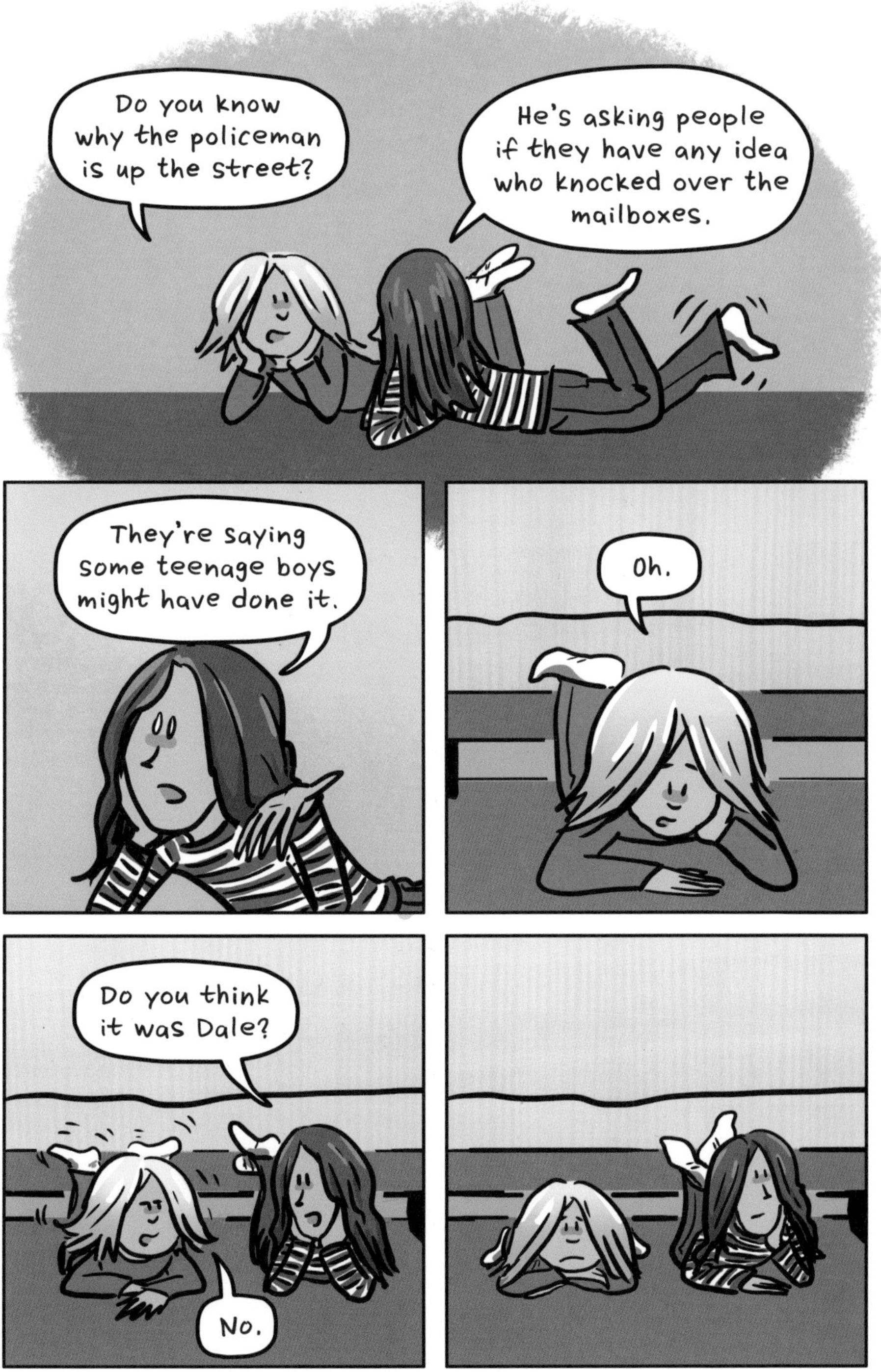
Do you know why the policeman is up the street?
He's asking people if they have any idea who knocked over the mailboxes.
They're saying some teenage boys might have done it.
Oh.
Do you think it was Dale?
No.

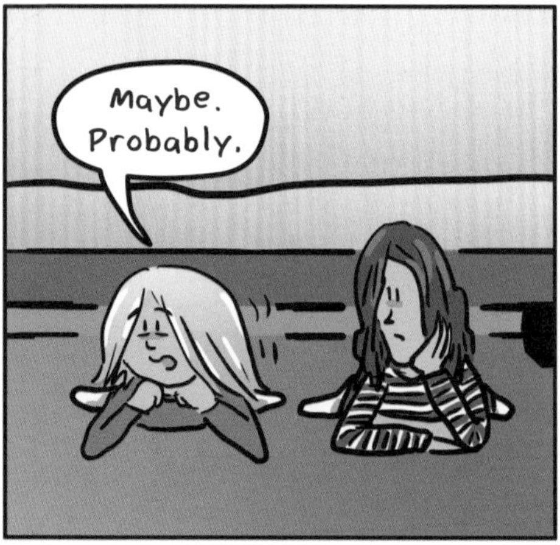
Maybe. Probably.

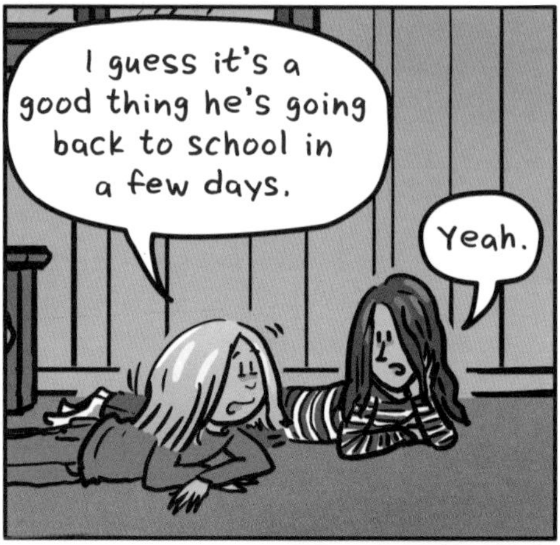
I guess it's a good thing he's going back to school in a few days.
Yeah.

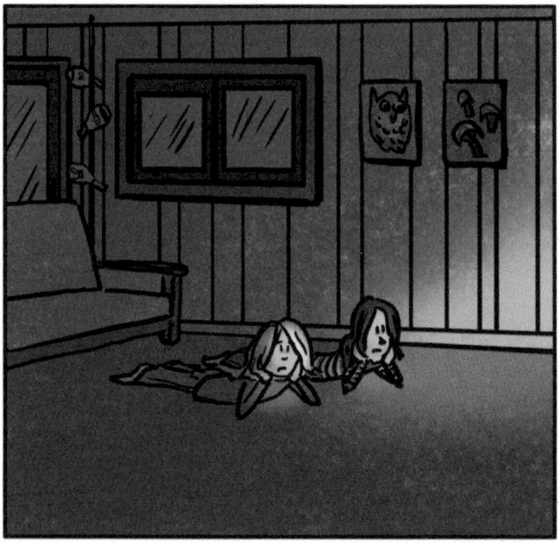

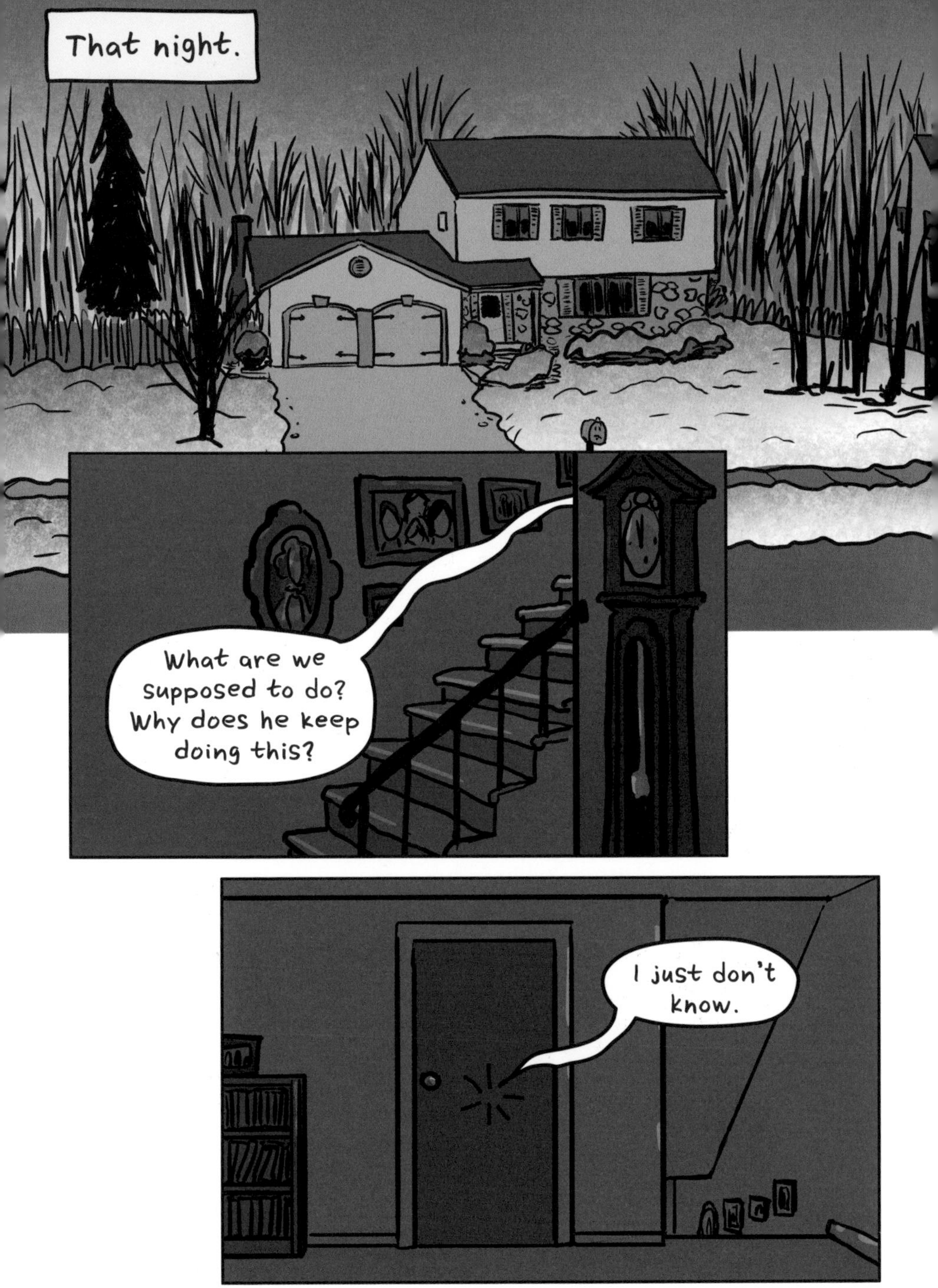
That night.
What are we supposed to do? Why does he keep doing this?
I just don't know.

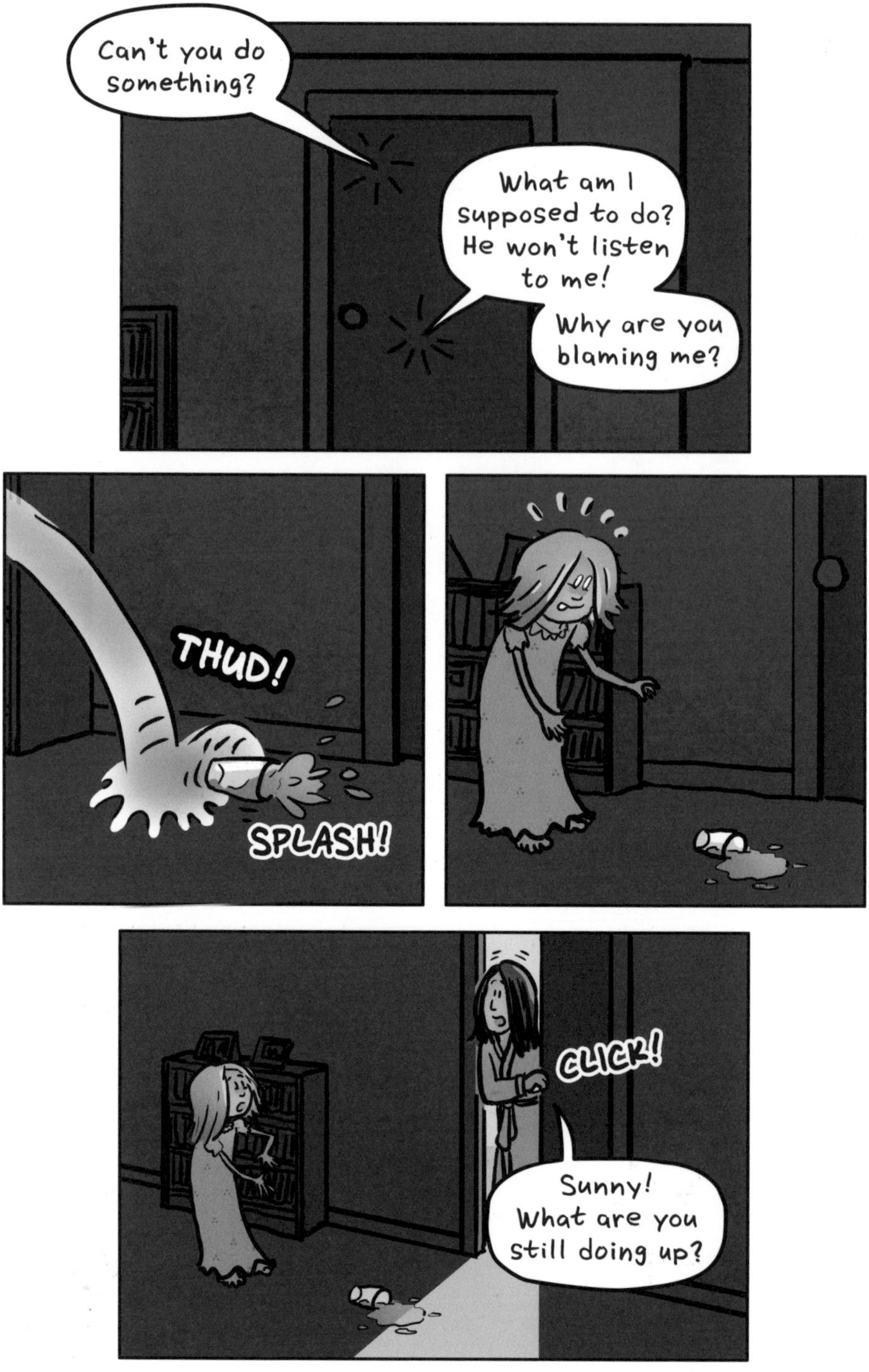
Can't you do something?
What am I supposed to do? He won't listen to me!
Why are you blaming me?
THUD!
SPLASH!
CLICK!
Sunny! What are you still doing up?

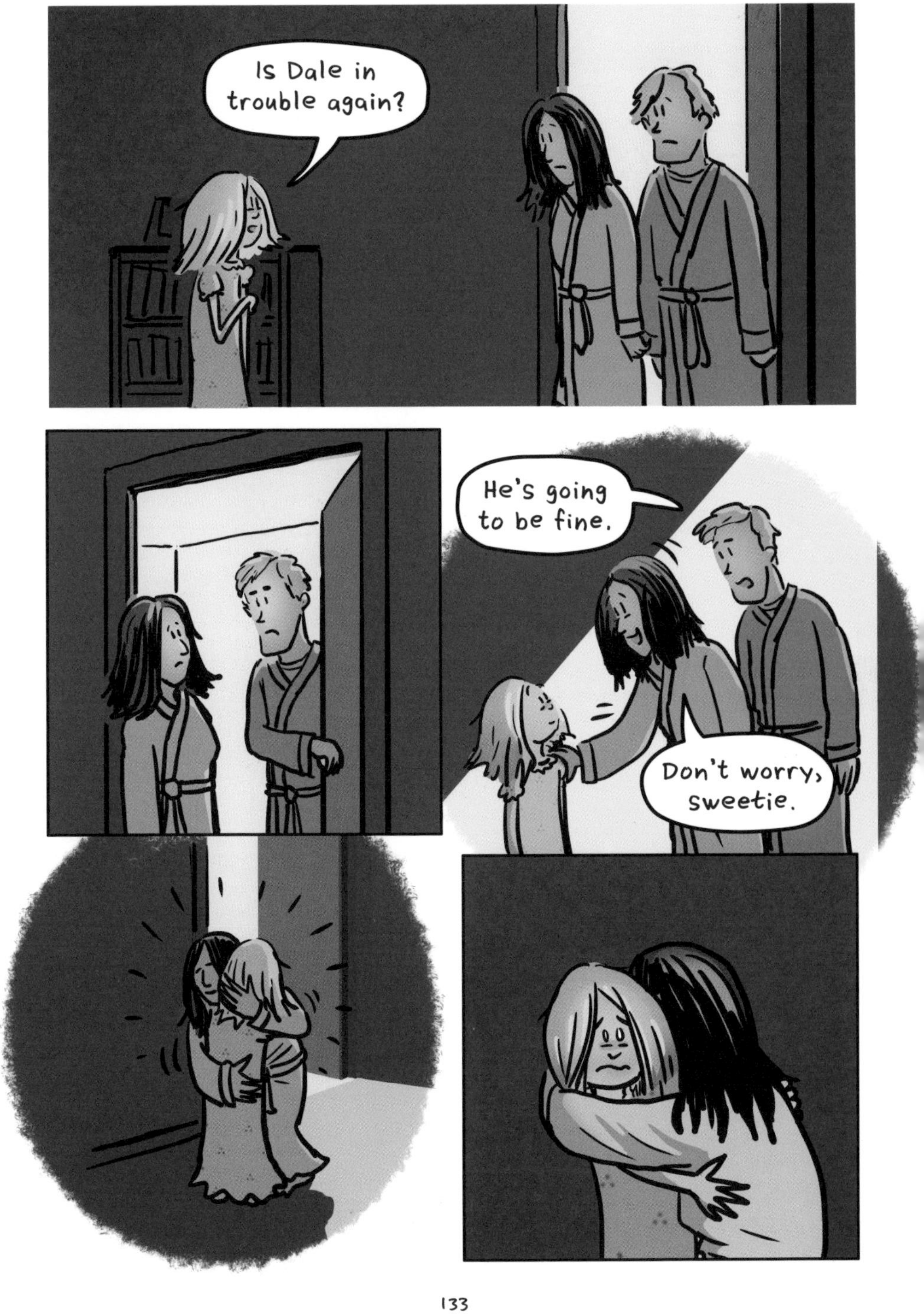
Is Dale in trouble again?
He's going to be fine.
Don't worry, sweetie.

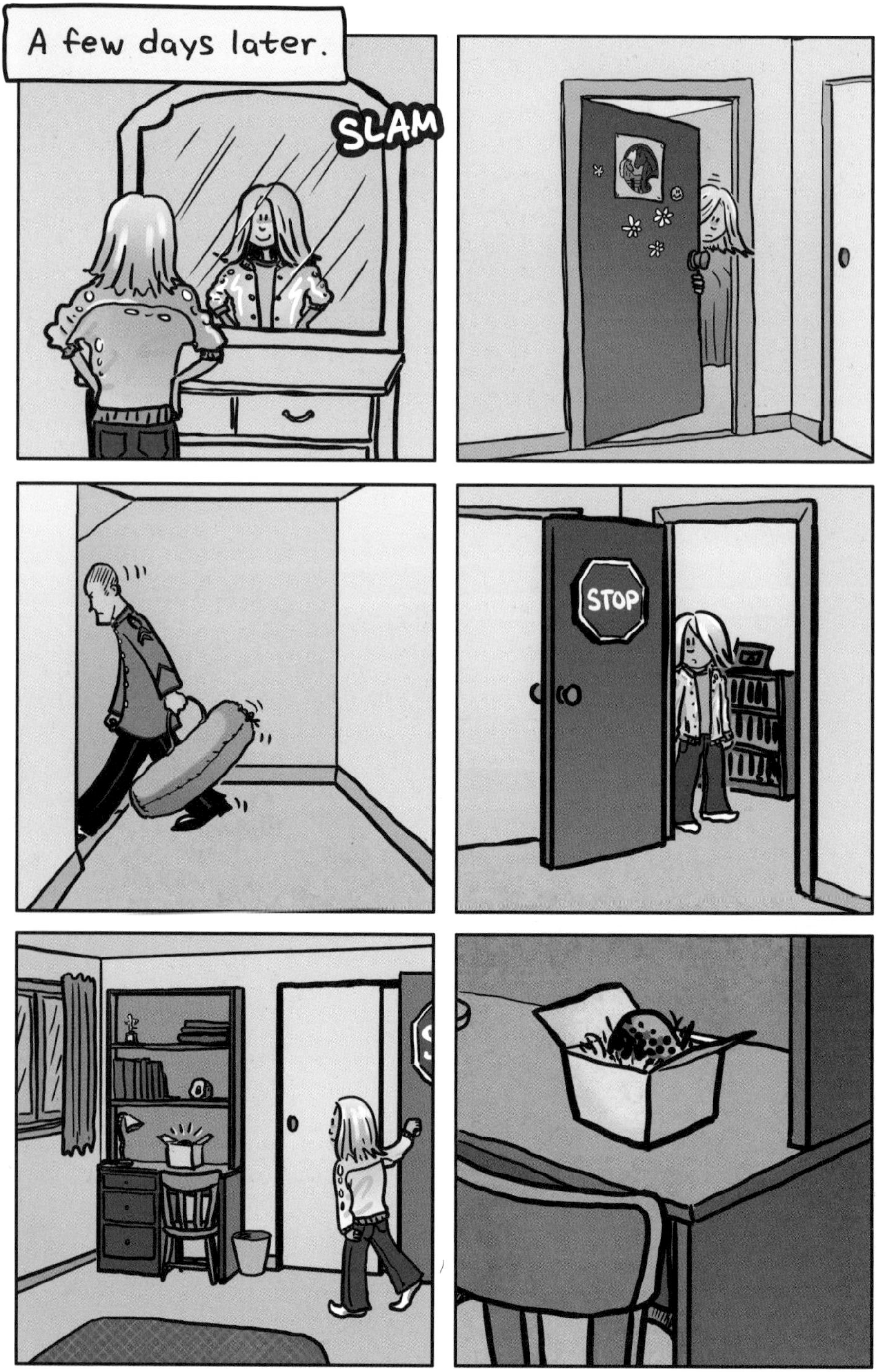
A few days later.
SLAM
STOP

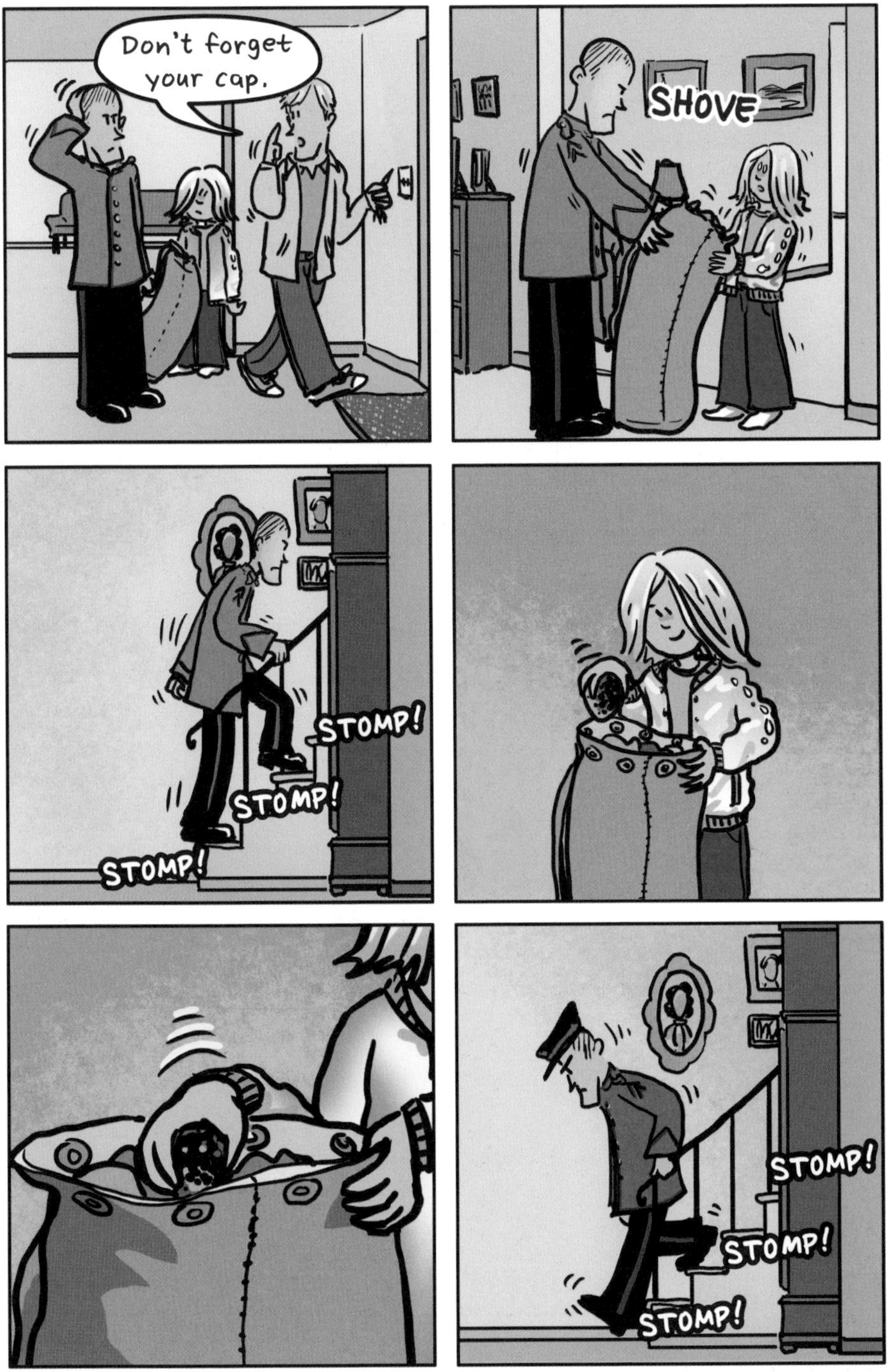
Don't forget your cap.
SHOVE
STOMP!
STOMP!
STOMP!
STOMP!
STOMP!
STOMP!

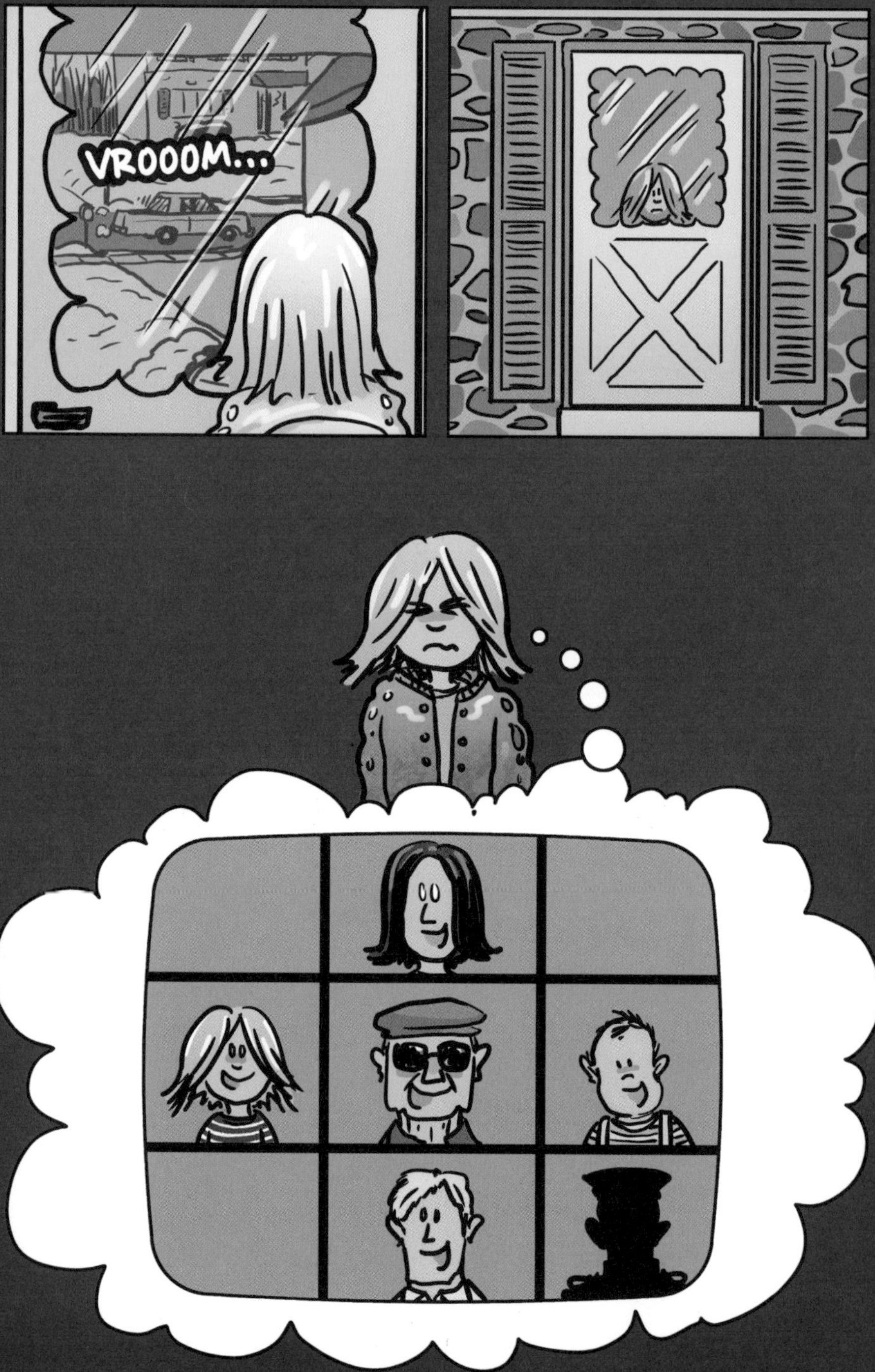
VROOOM...

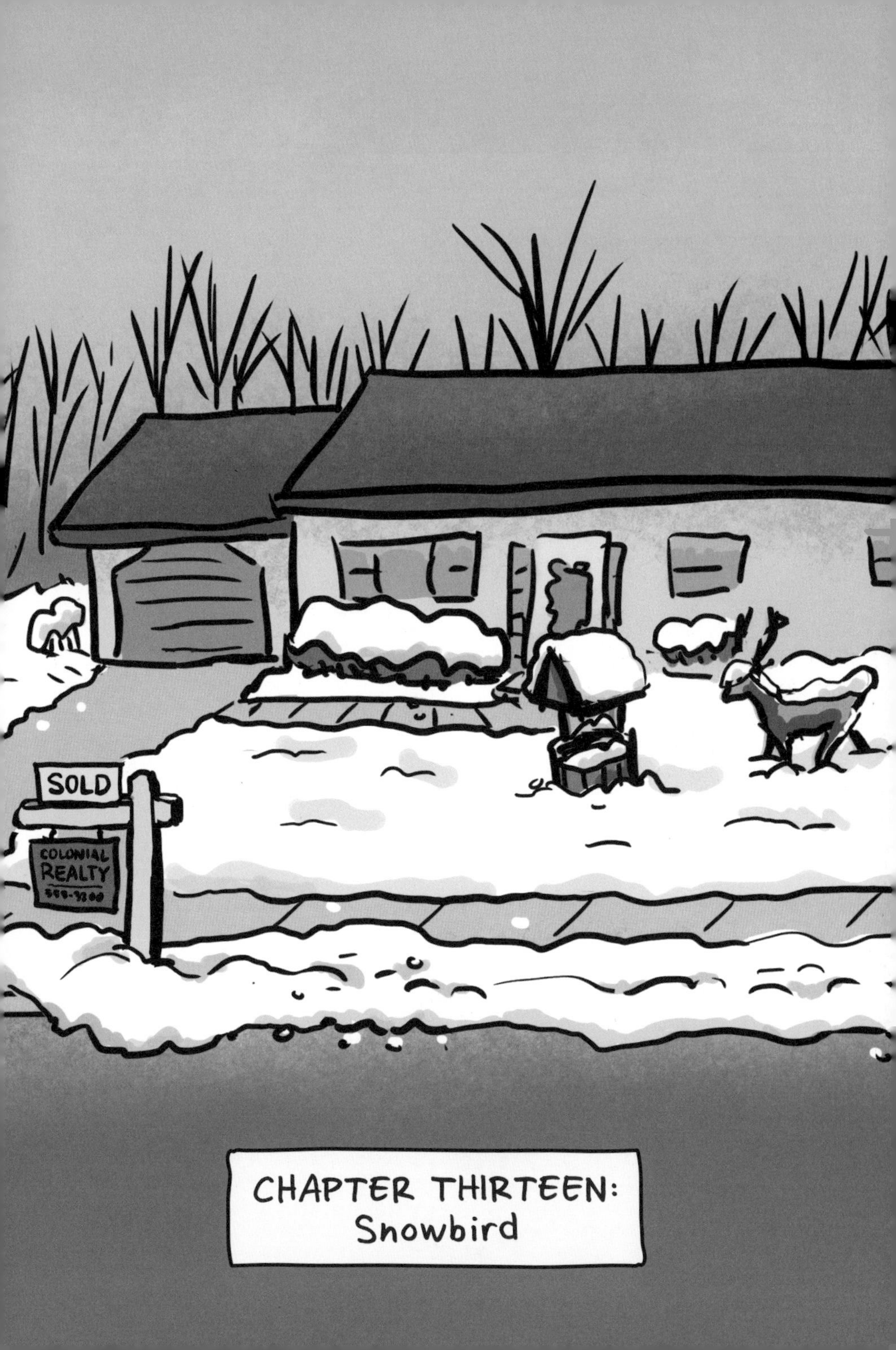
SOLD
COLONIAL
REALTY

CHAPTER THIRTEEN:
Snowbird

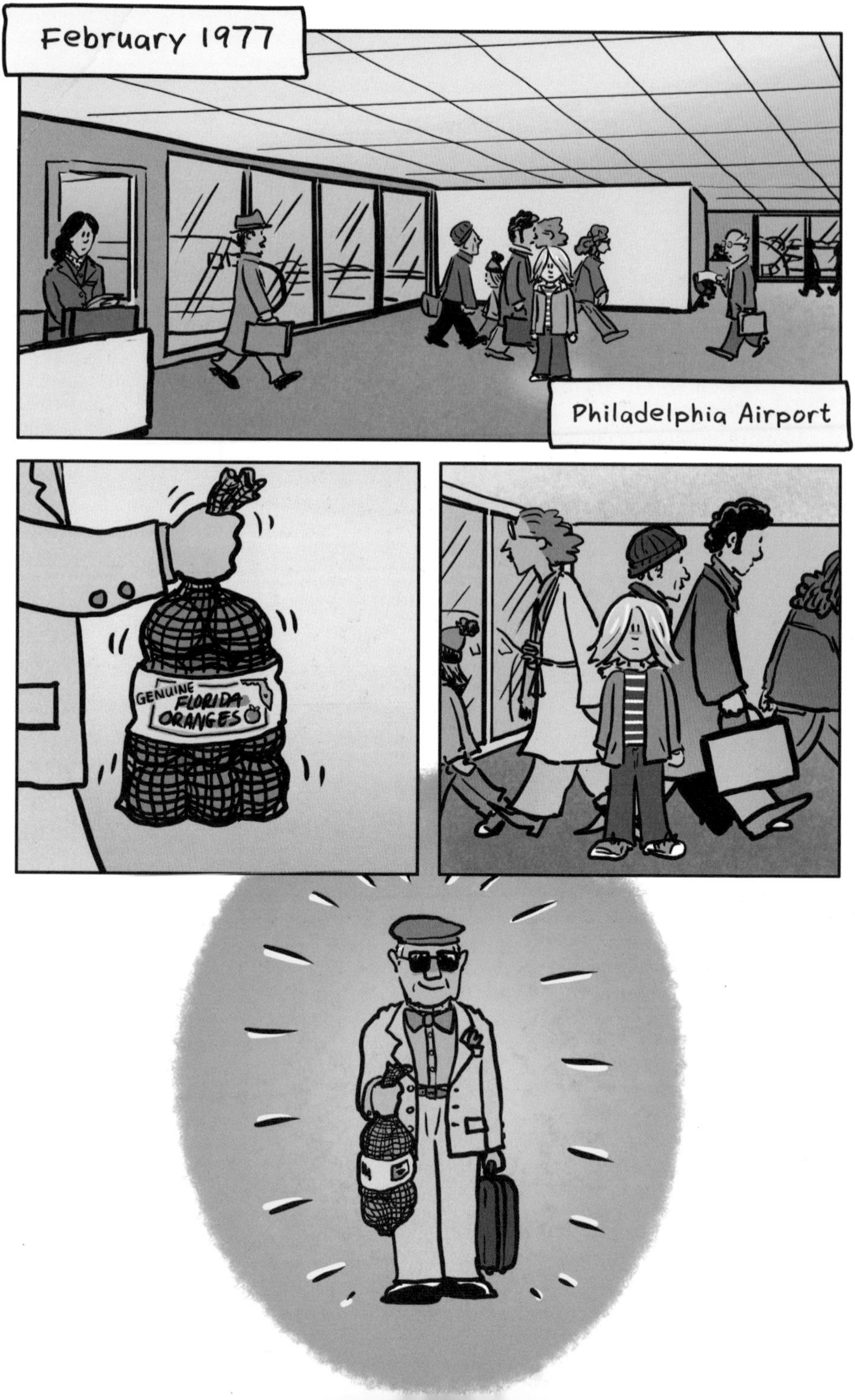
February 1977
Philadelphia Airport
GENUINE
FLORIDA
ORANGES

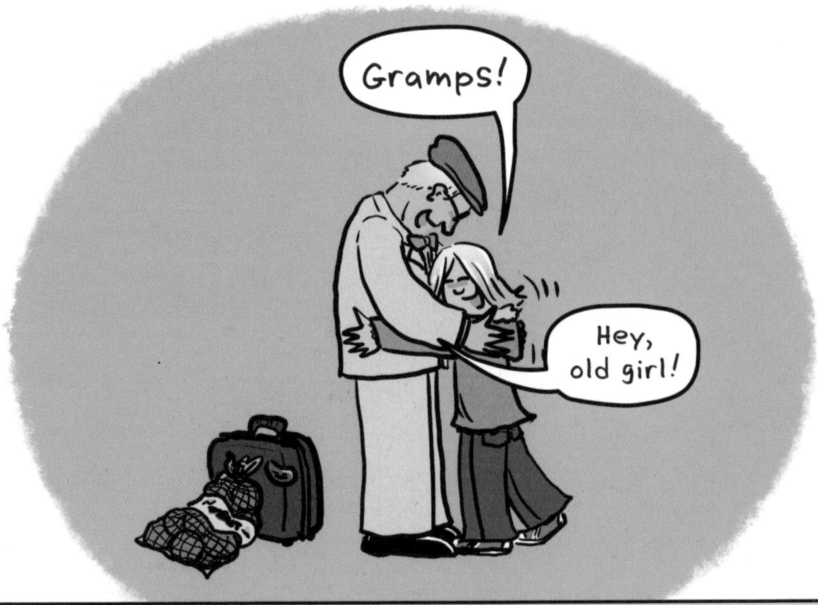
Gramps!
Hey, old girl!

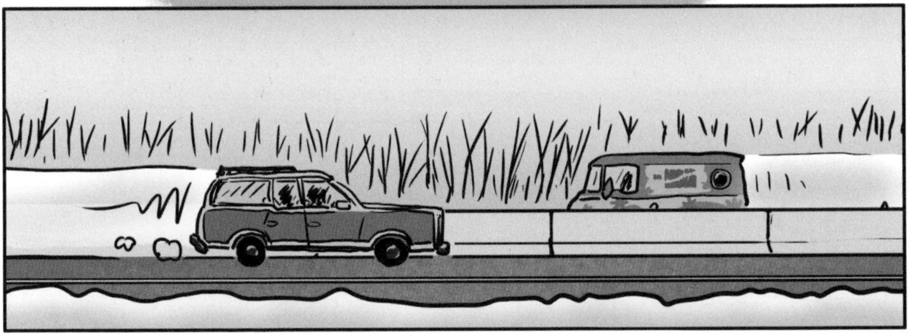

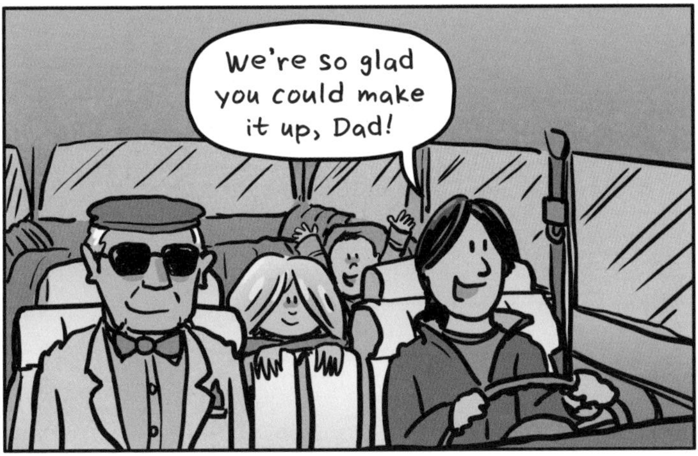
We're so glad you could make it up, Dad!

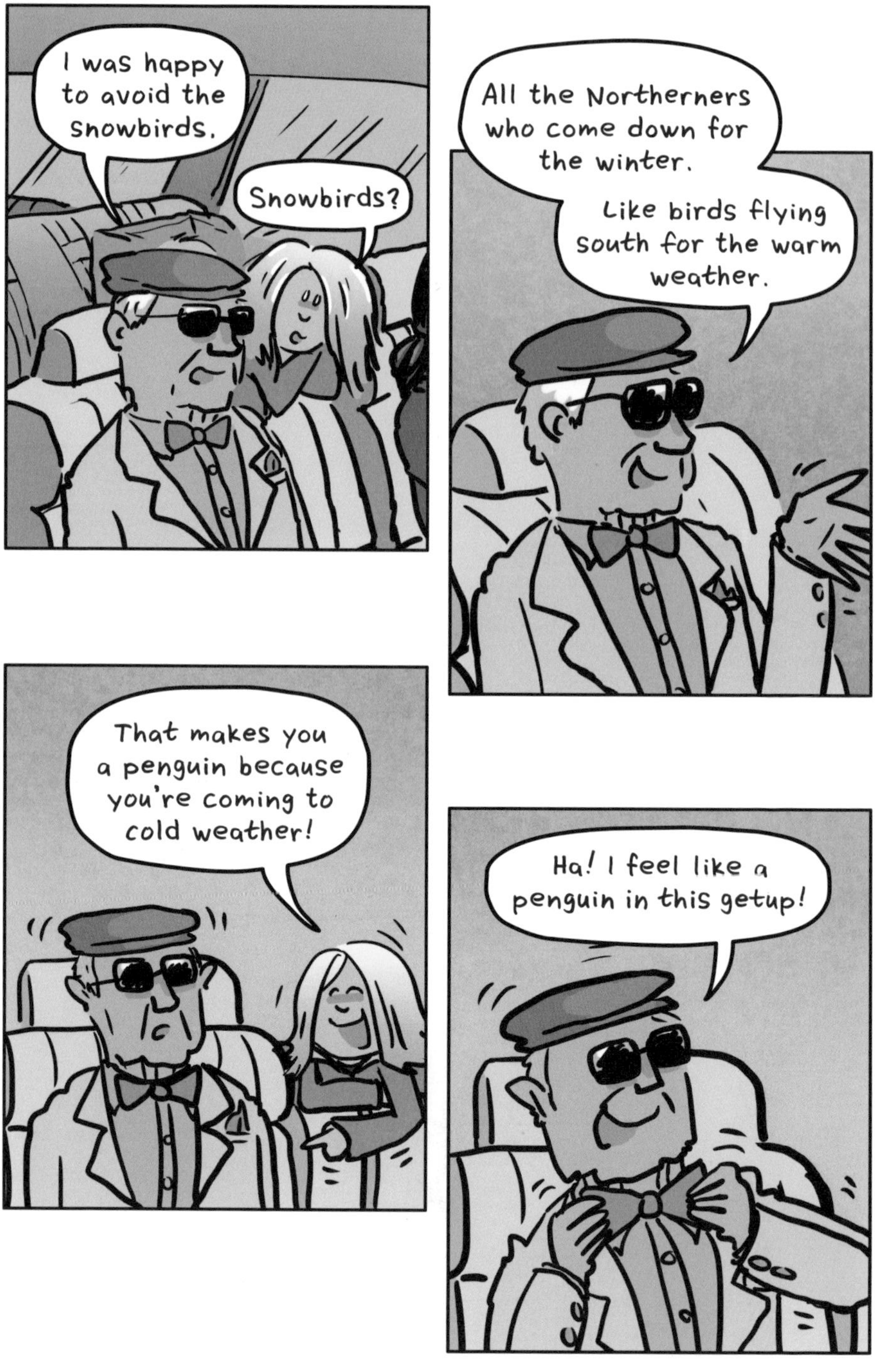
I was happy to avoid the snowbirds.
Snowbirds?
All the Northerners who come down for the winter.
Like birds flying south for the warm weather.
That makes you a penguin because you're coming to cold weather!
Ha! I feel like a penguin in this getup!

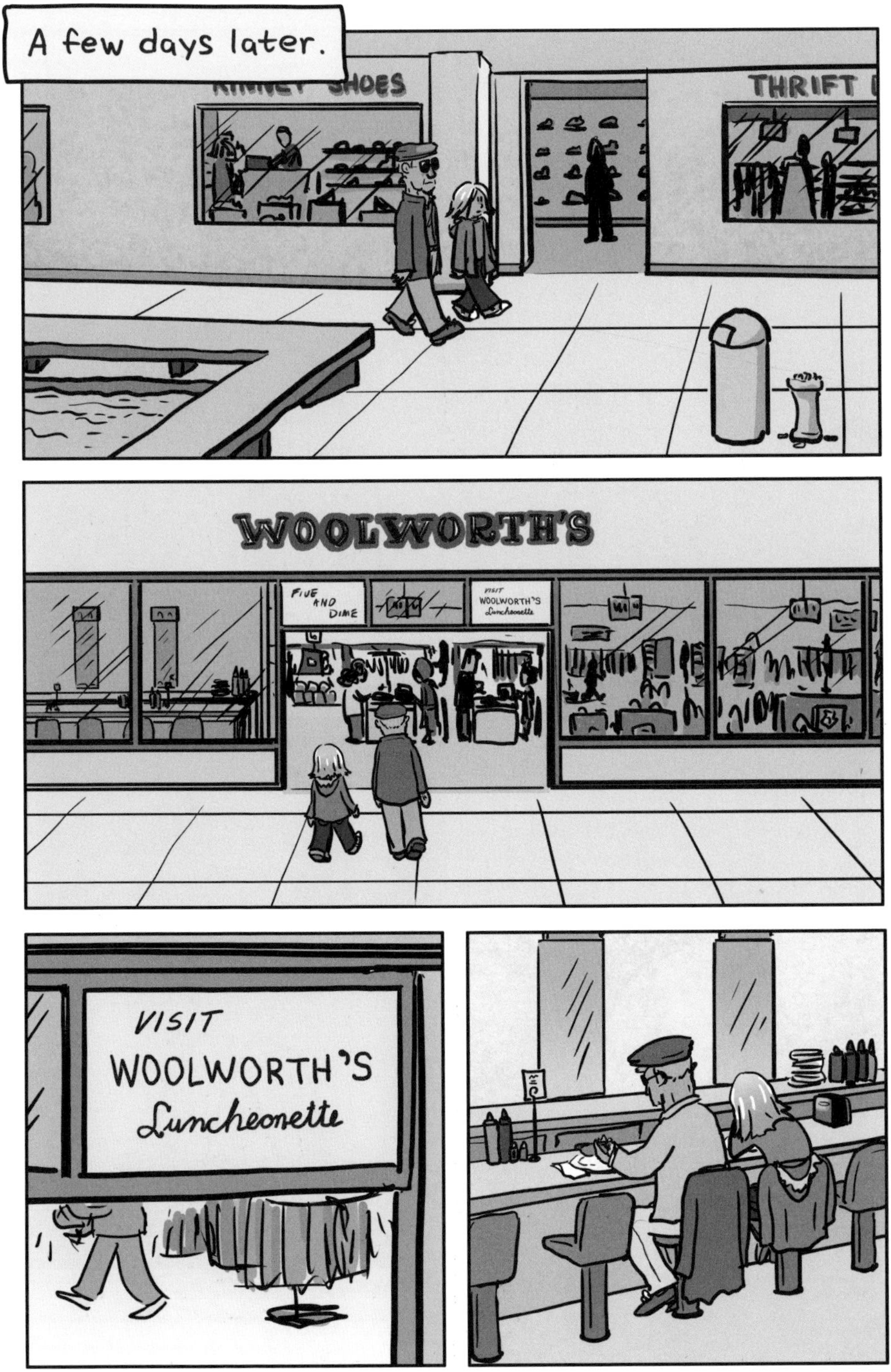
A few days later.
SHOES
THRIFT
WOOLWORTH'S
FIVE AND DIME
VISIT WOOLWORTH'S Luncheonette
VISIT
WOOLWORTH'S
Luncheonette

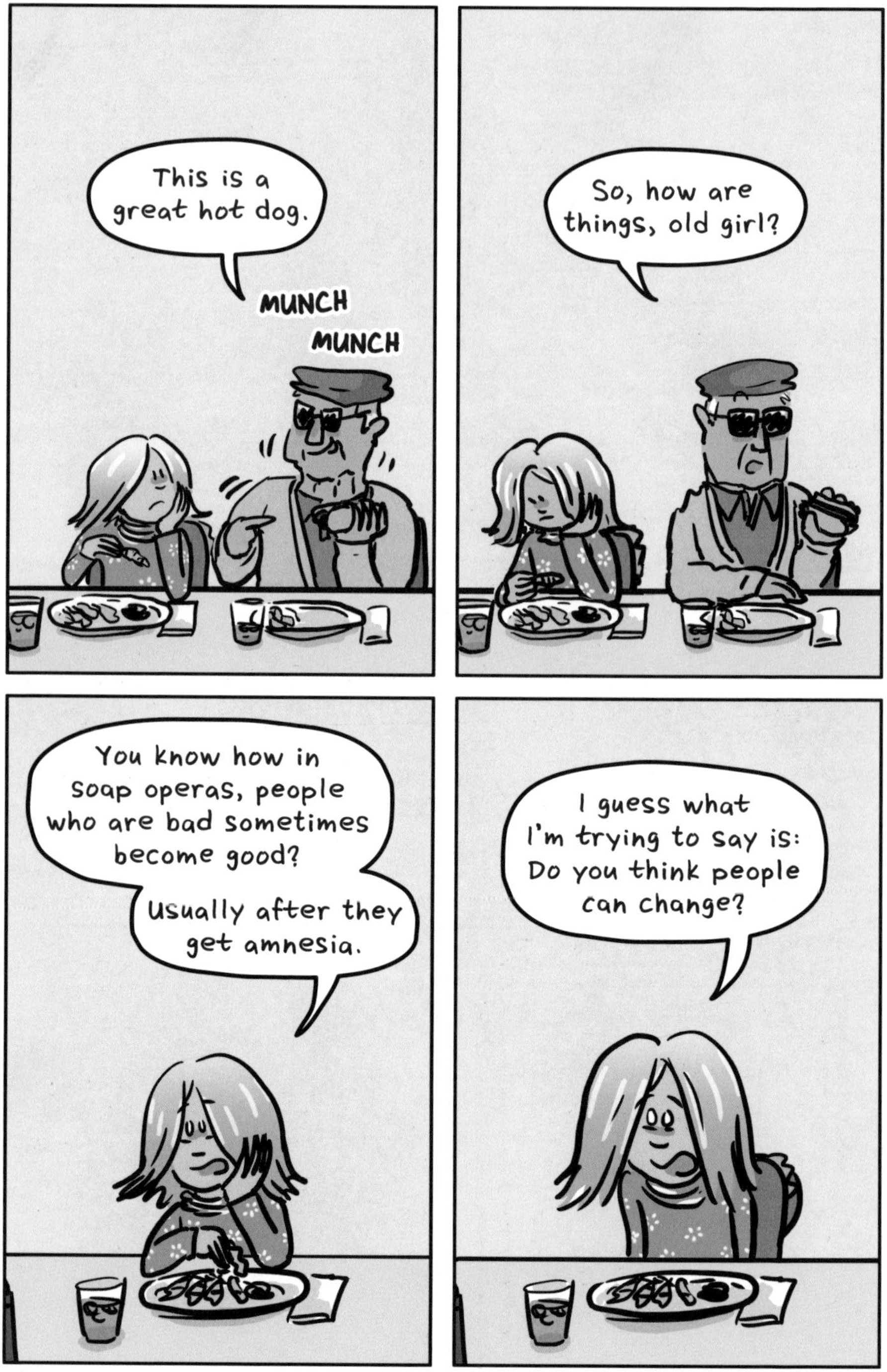
This is a great hot dog.
MUNCH
MUNCH
So, how are things, old girl?
You know how in soap operas, people who are bad sometimes become good?
Usually after they get amnesia.
I guess what I'm trying to say is: Do you think people can change?

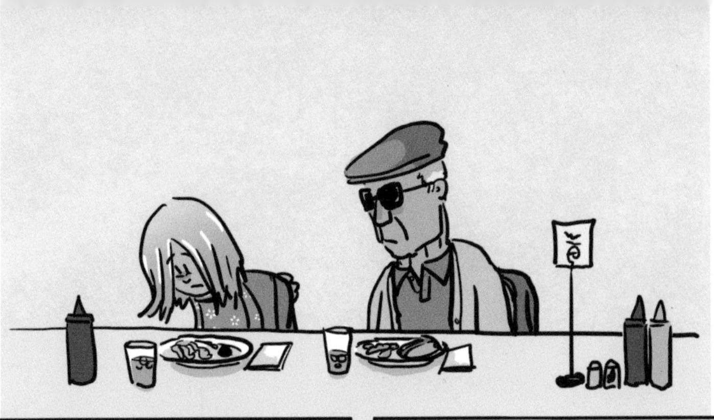

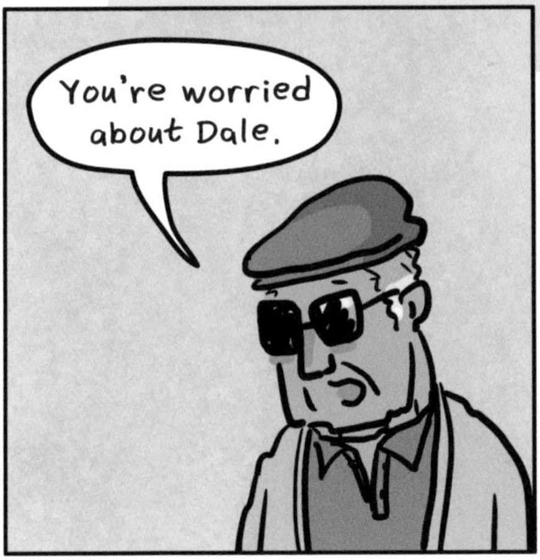
You're worried about Dale.

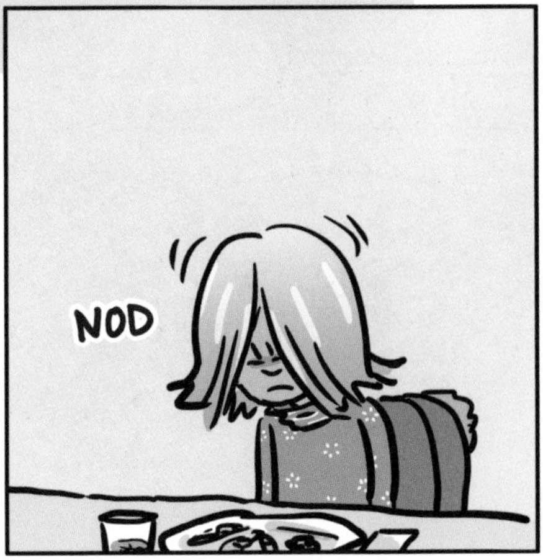
NOD

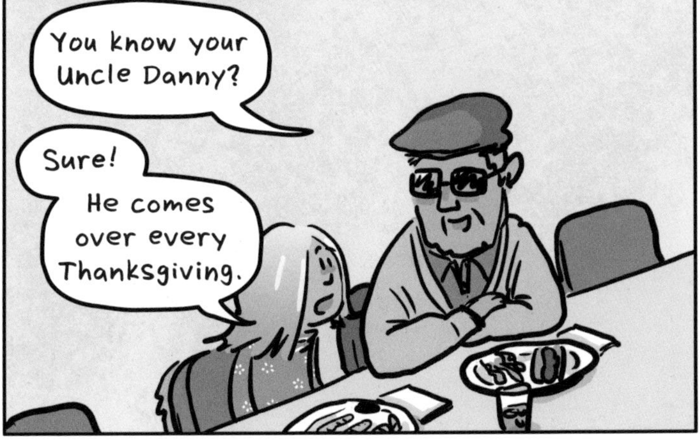
You know your Uncle Danny?
Sure!
He comes over every Thanksgiving.

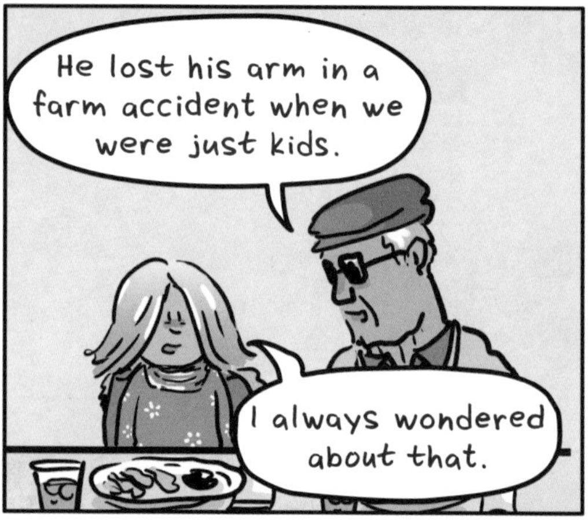
He lost his arm in a farm accident when we were just kids.
I always wondered about that.

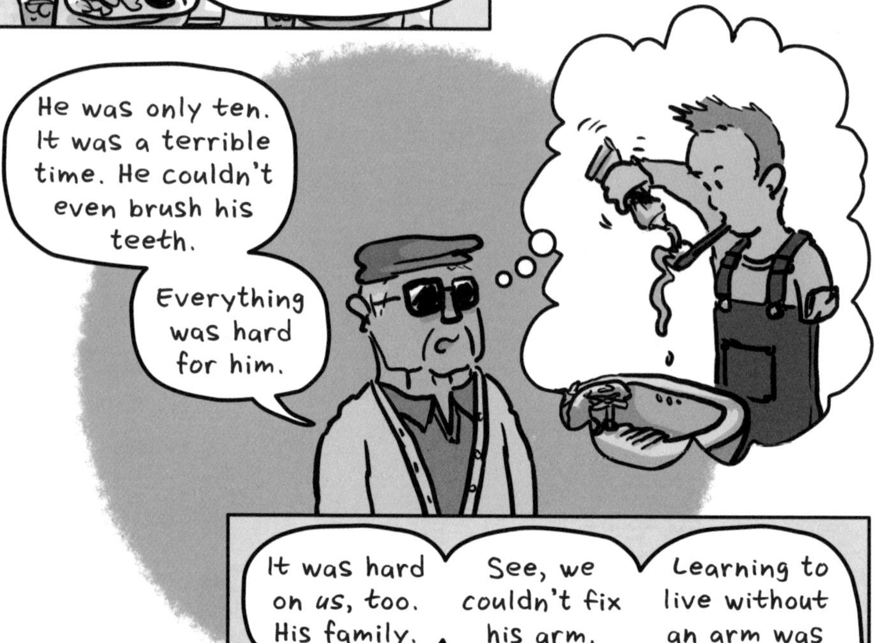
He was only ten. It was a terrible time. He couldn't even brush his teeth.
Everything was hard for him.

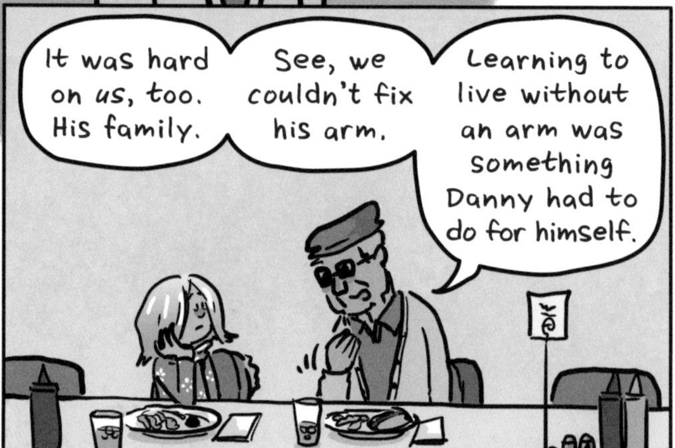
It was hard on *us*, too. His family.
See, we couldn't fix his arm.
Learning to live without an arm was something Danny had to do for himself.

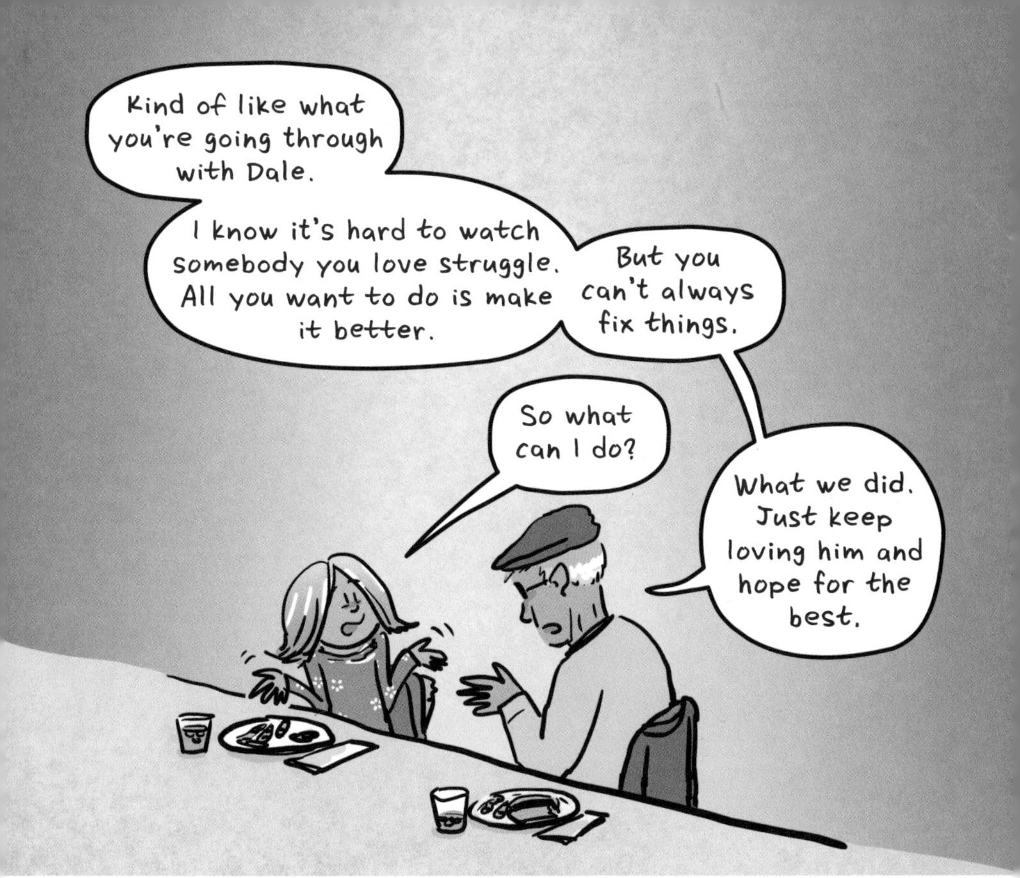
Kind of like what you're going through with Dale.
I know it's hard to watch somebody you love struggle. All you want to do is make it better.
But you can't always fix things.
So what can I do?
What we did. Just keep loving him and hope for the best.

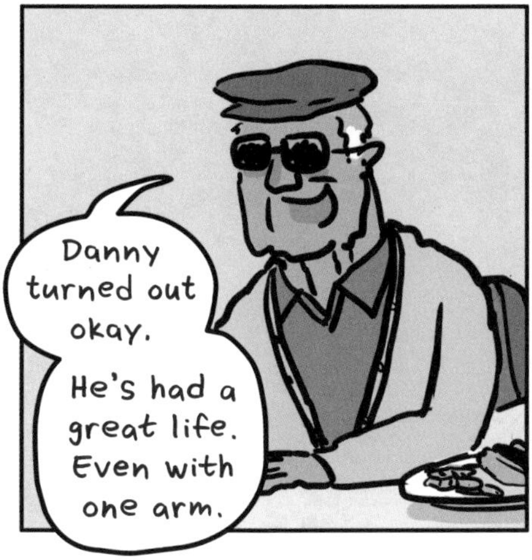
Danny turned out okay.
He's had a great life. Even with one arm.

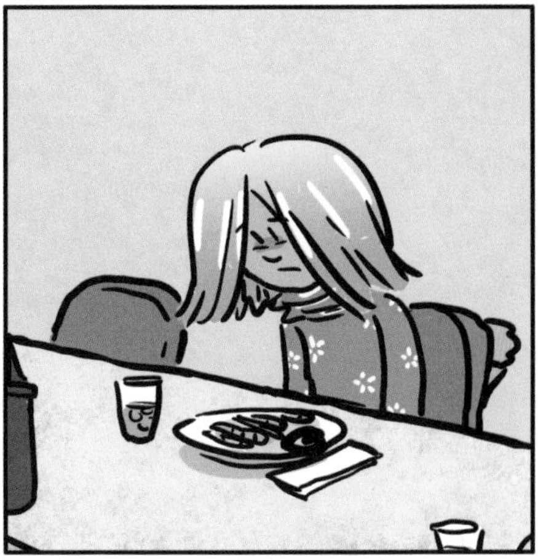

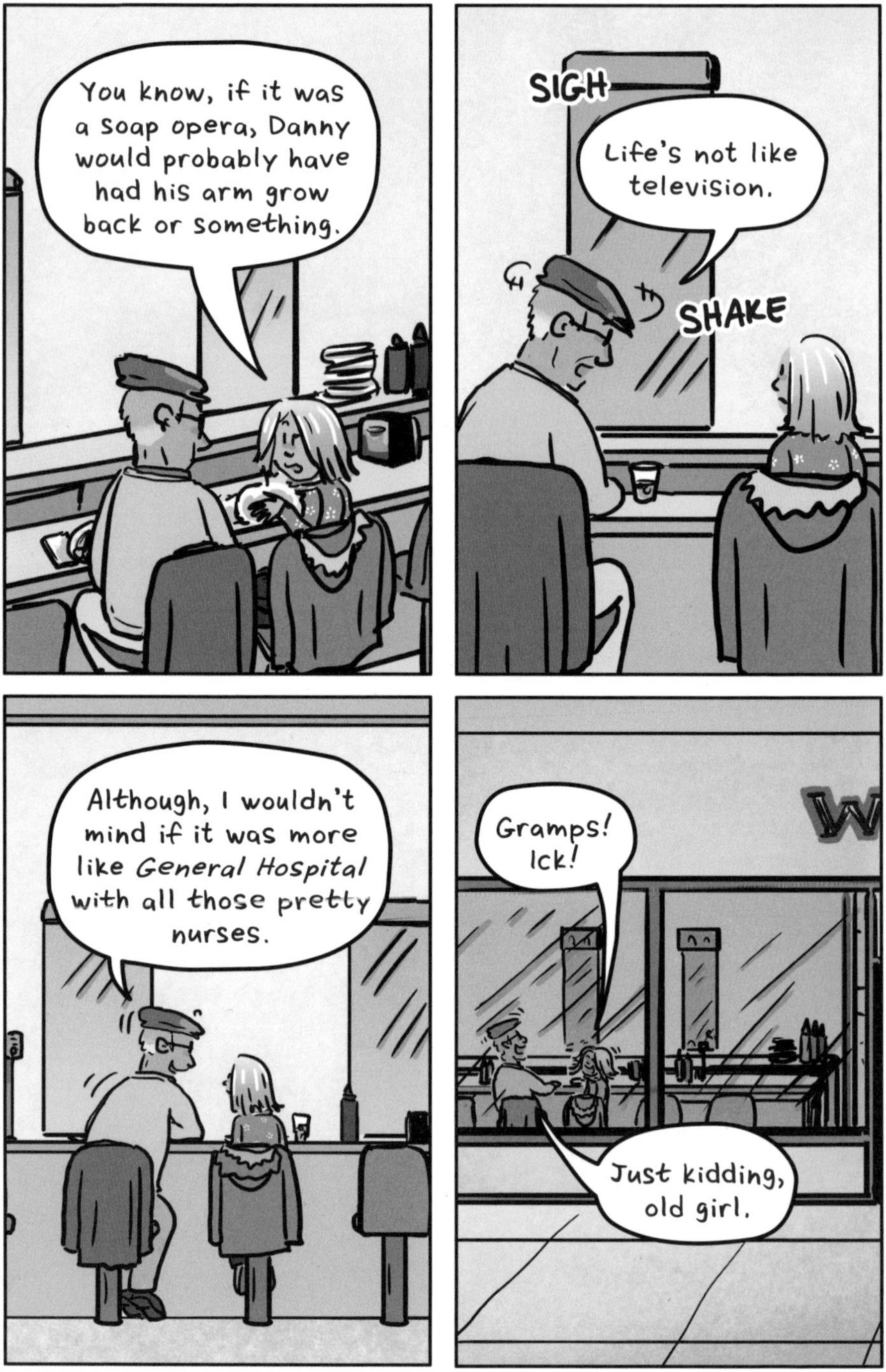
You know, if it was a soap opera, Danny would probably have had his arm grow back or something.
SIGH
Life's not like television.
SHAKE
Although, I wouldn't mind if it was more like *General Hospital* with all those pretty nurses.
Gramps! Ick!
Just kidding, old girl.

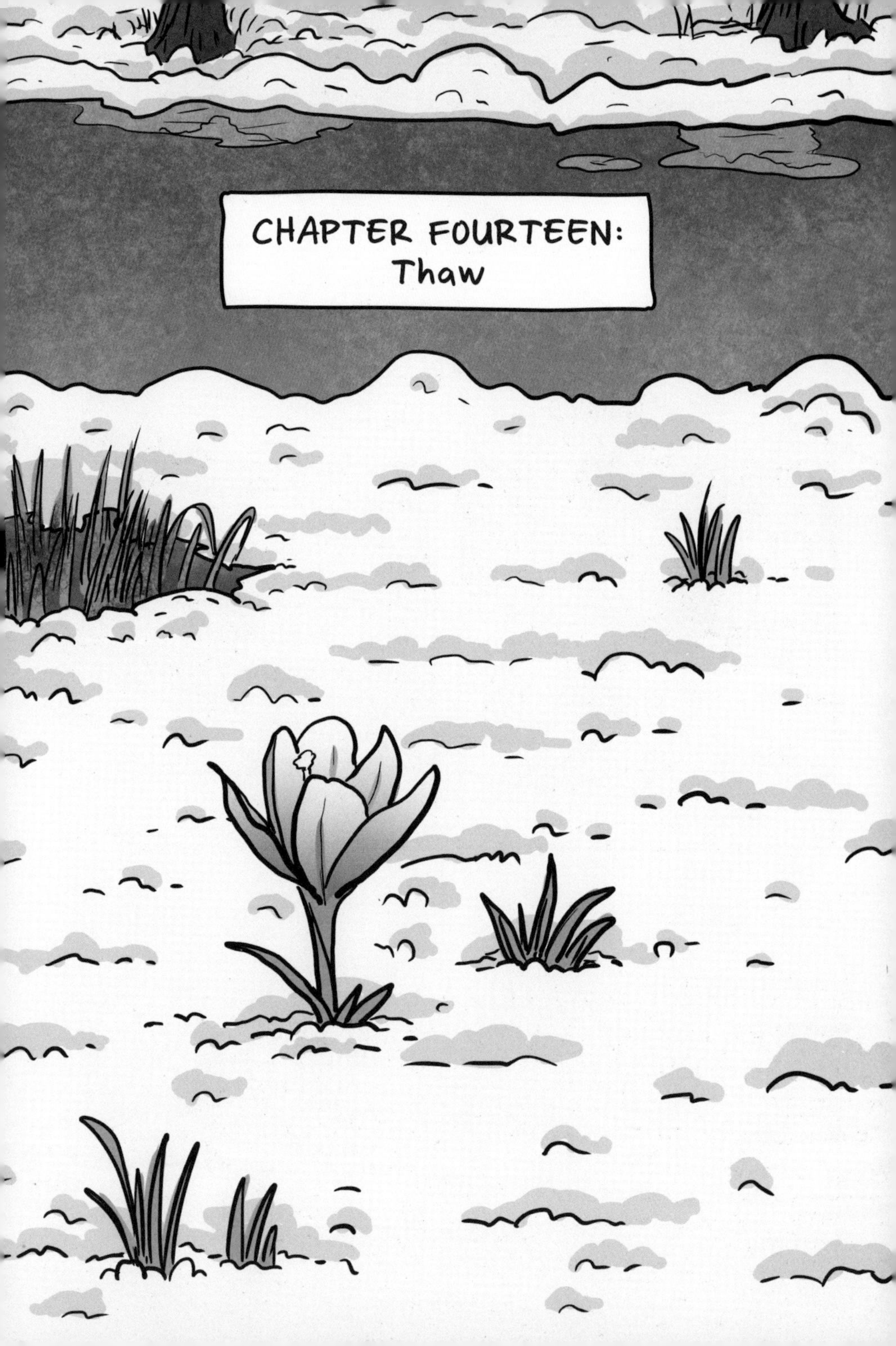
CHAPTER FOURTEEN:
Thaw

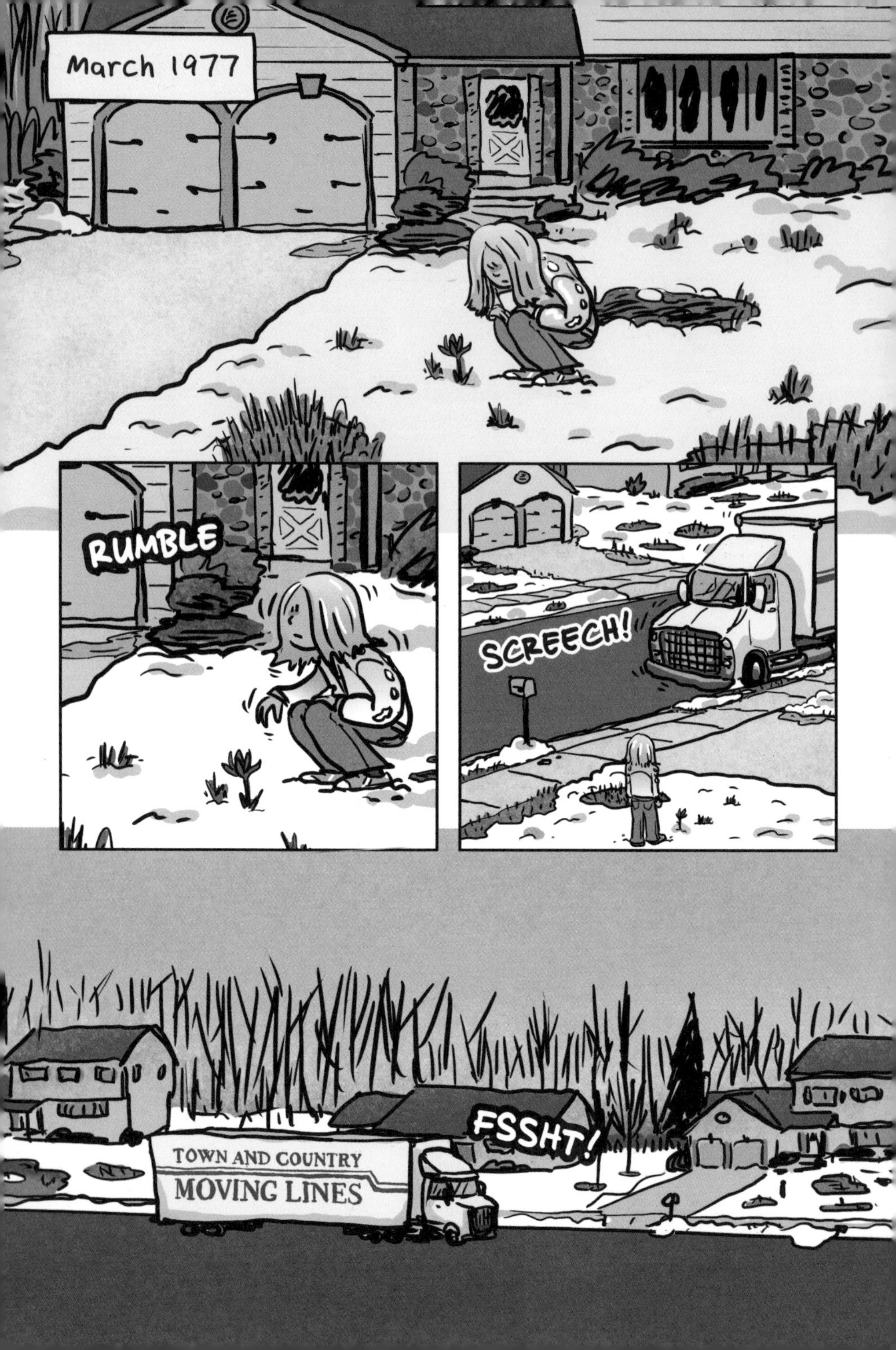
March 1977
RUMBLE
SCREECH!
FSSHT!
TOWN AND COUNTRY
MOVING LINES

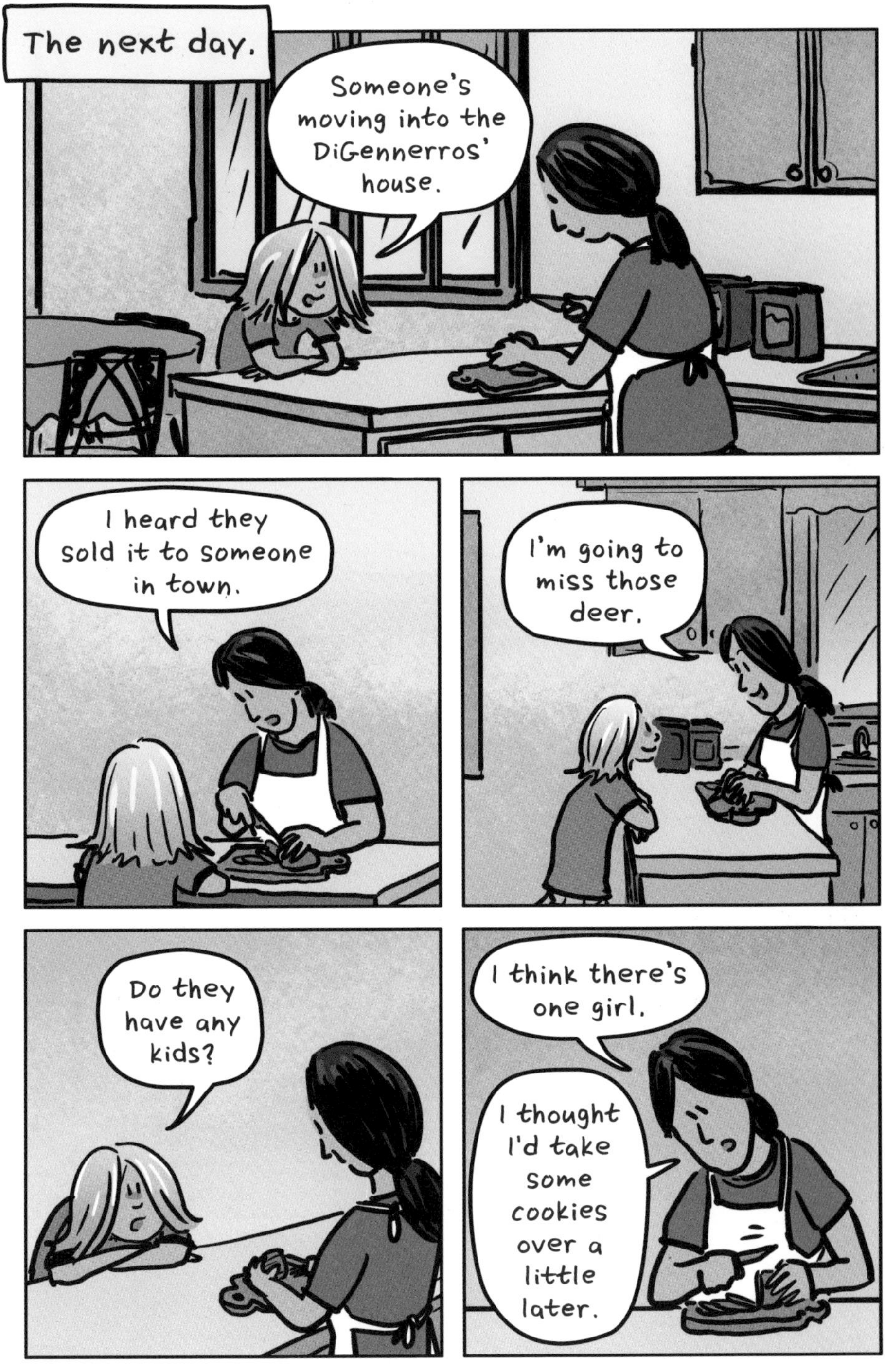
The next day.
Someone's moving into the DiGennerros' house.
I heard they sold it to someone in town.
I'm going to miss those deer.
Do they have any kids?
I think there's one girl.
I thought I'd take some cookies over a little later.

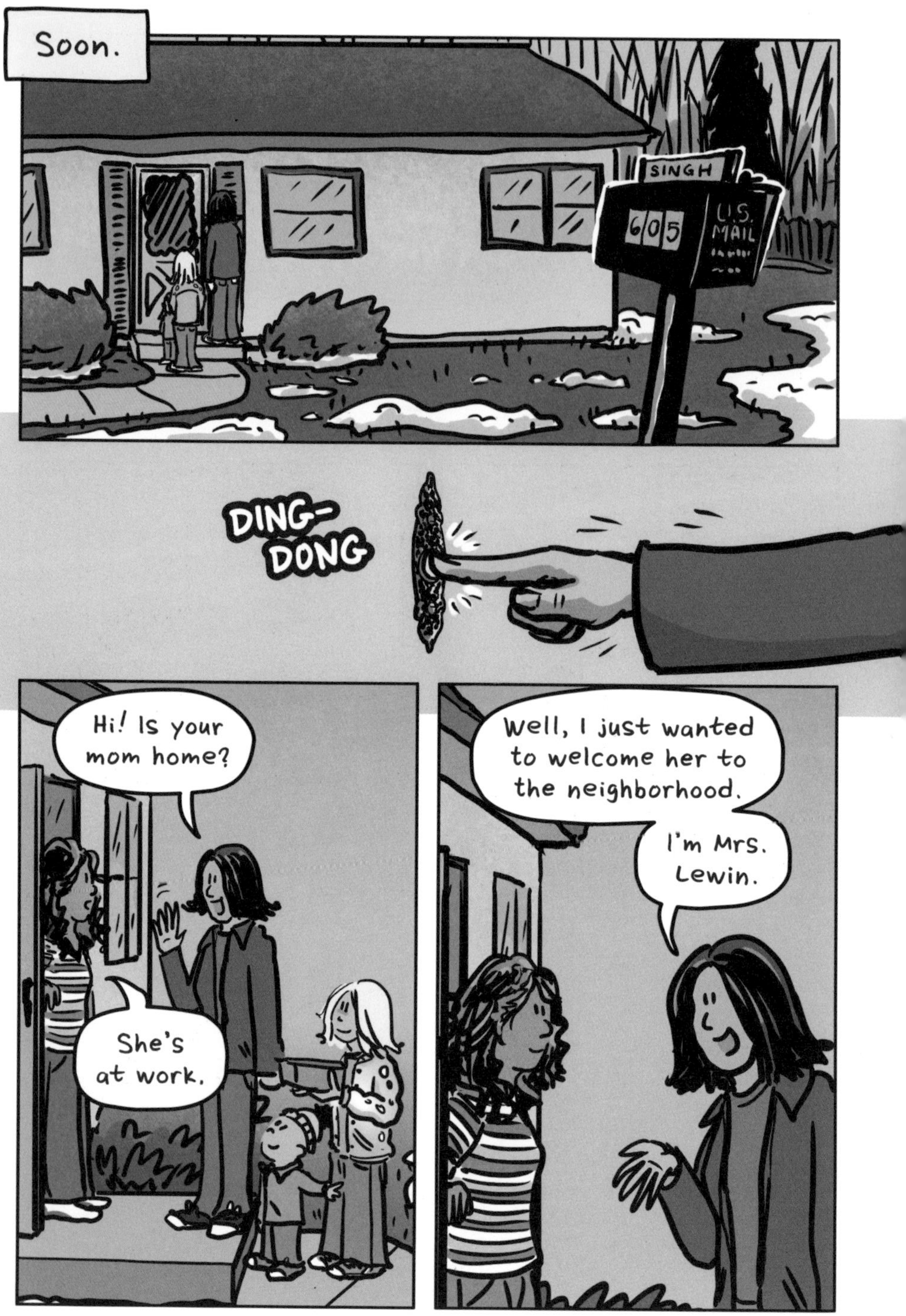
Soon.
SINGH
605
U.S. MAIL
DING-DONG
Hi! Is your mom home?
She's at work.
Well, I just wanted to welcome her to the neighborhood.
I'm Mrs. Lewin.

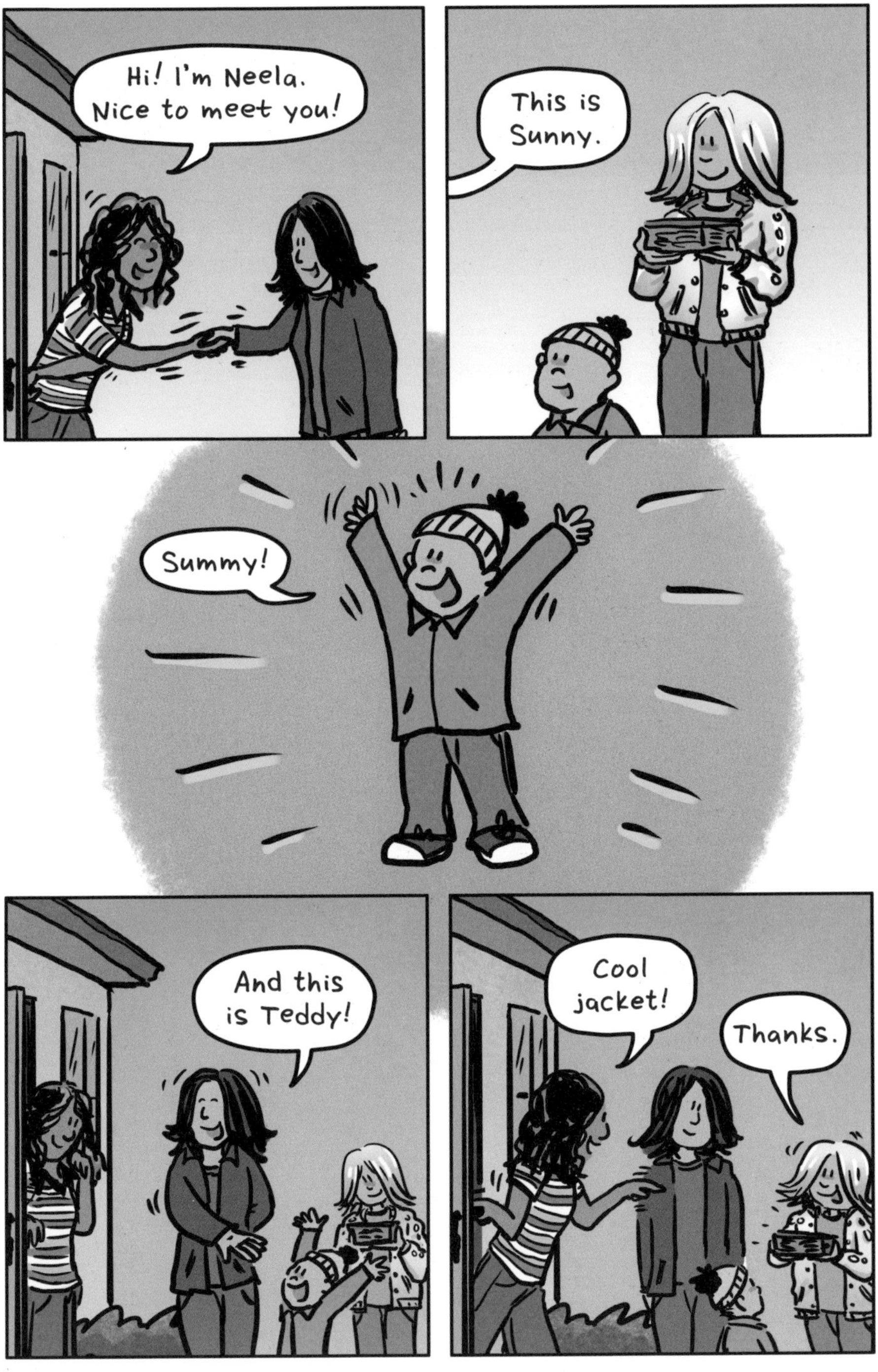
Hi! I'm Neela.
Nice to meet you!
This is Sunny.
Summy!
And this is Teddy!
Cool jacket!
Thanks.

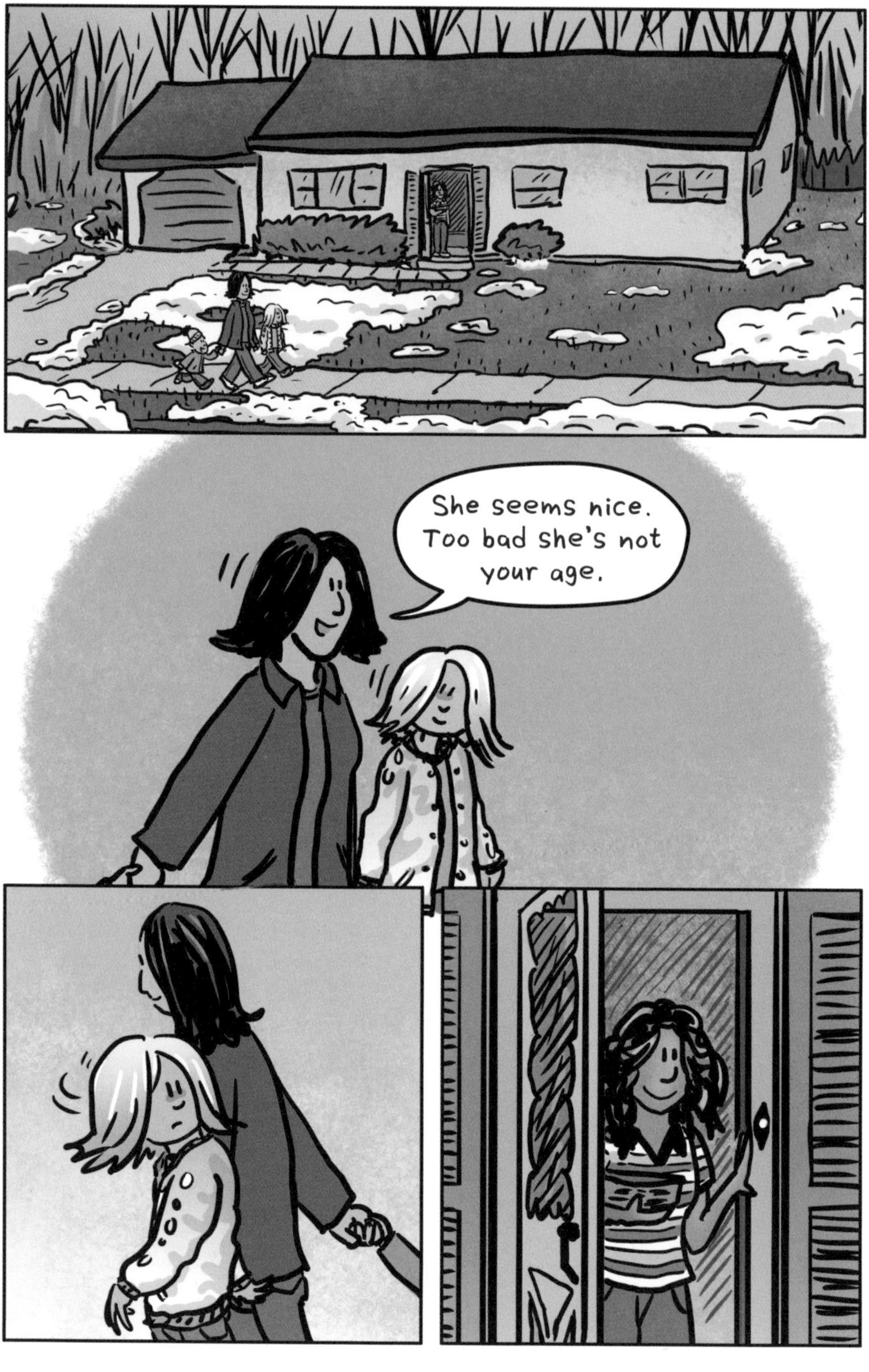
She seems nice. Too bad she's not your age.

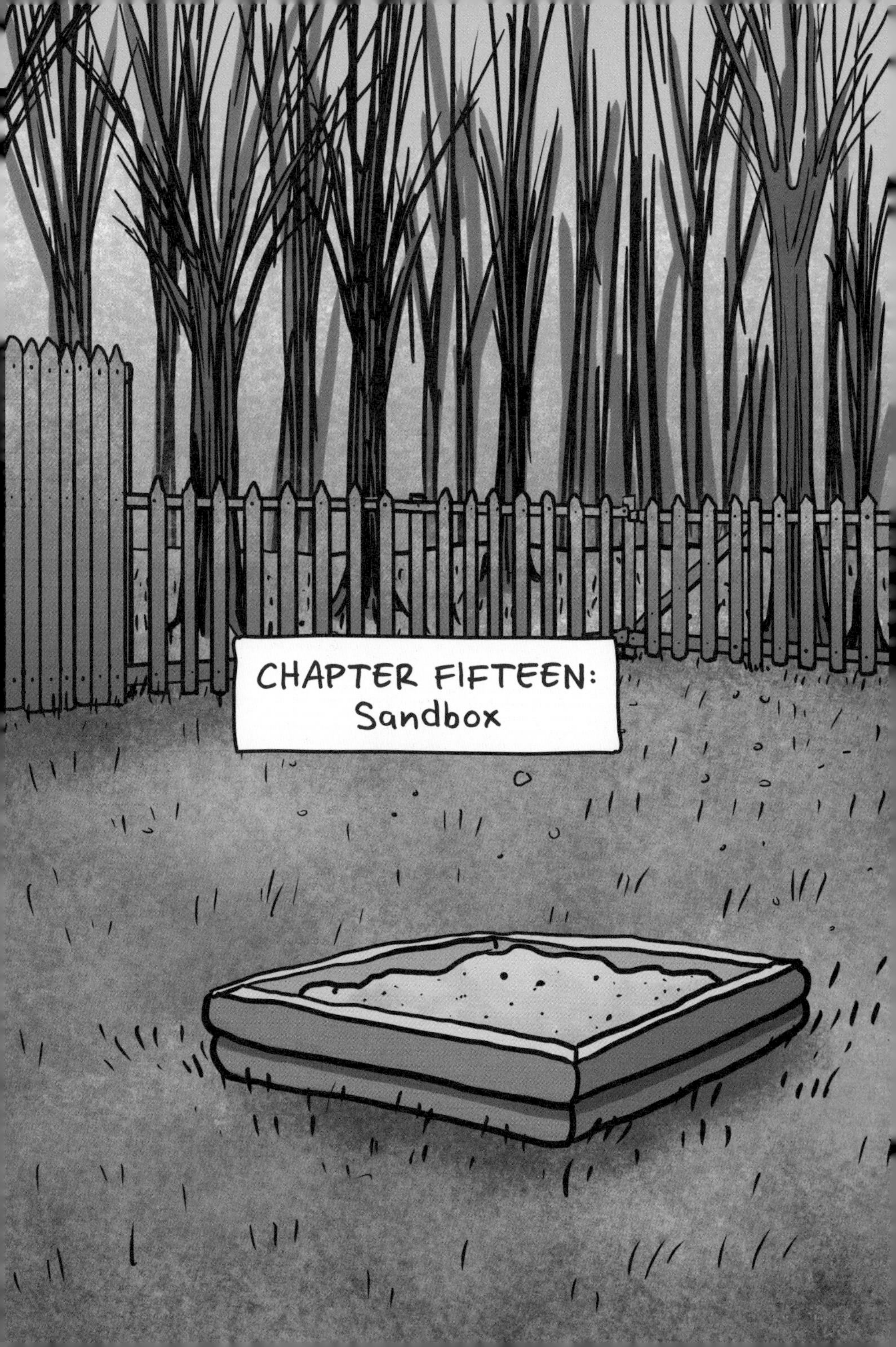
CHAPTER FIFTEEN:
Sandbox

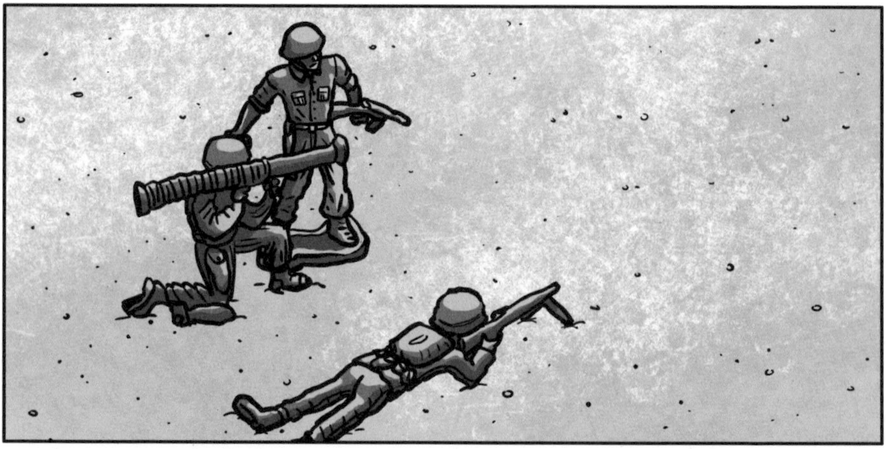

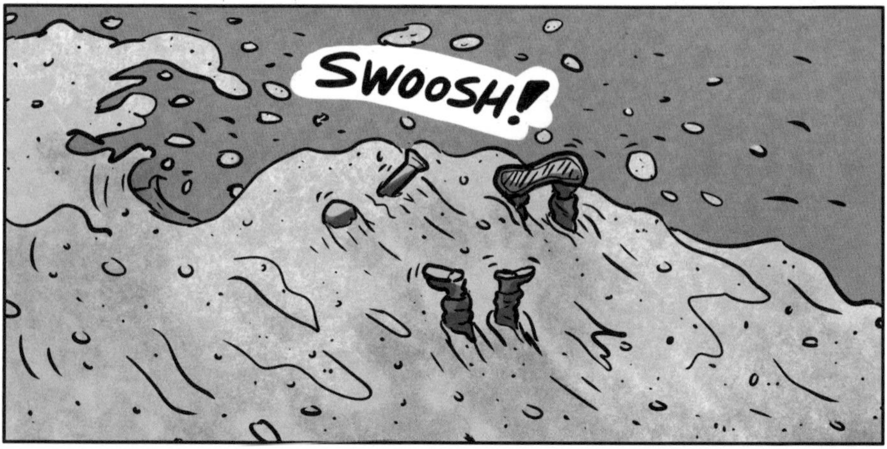
SWOOSH!

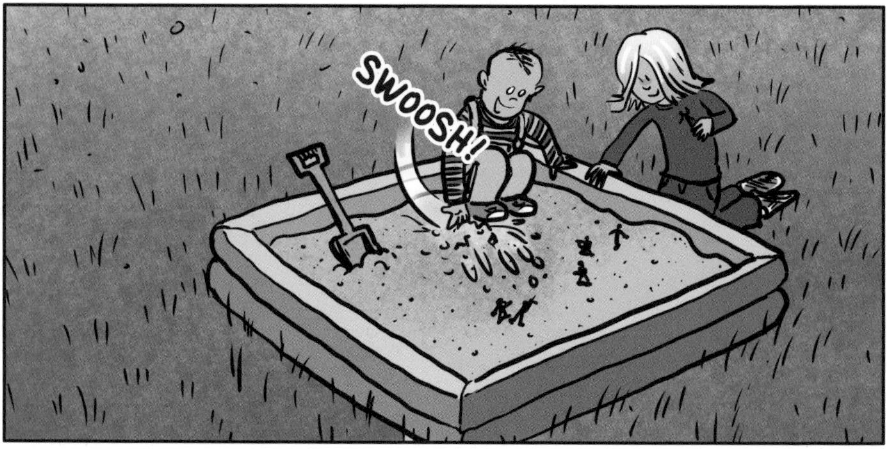
SWOOSH!

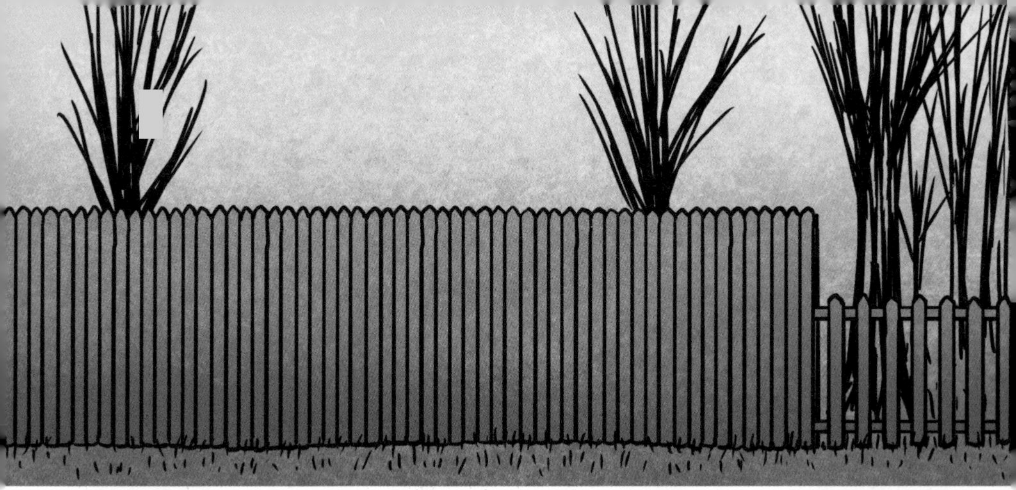

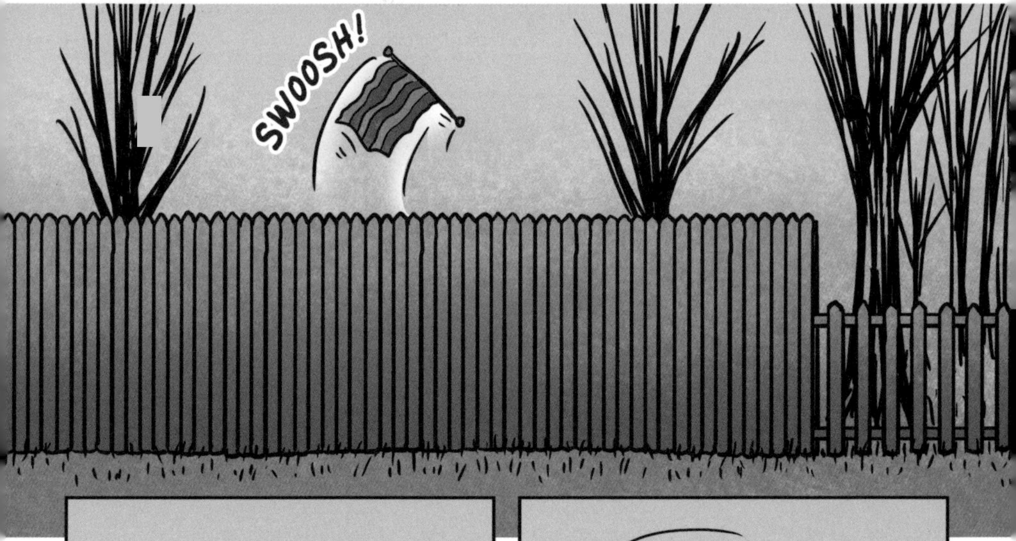
SWOOSH!

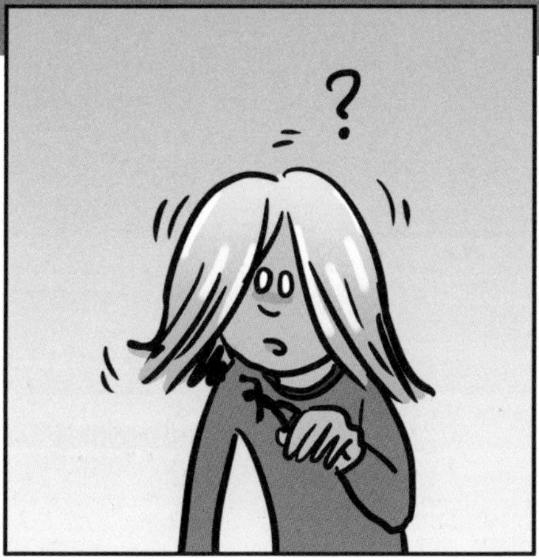
?

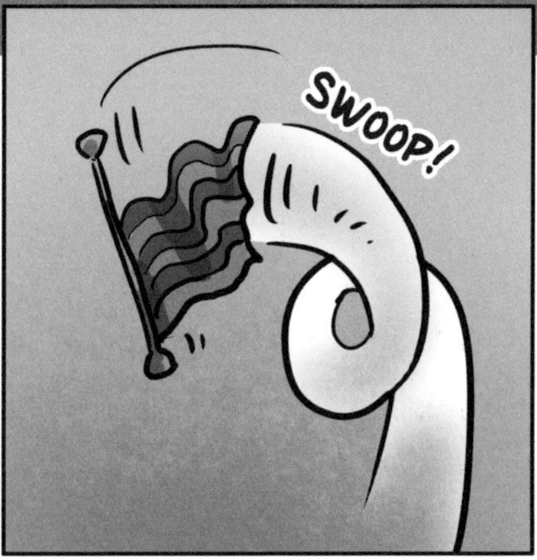
SWOOP!

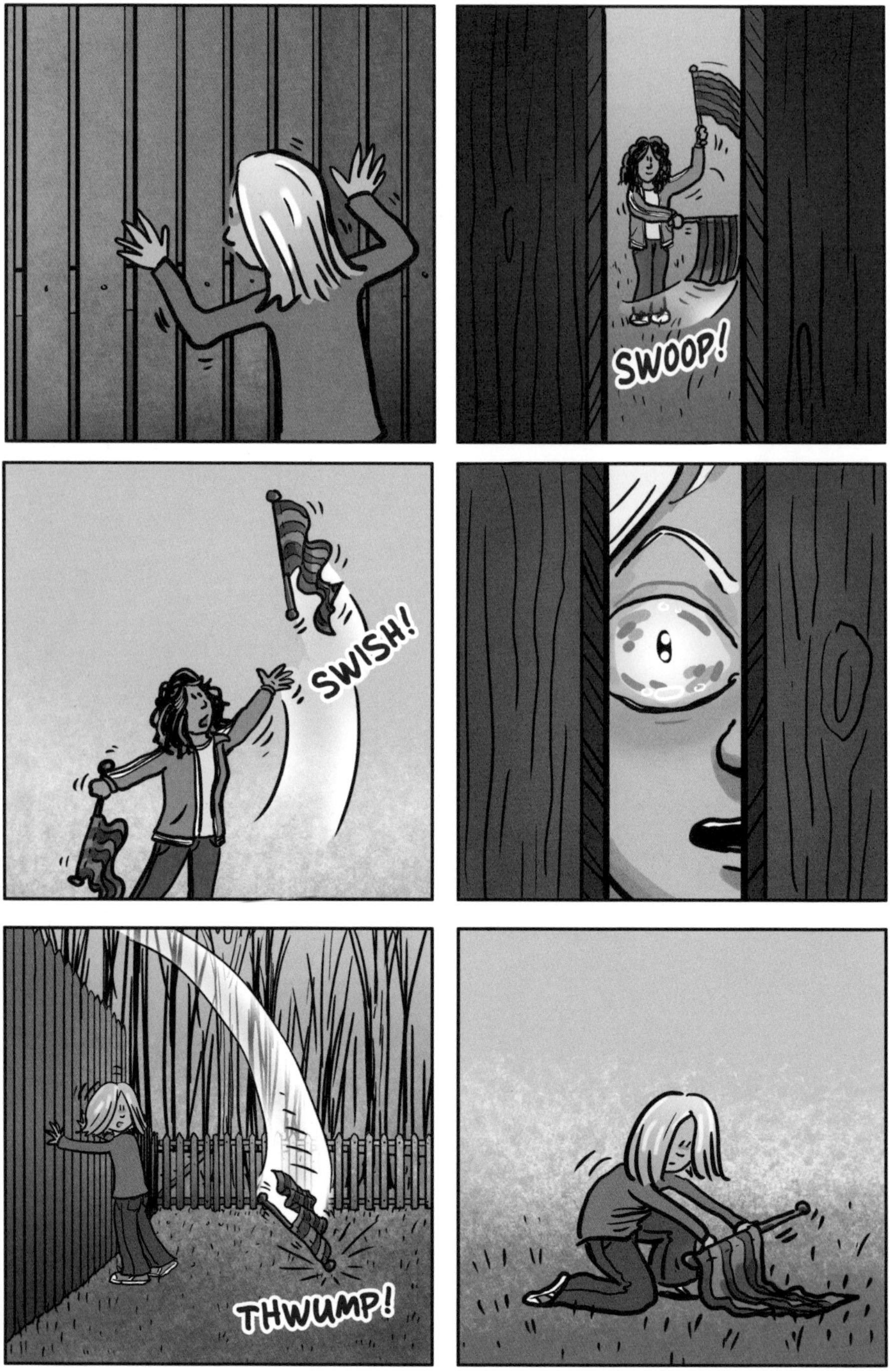
SWOOP!
SWISH!
THWUMP!

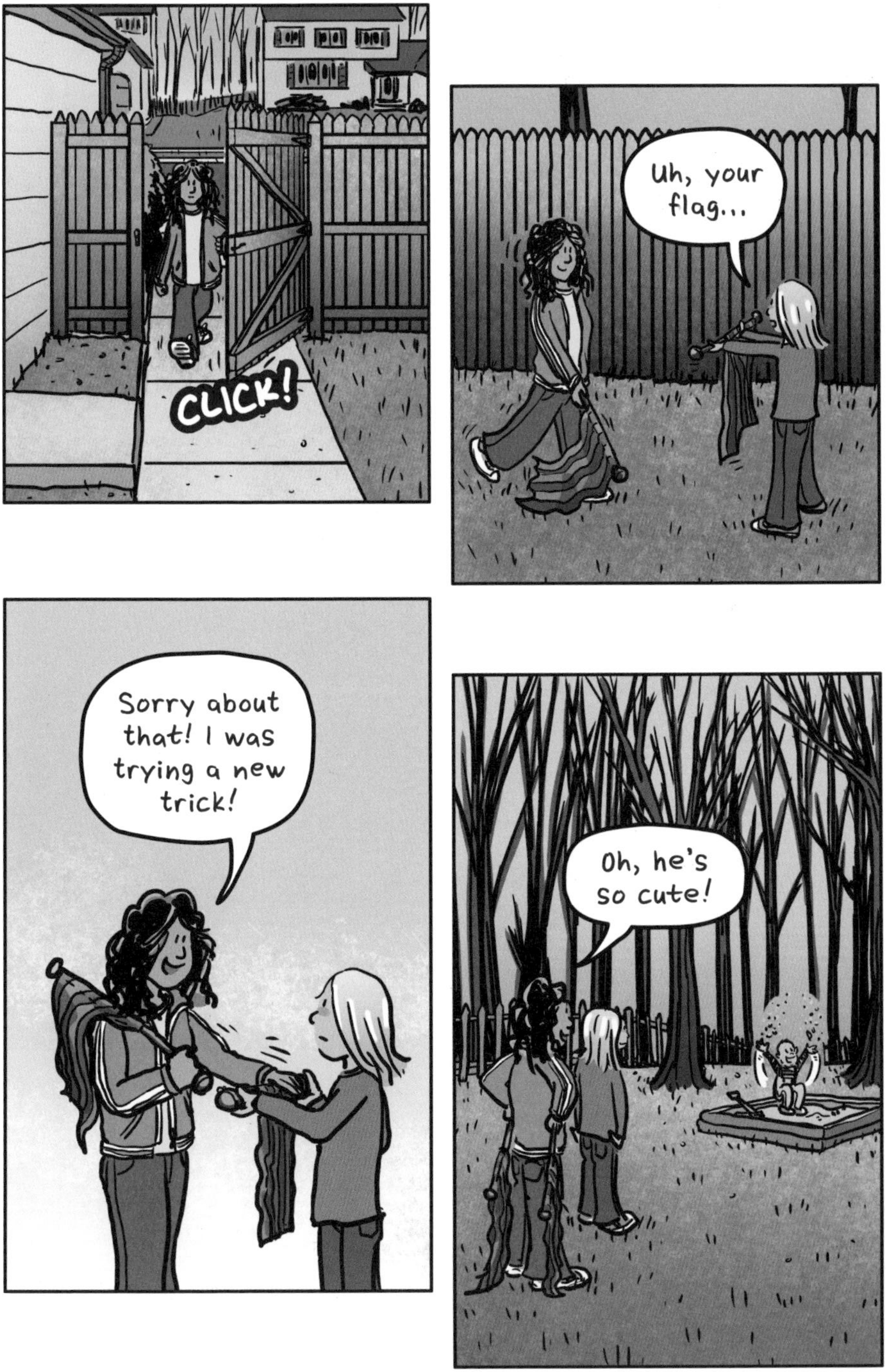
CLICK!
Uh, your flag...
Sorry about that! I was trying a new trick!
Oh, he's so cute!

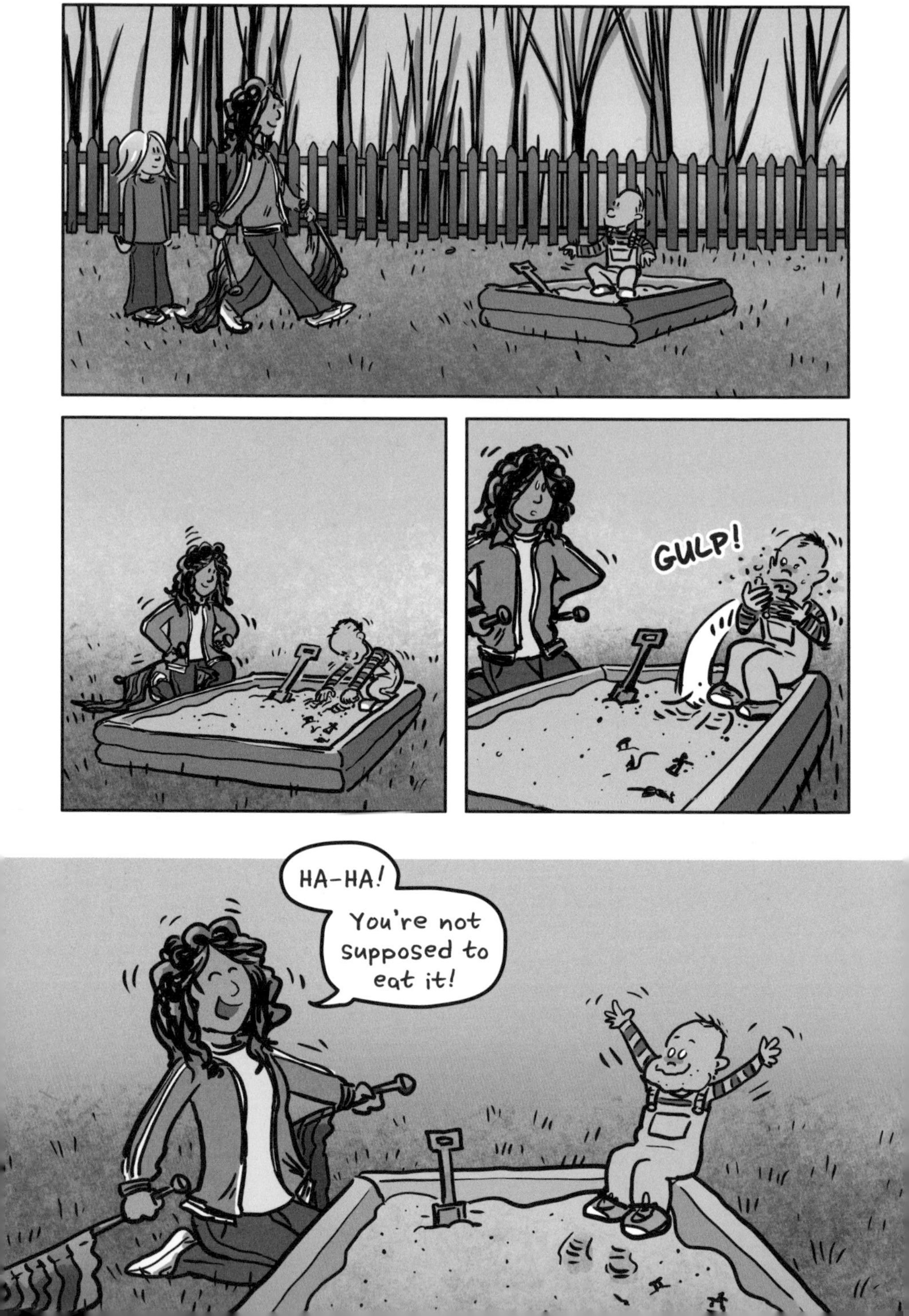
GULP!
HA-HA!
You're not supposed to eat it!

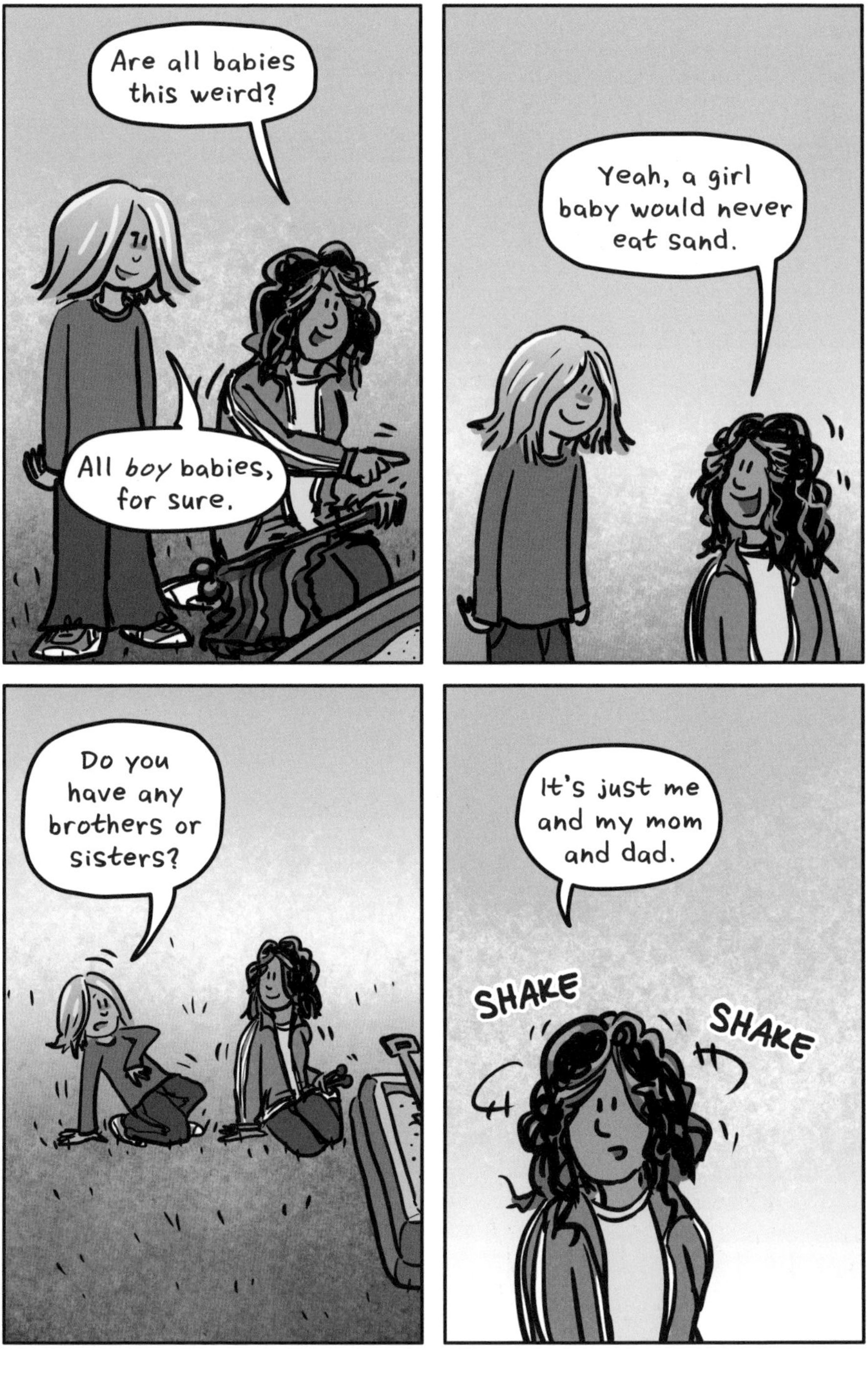
Are all babies this weird?
All *boy* babies, for sure.
Yeah, a girl baby would never eat sand.
Do you have any brothers or sisters?
It's just me and my mom and dad.
SHAKE
SHAKE

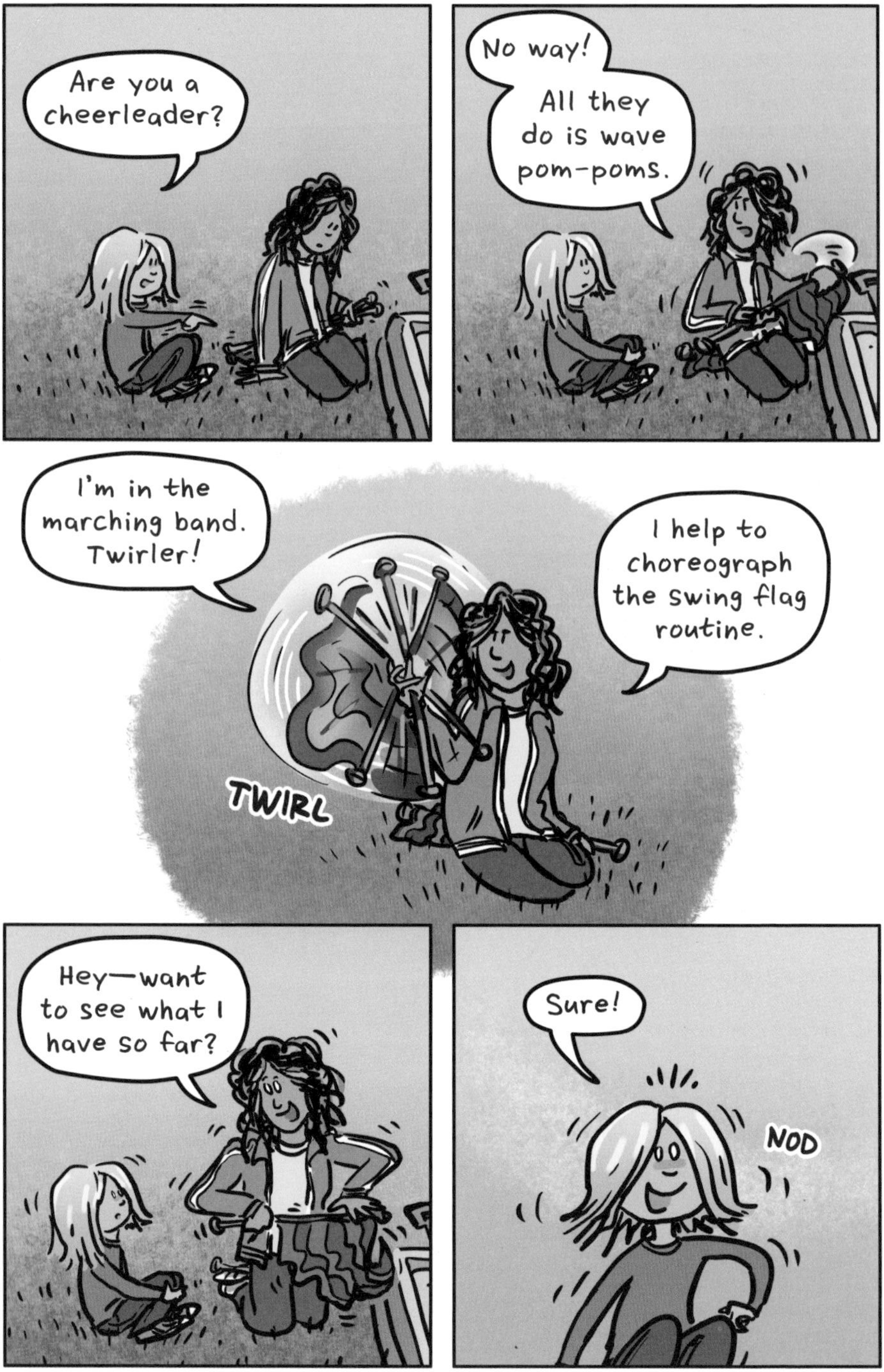
Are you a cheerleader?
No way!
All they do is wave pom-poms.
I'm in the marching band. Twirler!
I help to choreograph the swing flag routine.
TWIRL
Hey—want to see what I have so far?
Sure!
NOD

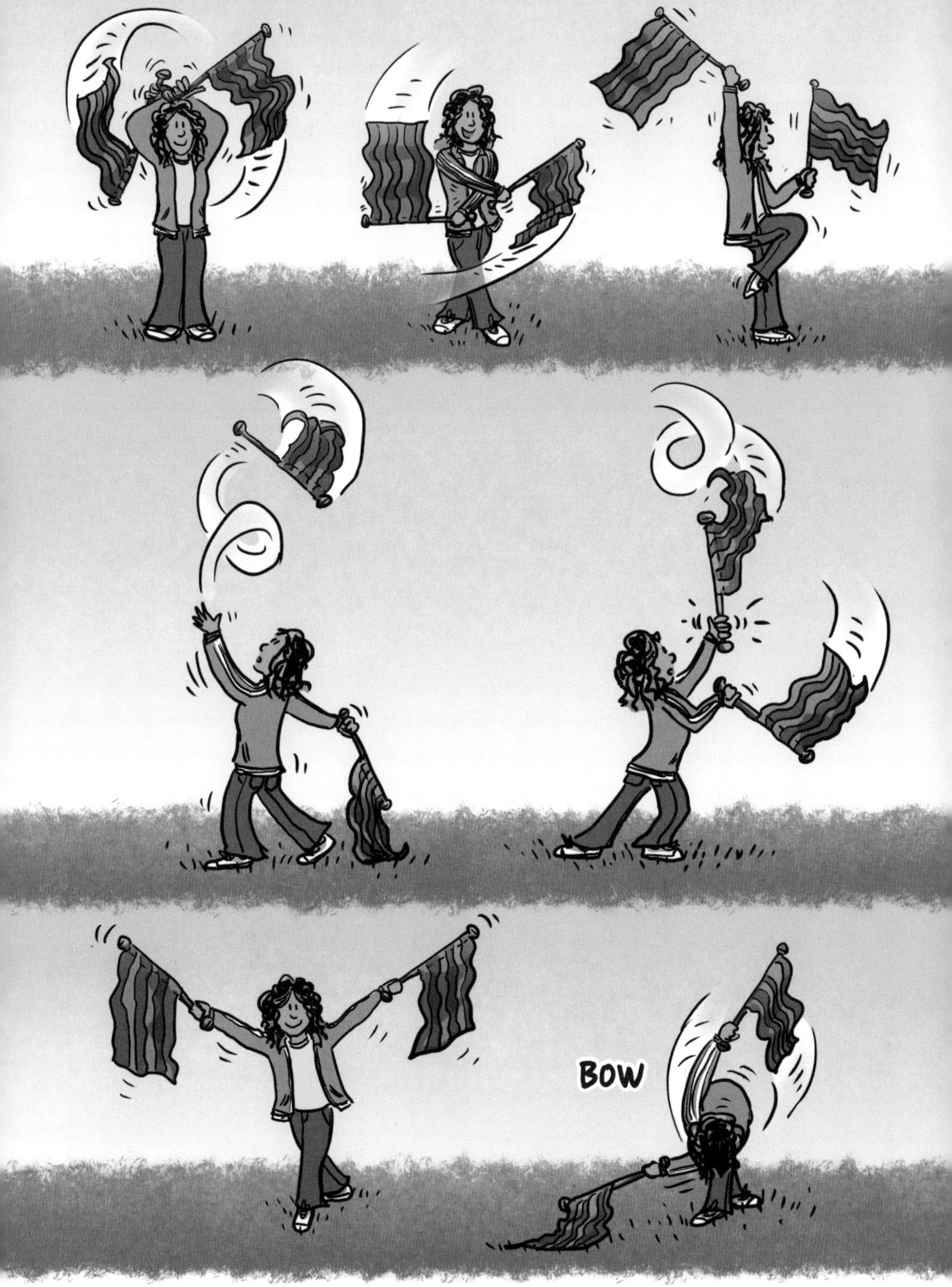
BOW

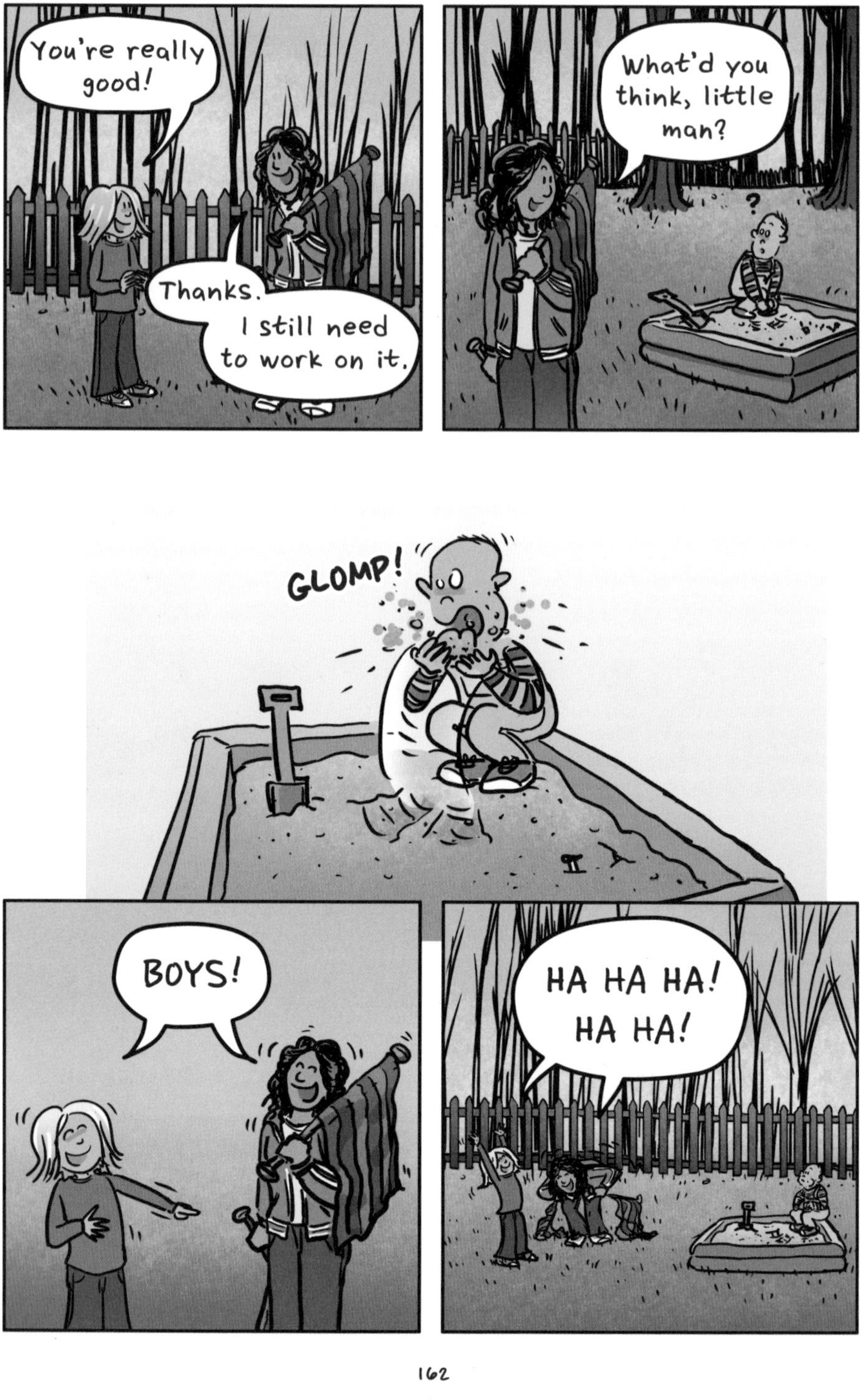

You're really good!
Thanks. I still need to work on it.
What'd you think, little man?
?
GLOMP!
BOYS!
HA HA HA! HA HA!

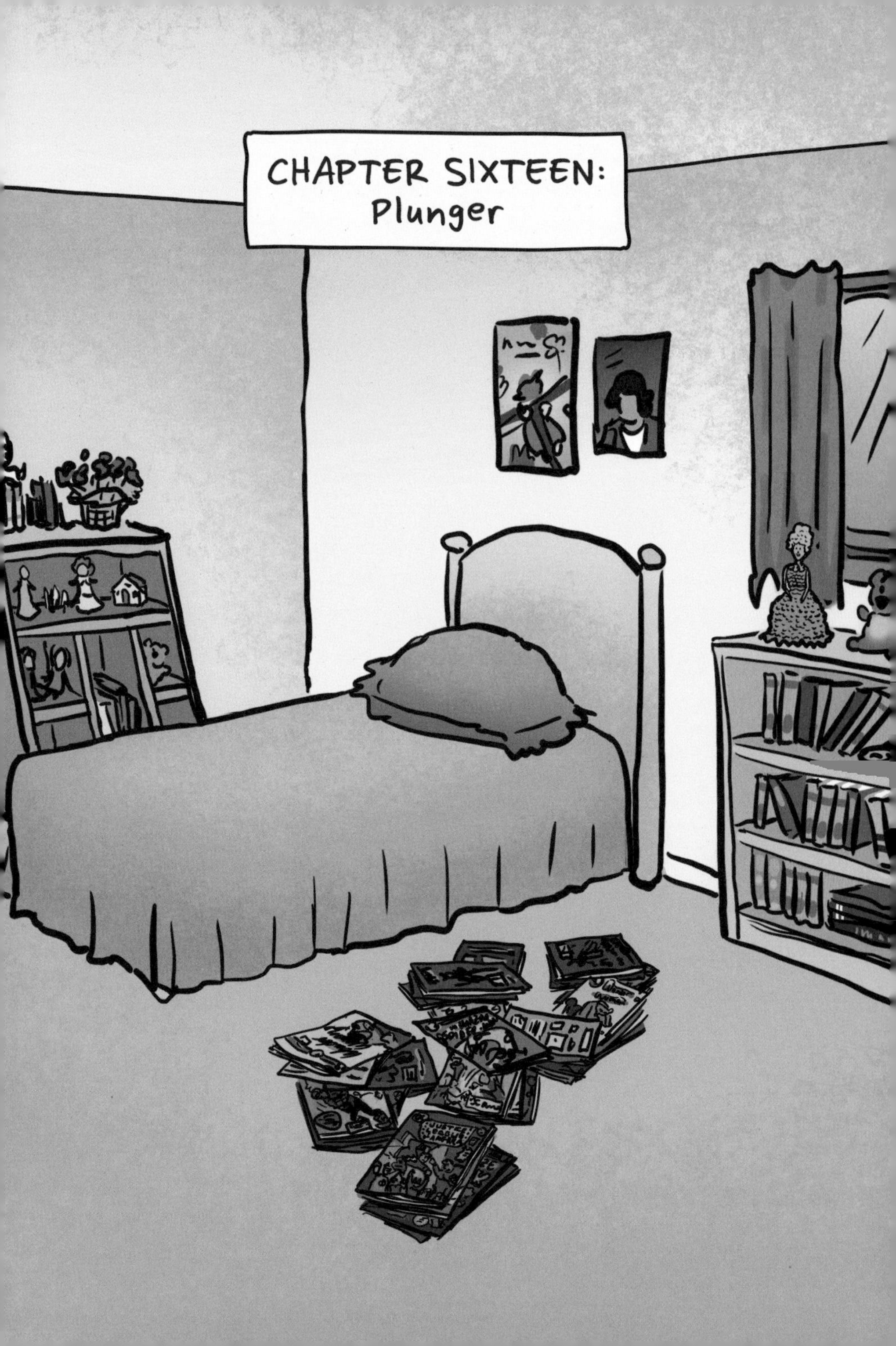
CHAPTER SIXTEEN:
Plunger

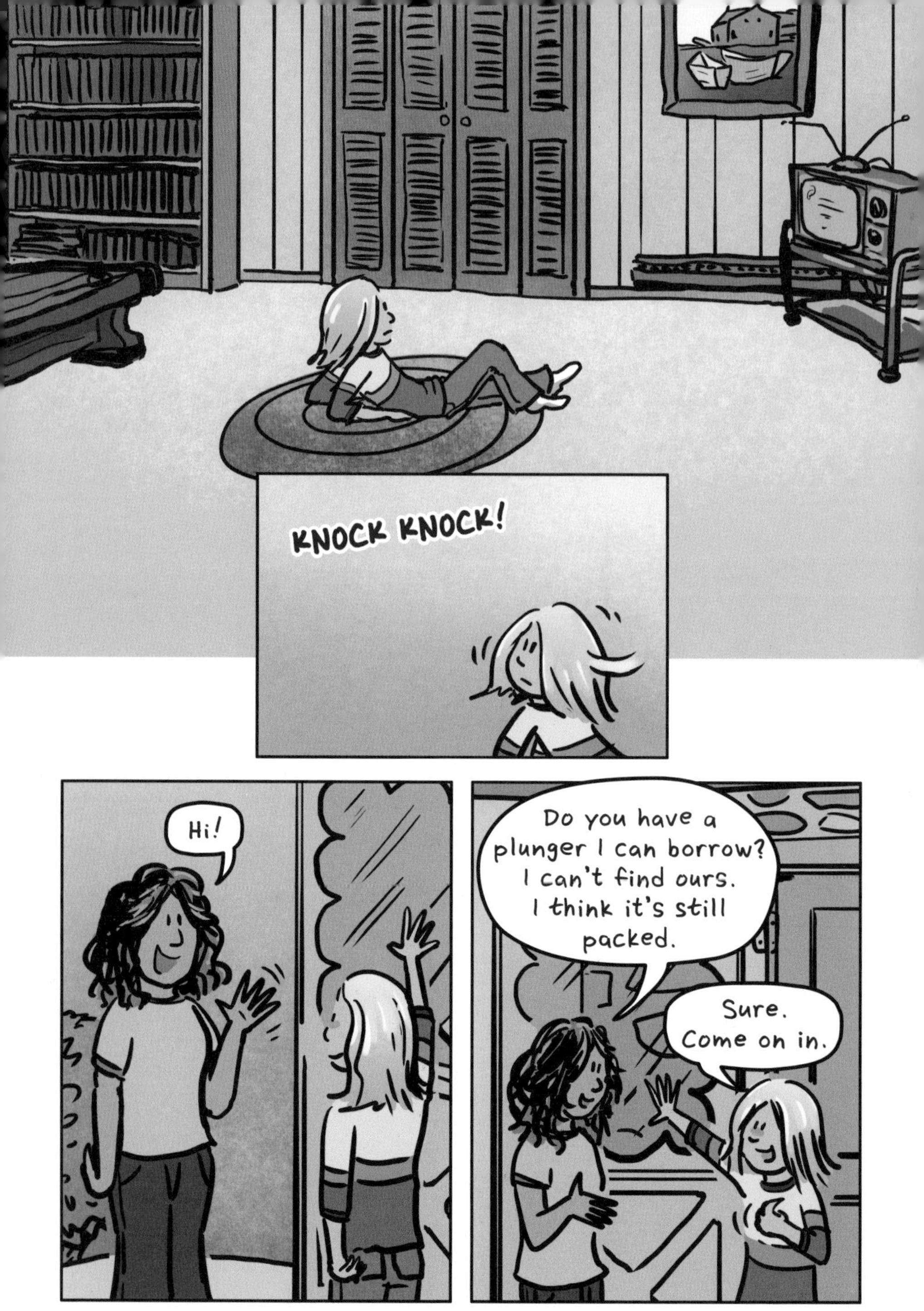
KNOCK KNOCK!
Hi!
Do you have a plunger I can borrow? I can't find ours. I think it's still packed.
Sure. Come on in.

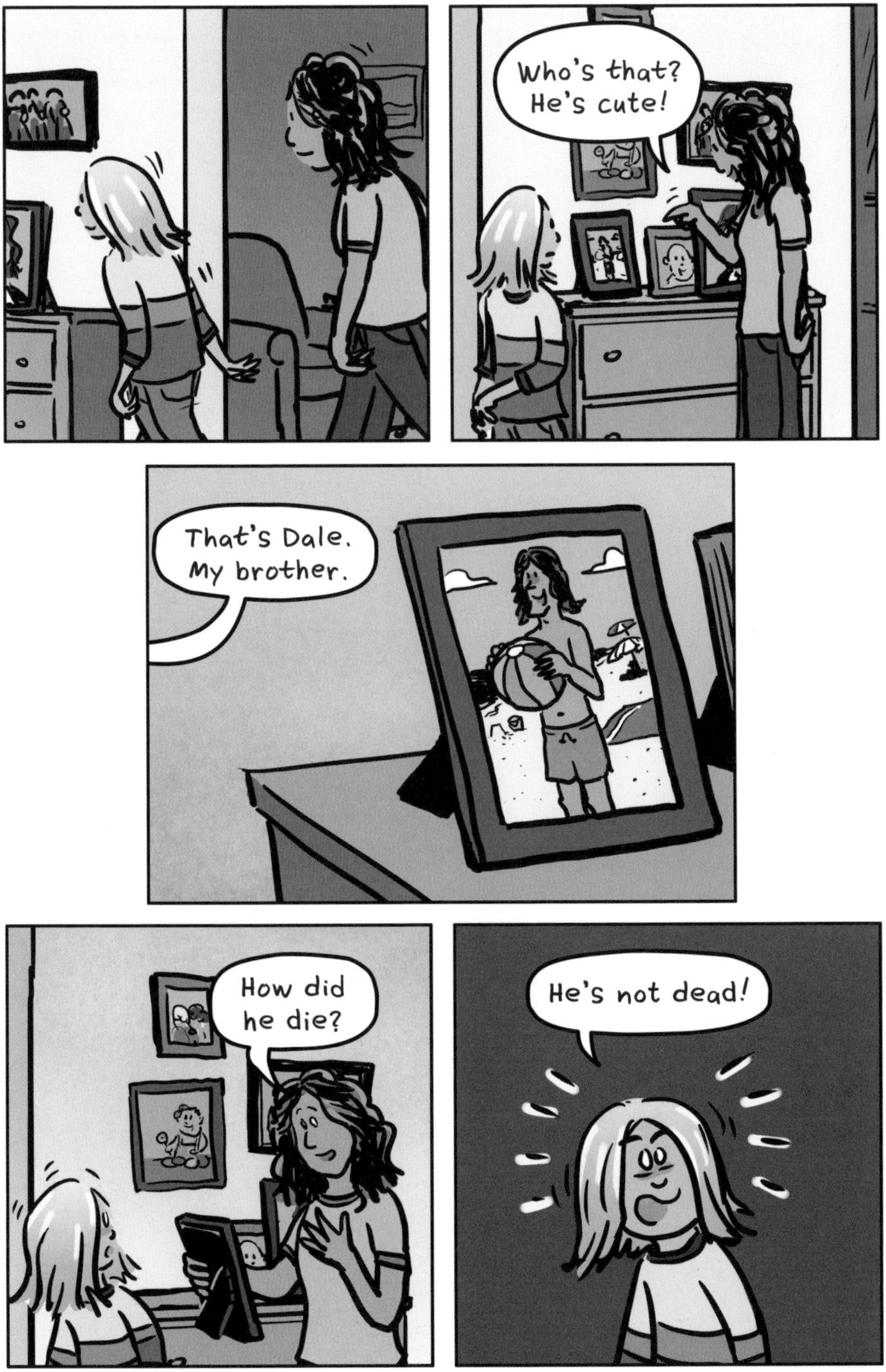
Who's that? He's cute!
That's Dale. My brother.
How did he die?
He's not dead!

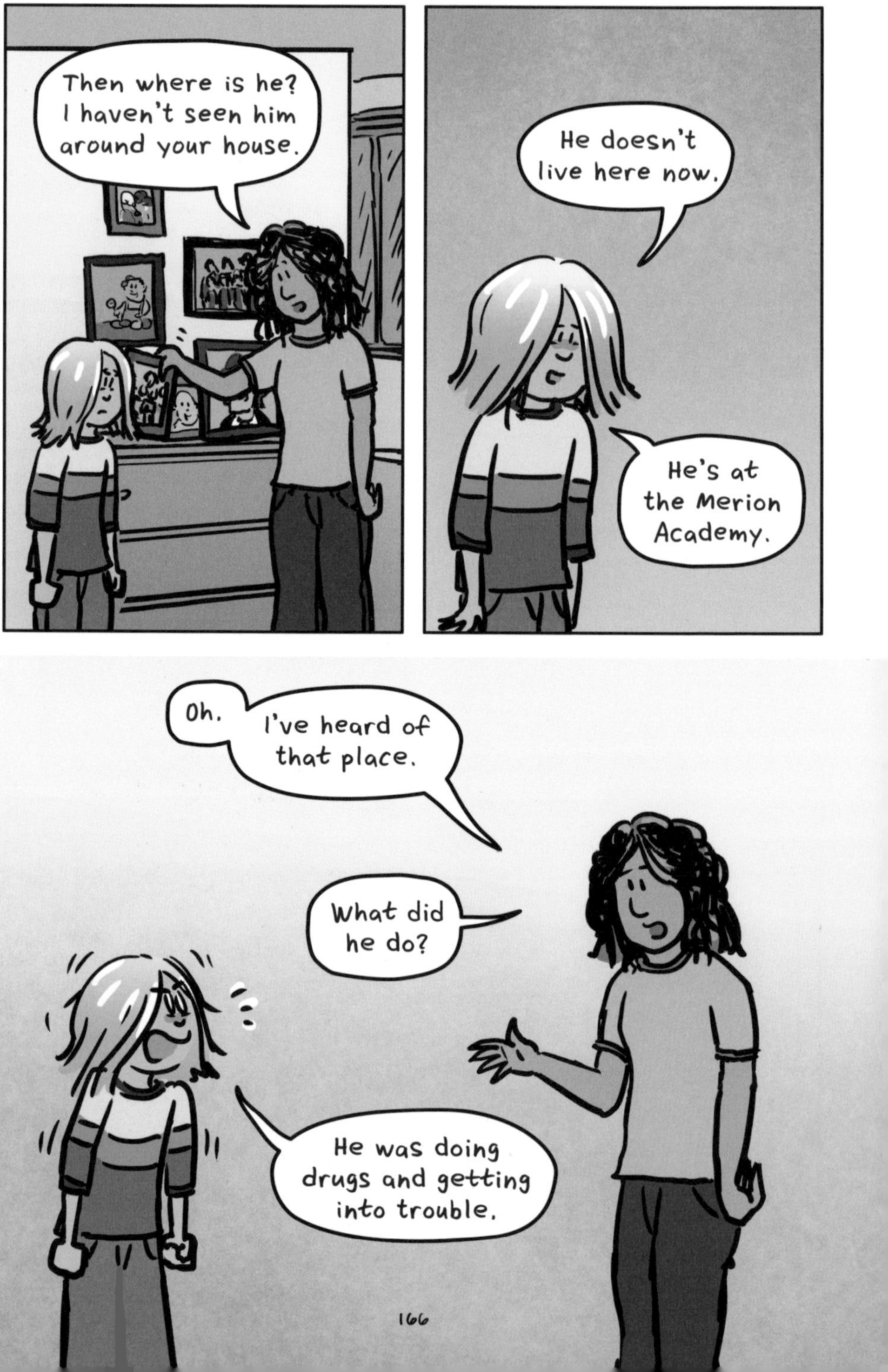
Then where is he? I haven't seen him around your house.
He doesn't live here now.
He's at the Merion Academy.
Oh.
I've heard of that place.
What did he do?
He was doing drugs and getting into trouble.

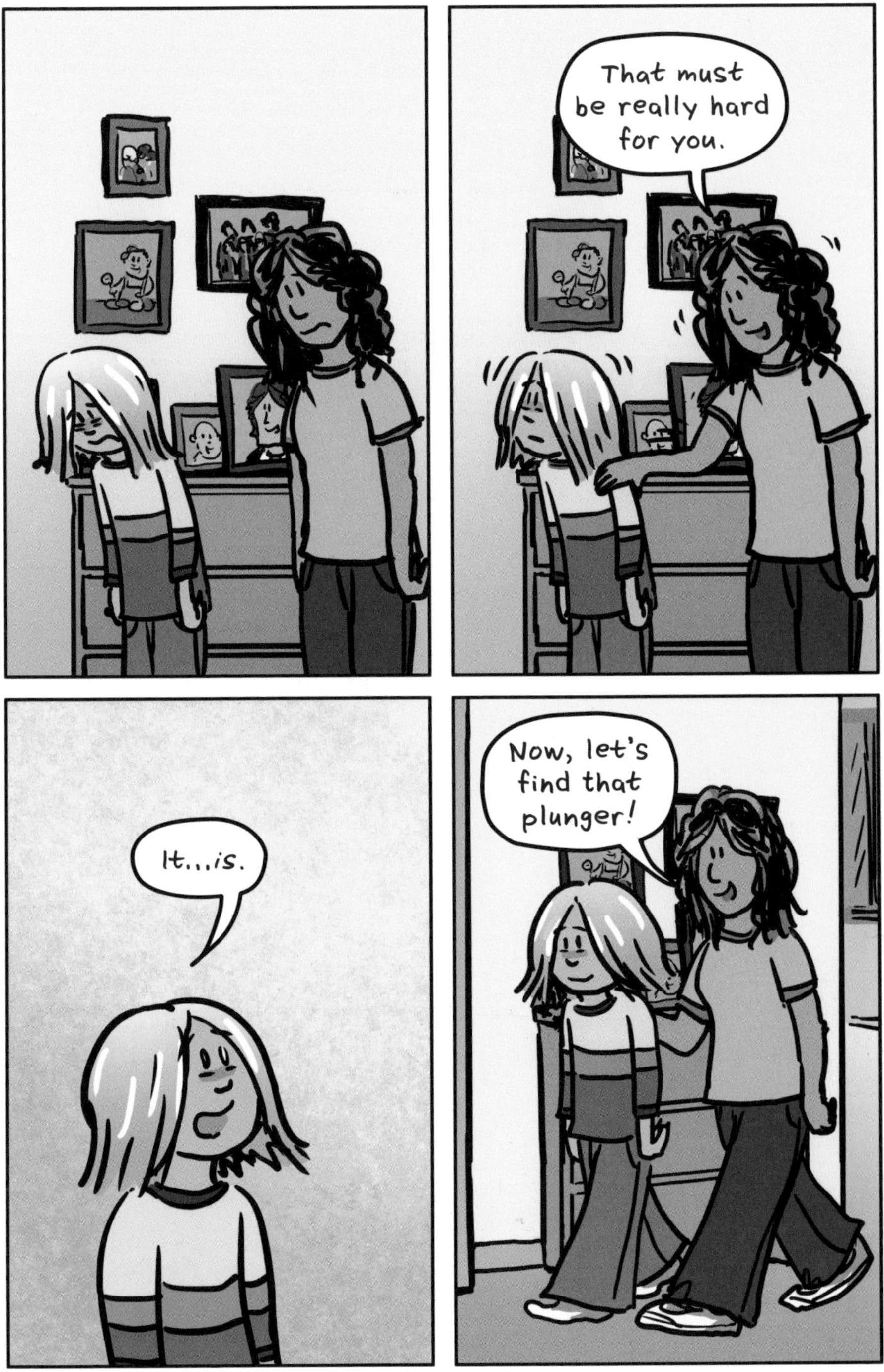
That must be really hard for you.
It...is.
Now, let's find that plunger!

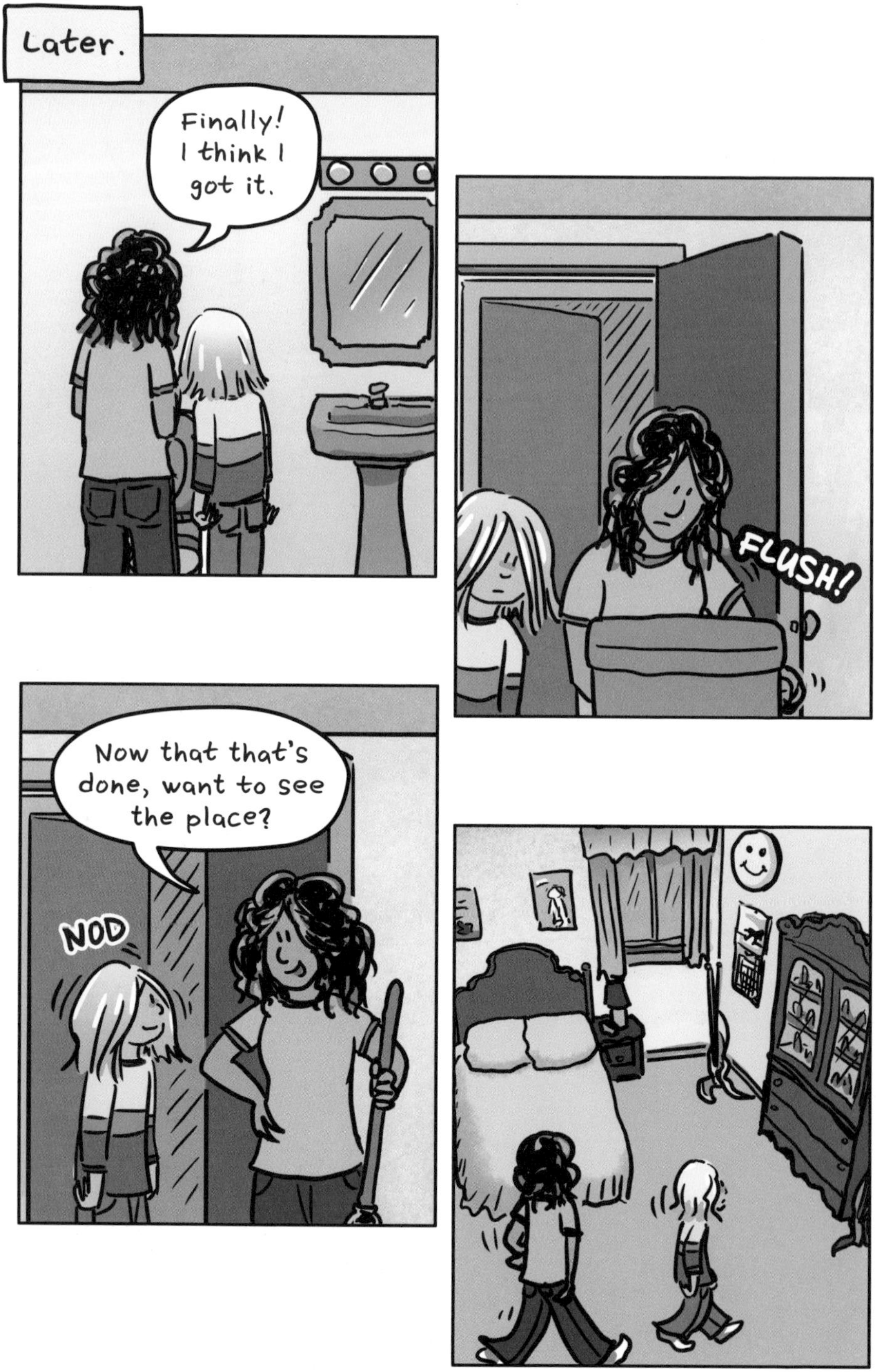
Later.
Finally! I think I got it.
FLUSH!
Now that that's done, want to see the place?
NOD

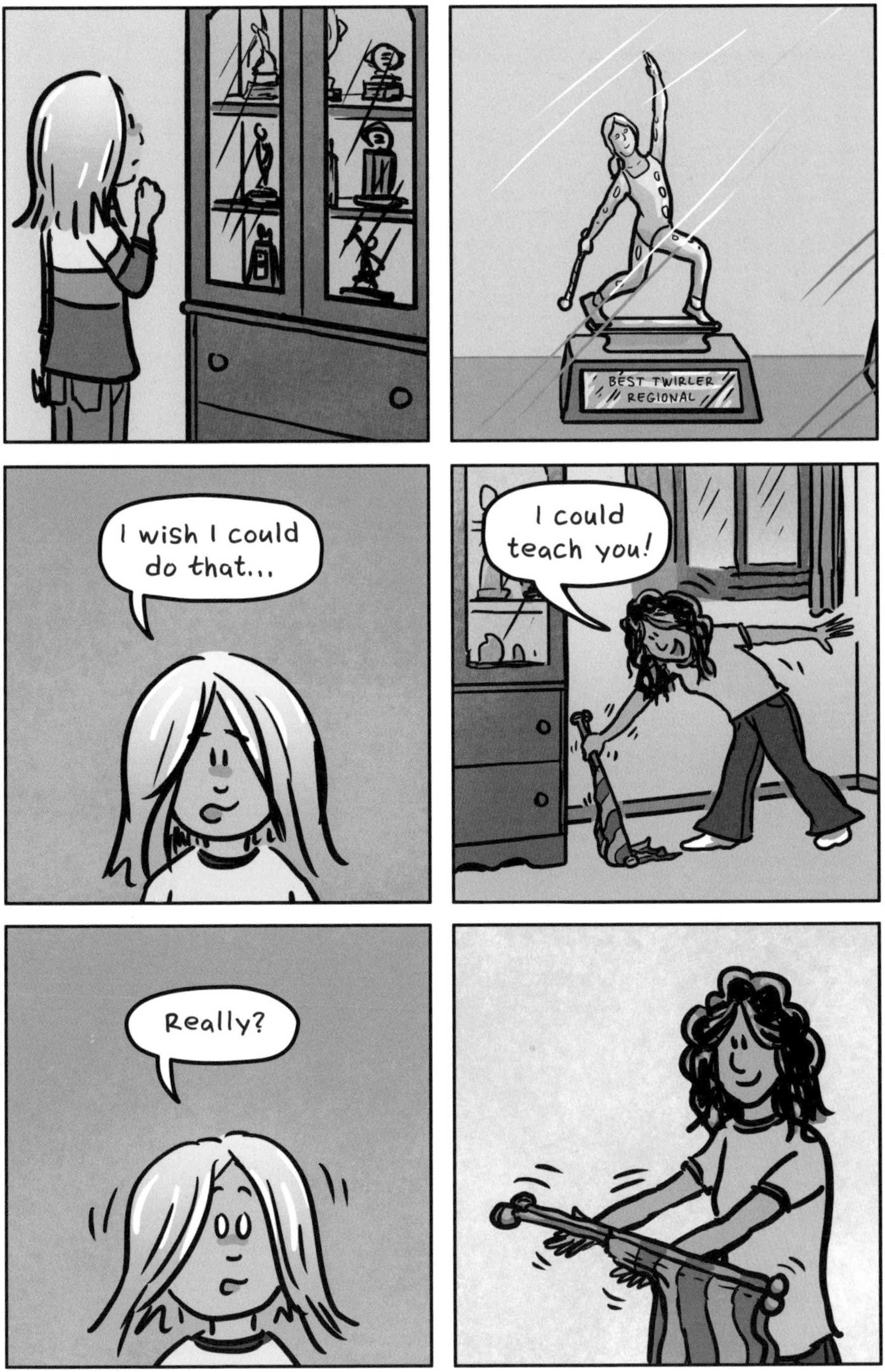
BEST TWIRLER
REGIONAL
I wish I could do that...
I could teach you!
Really?

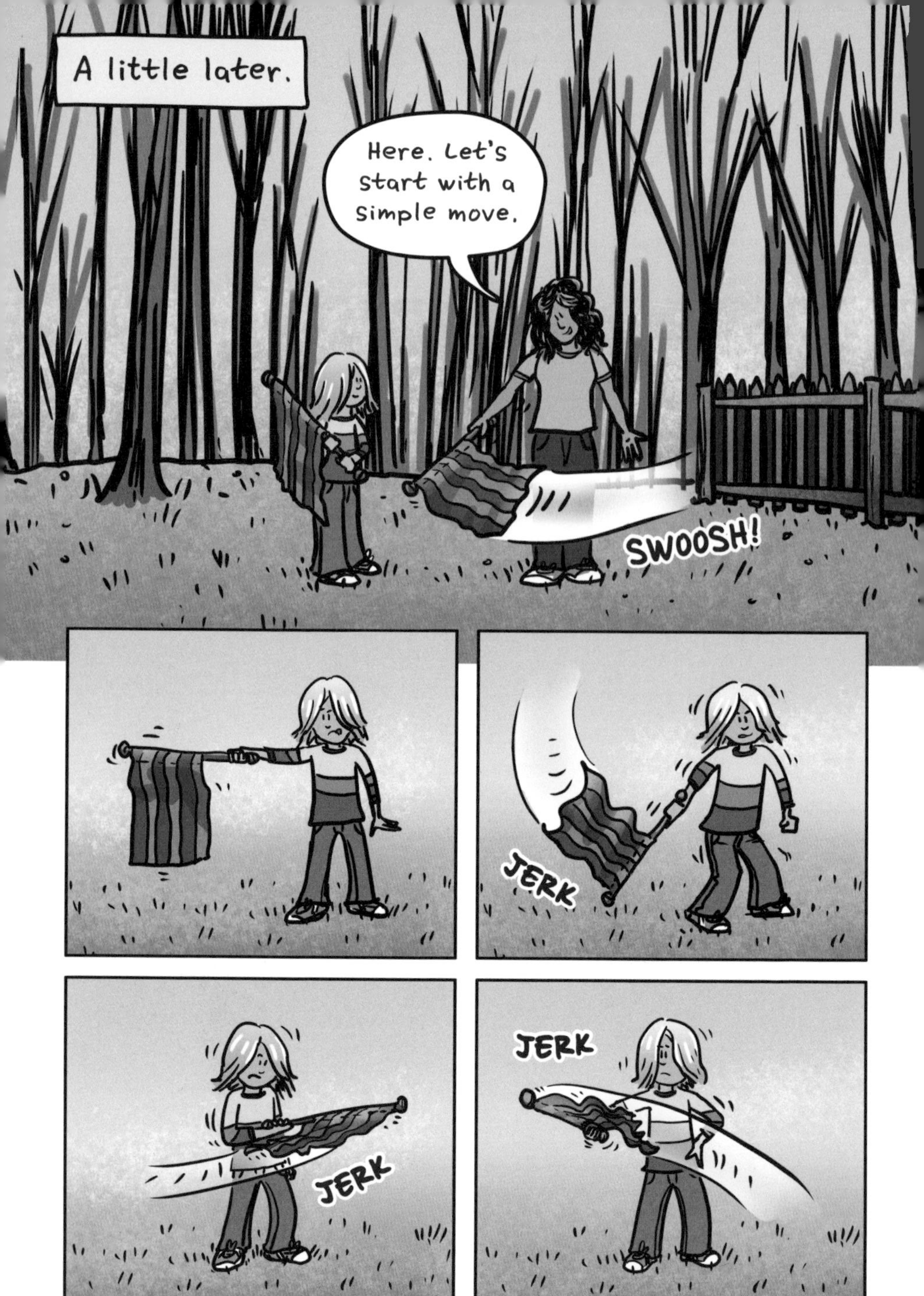
A little later.
Here. Let's start with a simple move.
SWOOSH!
JERK
JERK
JERK

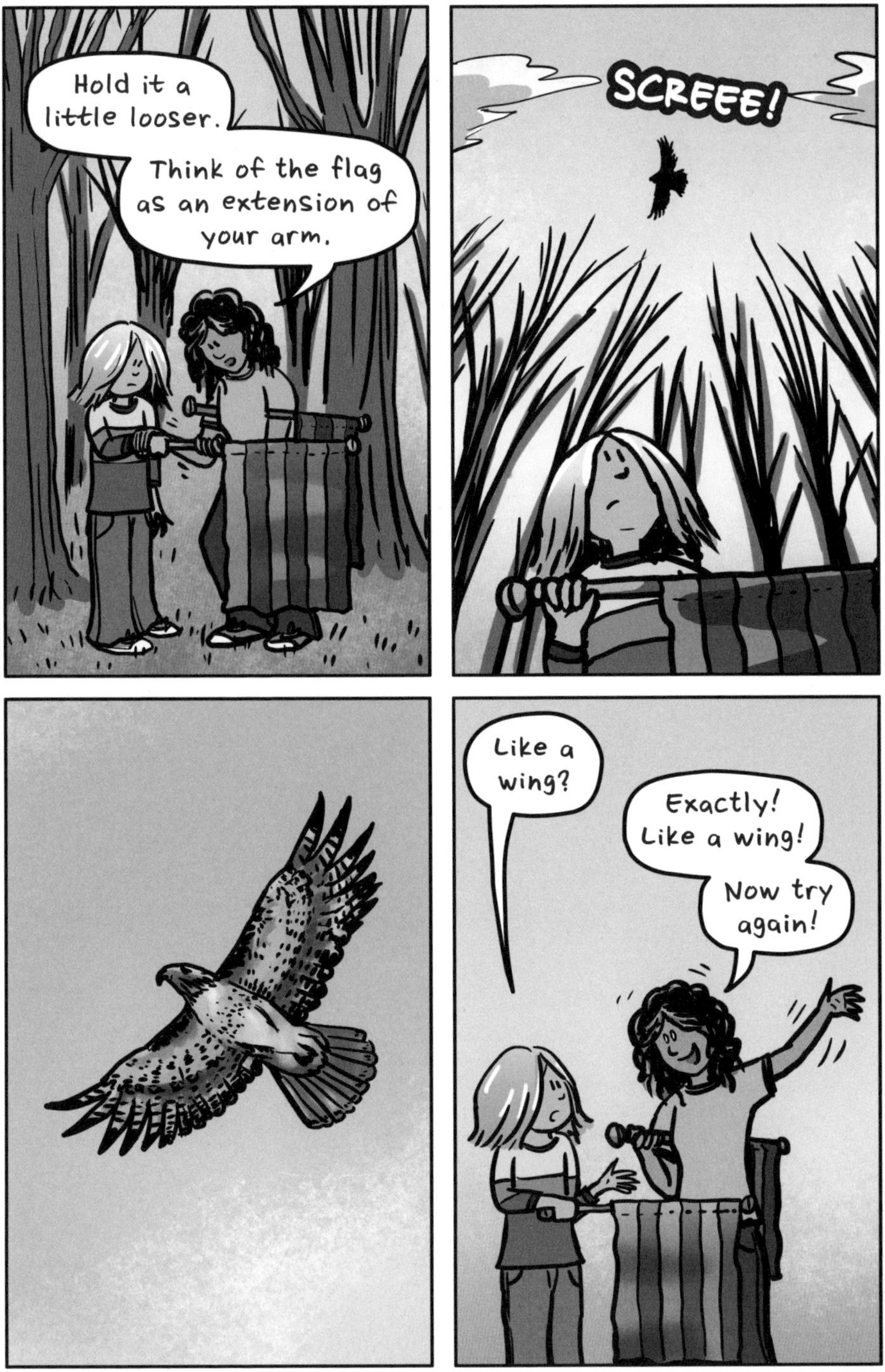
Hold it a little looser.
Think of the flag as an extension of your arm.
SCREEE!
Like a wing?
Exactly! Like a wing!
Now try again!

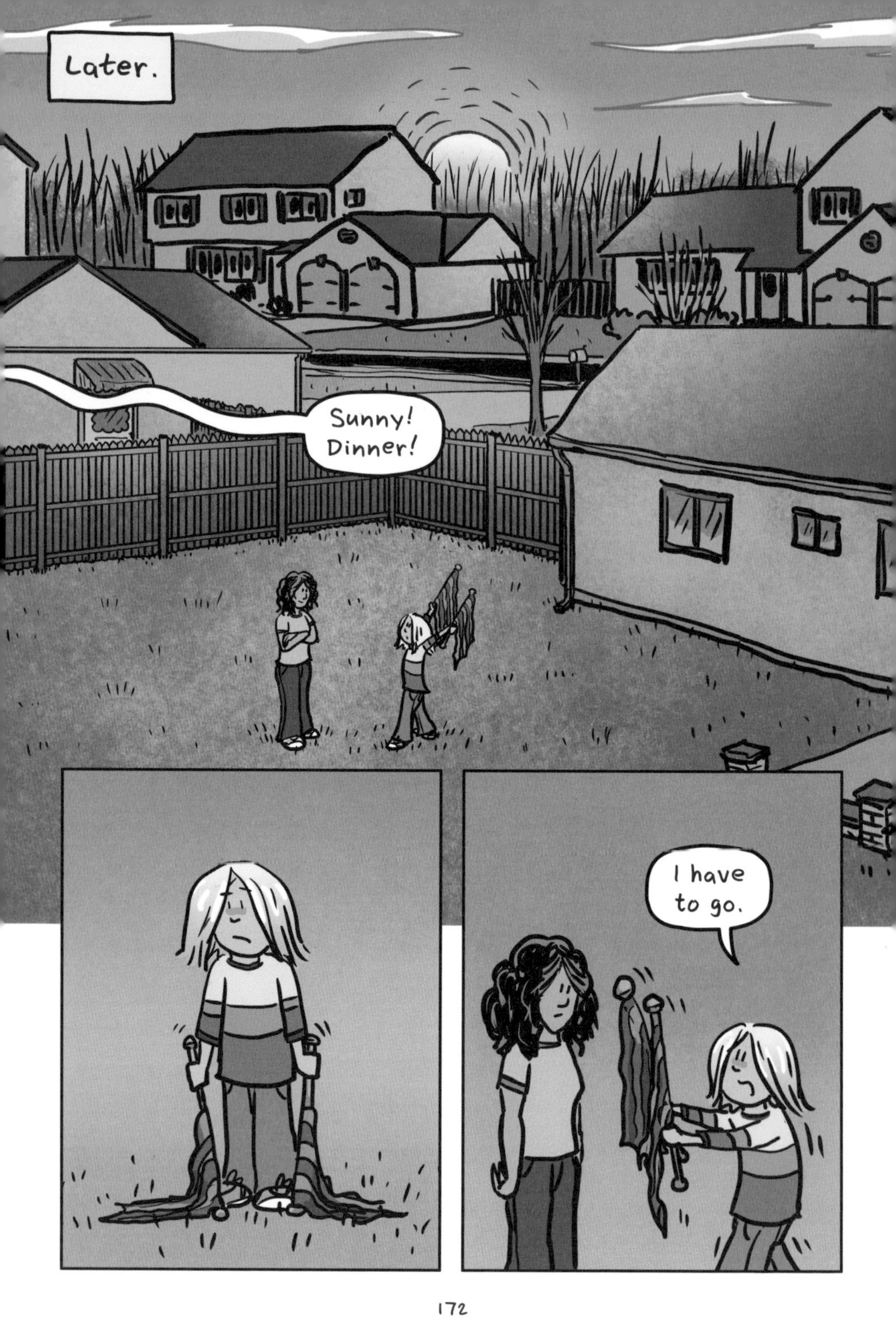
Later.
Sunny! Dinner!
I have to go.

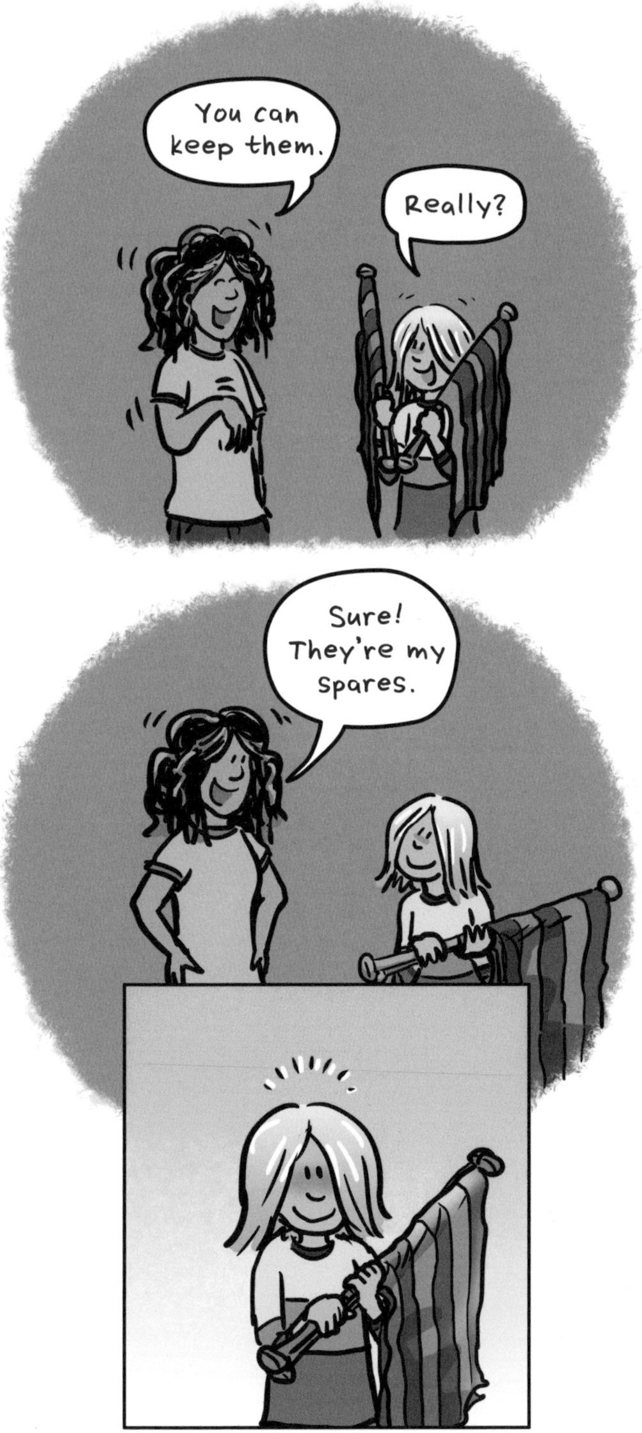
You can keep them.
Really?
Sure! They're my spares.

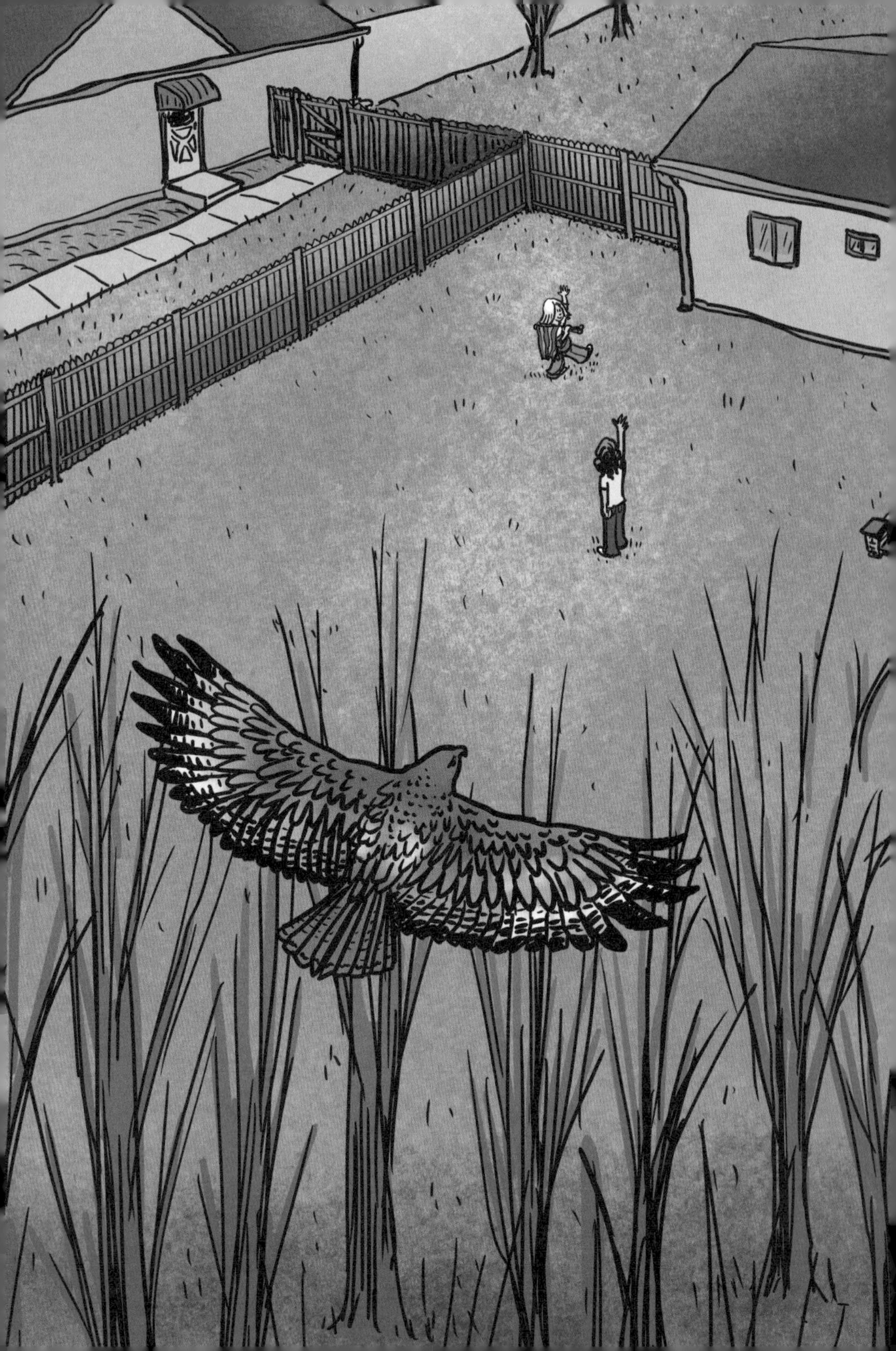

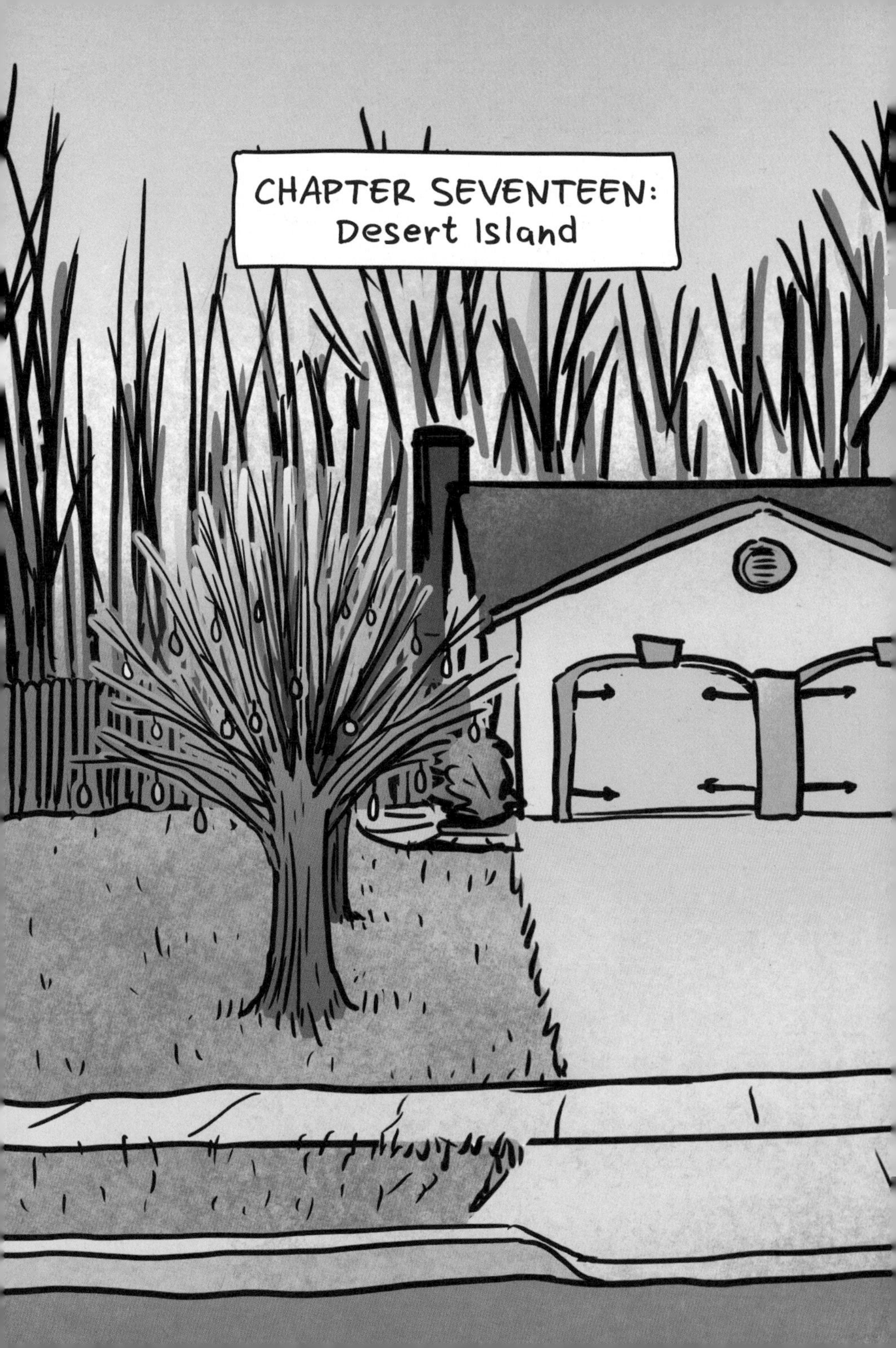
CHAPTER SEVENTEEN:
Desert Island

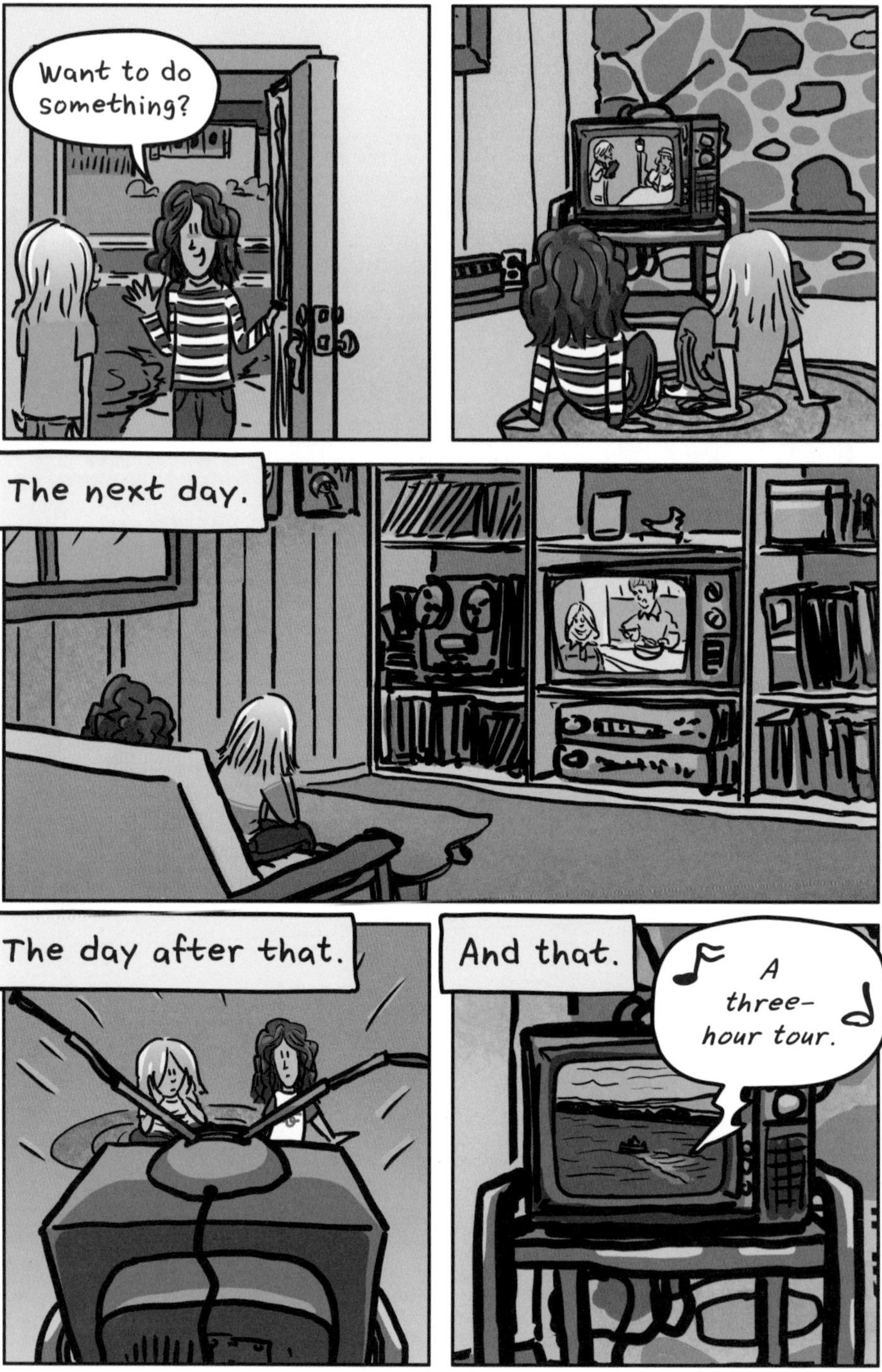
Want to do something?
The next day.
The day after that.
And that.
A three-hour tour.

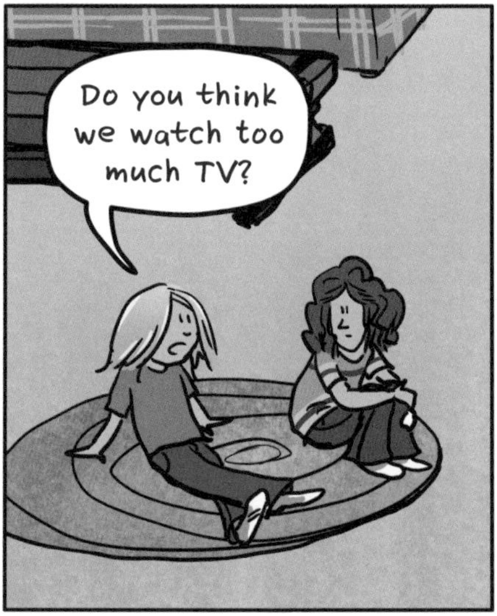
Do you think we watch too much TV?

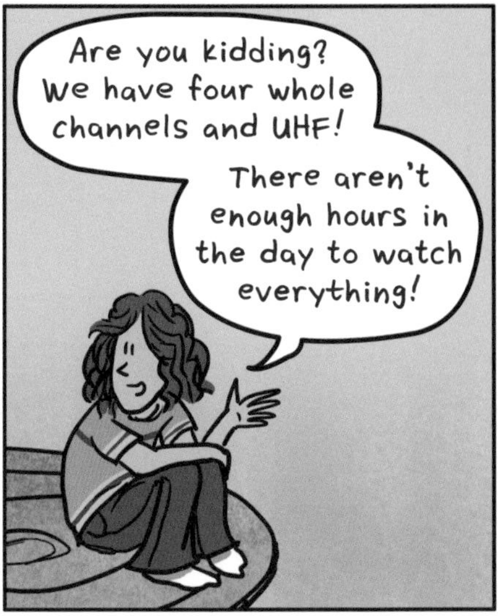
Are you kidding? We have four whole channels and UHF!
There aren't enough hours in the day to watch everything!

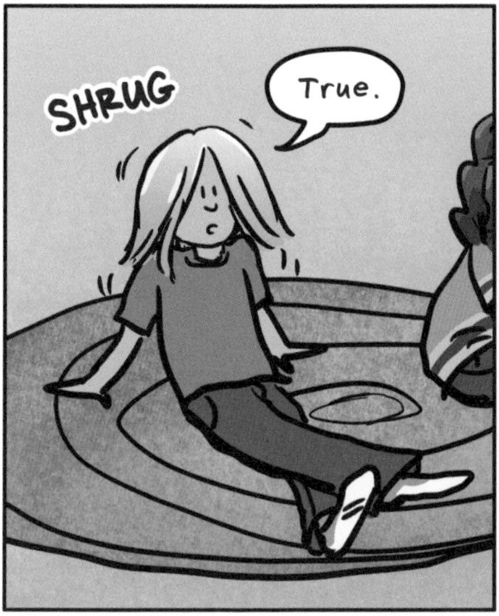
SHRUG
True.

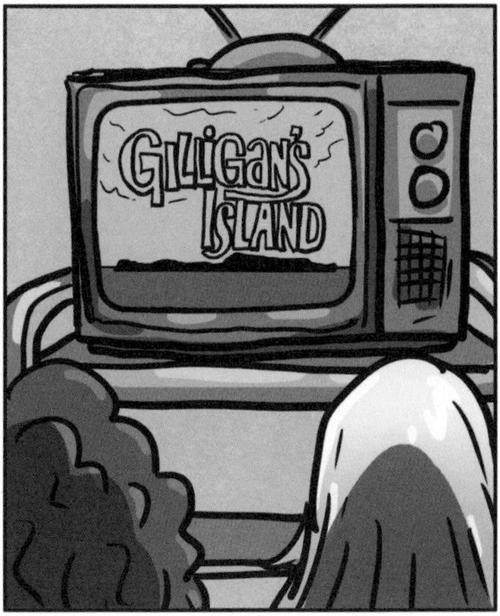
GILLIGAN'S ISLAND

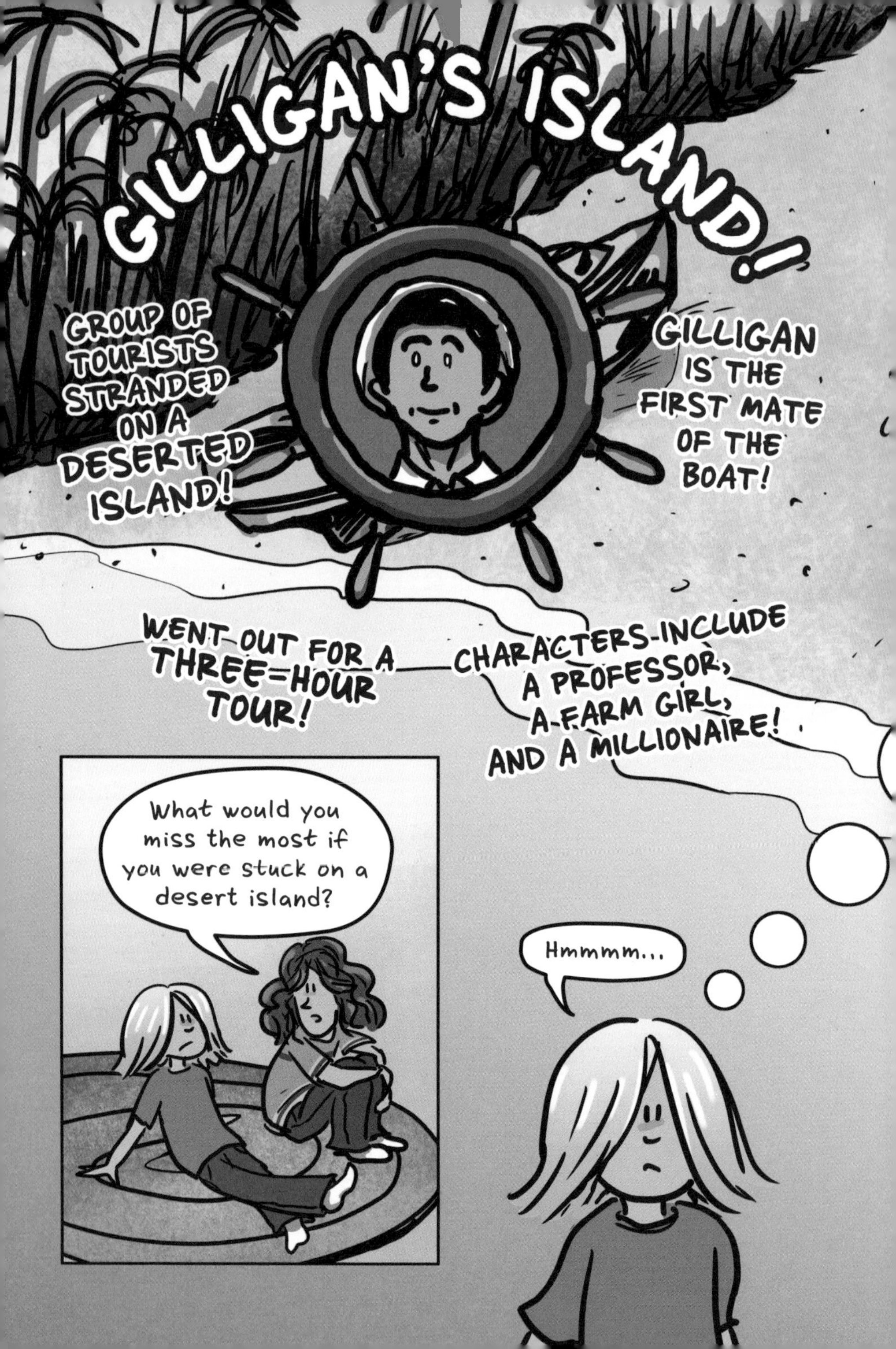
GILLIGAN'S ISLAND!
GROUP OF TOURISTS STRANDED ON A DESERTED ISLAND!
GILLIGAN IS THE FIRST MATE OF THE BOAT!
WENT OUT FOR A THREE-HOUR TOUR!
CHARACTERS INCLUDE A PROFESSOR, A FARM GIRL, AND A MILLIONAIRE!
What would you miss the most if you were stuck on a desert island?
Hmmmm...

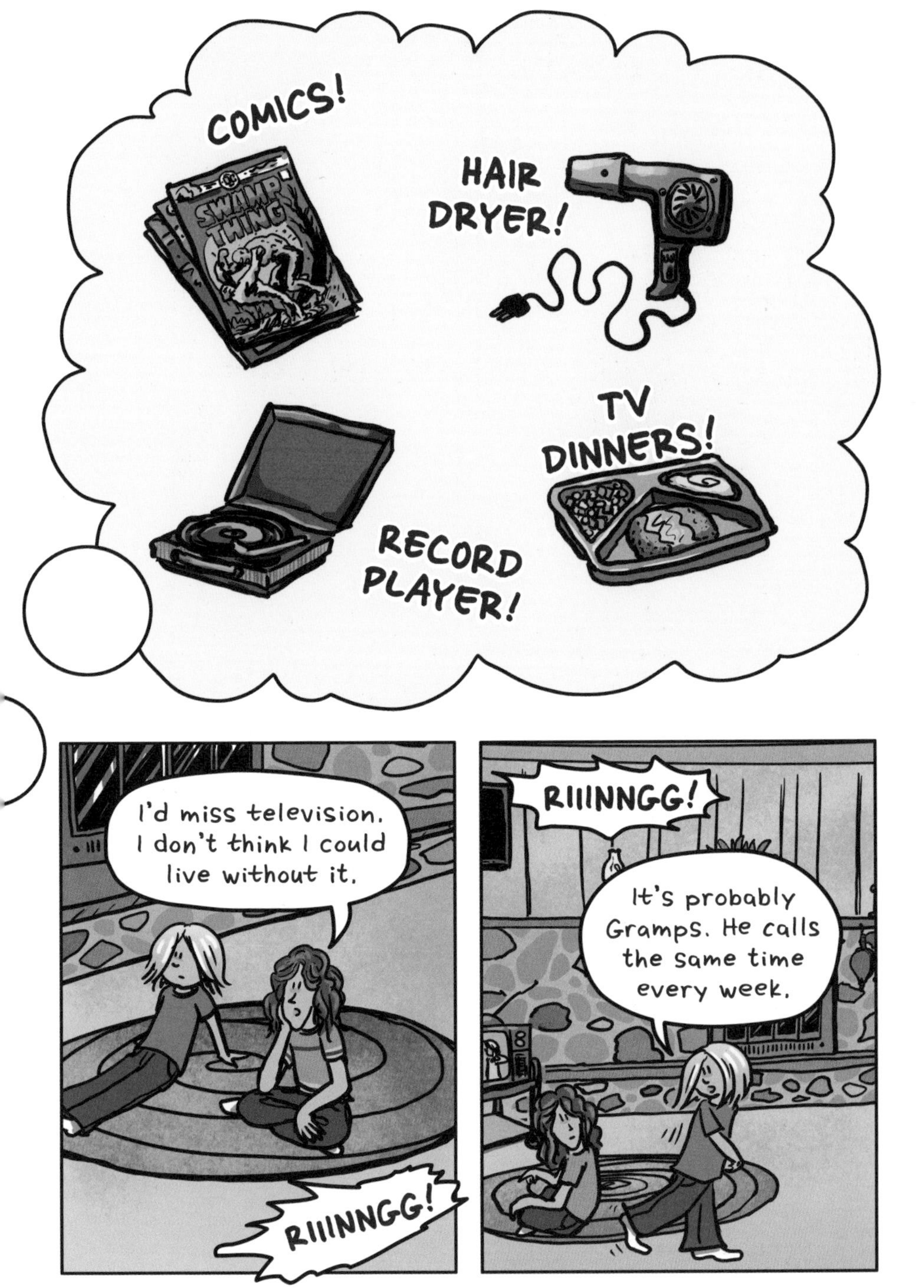
COMICS!
HAIR DRYER!
TV DINNERS!
RECORD PLAYER!
I'd miss television. I don't think I could live without it.
RIIINNGG!
RIIINNGG!
It's probably Gramps. He calls the same time every week.

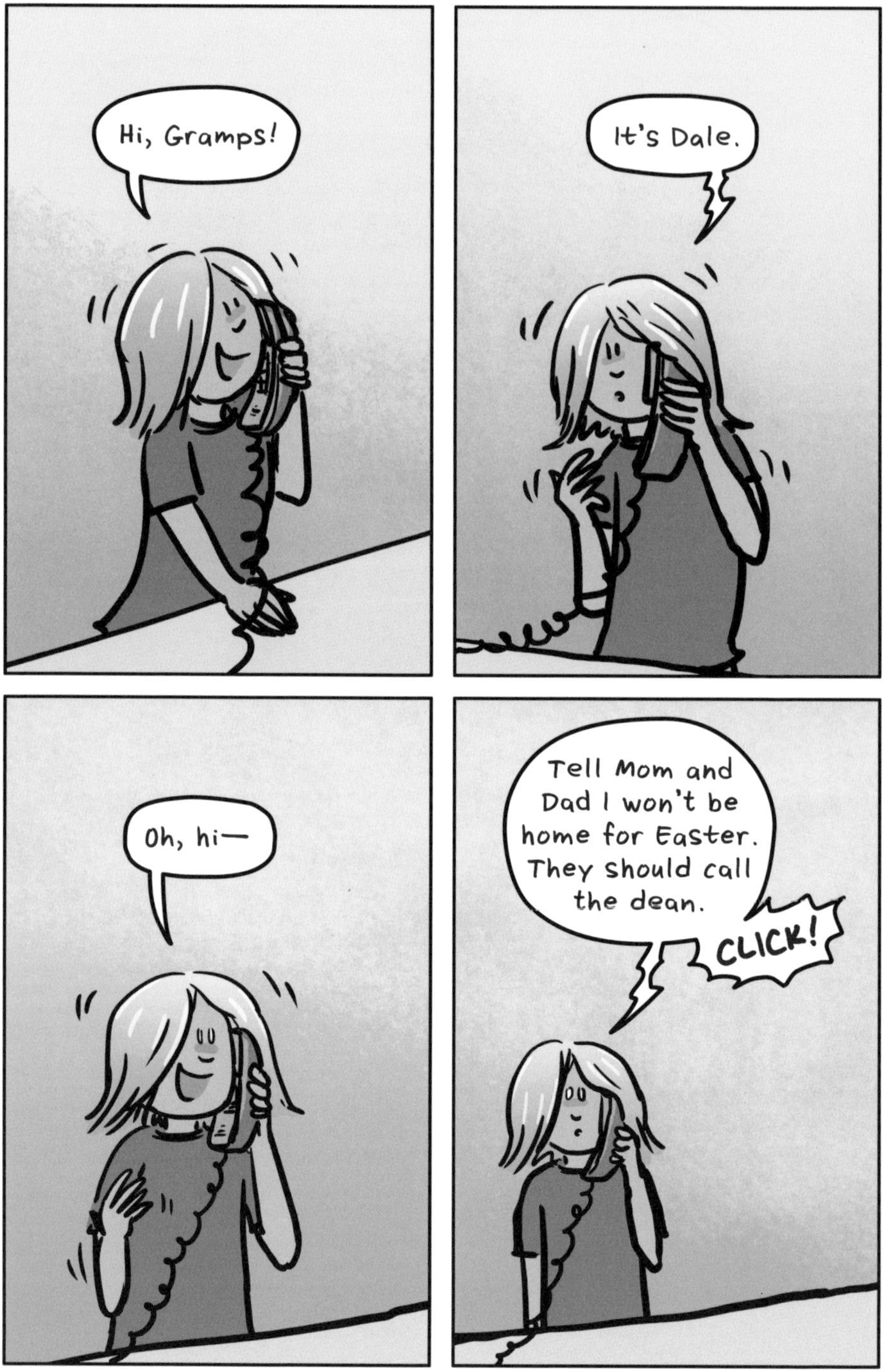
Hi, Gramps!
It's Dale.
Oh, hi—
Tell Mom and Dad I won't be home for Easter. They should call the dean.
CLICK!

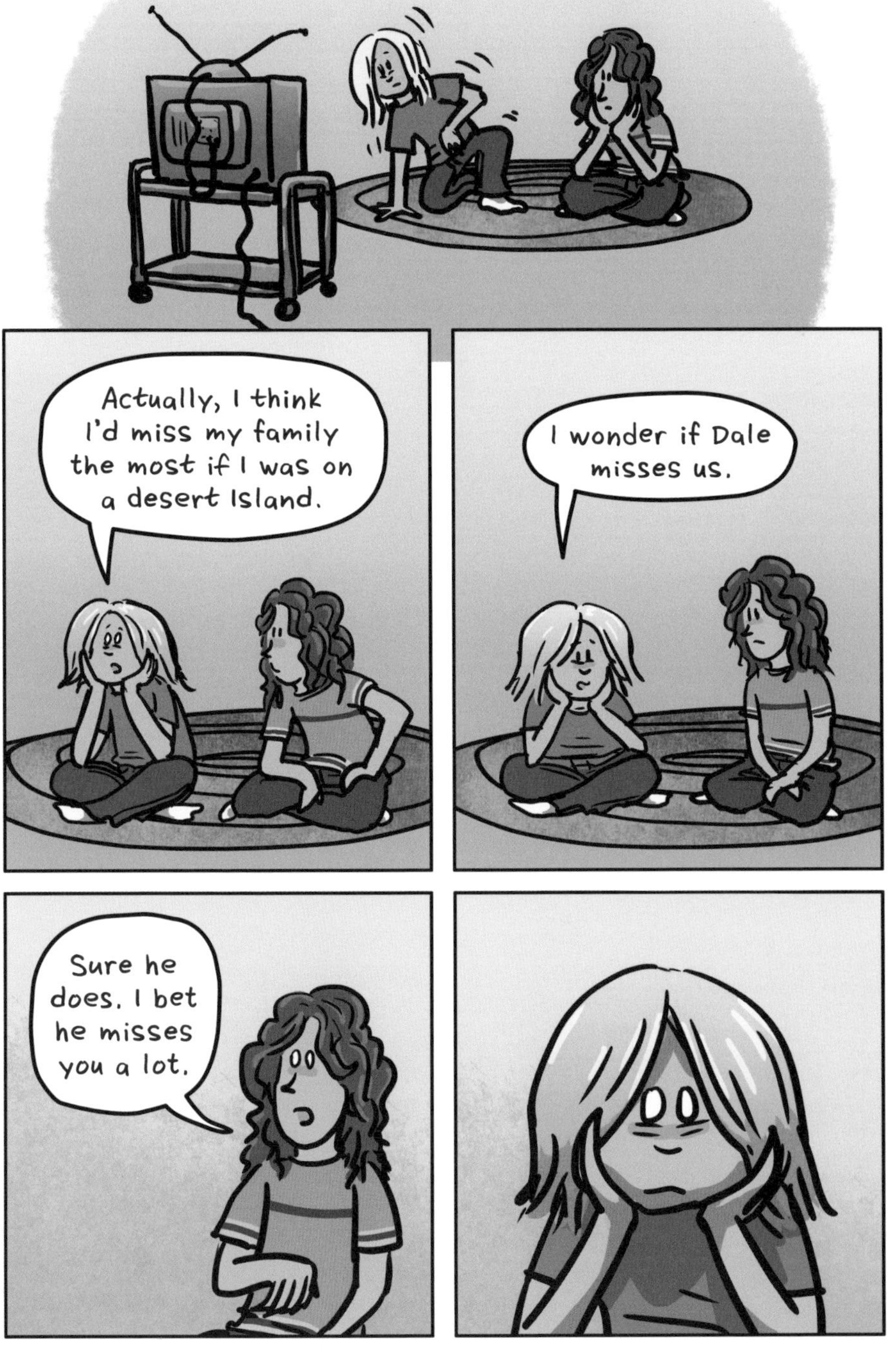
Actually, I think I'd miss my family the most if I was on a desert Island.
I wonder if Dale misses us.
Sure he does. I bet he misses you a lot.

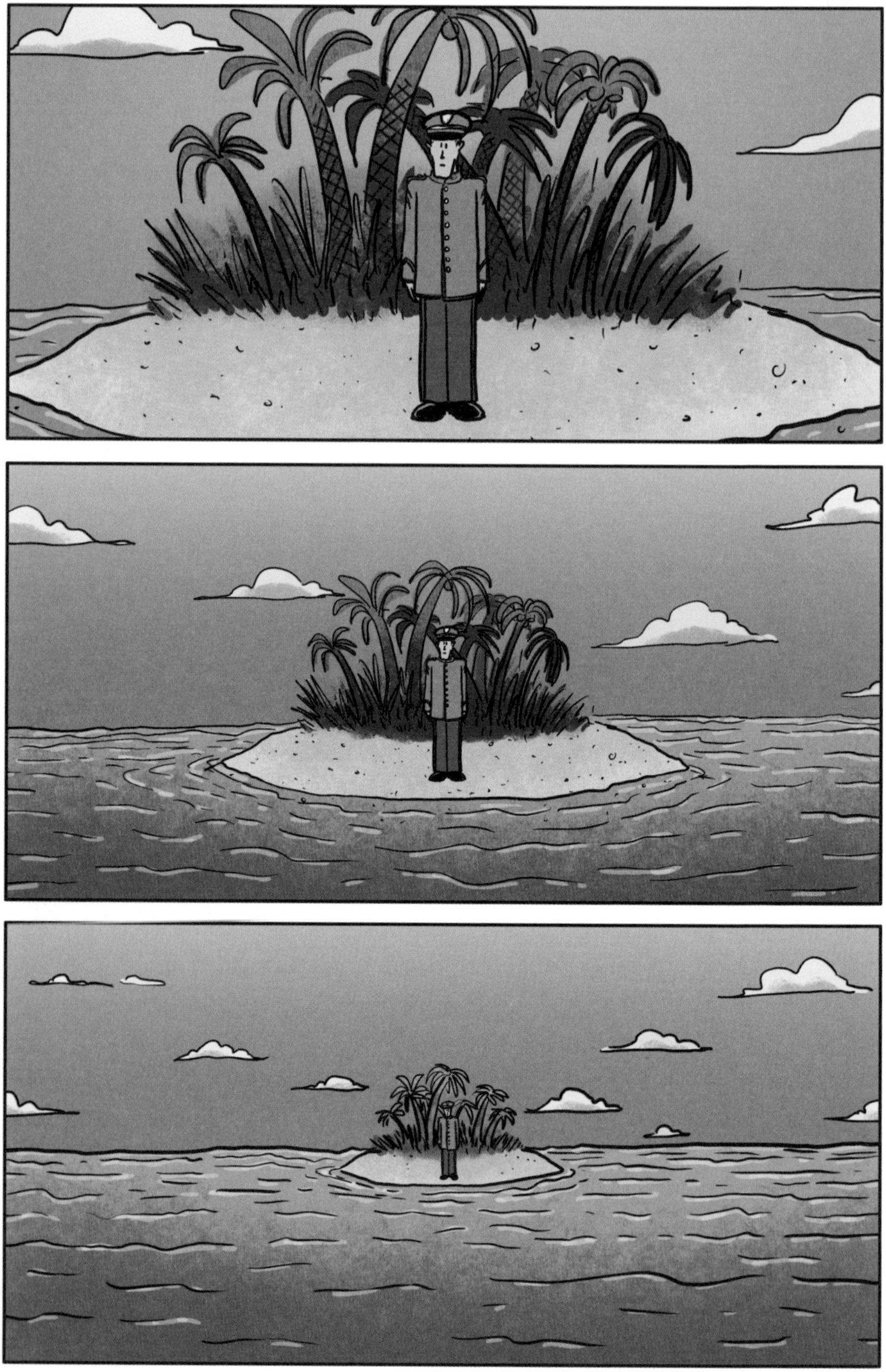

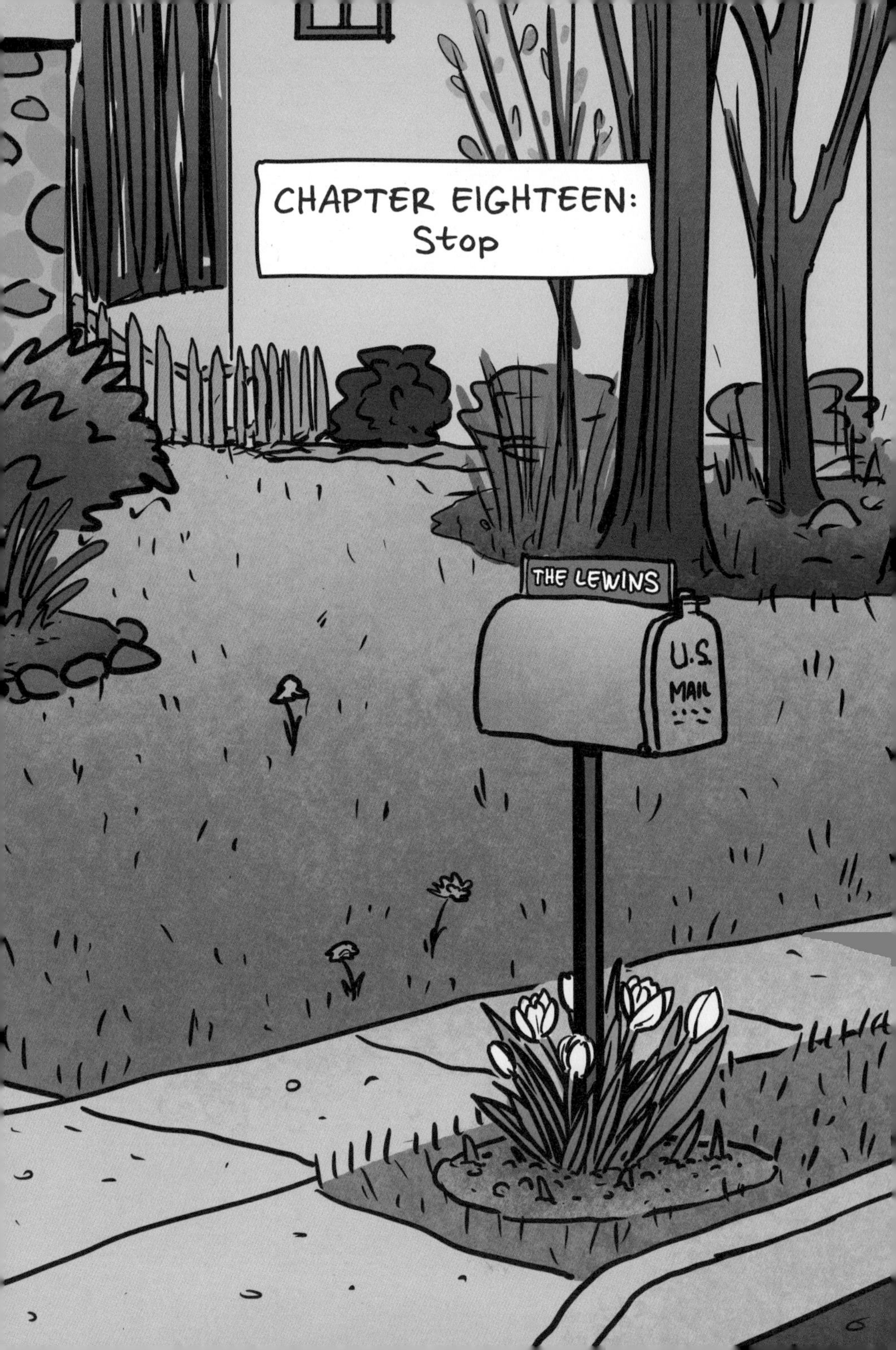
CHAPTER EIGHTEEN:
Stop
THE LEWINS
U.S.
MAIL

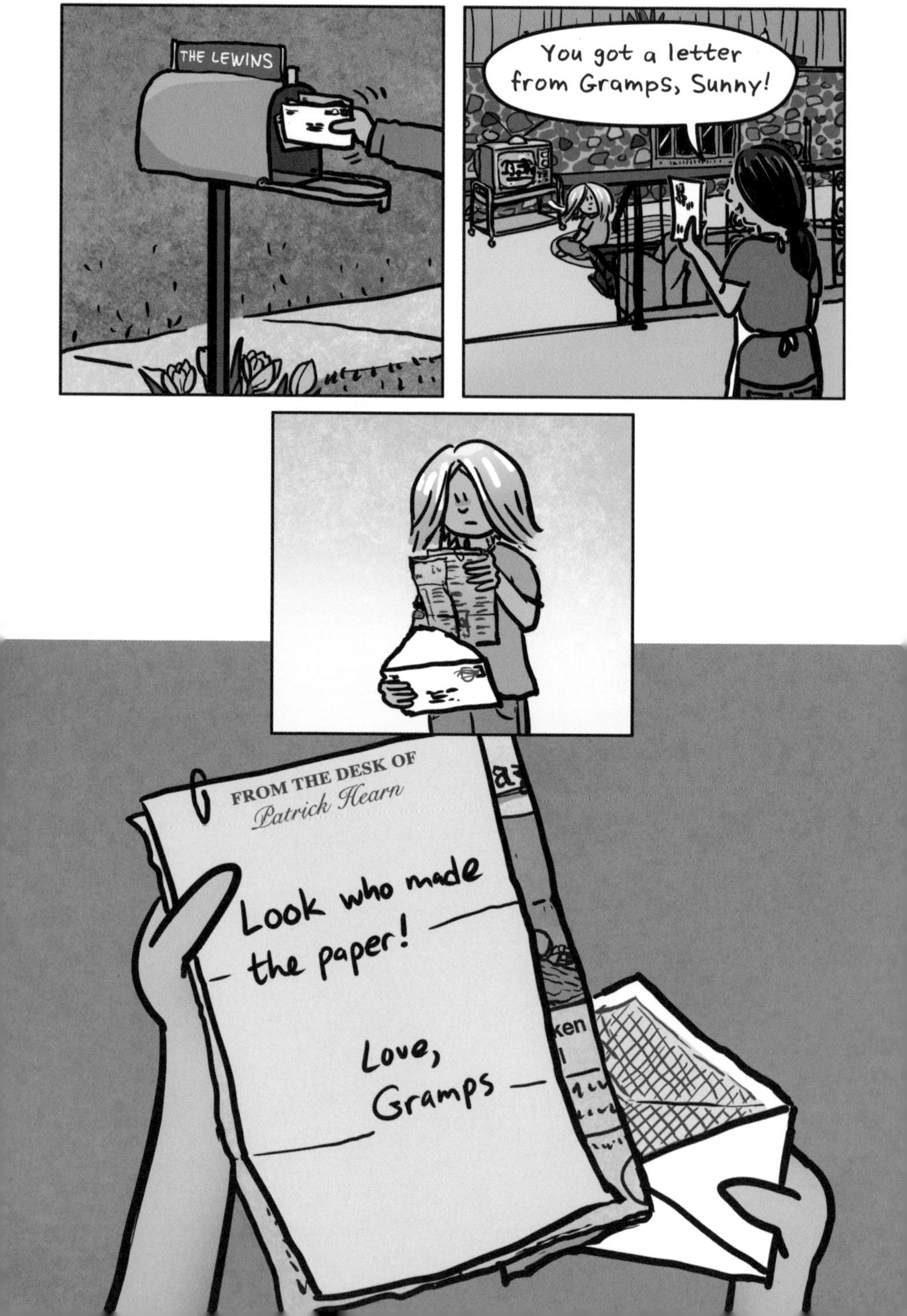
THE LEWINS
You got a letter from Gramps, Sunny!
FROM THE DESK OF
Patrick Hearn
Look who made the paper!
Love,
Gramps

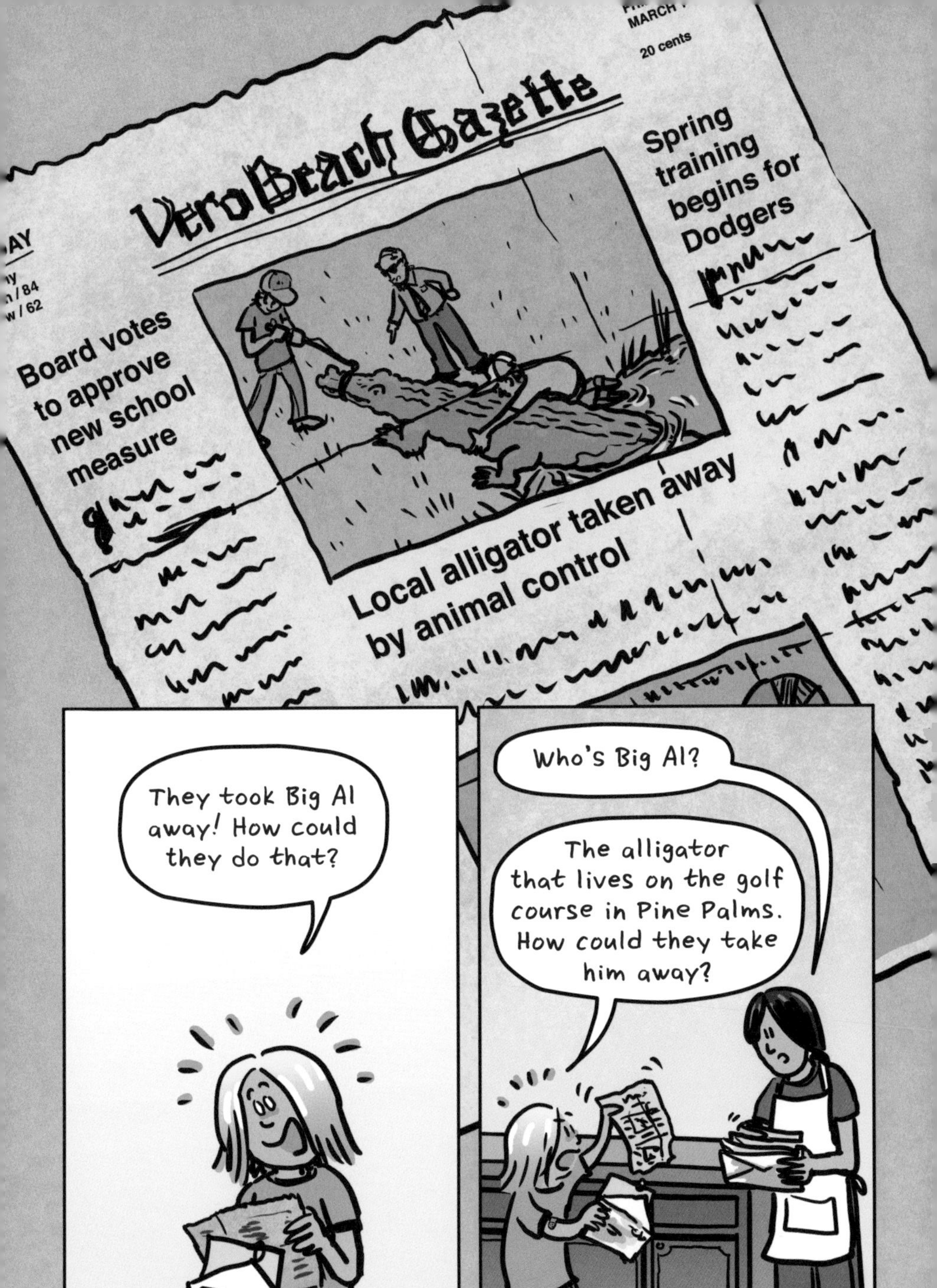
MARCH
20 cents
Vero Beach Gazette
Spring training begins for Dodgers
Board votes to approve new school measure
Local alligator taken away by animal control
They took Big Al away! How could they do that?
Who's Big Al?
The alligator that lives on the golf course in Pine Palms. How could they take him away?

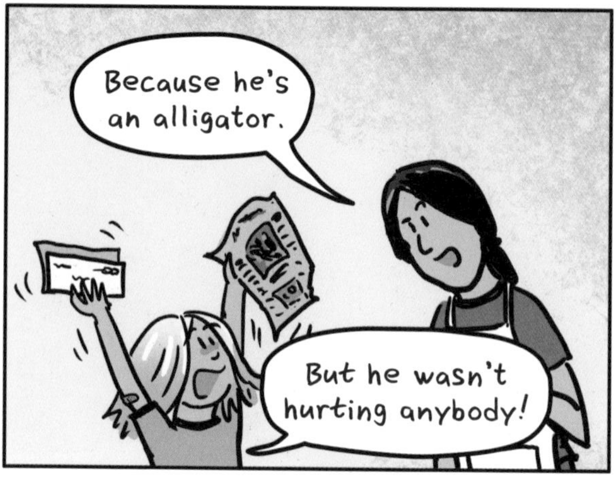
Because he's an alligator.
But he wasn't hurting anybody!

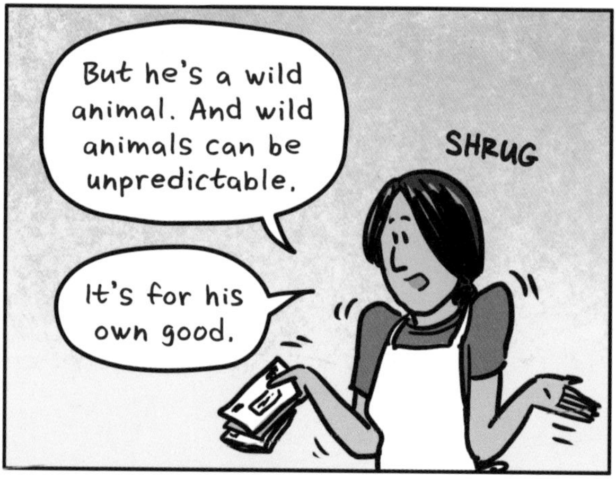
But he's a wild animal. And wild animals can be unpredictable.
SHRUG
It's for his own good.

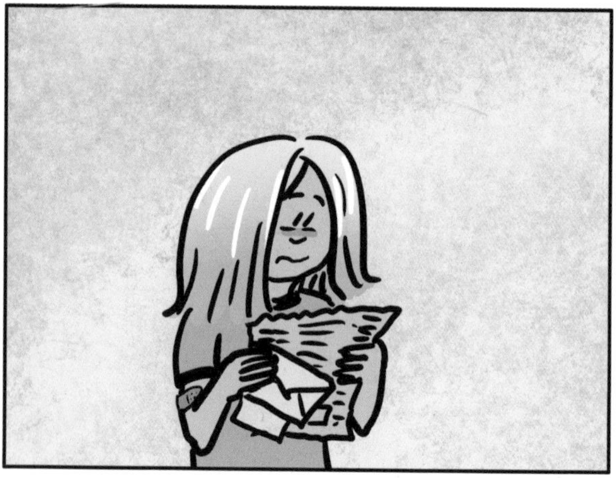

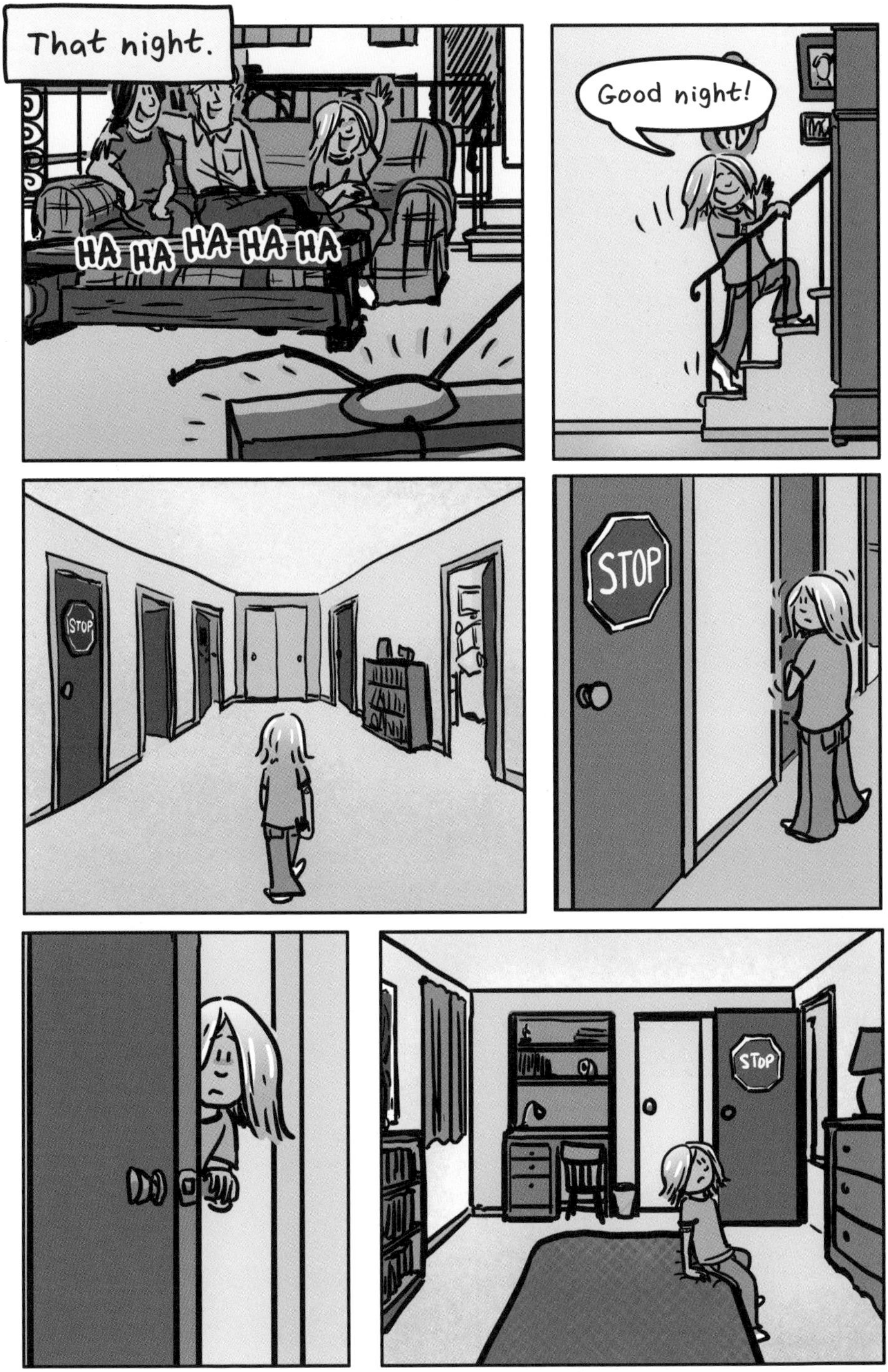
That night.
HA HA HA HA HA
Good night!
STOP
STOP
STOP

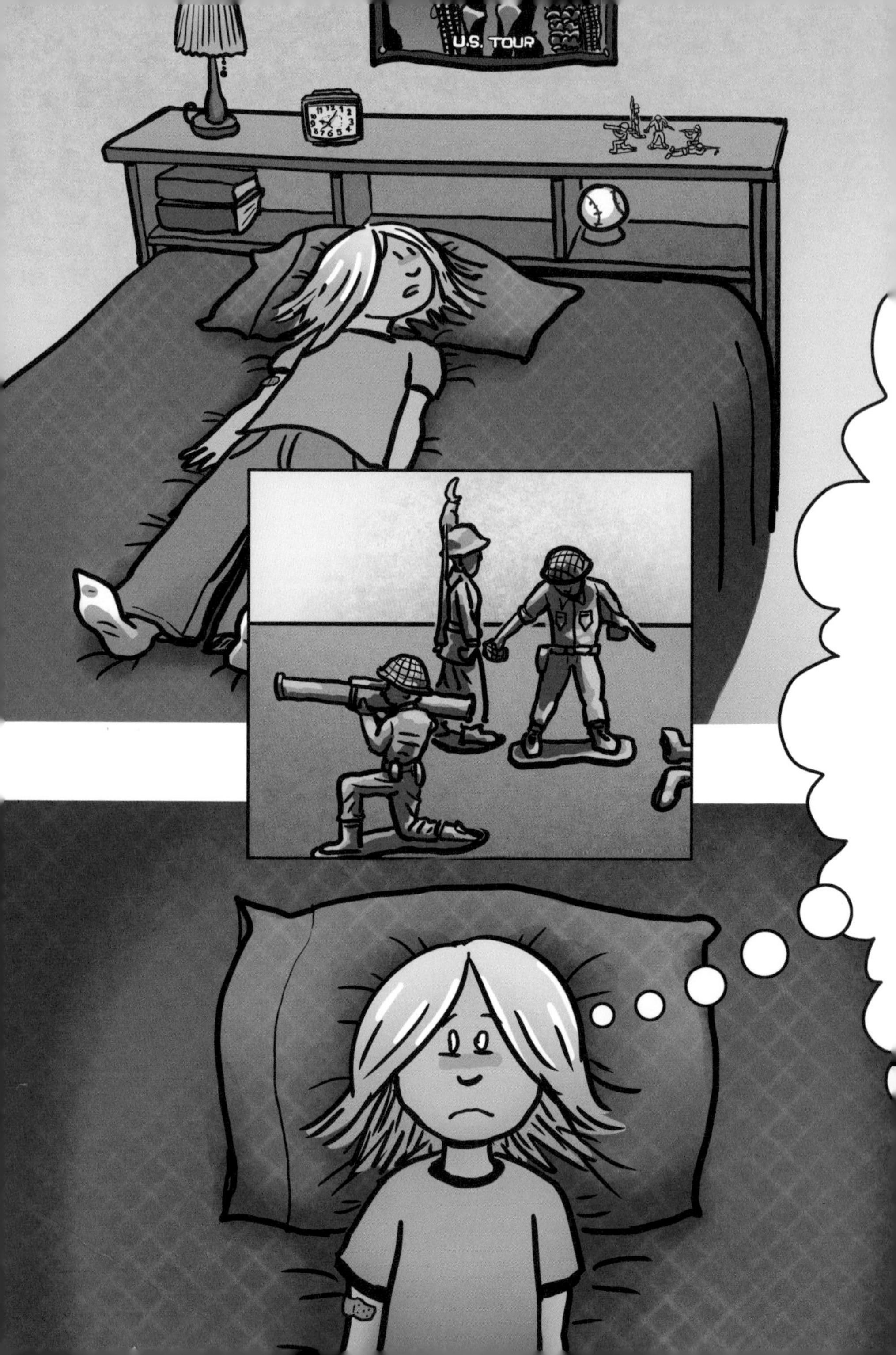
U.S. TOUR

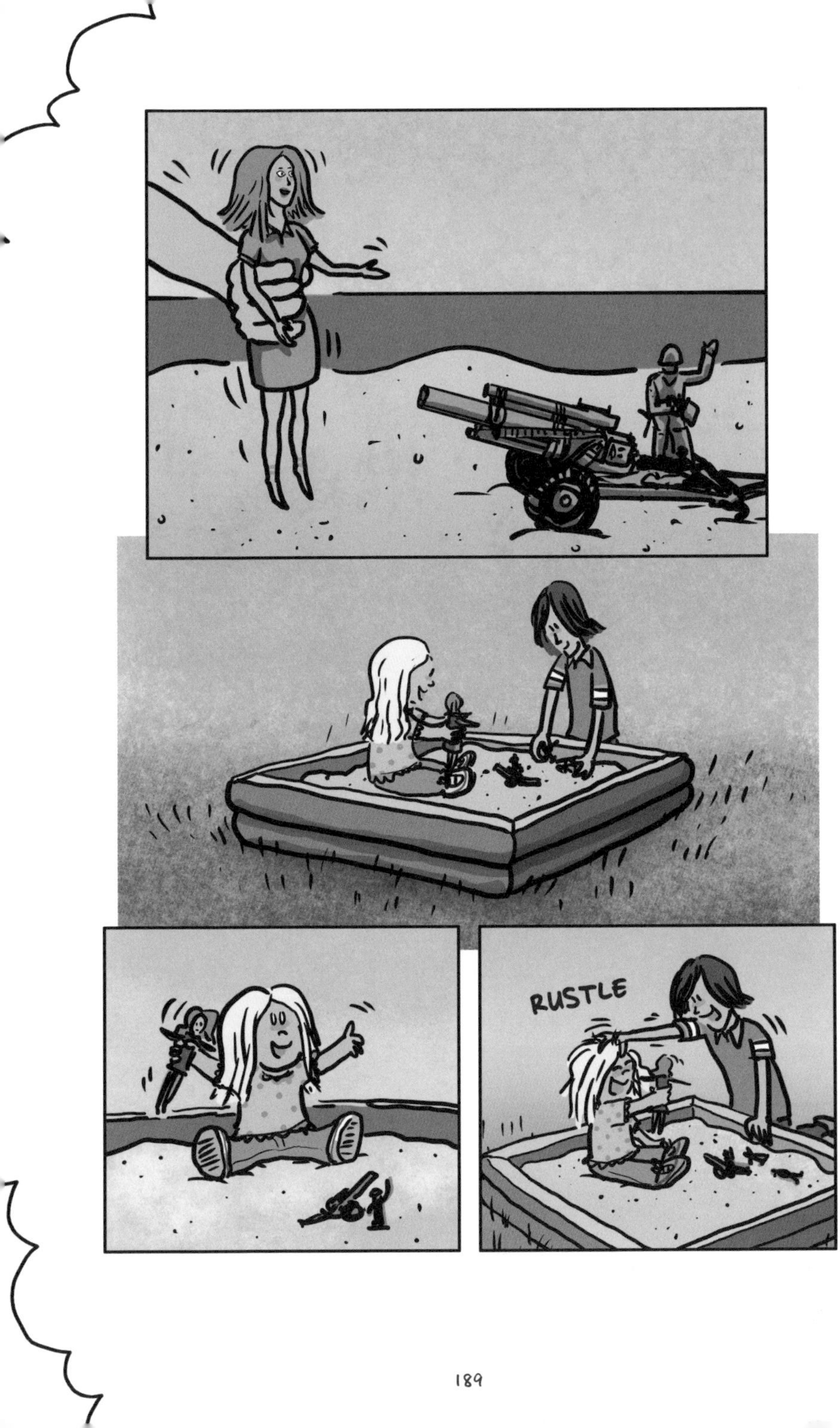
RUSTLE

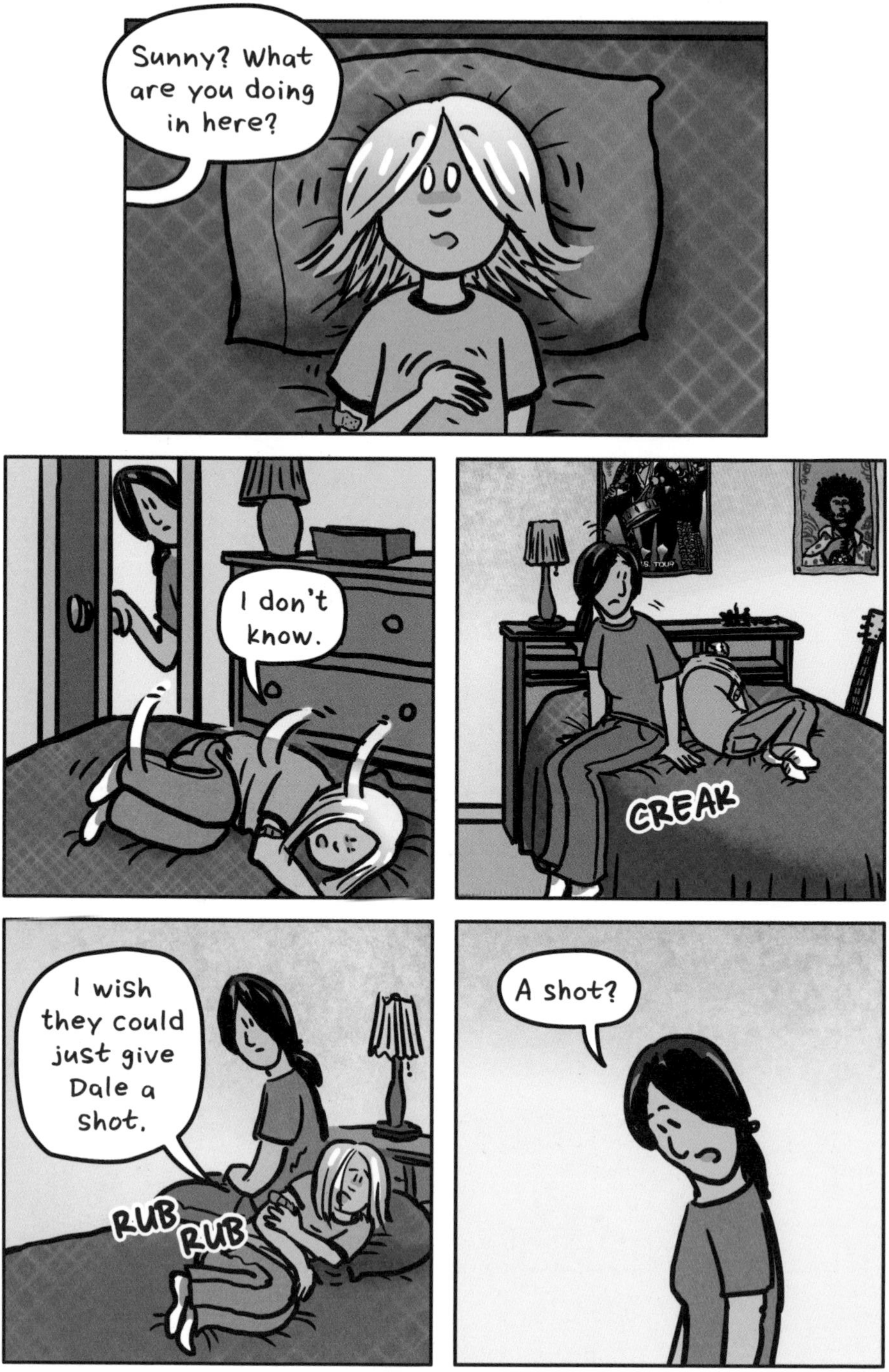
Sunny? What are you doing in here?
I don't know.
CREAK
I wish they could just give Dale a shot.
RUB RUB
A shot?

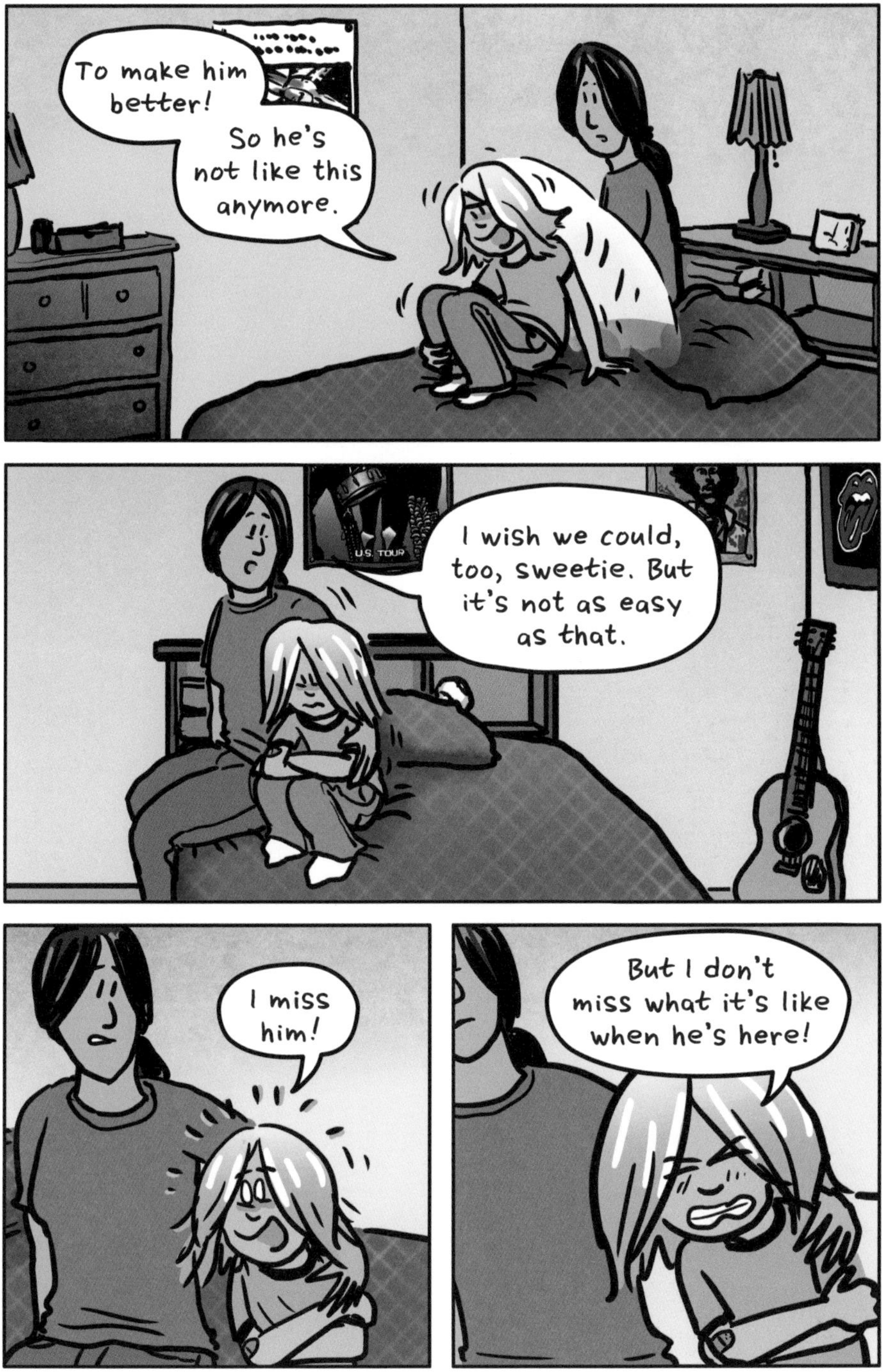
To make him better!
So he's not like this anymore.
U.S. TOUR
I wish we could, too, sweetie. But it's not as easy as that.
I miss him!
But I don't miss what it's like when he's here!

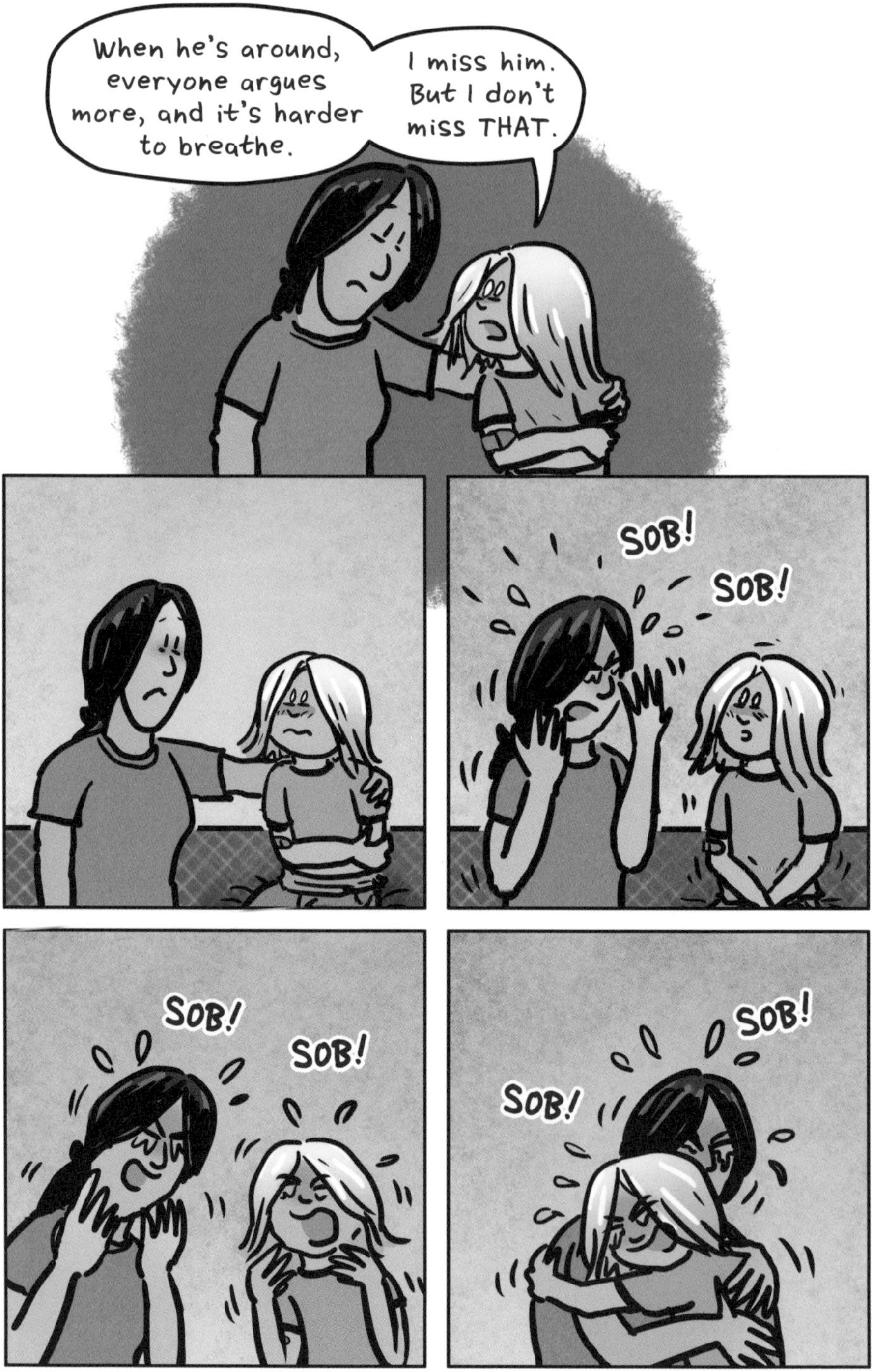
When he's around, everyone argues more, and it's harder to breathe.
I miss him. But I don't miss THAT.
SOB!
SOB!
SOB!
SOB!
SOB!
SOB!

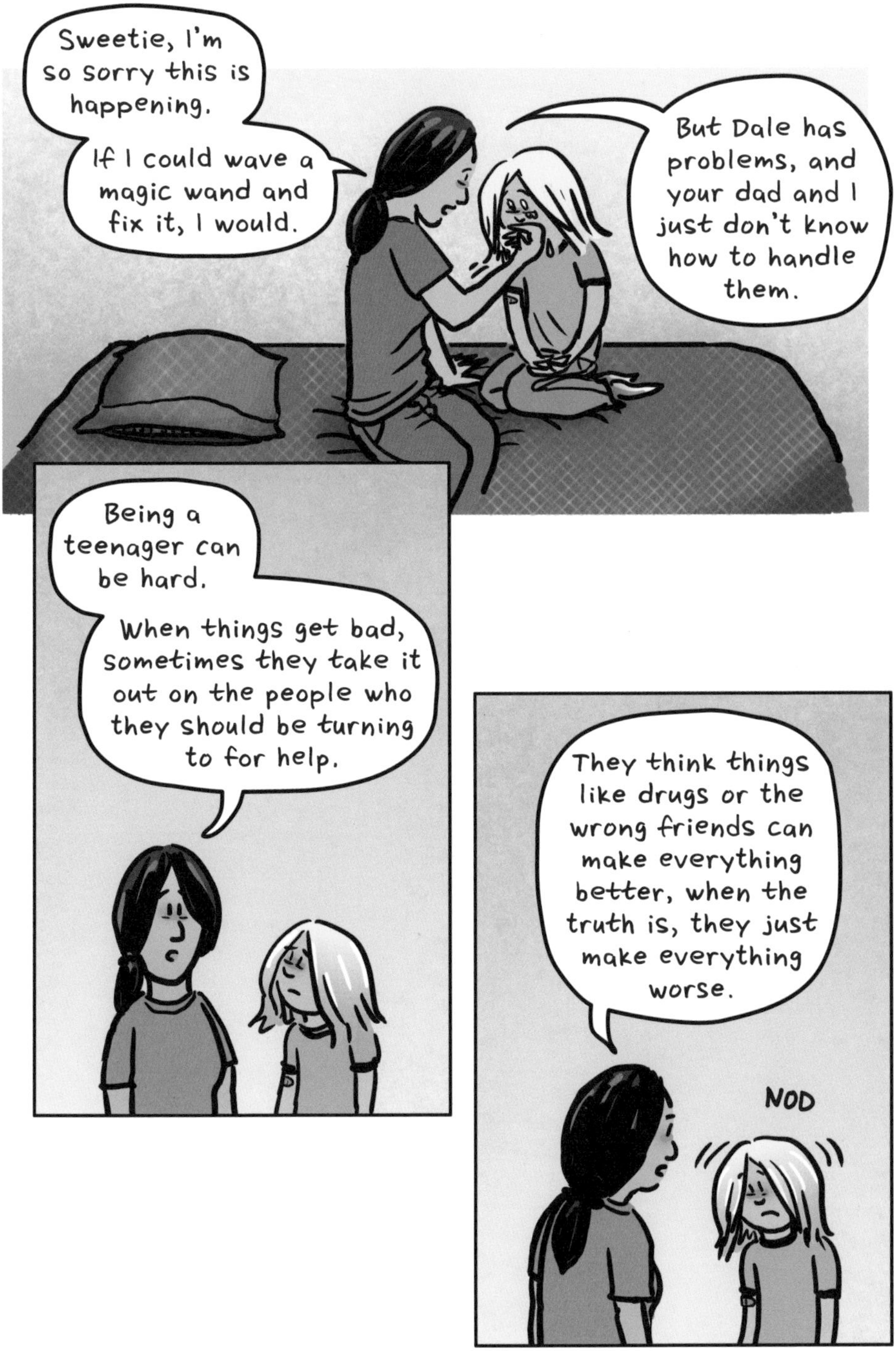
Sweetie, I'm so sorry this is happening.
If I could wave a magic wand and fix it, I would.
But Dale has problems, and your dad and I just don't know how to handle them.
Being a teenager can be hard.
When things get bad, sometimes they take it out on the people who they should be turning to for help.
They think things like drugs or the wrong friends can make everything better, when the truth is, they just make everything worse.
NOD

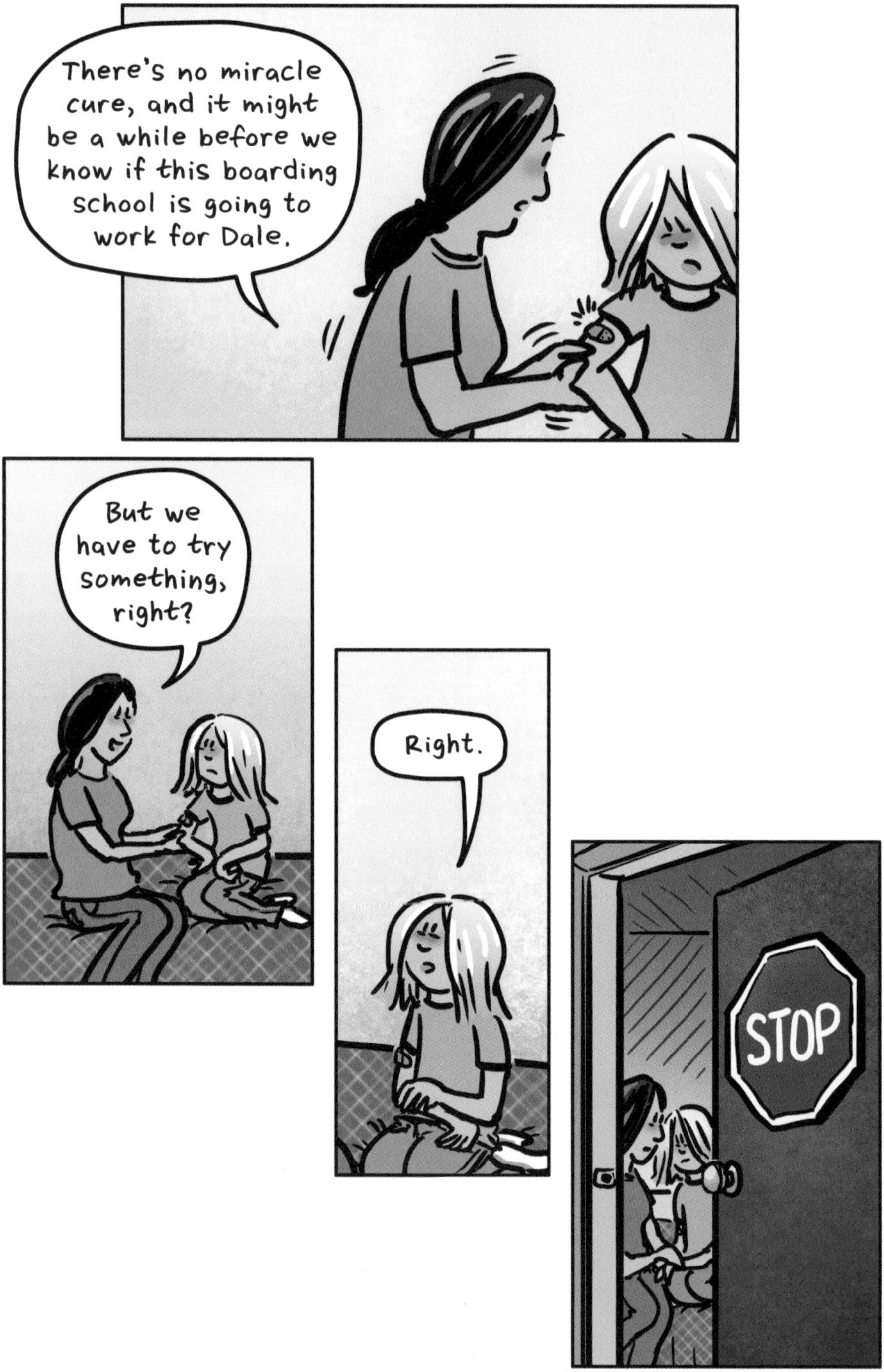
There's no miracle cure, and it might be a while before we know if this boarding school is going to work for Dale.
But we have to try something, right?
Right.
STOP

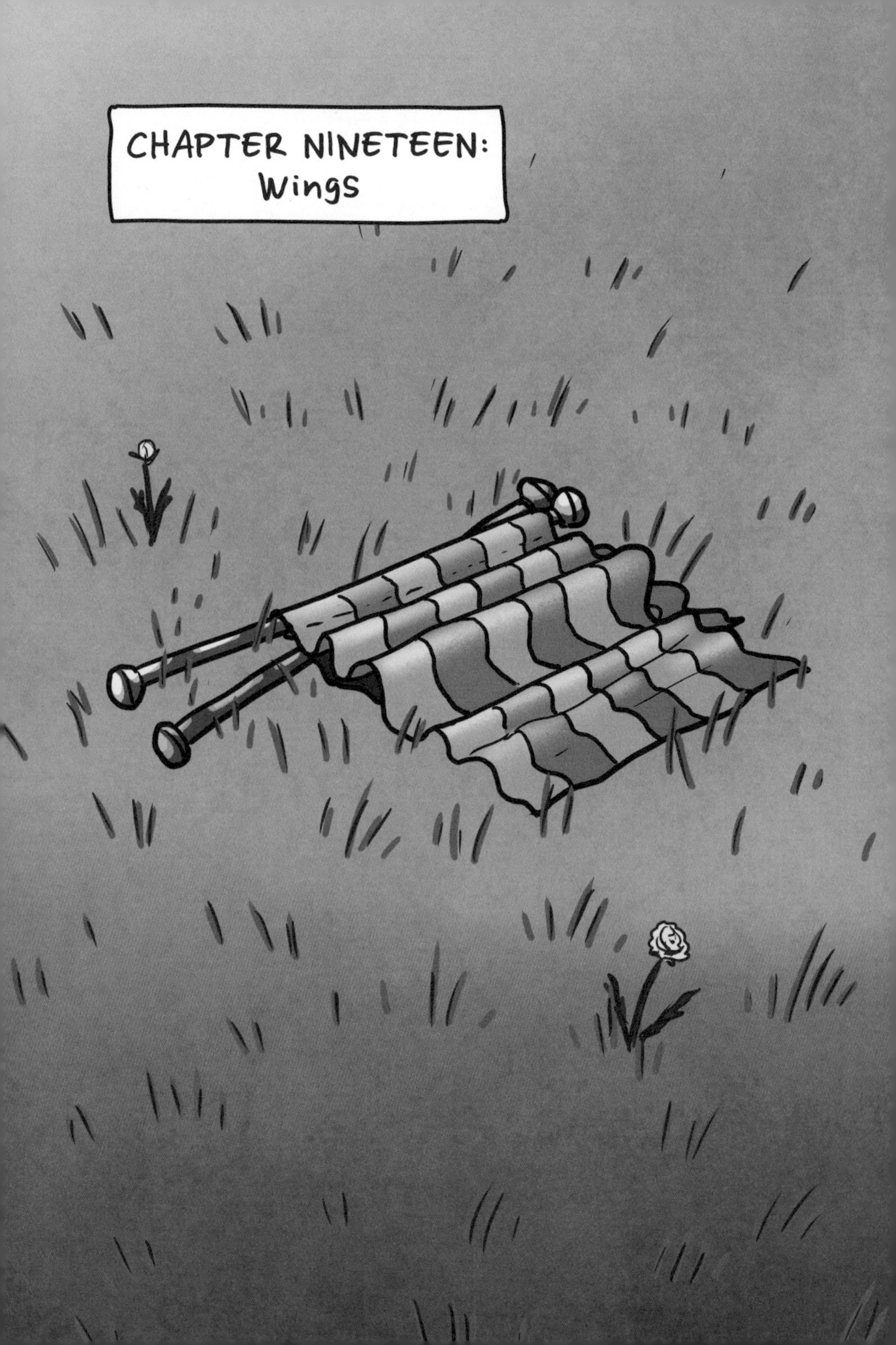
CHAPTER NINETEEN:
Wings

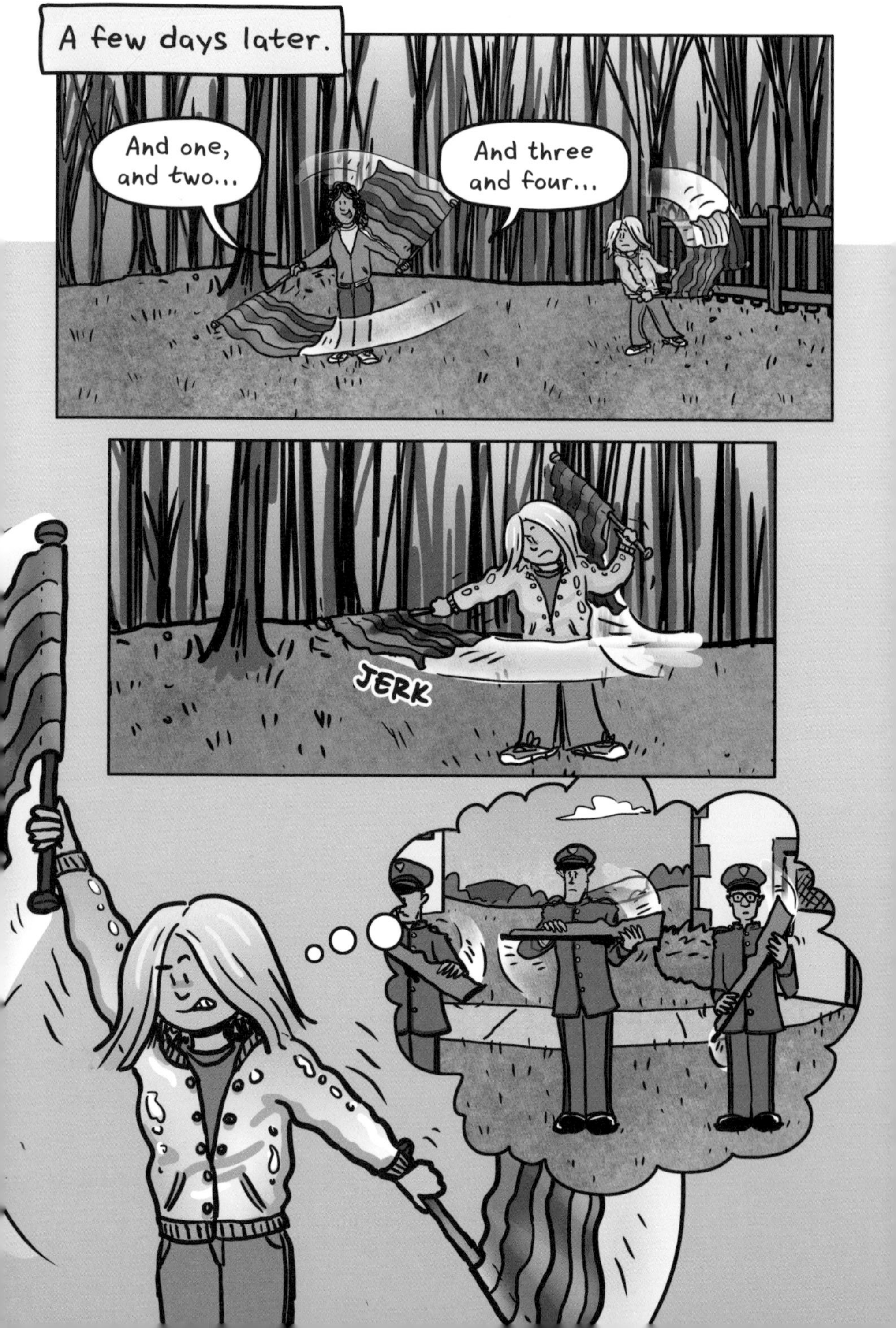
A few days later.
And one, and two...
And three and four...
JERK

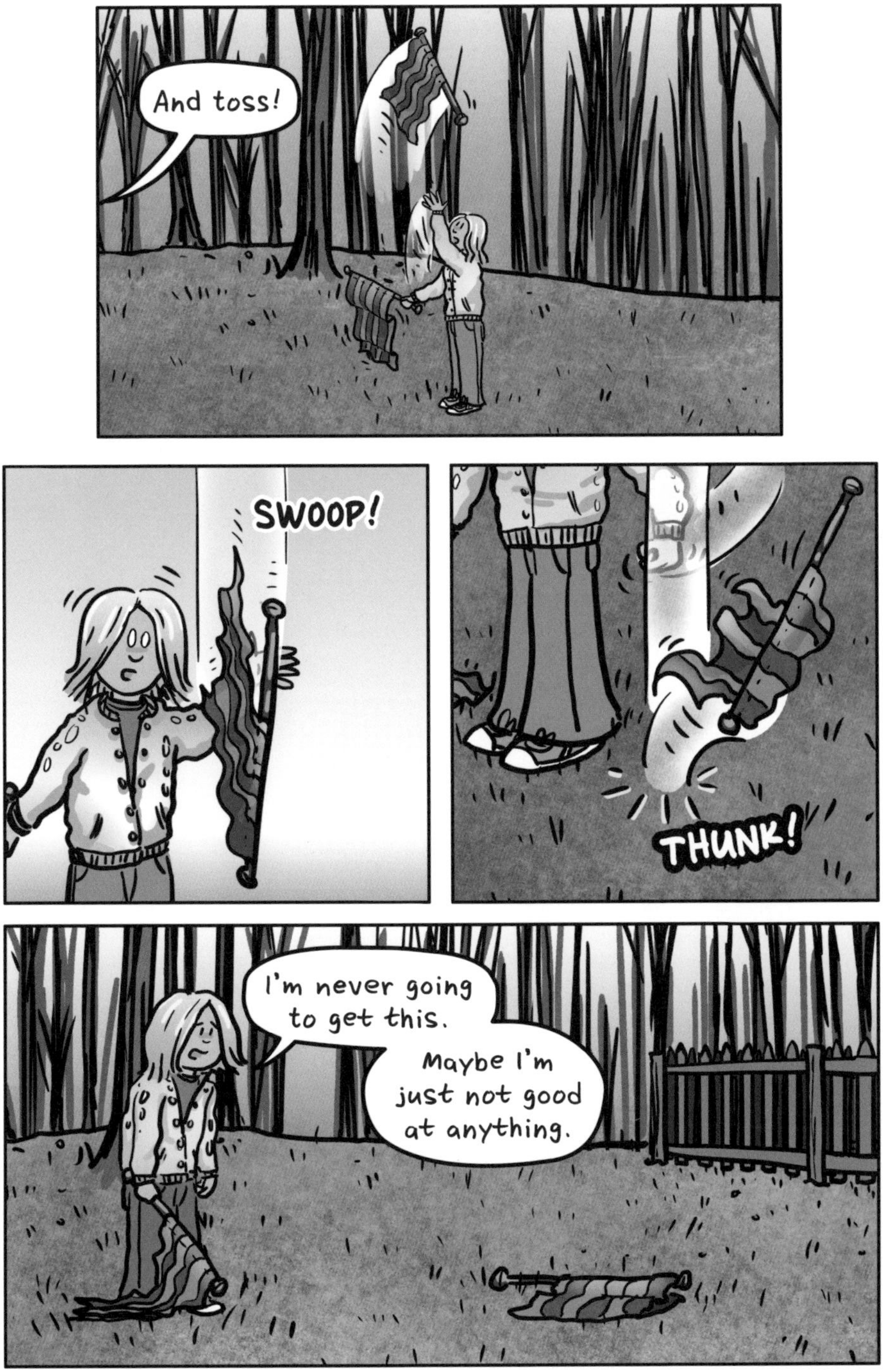
And toss!
SWOOP!
THUNK!
I'm never going to get this.
Maybe I'm just not good at anything.

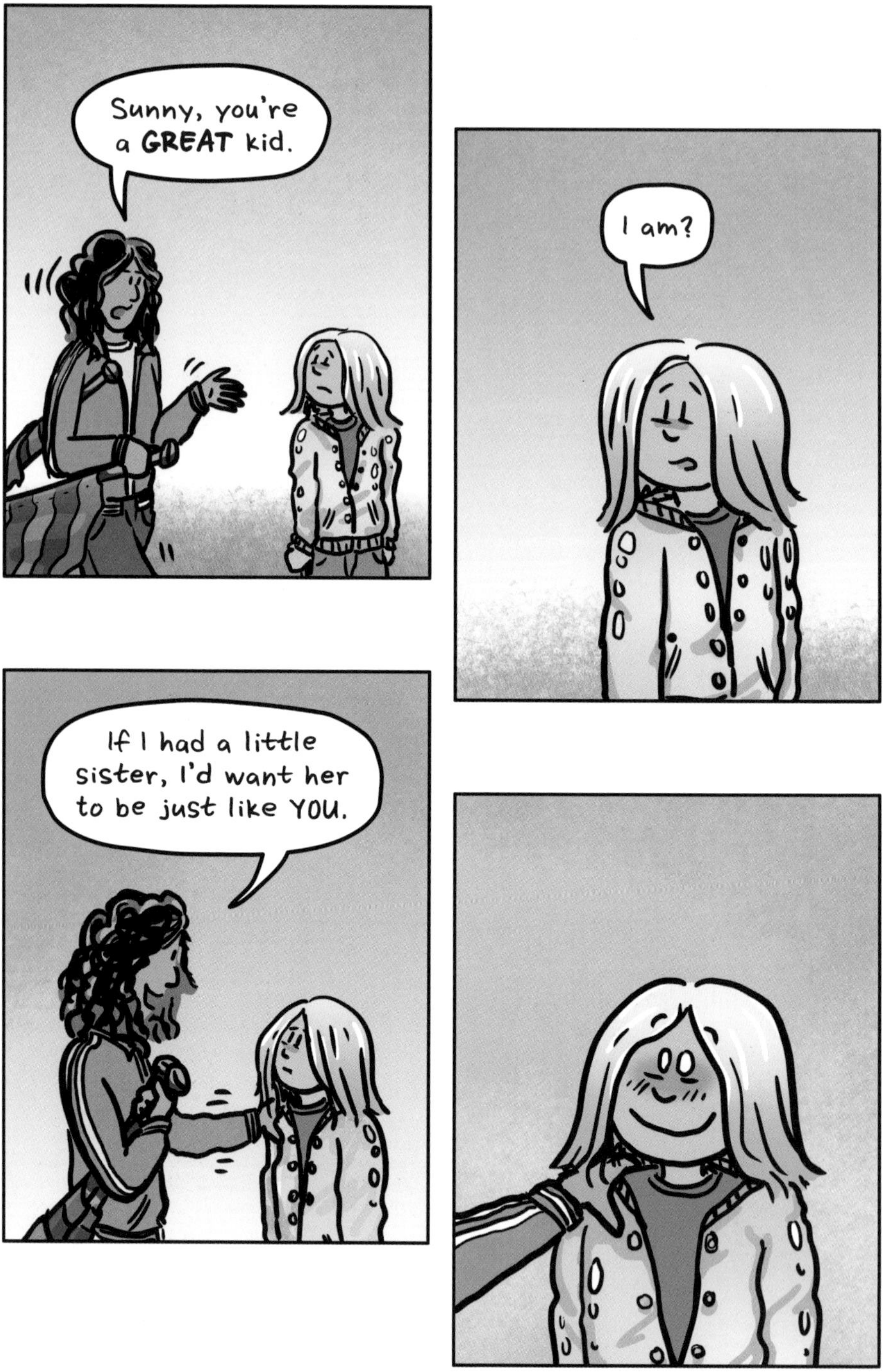
Sunny, you're a **GREAT** kid.
I am?
If I had a little sister, I'd want her to be just like YOU.

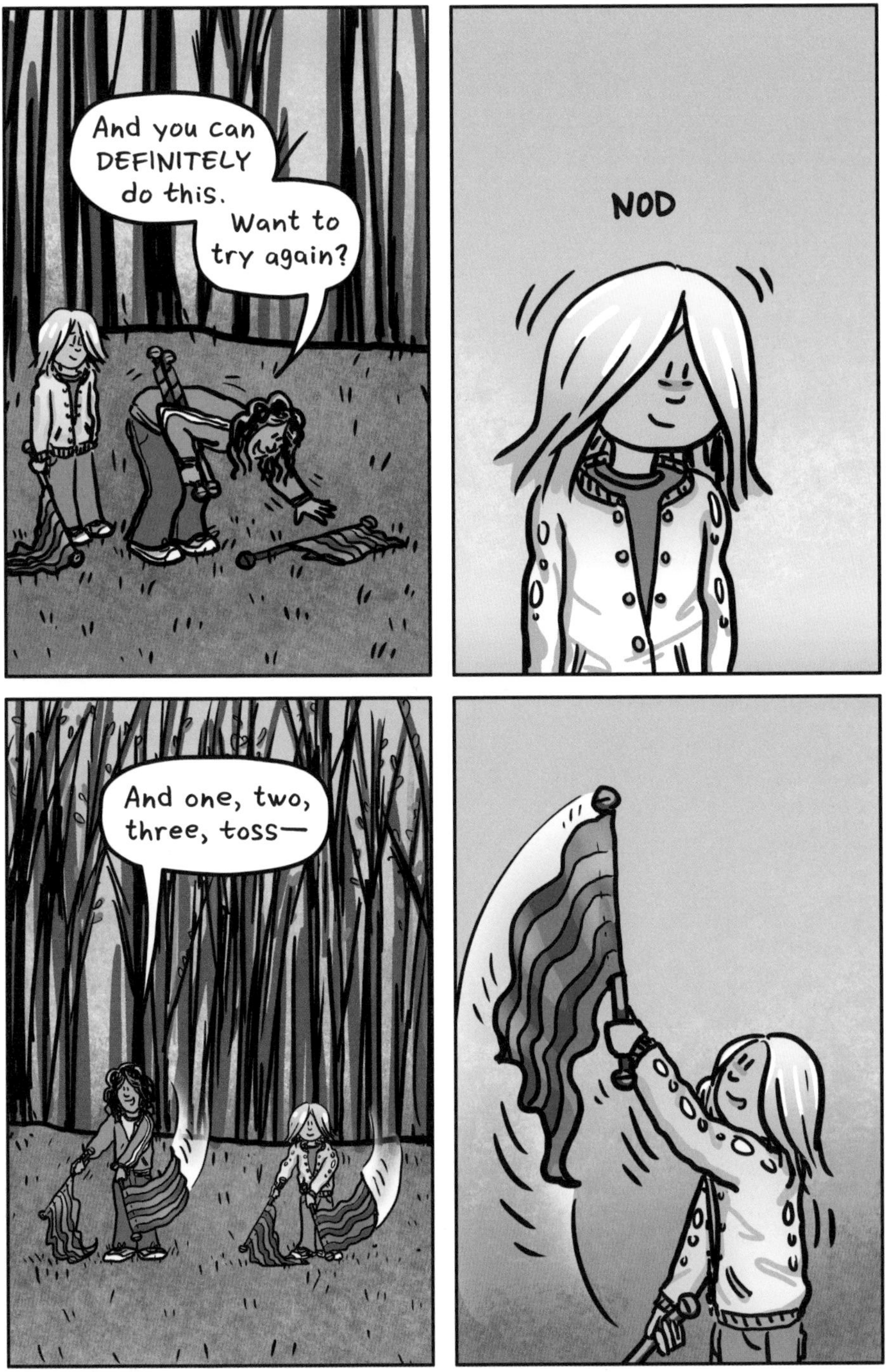
And you can DEFINITELY do this.
Want to try again?
NOD
And one, two, three, toss—

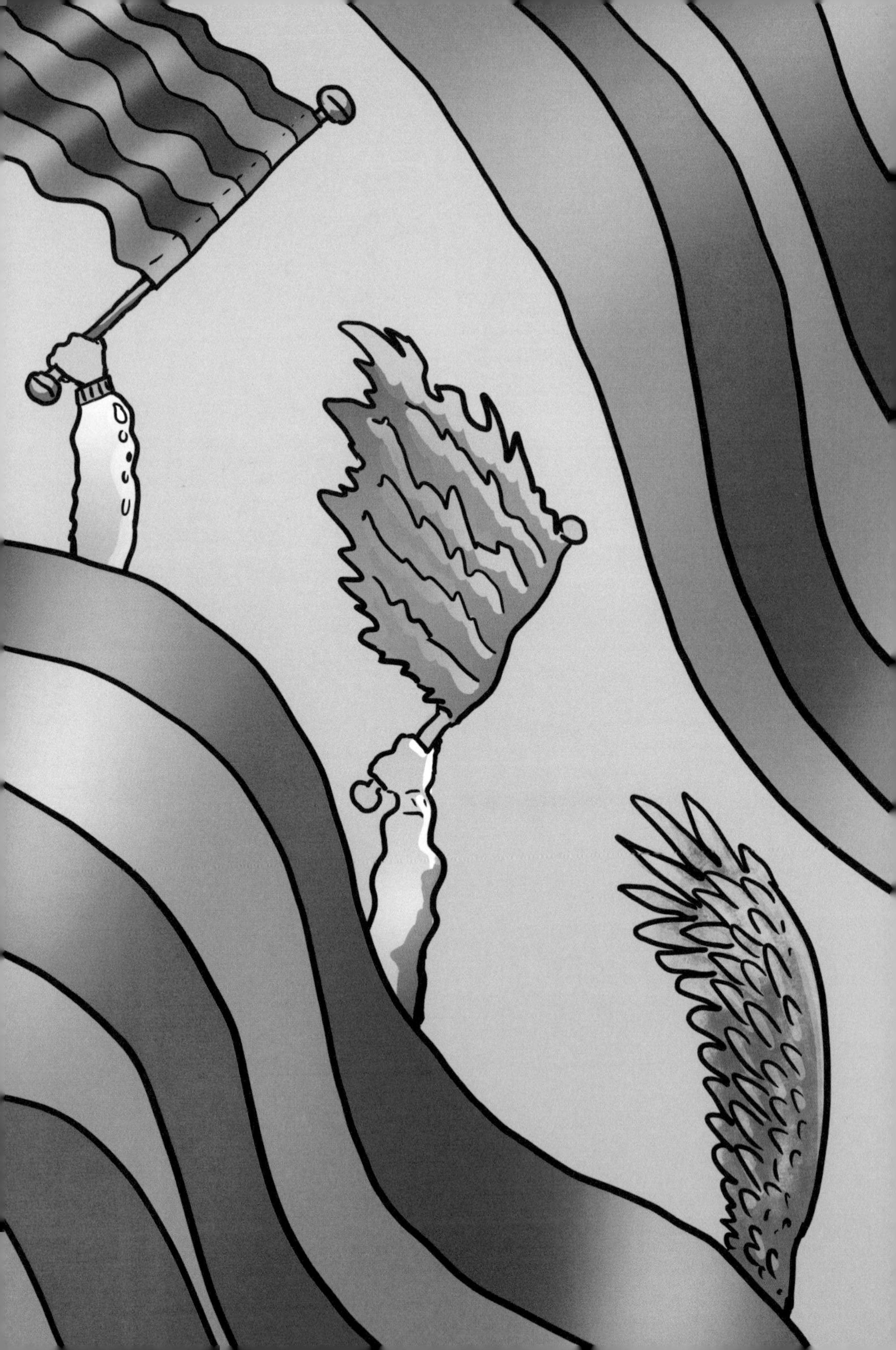

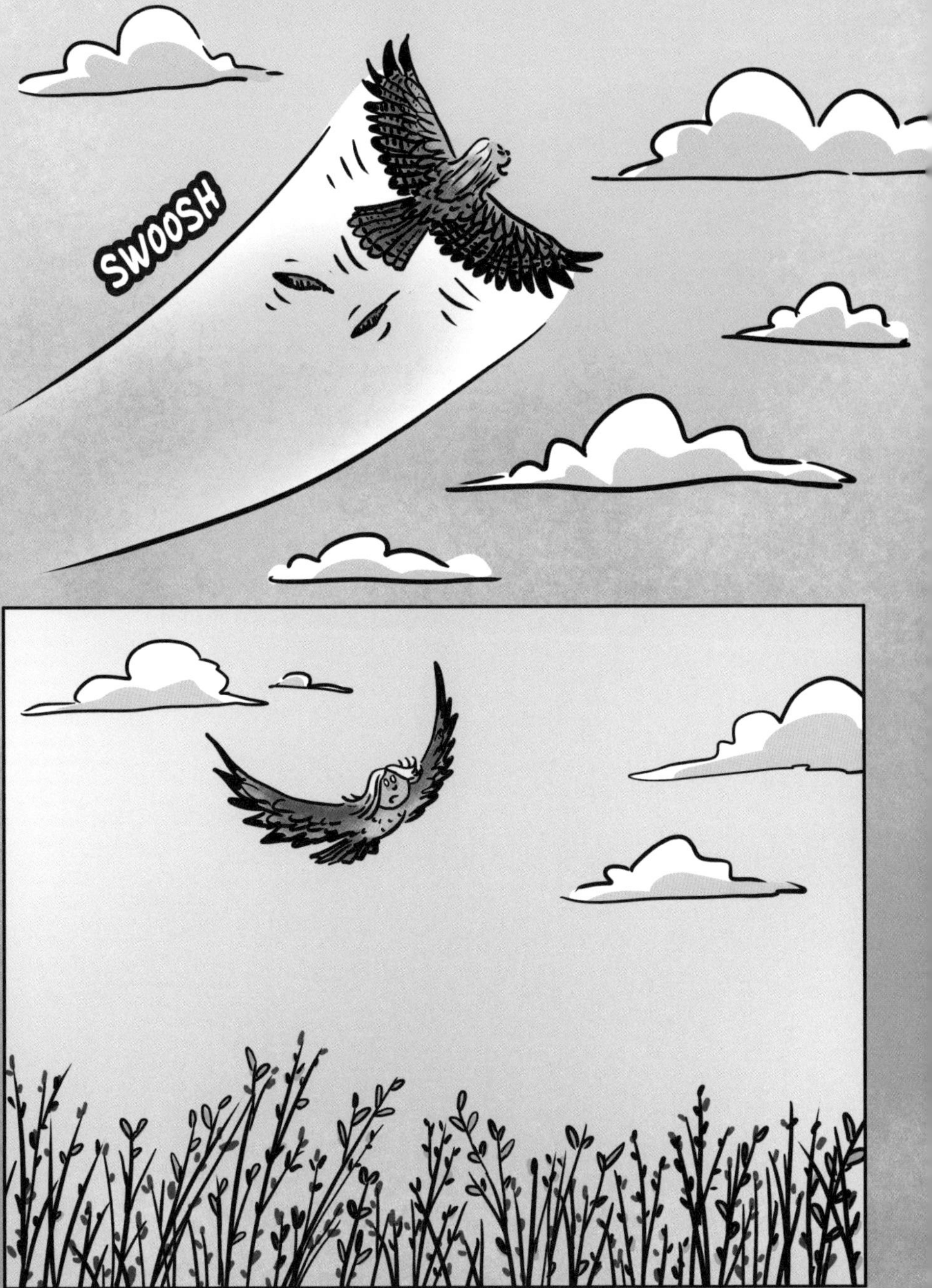
SWOOSH

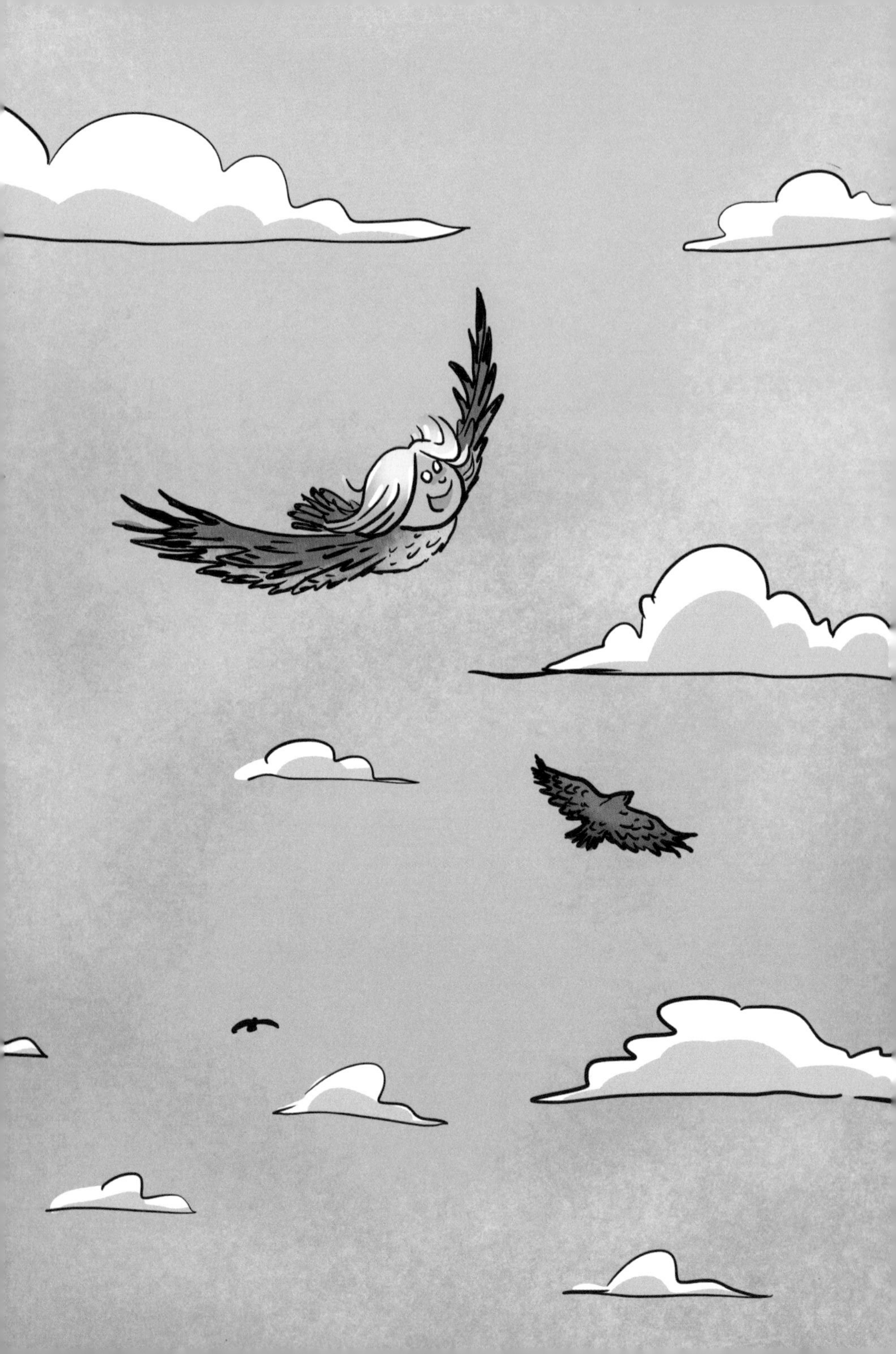

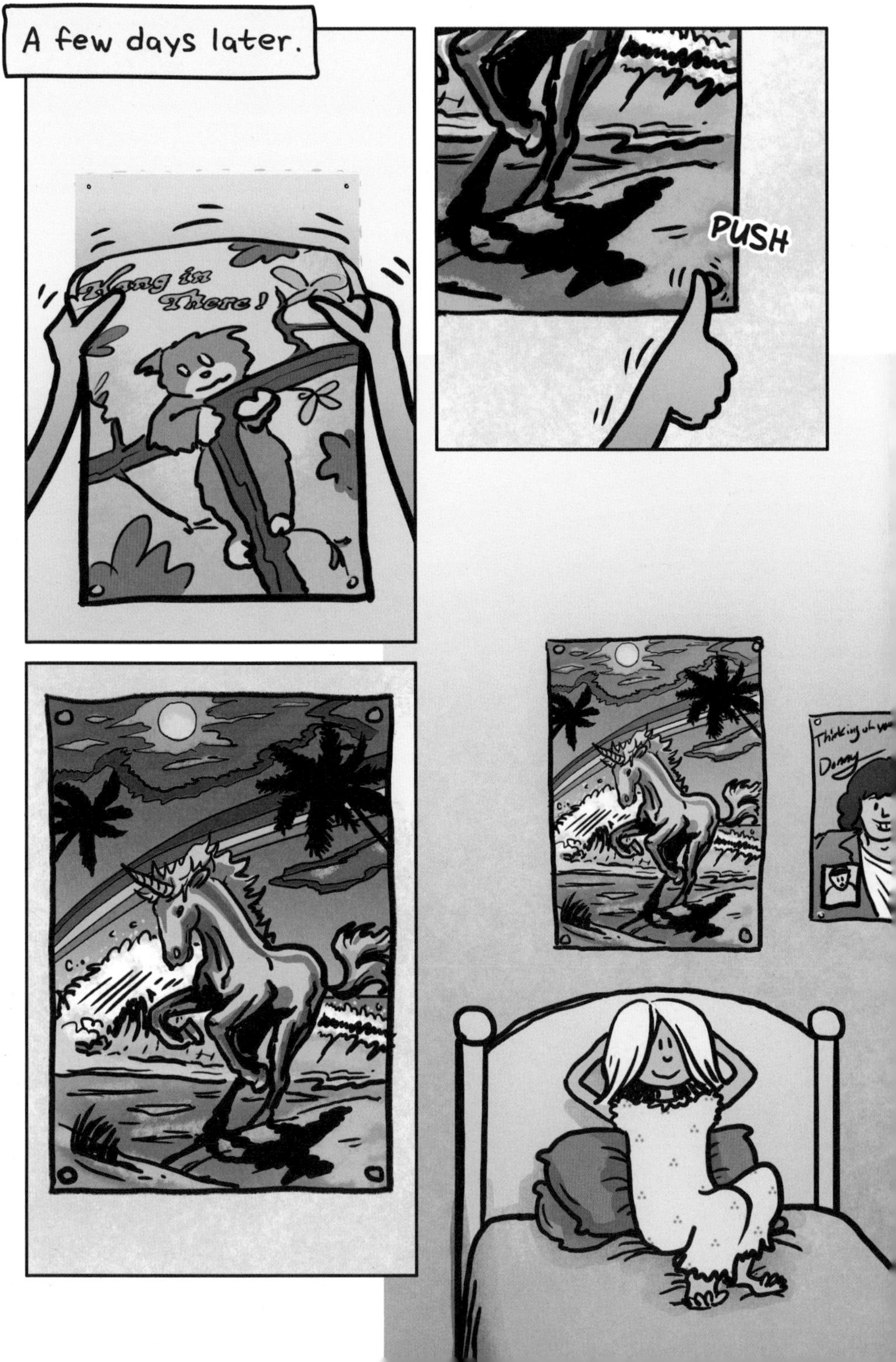
A few days later.
Hang in There!
PUSH
Donny

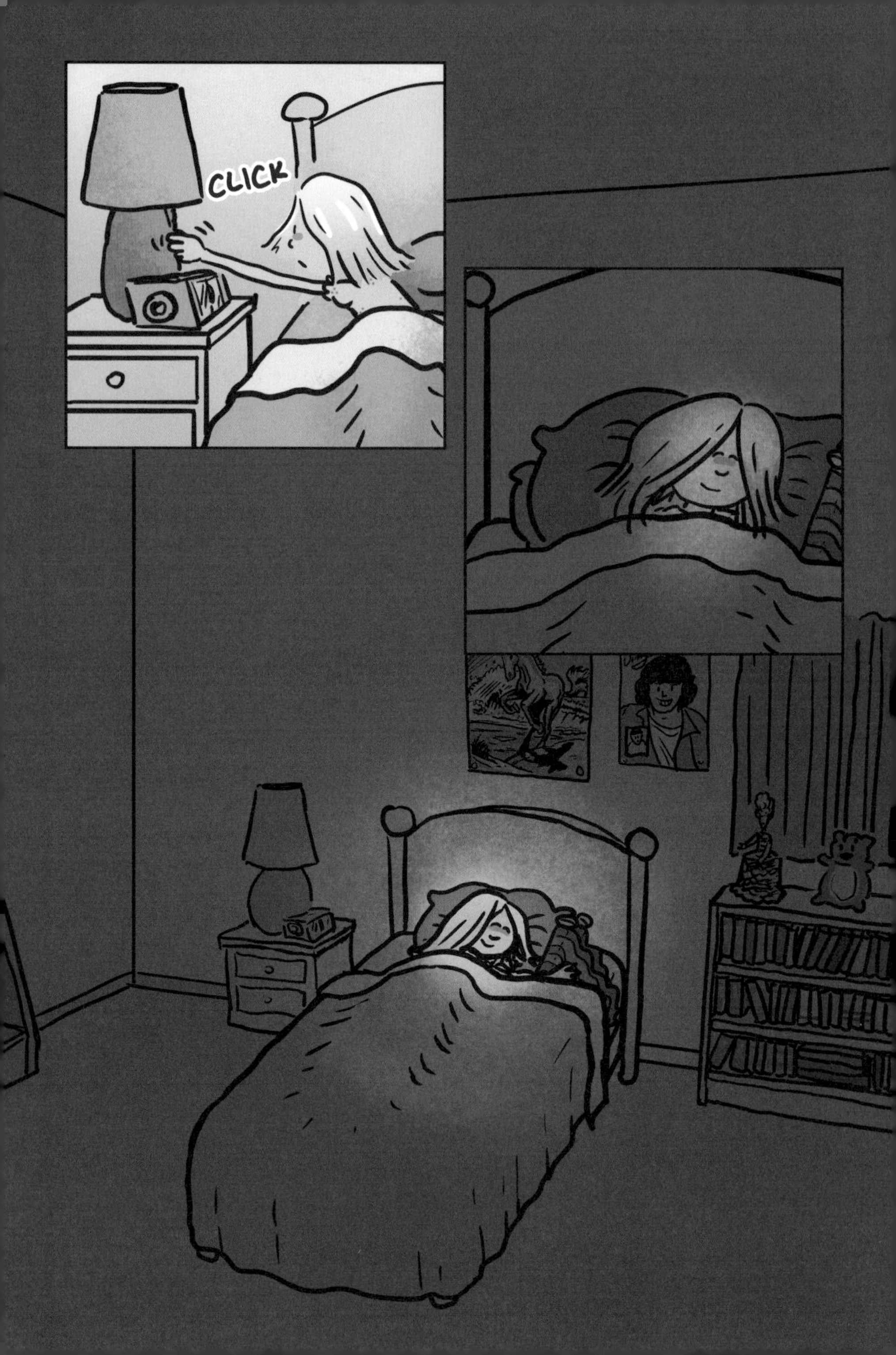
CLICK

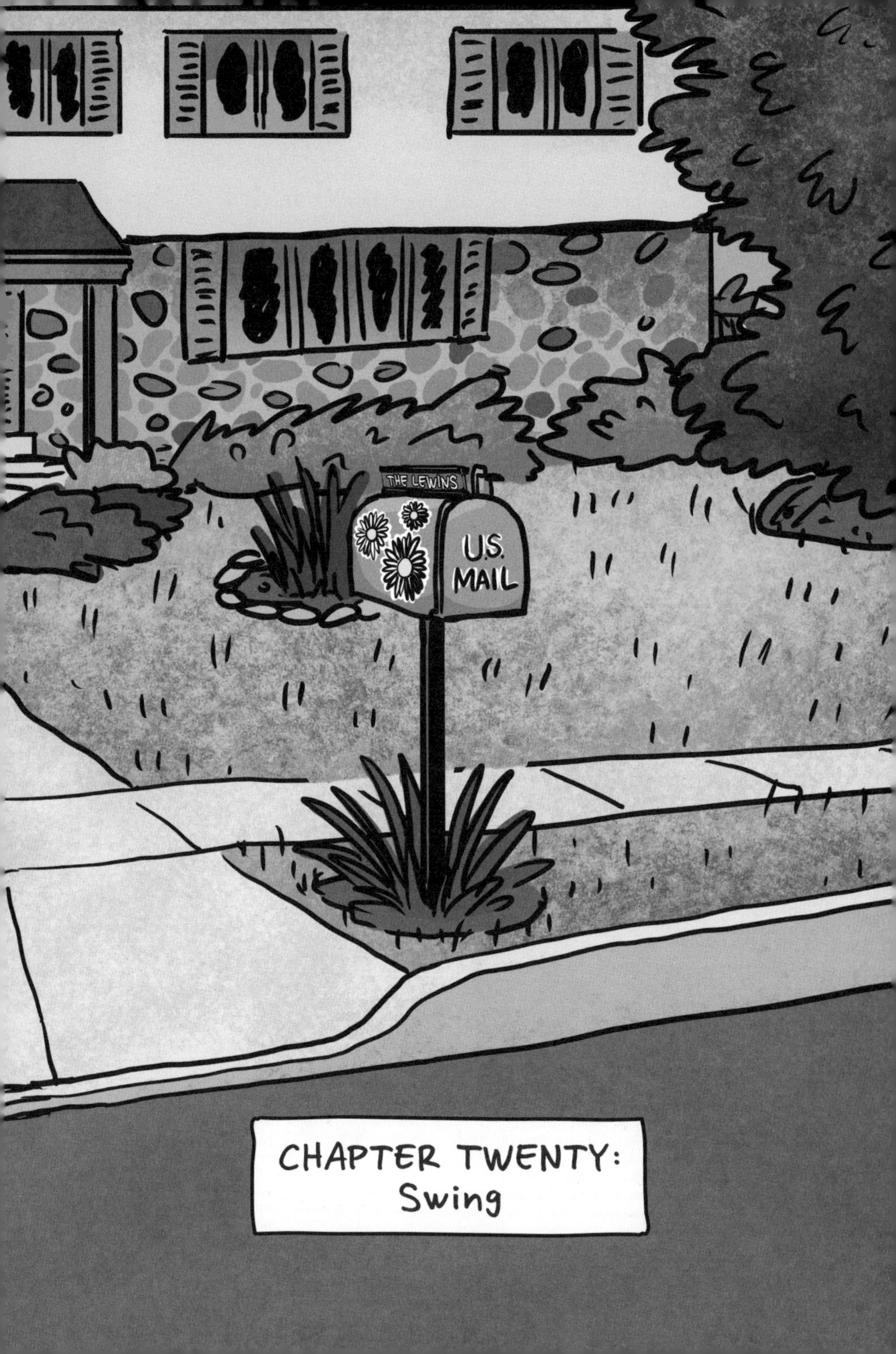
THE LEWINS
U.S. MAIL

CHAPTER TWENTY: Swing

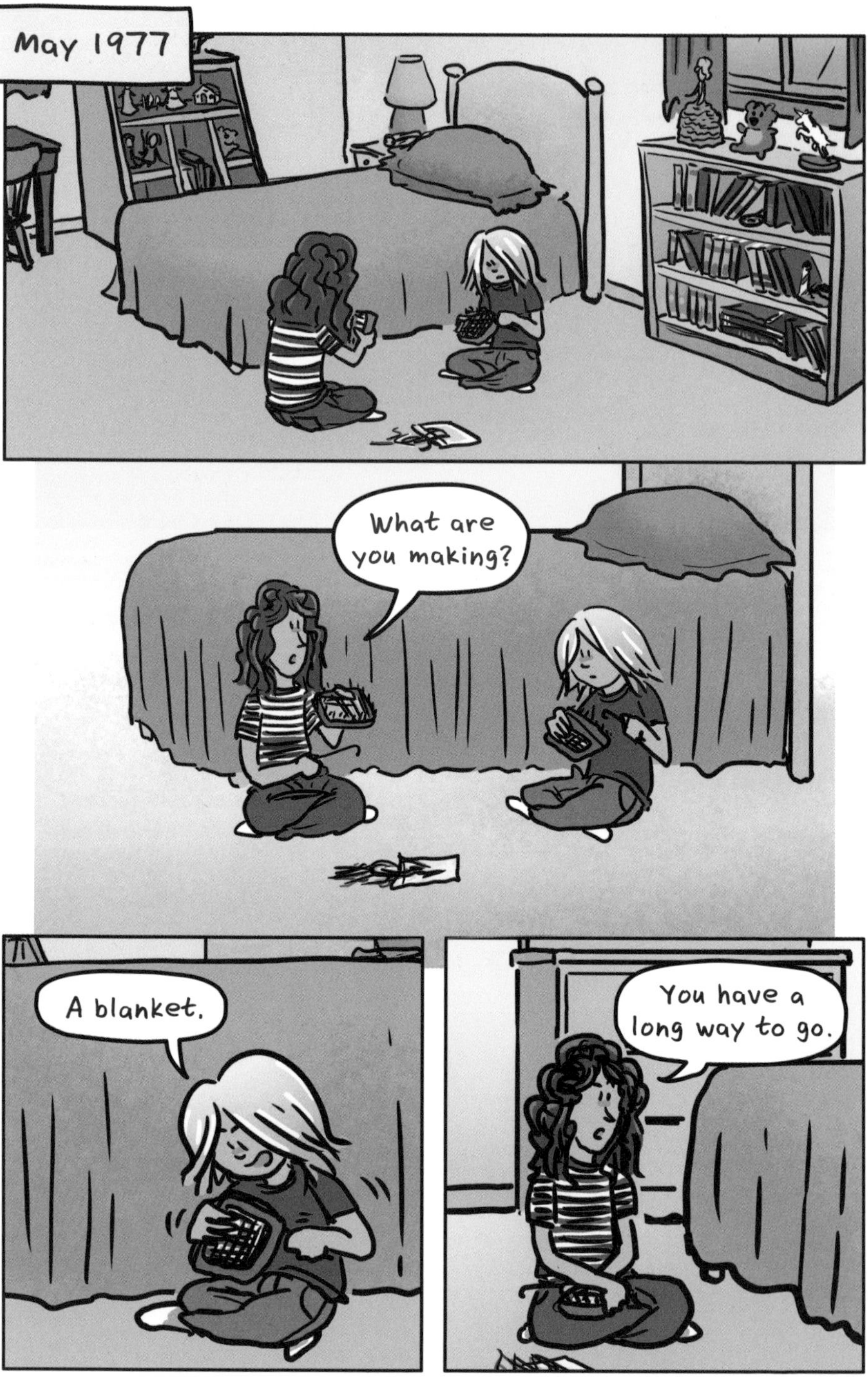
May 1977
What are you making?
A blanket.
You have a long way to go.

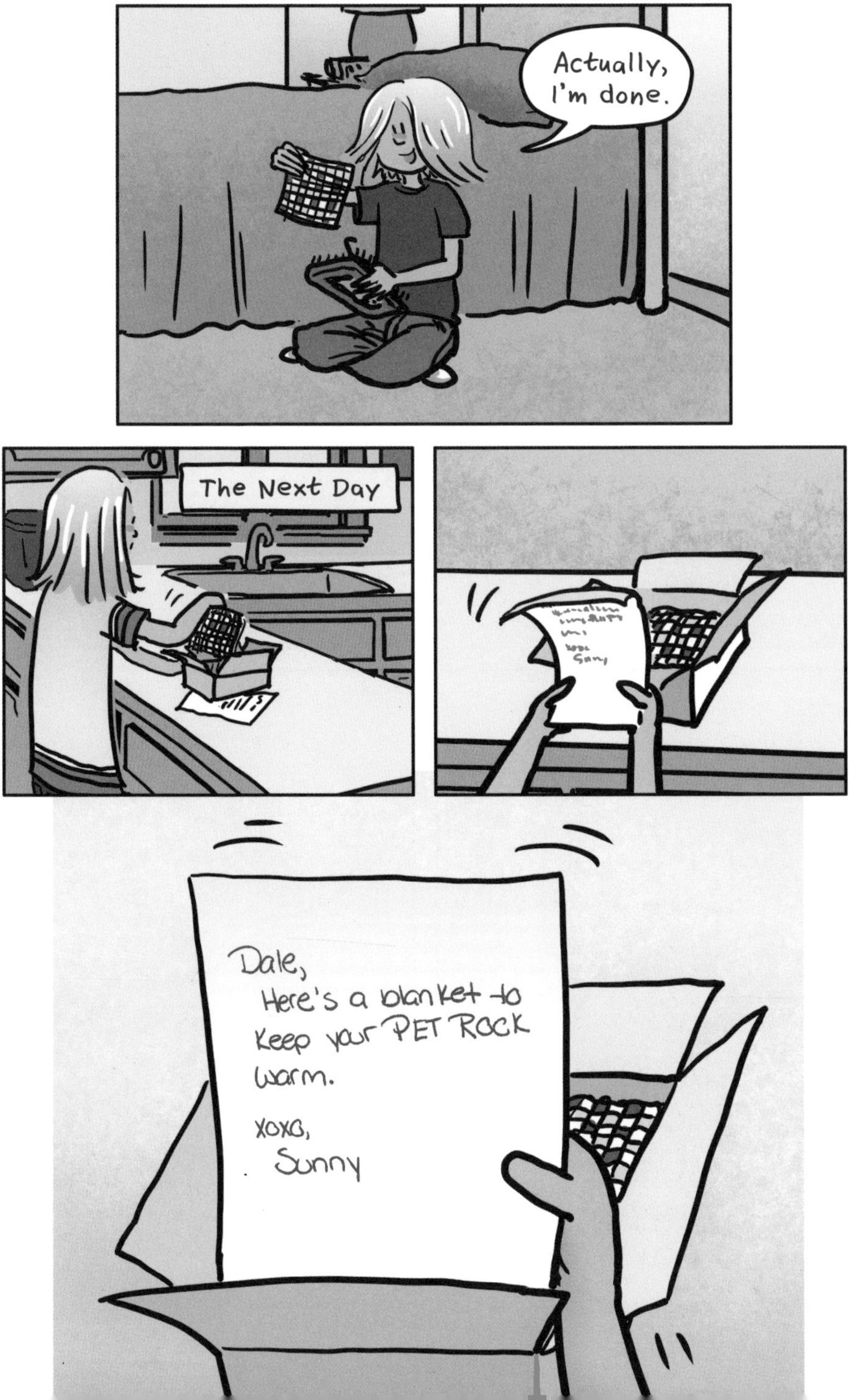
Actually, I'm done.
The Next Day
Dale,
Here's a blanket to keep your PET ROCK warm.
xoxo,
Sunny

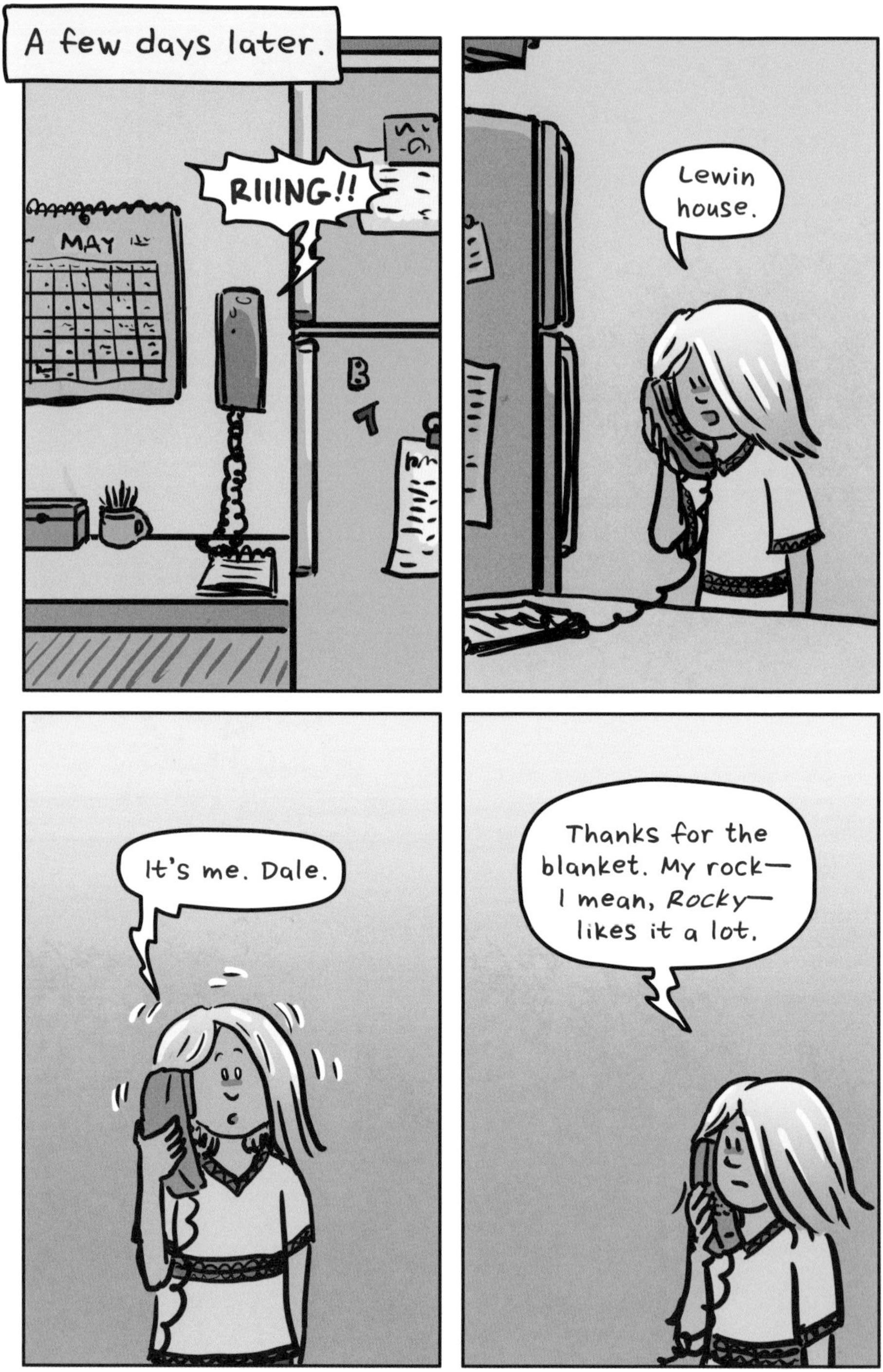
A few days later.
RIIING!!
MAY
B
T
Lewin house.
It's me. Dale.
Thanks for the blanket. My rock— I mean, *Rocky*— likes it a lot.

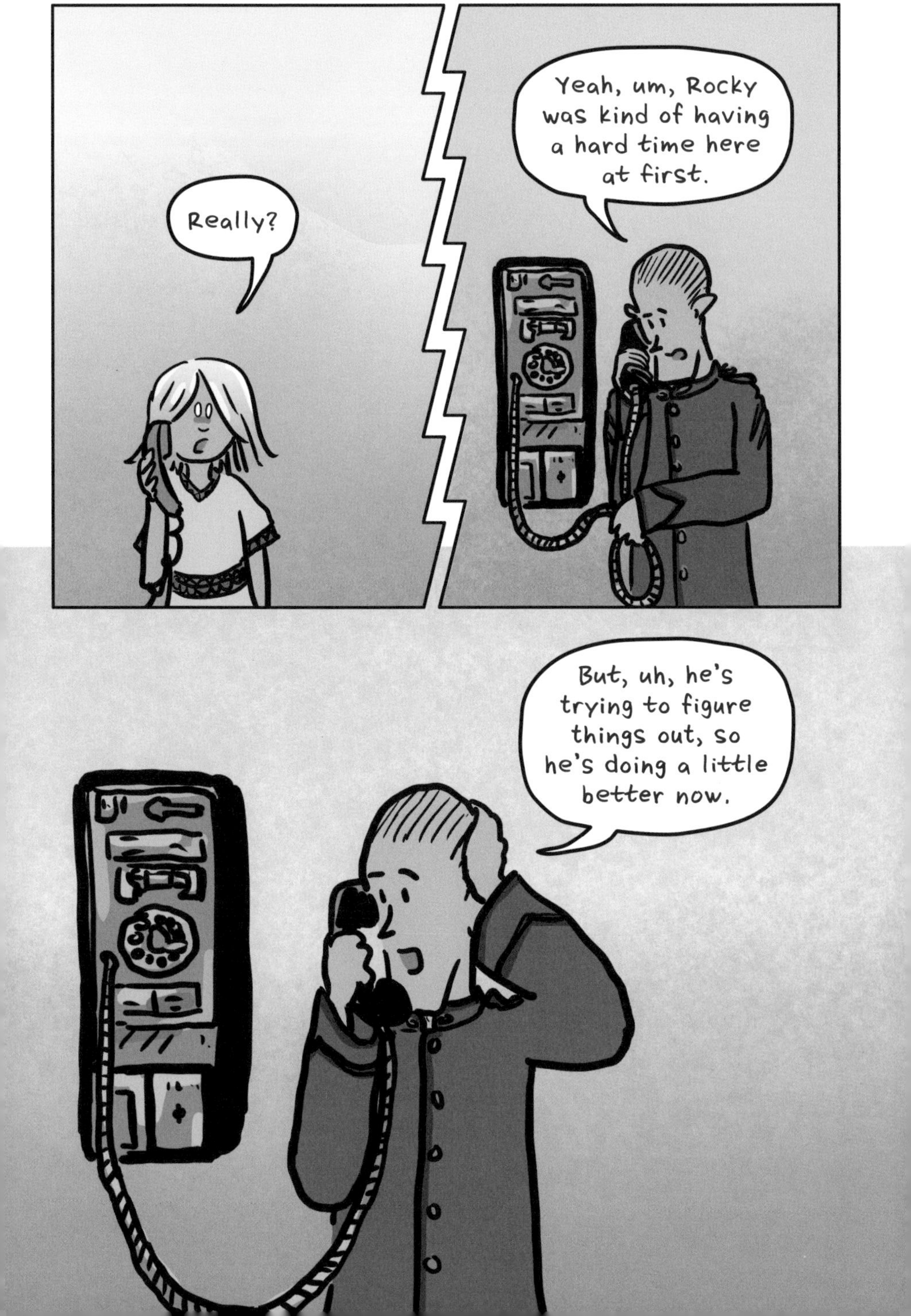
Really?
Yeah, um, Rocky was kind of having a hard time here at first.
But, uh, he's trying to figure things out, so he's doing a little better now.

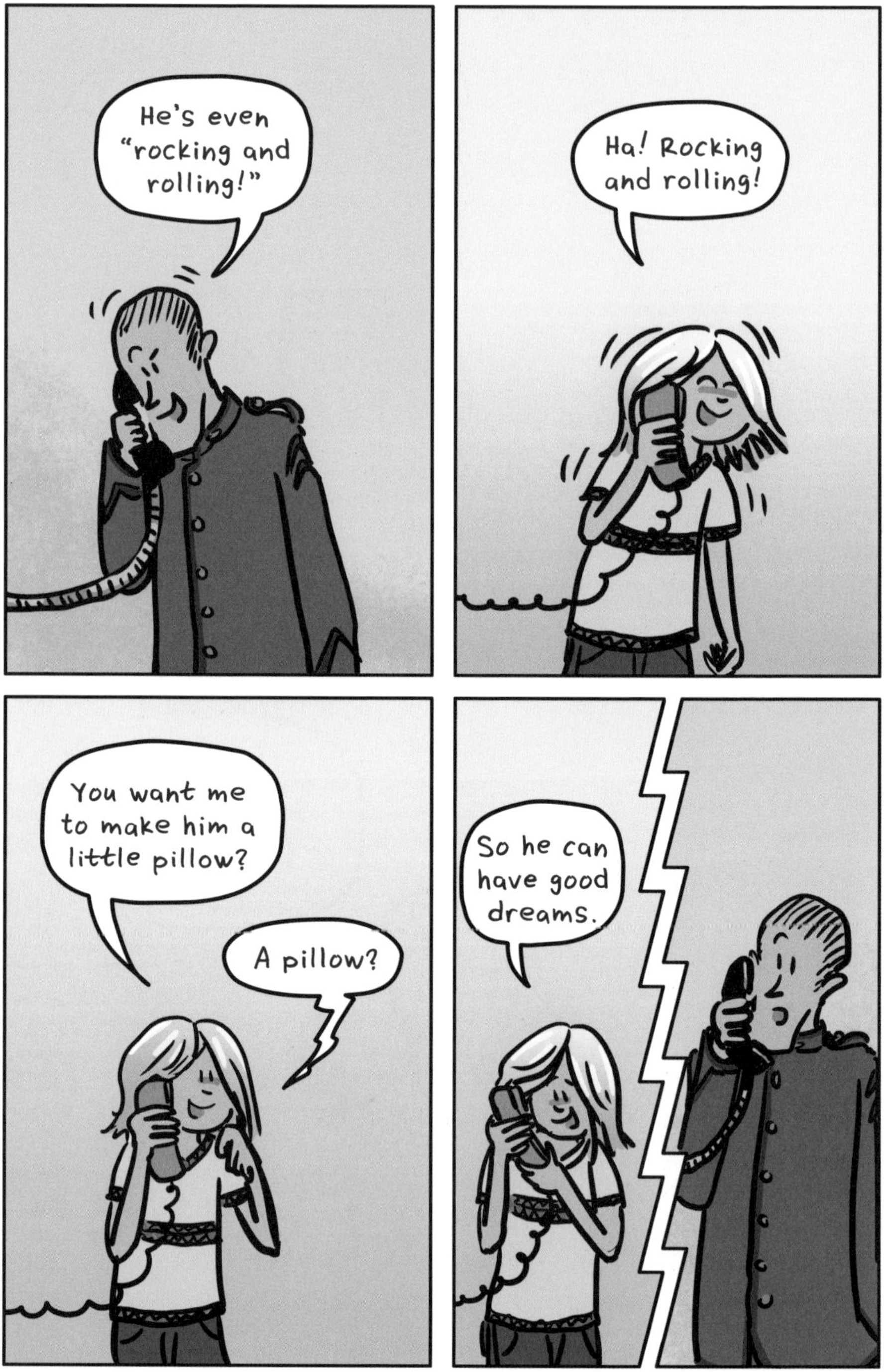

He's even "rocking and rolling!"
Ha! Rocking and rolling!
You want me to make him a little pillow?
A pillow?
So he can have good dreams.

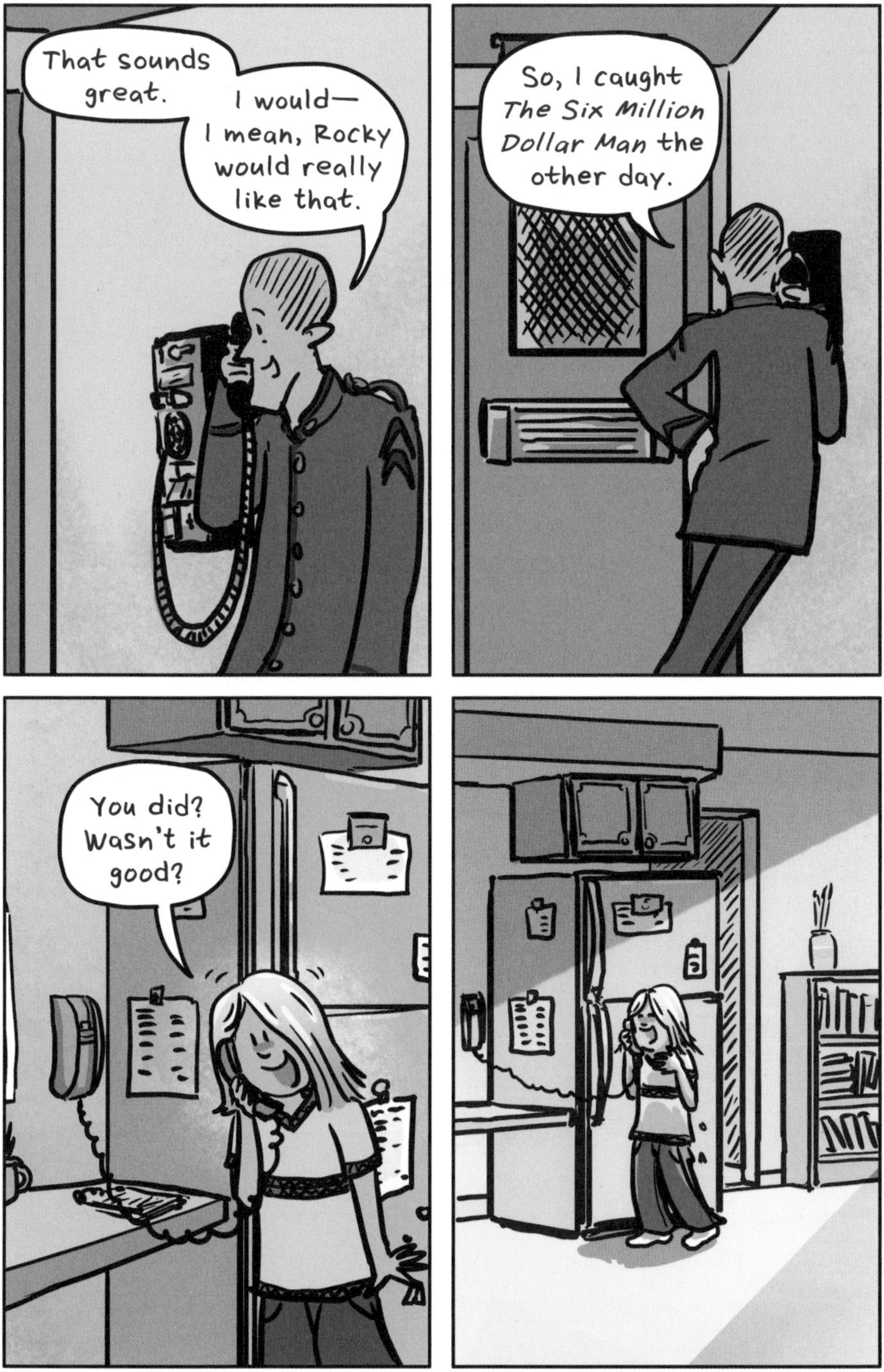
That sounds great.
I would— I mean, Rocky would really like that.
So, I caught *The Six Million Dollar Man* the other day.
You did? Wasn't it good?

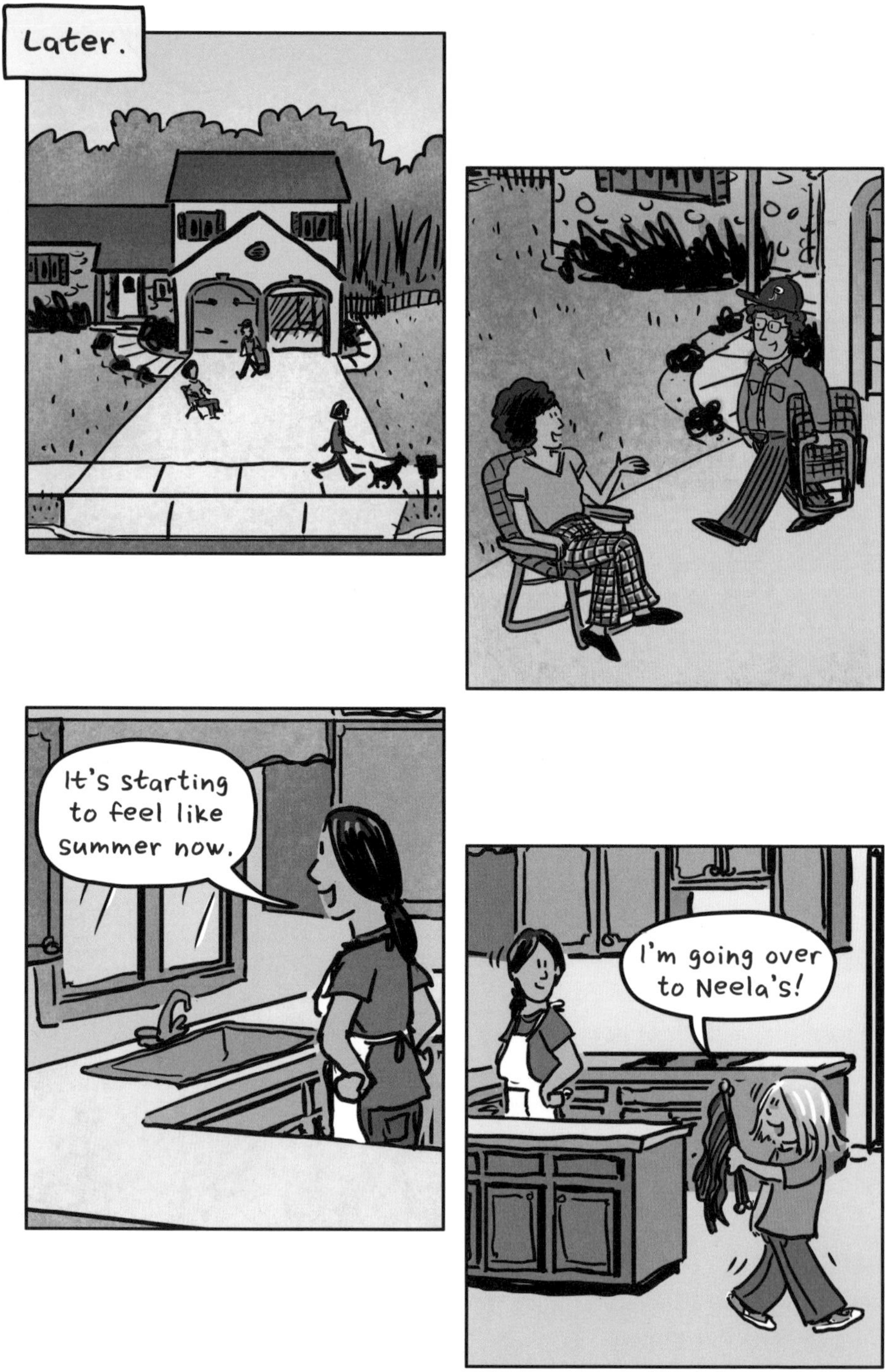
Later.
It's starting to feel like summer now.
I'm going over to Neela's!

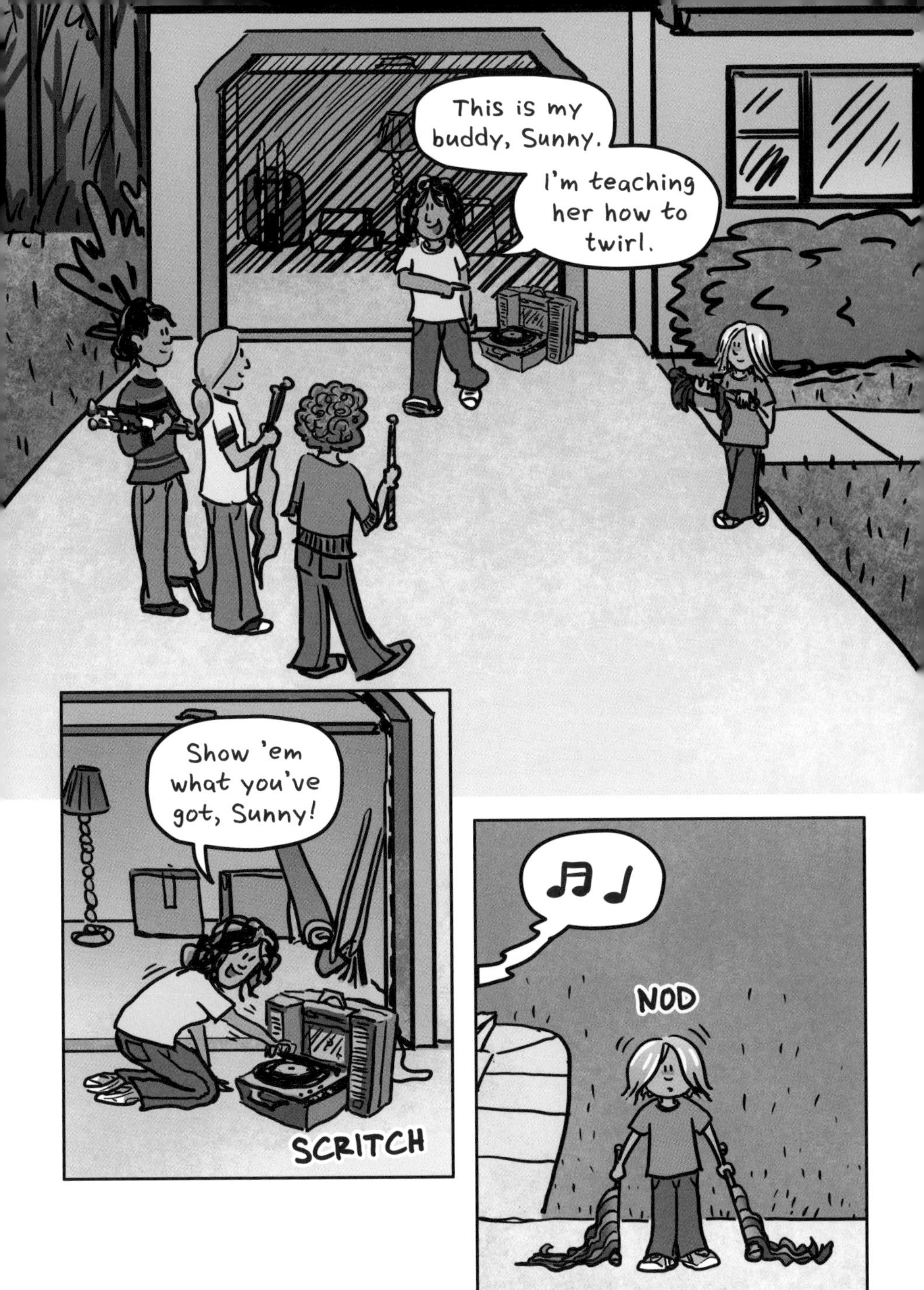
This is my buddy, Sunny.
I'm teaching her how to twirl.
Show 'em what you've got, Sunny!
SCRITCH
♬ ♩
NOD

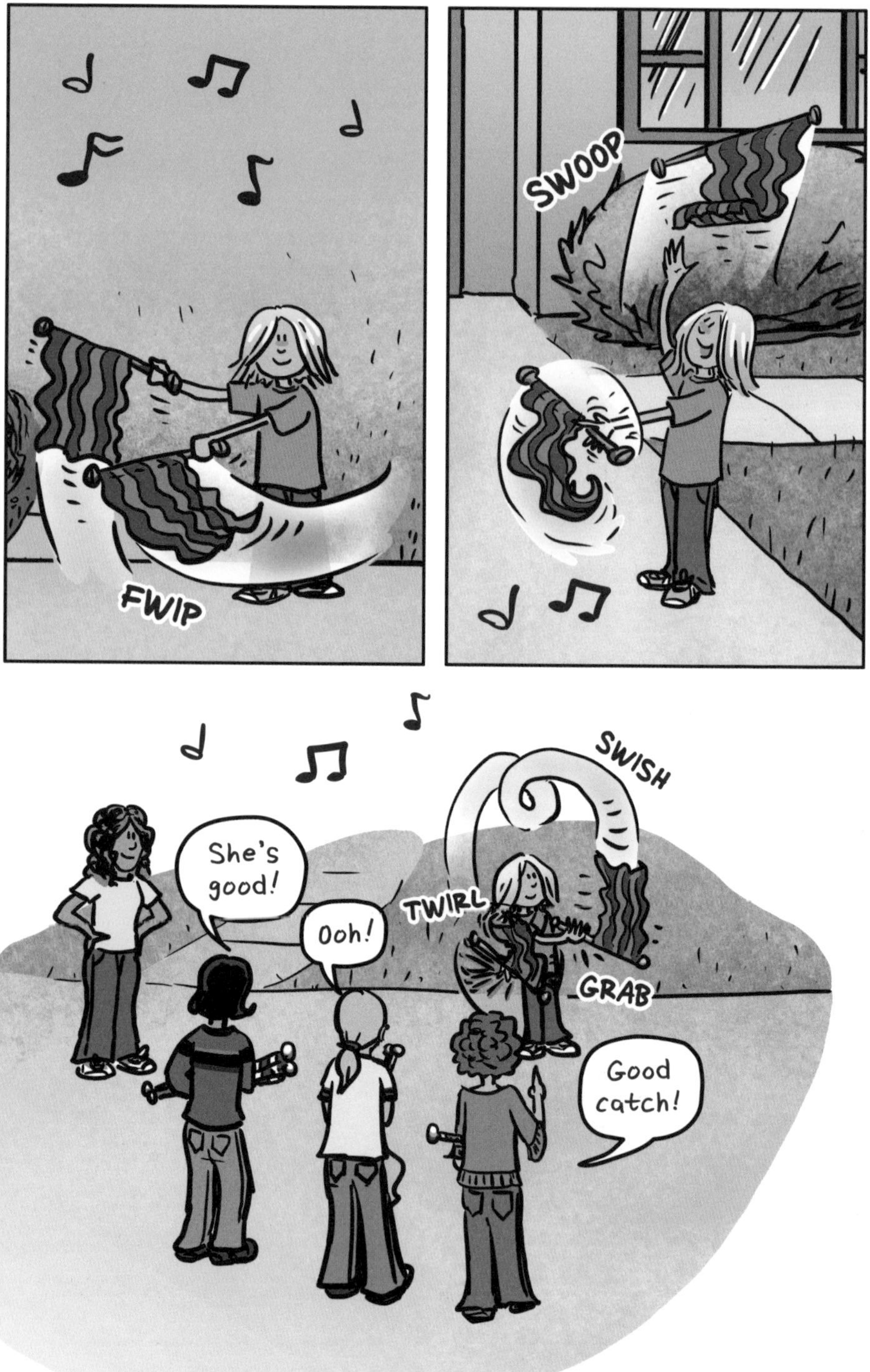
FWIP
SWOOP
SWISH
She's good!
Ooh!
TWIRL
GRAB
Good catch!

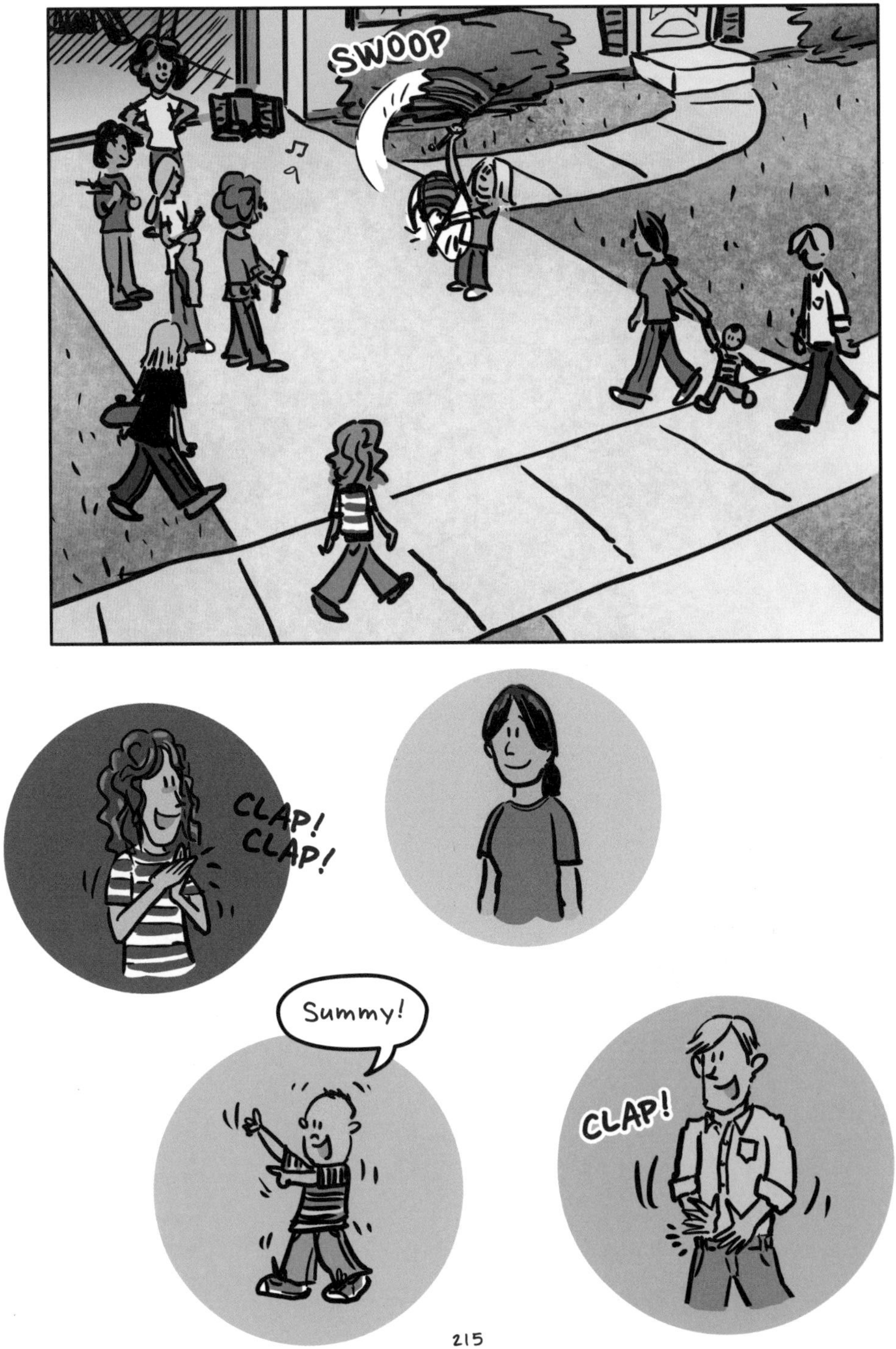
SWOOP
CLAP! CLAP!
Summy!
CLAP!

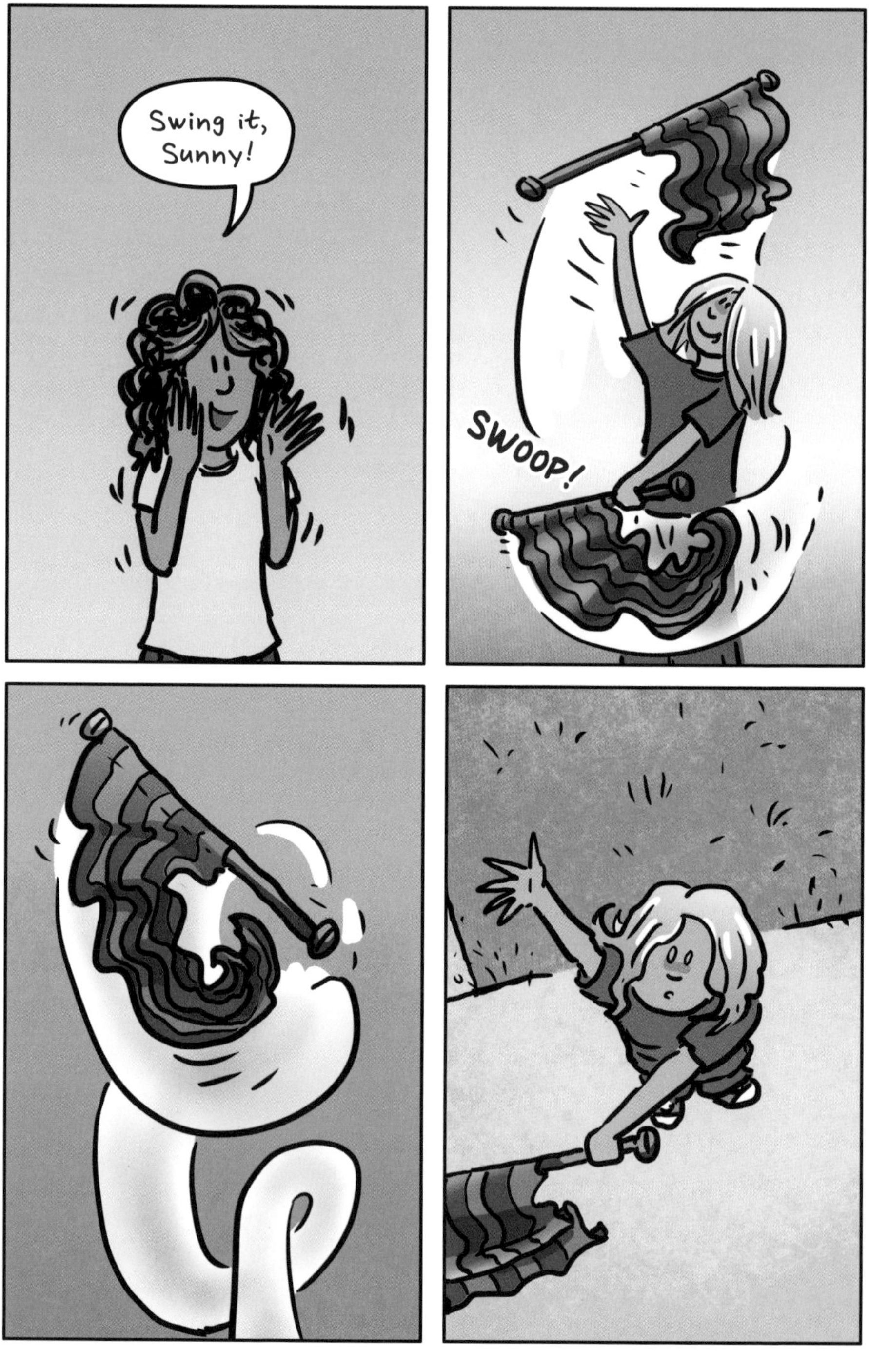
Swing it, Sunny!
SWOOP!

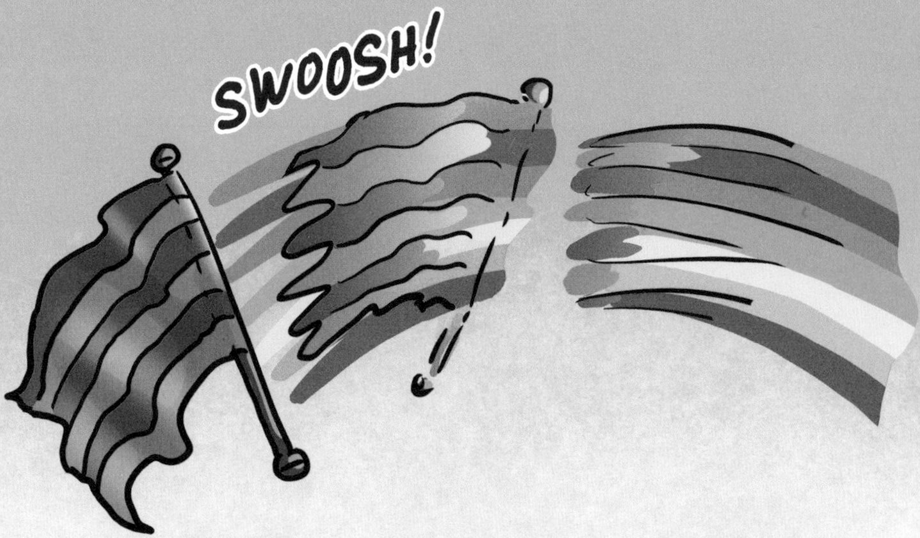
SWOOSH!

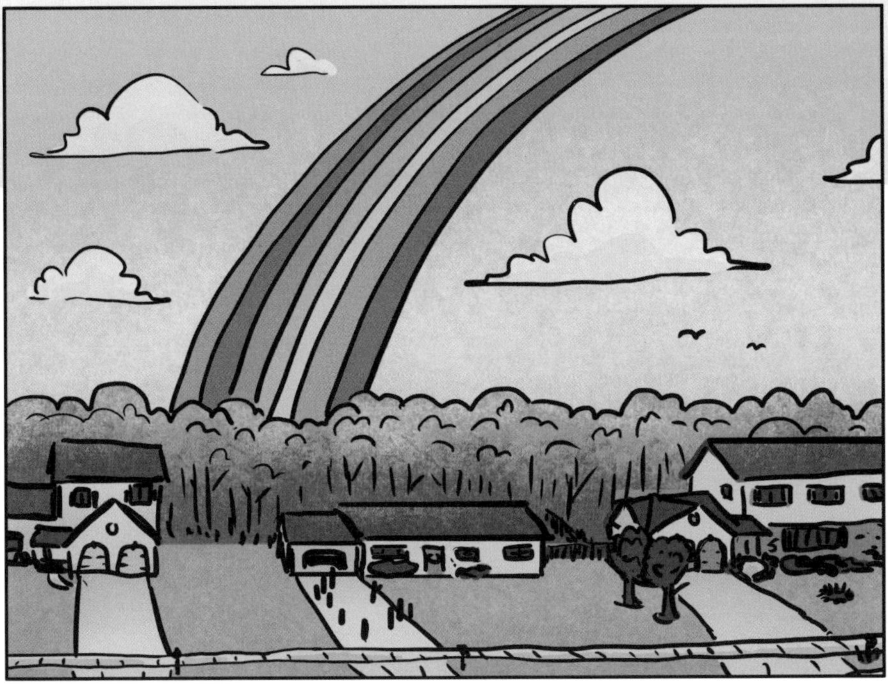

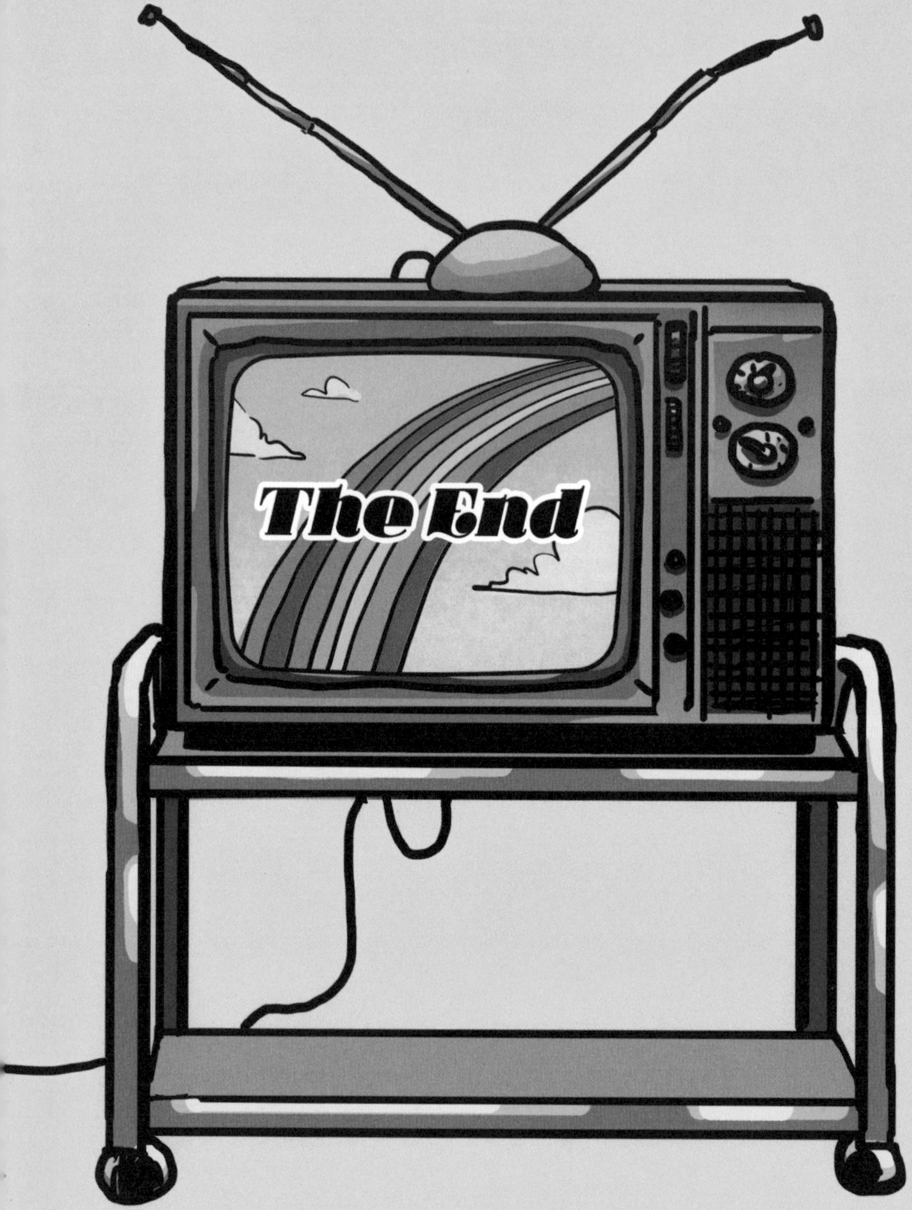
The End

A NOTE FROM JENNIFER L. HOLM & MATTHEW HOLM

We were inspired to have Sunny learn how to use a swing flag because Jenni used to do it herself!

ACKNOWLEDGMENTS

We are so grateful to all the wonderful people who help us to continue Sunny's journey. With special thanks to David Levithan, Phil Falco, Lark Pien, Fawn Lau, Cyndi Koon, David Saylor, Lizette Serrano, and Alexandria Terry. As always, many thanks to Jill Grinberg for her incredible support.

JENNIFER L. HOLM & MATTHEW HOLM are the award-winning brother-sister team behind the Babymouse and Squish series, as well as the first Sunny book, SUNNY SIDE UP. Jennifer is also the author of many acclaimed novels, including three Newbery Honor books and the NEW YORK TIMES bestseller THE FOURTEENTH GOLDFISH. Matthew's most recent novel is MARVIN AND THE MOTHS, written with Jonathan Follett.

LARK PIEN, the colorist of SUNNY SIDE UP and SWING IT, SUNNY, is an indie cartoonist from Oakland, California. She has published many comics and is the colorist for Printz Award winner AMERICAN BORN CHINESE, and BOXERS & SAINTS. Her characters Long Tail Kitty and Mr. Elephanter have been adapted into children's books.

A NOTE FROM JENNIFER L. HOLM & MATTHEW HOLM

We were inspired to have Sunny learn how to use a swing flag because Jenni used to do it herself!

ACKNOWLEDGMENTS

We are so grateful to all the wonderful people who help us to continue Sunny's journey. With special thanks to David Levithan, Phil Falco, Lark Pien, Fawn Lau, Cyndi Koon, David Saylor, Lizette Serrano, and Alexandria Terry. As always, many thanks to Jill Grinberg for her incredible support.

JENNIFER L. HOLM & MATTHEW HOLM are the award-winning brother-sister team behind the Babymouse and Squish series, as well as the first Sunny book, SUNNY SIDE UP. Jennifer is also the author of many acclaimed novels, including three Newbery Honor books and the NEW YORK TIMES bestseller THE FOURTEENTH GOLDFISH. Matthew's most recent novel is MARVIN AND THE MOTHS, written with Jonathan Follett.

LARK PIEN, the colorist of SUNNY SIDE UP and SWING IT, SUNNY, is an indie cartoonist from Oakland, California. She has published many comics and is the colorist for Printz Award winner AMERICAN BORN CHINESE, and BOXERS & SAINTS. Her characters Long Tail Kitty and Mr. Elephanter have been adapted into children's books.